THE BEQUEST

THE
BEQUEST

JOANNA
MARGARET

SCARLET
NEW YORK

THE BEQUEST

Scarlet Press
An Imprint of Penzler Publishers
58 Warren Street
New York, N.Y. 10007

First Scarlet Press edition

Interior design by Maria Fernandez

Library of Congress Control Number: 2022906582

ISBN: 978-1-61316-344-3
eBook ISBN: 978-1-61316-345-0

10 9 8 7 6 5 4 3 2 1

Printed in the United States of America
Distributed by W. W. Norton & Company

For Joyce

PROLOGUE

She shut her eyes and took a few steps closer to the edge. She didn't need to run away. Not yet. A cold, loud wind rushed into her ears. A branch snapped, and she felt a presence. Smelling a hint of familiar perfume, she opened her eyes and swiveled around.

"You startled me," she said, leaning forward, surveying the khaki-colored shrubs, the band of blue-black sea in the distance. Other than a few haggard trees, they were completely alone.

"Been curious about this view."

She dropped her arms by her sides and made an effort to lighten the tone of her voice. "Do you like it?"

"Gorgeous. But didn't you see the forecast? They're expecting a storm. You should be careful. Everything can change out here. Very, very quickly."

She looked up at the clouds. They were heavy, full. "I thought a couple of hours in fresh air, disconnected, might clear my mind. And I'm waiting for someone. Should arrive any minute."

A single laugh. "It's windy today! You're too close to the edge. Let's go somewhere warm where we can talk." She stood still. "Did you think over what we discussed?"

"Yes."

"Well?"

"I can't. I can't do it. I'm sorry." Crisp air swished through her hair, slapping it across her face.

"It's okay. I understand. Did you tell anyone about what you saw?"

She stepped back.

"No one will hurt you, I promise. But I need to know."

"Of course not." A dense fog hovered over them. Soon she wouldn't be able to see the horizon. She twisted her hair into a bun and glanced behind her. "You'll get along with my new student. She's very accomplished. Brilliant. She can help. With . . . anything."

Her scalp itched from chilled sweat. She loosened her wool scarf, and a current of fear coursed over the bare skin on her neck. She understood. It was too late. She lifted her hand to her cheek to still her trembling jaw.

The voice was gentle, consoling. "I only want to talk. There's no need to be afraid. I care about you, and will respect you, no matter what."

She stepped closer. "And you know how I feel."

A wordless struggle, a strong shove.

"*Je t'en pris*," she said, on her hands and knees now. "Please. I'm sorry."

With the second shove, a scrambling of gravel off the ledge, a choked cry melting into waves of wind, her body tumbled down, down, all the way to the rocks.

And then silence. Only some air whooshing through the thin branches of sparse trees and a crunching of footsteps, slow and unburdened.

PART ONE

CHAPTER ONE

I dreamt of St Stephens every night the month before I arrived. Imprints of its hallowed halls coalesced with images of mythical Brigadoon, that Scottish island that appears for one day once a century. Sometimes I was alone in my dreams, and other times Rose was there, except that I was Rose and Rose was me.

Rose Brewster. "Rose like the flower," she used to say when introducing herself over loud music. I hadn't seen her since college. I remembered the time we'd stayed up all night during finals week sharing a pack of Marlboro Lights as we fired exam questions at each other in the common room. Rose knew all the answers, even after three A.M. which is when my cognitive faculties shut down. Later that morning, Rose's makeup-free face looked so serene, blonde ringlets endearingly messy, that my roommate asked if she'd had her hair styled, and I just laughed. If I were a different kind of person I might have hated Rose, but it was never like that between us. After getting an A on the test, she'd written to me that she wouldn't even have passed without our last-minute study session.

Rose was the only person who knew me in Scotland. And even she didn't know what I'd done.

It was 2006, I was twenty-three, and I had plans, which began with leaving the old me back in Boston. On a damp afternoon in late August, I stepped off the train and into my new life.

St Stephens is perched on a hill above the North Sea, granite bulwarks relentlessly battered below by raging, freezing water. Many of the buildings appear medieval but are in fact neo-Gothic, with towering spires, pointed arches, and mock fortifications. The color grey defines the architecture, the weather, and the town's character. St Stephens is famous both for having been a center of the Reformation, and for being home to the revered 600-year-old university. St. John's Quadrangle constitutes the oldest preserved part of the campus, where on sunny days students sit on benches flanked by ornate fifteenth-century buildings and watch the ivy crawl up and down the facades.

St Stephens boasts one of the most competitive history departments in the world, but what had drawn me to the university was the opportunity to work with Madeleine Grangier, French feminist extraordinaire, expert on the soft power that women wielded in European courts during the sixteenth century. Grangier spoke six languages fluently and had made waves in my field. She was a recent hire who had been at St Stephens for only two semesters.

The morning after my arrival I dressed carefully for my meeting with Professor Grangier. Not that I was trying to impress her, but maybe I wanted to seem more European than American. I had read somewhere that the act of smiling sent signals to the brain that make you feel happy, so I tried in front of the mirror. Then I walked to the history department, weaving through the corners of the Quad, rehearsing what I wanted to say to my new advisor.

Three streets south of the Quadrangle I found the red-brick history building sandwiched between sandstone houses. Entering through an iron-barred gate, I climbed four flights of stairs and found Professor

Grangier's office at the end of the hall. I knocked lightly, and the door was opened by a grey-haired man in a burgundy sweater. When he saw me the flat expression on his face rearranged itself.

"Professor . . . Endicott?" I recognized the chair of the department from the website and numerous book jackets. I reached out my hand to shake his, which he did not offer in return. "Isabel Henley. I greatly admire your work, it's a pleasure to meet you."

"Right, nice to meet you, too." He looked over my shoulder as he said, "Do come in." He gestured with his hand, "Please sit in one of those chairs by the fire, Ms. Henley." I slipped off my coat and sat down. "When did you arrive?"

"I flew in from the States yesterday. Is this not Professor Grangier's office?"

He pushed his glasses up his nose. "Did you . . . receive our email?"

"No. But I changed my email address about a week ago. I probably should have alerted someone."

He pursed his lips before continuing, "Ms. Henley, I have some very sad news. Just last week Professor Grangier . . . lost her footing while hillwalking and suffered a fall. A fatal fall."

The room blurred out of focus for a few seconds. "What?"

"I'm so sorry. Madeleine's death has been a tragic shock to us all. We've arranged for you to study with me, which I hope will be satisfactory. I was impressed by your application, and the academic achievements described therein."

I gripped the armrests on the chair. "Yes, of course. I . . . I look forward to working with you. Professor Endicott."

He continued speaking, but the only thing I heard was a low drone as I considered what he'd just told me. He looked at me expectantly. "Well then, please tell me about yourself."

"In college I studied . . . I mean *read* French and History," I said. "I worked in the archives in Paris and on Franco-Tuscan relations . . ."

Endicott glanced at the door, then back to me. I heard a knock and exhaled.

"Come in," said Endicott.

She was slim and masculine in faded jeans and an argyle vest. Her arms were cradling the six-volume set of Enrico Davila's *Istoria delle guerre civili di Francia*. The four flights of stairs must have been difficult to climb, especially in heels.

"Terribly sorry to interrupt," she said, crossing the room. "I promised to bring them back," she added, dropping the books on his desk. A chunky gold ring with a red stone sparkled on her index finger.

"Catrina Parker was here as an undergraduate and knows the lay of the land. She works on peace treaties of the 1570s," Endicott said, and I stood up and shook her hand. She looked down at my shoes and took in the rest of me in a quick glance.

"It was nice to meet you, Isabel Henley," said Endicott. Catrina stepped closer to him and then they turned to face me.

"I'm looking forward to getting started," I said, shrugging my coat on. "Where is Rose Brewster's office?"

"It's just downstairs but don't think she's back from her trip yet," Catrina said. "If she is, she'll be at the event tonight." She tilted her head, "Do you know each other?"

"We were undergrads together. Thanks again."

I walked out and pulled the door shut.

Nigel Endicott was an excellent scholar, but somewhat removed from my area. I'd been looking forward to working with a woman advisor. Now she was dead.

I heaved in a deep breath. You're okay, Isabel.

It was another of many lies I'd told myself over the past year.

CHAPTER TWO

Outside, the light grey sky had blackened, and it was drizzling. I continued down South Street until it converged with North Street and Market Street. At this meeting point between streets stood the old cathedral.

St Stephens Cathedral had been burned down during the Reformation, an ever-present reminder of the early Protestants' zeal. The cathedral, whose high spires were visible from any part of town, had soaring walls but no roof. Breezes flowed freely out of arched window frames, long empty of glass panes. Tombstones, half-sunk into patches of grass, sprouted up here and there inside the walls. I crouched down to read one of the inscriptions but only a few lines poked through a grimy layer of moss. The wind began to pick up.

I passed a group of chattering Spanish tourists, shivering in T-shirts, cameras slung around their necks. At the opposite end of the cathedral was an open door through which I could glimpse the navy-blue sea.

After zigzagging among the gravestones, I exited through the open door. Outside the cathedral walls, unprotected from the elements, I gazed at the distant froth of the North Sea. Pulling my coat around me, I turned. Someone was standing there, smiling at me, hands inside his coat pockets. Taking a step back I flicked my eyes left and right. Would those Spanish tourists hear me if I screamed? Doubtful.

"You're the new PhD student, aren't you?" he asked.

"Yes," I answered.

"I'm a lecturer in the department, William Anderson. Isabel Handley, right? Welcome to St Stephens."

He was tall, with chestnut-colored hair and greyish dark eyes not unlike the color of the North Sea. Probably in his mid-thirties. I didn't recognize his accent. Wales? His long black coat looked soft and warm. And expensive.

"Henley," I said. "Not Handley." Although I didn't mean to sound unfriendly, as the words left my mouth, I heard a bit of a growl. "Funny bumping into you out here. In the rain."

"Ahh, you'll get used to it. That's what it's like in St Stephens. Bumping into people, I mean. It's a small town." As he raked his hand through his wet hair, I checked for a wedding band. He wasn't wearing one.

"I've got to run," he said. "See you soon." I watched him walk away and headed to my apartment.

My flat occupied the second floor of a small building in the back of a parking lot. I had signed the rental contract online and was pleased with the result—although the building was decidedly run down, and it certainly wasn't in the posh part of town. But the price was right. I unlocked the main door on the ground level and went up the stairs. I couldn't afford to keep the radiators on all the time, and the outside air seeped in through gaps around the thin, ill-fitted windowpanes. I decided to make tea.

Unable to find a kettle, I filled a pan with water and put it on the burner then went into the bedroom. The space heater click-click-clicked as I switched it on.

The department meet-and-greet didn't start until five o'clock so I climbed into bed with my coat still on and stared at the ceiling. It didn't seem possible that Professor Grangier was dead.

Although the opportunity to work with Grangier had been my main reason for coming to St Stephens, it wasn't the only one. While researching the top graduate programs in history outside the United States, I'd recognized Rose Brewster's name and photo on the St Stephens website. We'd attended the same liberal arts college outside Boston, where she was two years ahead of me.

Even though our classes had been small I hadn't been sure how well Rose would remember me. I remembered her well, in the way that younger students keep tabs on their older classmates. Rose had been president of the French Society, the Italian Society, and the Drama Club at school. At the club meetings she had come across as poised and assertive without being bossy. She was a great storyteller, and we all hung on her every word. One year I'd helped her organize the Italian Society's holiday party, a benefit for local charities. I'd worked as cashier that night, and Rose had checked in every hour—asking if I needed anything, and bringing me drinks until the party wrapped up around four in the morning. In between shots of grappa, she introduced me to a guy I'd had a fling with.

Rose was a beautiful *wunderkind*. People talked about her a lot, mostly behind her back. I thought she was really kind and irresistibly charming. She didn't take herself too seriously, and she wasn't afraid to be self-deprecating.

On campus she had always been surrounded by an entourage, including a new guy on her arm seemingly weekly. Like Rose, I'd been a History and French double major. The leader of our seminar, Denis Viret, specialized in sixteenth century French history, and he became a mentor for me, and for Rose before me.

Unlike Rose I'd kept a very low profile at school, and the people who knew me best were the librarians. As a sophomore I'd attended the French department's graduation reception, when Rose had won the prestigious

French prize. I won the same award two years later, and Rose sent me a lovely note welcoming me to "the club."

A year after graduation, in the midst of the worst time in my adult life, I'd written to Rose and asked about St Stephens. I'd kept track of her, and had seen her name in a conference booklet, so I knew she'd gone into the same field. She remembered me well, and recommended St Stephens wholeheartedly. She'd sung the praises of Madeleine Grangier and the entire faculty, as well as the other students. She'd waxed lyrical about windy beaches and history that permeated every corner of town, although she made a point of saying that it rained all the time, and recommended I bring a sturdy umbrella, an assortment of Mackintoshes, and rubber boots. She said St Stephens was everything Americans dreamed a British campus could be, and asked if I knew the Harry Potter movies were being filmed in Scotland? She could even help me find funding, whatever the department couldn't cover, so it would basically be a free ride.

"It sounds perfect," I'd replied. "I like the idea of being far from the States and close to the European archives."

She didn't know it, but it wouldn't be an exaggeration to say that Rose Brewster saved my life.

My eyes were closing when I heard four sharp knocks on the door, followed by a set of keys jingling, and the front door unlocking. The light flashed on in the living room.

"Someone's left the hob on." I jumped out of bed and pushed the bedroom door open a few inches. A man in a burgundy velvet jacket was standing across the room.

"Don't be frightened," he said, "I'm your landlord, Charles."

I opened the door some more. "Pleasure to meet you, too," he said. "Feel free to take off your coat. Or maybe you were heading out? In that case best brush your hair. I wanted to show you how a few things work, the hob, the tub, that sort of thing." He led me on a brief tour, during which

I wondered if he could tell I wasn't listening. "I hear of strange goings on in St Stephens," he said. "I graduated over twenty years ago, and much has changed. Have you walked around town? It's my duty to warn my student tenants not to step on the letters, 'TP,' carved near the cathedral. The initials of a Protestant martyr burned on the very spot. Any student who walks across will fail his exams."

"Good to know," I said. "What did you mean by strange goings on in St Stephens?"

"Most recently a Newton book went missing from the library. One of our oldest, most valuable texts. Belonged to the collection of a professor of chemistry who bequeathed it to the University in the nineteenth century."

"That's terrible. Do they know what might have happened to it?"

"They'll track it down eventually—St Stephens is like an island; secrets are impossible to keep. I didn't mean to alarm you, the town is very safe, even for a woman living alone. In short order I'm sure you won't lack friends to keep you company. Many of your compatriots, too. They aren't the most visible component of the student population, but they're the most audible one, eh eh."

I coughed a laugh and tapped my foot on the floor.

"I'll be on my way, but do buy yourself an electric kettle, Isabel. If it isn't too much of a hardship, that is," he said. "American girl last year almost burned the place down. Anyway. I trust you don't host wild parties?"

"You have nothing to worry about. I'm here to study, not to throw parties."

His eyes narrowed. "That's right. Don't you read history? A professor from the School of History died in an accident last week. Peculiar."

"Peculiar in what way?"

"I'm not convinced it was an accident, not with what was being said about her in town. I met her once, handsome woman. . . . Only she wasn't much . . . liked in St Stephens. Her reputation—"

"—What do you mean, she wasn't much liked?"

"For one thing she sought membership in a private club that's been men's only since its inception. Made a fuss when they wouldn't let her in, ruffled some feathers."

I put my hands on my hips. "Can't say I blame her."

"Never mind. Lastly, please don't forget to lock up. Dodgy lads hang about that car park at night. Don't hesitate to ring if you need anything. You have my number."

Before I could say anything further, he left, locking the door behind him, and I dismissed what he had said as simple warnings to a foreign student.

I filled my mug, took off my coat, went back into the bedroom, and crawled under the covers. Reaching over to put the mug on the table I toppled over two bottles of Effexor and Wellbutrin. Tiny white pills spilled out on the table and bounced onto the carpet, a psychotropic avalanche. I didn't pick them up. Ten minutes later, half asleep, I wondered whether I'd imagined Charles. I had so many questions for Rose, wherever she was.

CHAPTER THREE

When I woke up it was dark. I primped quickly, worried I'd be late for the meet-and-greet, and ran out into the rain, this time with an umbrella. It was difficult to trace my steps back to the history building. The streets had emptied, and the lights were off in the shop windows. Even with the umbrella I was drenched by the time I found the entrance, locked behind a barred gate. After waiting for several minutes for someone to walk by, I found a security guard who said he would show me the side entrance.

"You're American?" His Scottish accent was thick, but I could understand most of what he said. "You seem like a nice lass. I've been a custodian here for thirty years. Seen my share of clatty behavior. Lots of mad bampots about. Mind yourself. Don't let 'em beflum you, aye?"

I nodded, whispered thank you, and walked into the overheated room with deliberate, soft steps, but the floorboards squeaked, and when Nigel Endicott saw me, he stopped talking. I put my hand up in a tentative wave, which he did not acknowledge before returning his attention to the group of forty or so scholars, fluorescent lights buzzing overhead. Standing close to the door, I tugged off my water logged coat. The musty book and wet carpet smell was oddly comforting.

"In conclusion," Nigel said, "I would emphasize that when you graduate, *if* you graduate, there will be but a scant few academic positions. The academic process works as a funnel, allowing only those who are serious to pass through. I say this to encourage you and wish you the best of luck." Hands clapped reluctantly, and there was a brief silence as William Anderson walked to the front.

"Well, that was cheery," William said. A murmur of a laugh rippled through the group. "Welcome, do help yourselves to drinks, and please introduce yourselves to our newest postgraduate students." Those sitting rose to their feet and polite chattering commenced. I smiled at everyone and no one and reached for a glass of white wine on a table nearby. I scanned the audience. No Rose.

Most of the history faculty stayed clustered together at the front of the room. William introduced me to the second-year with whom I would share an office. "Mairead. That's a beautiful name," I said. "Where are you from?"

"I've been living in the UK for the past twenty years, but my mum comes from County Mayo and my dad is Italian." As we talked, her eyes darted around the room.

"Sorry about your advisor," she said. "I had just started working with her."

"I'm still in shock."

"Me too. Everything's gone pear-shaped." She sucked her cheeks into a fish face. "And you came all this way to work with her," she said. "I've been reassigned to William Anderson. You?"

"Endicott."

"Oh. And sorry about your office," she said.

"My office? What about it?"

"Rose is still writing up. Have you met Rose? Don't worry. She's been told to surrender her desk by November."

"November? Is Rose coming? I've been looking for her."

Mairead shifted from one foot to the other.

"She'll be back any day now. I wish she didn't go away so often. She's burning up a lot of carbon."

"New girl. Join us for drinks later at the Quake," said Jeff, a third-year from Inverness, studying French-Scottish trade relations. He gestured to the burly Bertie, a second-year, standing next to him. Catrina joined us. "We have to take care of our new Pet."

"Pet? I'll take it as a term of endearment," I said, and they all laughed.

I met Sean, from Northern England, and Luke, from Northern Ireland. I liked the way he pronounced his name, "Lyoook."

William circled back to me as I was putting on my still-wet coat. "Coming?" he asked.

I had hoped to sneak out, but surprised myself. *"Bien sûr!"*

In small groups we walked over to the pub. William fell in next to me as I walked with a friendly Scottish lecturer, Claire Miller, until she said goodnight and went home.

The "Quake" was actually the Quaich, and inside, where the reek of cigarette smoke competed with the odor of stale beer, I learned that a *quaich* was a drinking cup.

I ordered a glass of water. "Sparkling. No ice. Thank you."

William turned to me. "In this country, Isabel, water is for bathing or tea."

"Okay, I'll have a whiskey," I said. "Straight up."

"What kind would you like?"

I looked behind him at the bottles lined up and read the first label I could make out. "Bowmore," I said, confident I had pronounced it correctly.

"A woman who knows her single malts," he said. I grinned. "A dram of fifteen-year-old Bowmore for the lady, and for me. On my tab if you will, Pete," William said to the bartender, who poured two healthy servings into thick tumblers.

"Bowmore," William said. "Has the perfect balance of smoke and peat. It's from Islay, the most untamed of the islands, home to eight distilleries. Close your eyes before you take a sip. Trust me on this."

It felt silly but I tried it. When I opened my eyes his silvery-blue ones were looking straight at me.

"Did you taste the sea?"

"To be honest, no. Are you some sort of whiskey connoisseur?"

"Evidently I have a rather amateur palate."

I smiled. "Shall we join the others?"

Mairead, back to the fire, was participating in several conversations at once. I was standing next to Bertie when Catrina sidled up and slapped his ass. "Bring me a whiskey sour?" he said, and she sashayed to the bar.

I leaned over to Bertie, "You guys are a couple? I thought she was with Jeff."

His nostrils flared. "Ah, you mean the good-looking Scot? Jeff's with Danny. Sometimes. He prefers older women. Like Madame Ooh-la-la," he said, in an exaggerated French accent. "Danny was jealous of your late supervisor—Madame Ooh-la-la was fit."

"Do you mean Madeleine Grangier?"

"Who else?"

"That seems a disrespectful way to refer to an esteemed professor. Not to mention someone who's dead."

"I meant it as a compliment. Madame *la professeur* had that *je ne sais quoi*. But I am sorry she's not here to defend herself. If you'd met her, you'd know she's the sort who invited speculation, tight skirts and stilettos. She was up for it."

I frowned. "I don't think anyone *invites* speculation. Is Danny here tonight?"

"She's in the Highlands, researching 'Catholicism in the clans.'" He bent his fingers to make quote marks and excused himself to join Catrina.

Sean and Luke were standing in the corner, and Luke took my arm and told me that Sean's girlfriend had left him to become a cloistered nun.

"I'm sorry," I said to Sean.

"What for? Because my ex gave up humans after going out with me?"

"I'm sure it wasn't because of you, specifically," I said.

"You don't know me," he said, with a wink.

I turned to Luke. "What's Bertie's deal? Did he have something against Madeleine Grangier?"

Sean sighed. "Ignore him, he's a tosser, a rich man's son who uses fivers to wipe his nose. Grangier was on the panel that failed Bertie's second-year review, and he's been whinging ever since."

"That's awful," I said.

Luke nodded. "Yeah, he's practically gloating she's gone. Hardly her fault Bertie skived off school last year."

William came up to us and asked if we wanted another drink. We ordered a round of whiskey shots.

"My turn," I said, clenching my jaw while signing the credit card slip.

Catrina joined us just as Luke asked what my dissertation topic was.

"I'm re-examining the women of Catherine de' Medici's court, her so-called 'flying squadron,' from a feminist perspective, and the way these historically slut-shamed women did serious political work behind the scenes."

"Isabel, my Pet," Catrina interrupted Luke. "This might not be terribly polite to bring up, but when I was working in the British Library a few months ago I trained up to Cambridge and heard a lecture on that exact subject." She reached out and touched my arm. "We women must look

17

after one another. It would be a shame to get invested in a topic that's been covered."

"I wonder why Professor Grangier never mentioned this to me," I said aloud, my face feeling hot.

"Or Endicott," said Catrina. "Then again, Endicott's students were rivals of hers, just like the two of them were . . ."

Bertie walked up behind Catrina and threw his arm around her. "Cat, I know that look of yours. Were you stirring the pot?" He clapped a hand on my shoulder, and I jerked back. "If she's bothering you, Isabel, do let me know."

"She's not bothering me," I said. "Excuse me. I'm going to run out for a cigarette." Walking toward the exit I saw Bertie grab Catrina's wrist. William was talking to them in a low voice.

Outside, the bitter wind wormed into my cardigan, beginning to sting after a few seconds. The door opened and warm air blew in my direction. William walked out.

"Already finished your cigarette?"

"I haven't smoked since college."

"You don't drink, you don't smoke. Americans are so healthy these days."

"Just needed a break."

"Shake it off. What Catrina said," he said, correctly guessing my thoughts. He ran his hand through his hair. "You know what you should do instead? Buy me a drink."

I followed him back inside, and a few whiskeys later the staff lowered the lights and turned up the music and we started singing 80s songs, our liquor-bolstered courage leading us to presume we knew all the words.

Leaving the pub a few hours later I concluded that the whiskey had helped me understand I had something in common with the room full of strangers that extended beyond our field. By the time I reached the parking lot I wasn't so sure.

Still singing, "I Just Died in Your Arms Tonight," the raw chords bringing the events of the past year back into focus, I stood shivering in the wet darkness, dodging empty liquor bottles.

I unlocked the door and went upstairs to my flat, which seemed so quiet. In the bedroom I saw the pills spilled out over the table and floor. With a grunt I bent down and picked them up one by one and put them back in their respective bottles.

I threw my nightly dosage in my mouth. I wasn't supposed to drink on the meds. Hot tears filled the spaces behind my eyelids.

Taking only a sip out of a water bottle I tried to swallow and started coughing. After a few seconds the pills disintegrated into chalky bitterness. Who would even know if I choked? I'd be one of those solitary people, my body discovered weeks later. I spit the powder into the sink, swished water in my mouth, grabbed both bottles from my room, and emptied the contents down the toilet.

Then I let the tears come.

CHAPTER FOUR

The next morning, I stood in front of the history building with a throbbing headache. Before climbing the second flight of stairs, I took a moment to catch my breath. Everyone who had been at the pub the previous night was already in their offices, clicking away on their keyboards as if they hadn't been boozing until the wee hours.

"Good morning," Catrina called as she passed me. Her hair was as smooth as it had been the day before, and she appeared even more energetic. "Feeling a bit rough today, eh?"

"I feel great," I said. "So much fun last night."

After my crying jag I'd read an email from Rose, who'd just returned, and arranged to meet the next day. I stayed awake until five searching the Internet for the lecture that Catrina had mentioned, and found Christina Yee, "The Myth of the Flying Squadron: Catherine de' Medici's Female Court." Under "Publications," she had listed the same title, with the subheading, *Monograph, Redding Press, forthcoming, 2007.* I couldn't build on Yee's research, since her book wouldn't be released for a year, but it was already under contract with one of the best publishers.

The one good thing about living in an isolated apartment in the back of a parking lot was that no one could hear me scream "FUCK," over and over until I could only squeak it.

"Thanks for the heads up about the other scholar working on Catherine de' Medici's court," I called out to Catrina. "Really useful."

"Anytime," Catrina said, descending the stairs. "Whatever I can do to help."

I knocked once on Endicott's door. What would I tell him? Leaving the program wasn't a viable option. I could barely afford my flat, or heat, and had been preparing to sacrifice my Internet. I needed to find a job, the sooner the better, and all the TA positions were allocated to second-year students. Inside Endicott's office a woman was speaking in a low voice, so I headed down to the lounge, where Rose had suggested we meet in a half hour.

The department lounge reminded me of a subterranean cave, dark and damp with a curved ceiling. I chucked two teabags of English Breakfast into a cup and filled it with hot water. Waiting for it to steep, I leafed through a student brochure on the table with the tea packets. Under the brochure was a fat, red, hardcover book. I picked it up and read the title on the spine, *Illustrious Members of the Sixteenth-Century French Court.* There was no call number. The pages smelled sweet and floral. Ripples of steam floated up from my cup.

I sat down on the couch and flipped through the book, which kept opening to the center, where a single page was dog-eared. A name on the top of the page was highlighted in mint green. *Falcone.* I said the name out loud, whispering it and then sounding it out the Italian way, "Fal-COE-nay."

My head was still throbbing, so I leaned back and laid the book down next to me. My eyes fluttered shut.

"There it is!" a metallic voice bounced through the space, and I jumped. "Izzie! Isabel! Is that you? Oh my . . . wait, were you . . . napping? Sorry!" Rose was wearing a Burberry trench coat and the tousled hair that used to fall to her waist was now chopped shoulder-length in a sophisticated cut appropriate for her glam-academic look. I remembered her effortless beauty in college, but today she had on full makeup.

"You made it!" she said, hugging me hard. "It is so, so good to see you. How was the trip over? Settling in okay?" Her inflections sounded British.

"Jet-lagged but . . . I've been all over looking for you!"

"You look great!" she said, her smile a little higher on the right side.

"So, this belongs to you," I said, handing the red book to her.

"Beautiful binding, right? And they say not to judge a book by its cover," she said. She looked down at her watch. A Rolex. "I should head back to the office. I'm prepping a paper. We must get together soonest!"

"What are you working on?"

"A Genovese family who lived in France in the sixteenth century. The Falcone. I was the first modern scholar to work in their private archive in Genoa." She shook her head and draped her coat over one arm, as she went into full professorial mode. "What I most enjoy about being an archival historian is that, for all the painstaking labor and paleographical challenges, there's a possibility of finding one slip of paper that could forever change our understanding of the past. As you well know, most of the time archival work is looking for the proverbial needle in the haystack."

"Find any needles?"

"I could tell you, but I'd have to kill you," she said. "By the way, I wanted to apologize. You're welcome to use my office and computer anytime. My desk will be yours soon." She heaved an exaggerated sigh of relief.

"Thanks very much," I said, unable to imagine how we could share a desk or a computer.

"You're working on Catherine de' Medici's court, right?"

"Word gets around."

"Are you kidding? You're the talk of the town!" She stepped closer.

"Who's your advisor?" I asked.

"William. Go introduce yourself if you haven't met yet. He's incredibly knowledgeable. I'm really sorry about your advisor. Madeleine Grangier was amazing. I would've loved to work with her, but I'd already started by the time she arrived. You're in good hands though, Endicott has a world-class reputation. He might seem intimidating, but he'd do anything for his students."

"What happened to Professor Grangier? I heard she fell down a mountain?"

"It was bizarre because she's an experienced climber. Then again, it could happen to anybody. Scottish weather is so unpredictable, you know? Still, a heartbreaking loss, for all of us. She didn't have any family, which is the tiniest of consolations."

"This may sound strange, but my landlord suggested her death might not have been an accident. That she wasn't well liked?"

"Your *landlord*? There was friendly competition between her and the other professors, sure, but the idea that her death was anything other than an accident seems far-fetched." She looked down at the chipped red polish on her nails.

"Endicott was oddly cold when he delivered the news to me."

"That's just his way."

"Okay, good. Bertie said something weird, too."

"Bertie is mediocre and bitter. Keep away from him."

"I will. My landlord Charles also told me a valuable Newton book was stolen from the library."

"Who exactly is this Charles guy?"

"Just the owner of my apartment. That he lets himself into on occasion. He's an alum, seemed very protective."

"Sounds like a weird dude. Consider the source? I haven't heard any-thing about a stolen book and I'm in the library all the time. Relax. Don't worry about anything. I'm excited you're here. We're going to have fun." She saluted and left me alone with my cold tea.

I poured the tea down the sink and was on my way to Endicott's office when Mairead passed me. Apparently, she had been the woman in his office. Her eyes were bright red, and she looked as if she'd been crying.

I went to William's office instead and knocked. "Yes?" he called. As I walked in, he stood up, and gestured to the chair opposite his desk. He waited to sit until I did and smiled that already endearing smile of his. Wearing a crisply ironed shirt with tiny pink checks, and a navy tie, he looked like a model for a French designer.

"Would you like to . . . grab a cup of tea together?" I asked. He glanced down at the papers on the table.

"Guess I've done enough marking for one morning," he said. "Give me just a minute, would you?"

As William typed I scanned his bookshelves. In addition to hundreds of academic history books, he also had a section dedicated to philosophy and game theory, and an entire shelf of Italian and French literary classics, including a leather-bound collection of fairy tales by Perrault, which I hadn't read in years.

"Quite a variety of books," I said, after he pushed his chair back and stood up.

"I like to read widely," he said. "Gives perspective. On everything."

"Agreed. I read a lot in my spare time."

"Is that so? We'll have to compare titles."

He pulled a trench coat off the back of the door, and we walked downstairs.

Outside, the sun was shining, and I didn't mind the cool breeze.

"The coffee at Gianni is good. How does that sound?" he asked, and I smiled in assent.

At the faux-Italian café, I ordered a double Earl Grey tea and William ordered a macchiato. When I reached in my bag for my wallet, he put his card over the tab.

"I should pay since I dragged you out," I insisted.

"*I* must pay, since you dragged me out," he countered.

"But you bought me whiskey last night. Bowmore."

"You are being kind, Ms. Henley, to pretend not to remember that you bought me *three* whiskeys."

We found a small table in the back of the empty café.

"I thought you'd want to try their coffee," he said. "It's not bad for Scotland."

"I recently gave up coffee," I said, sipping my tea.

"Graduate school without coffee? I'm fairly certain that's never been attempted."

"Long story."

"Mysterious," he said, lifting both eyebrows.

"Speaking of mysterious, I still can't believe what happened to Madeleine Grangier."

He swallowed hard. "It was sudden and devastating. We're all still reeling. You must have been so disappointed; I feel even worse for you. Is that what you wanted to discuss?"

I did want to. "Not now. But, another time. That would be great."

"Anytime, Isabel. I'm here. I mean that."

His offer seemed sincere, if merely courteous. No indication he was interested in me romantically. Pushing that thought aside I launched into what I'd wanted to tell Endicott. "Catrina was right. Someone at Cambridge is working on Catherine de' Medici's female circle. Thought I'd run an idea by you before I discuss it with Endicott. You published quite a bit about the Medici, back in the day."

"Back in the day, indeed."

"Now it's Machiavelli. But anyway, you're still an expert in the field."

"You flatter me," he said, "although you are correct that I am a humble scholar of Niccolò il Principe." Then he swallowed the rest of his macchiato in one gulp and said, "I've always thought scholarly topics were like novels. Or love affairs." He lowered his head and looked at me. "If you put them aside once, but then return to them, a certain magic is gone. Or perhaps there wasn't enough to hold your interest in the first place." He glanced at his cell phone, then back up at me. "So, how can I be of help?"

"What's your professional reaction to me modifying my topic? Maybe I could shift to working on the family of one of the women at court? Maybe a family like Rose's Falcone? By the way, I saw your advisee Rose earlier." I cradled my teacup between my fingers.

"Let me guess. She give you any unsolicited advice?"

"She suggested I introduce myself to you. Actually, we were in under-grad together. She was a couple years ahead of me, the star of our French department."

"Rose is . . . a diligent student, and among the cleverest I've ever known," he said, and stared down the bit of foam left in his tiny cup.

A dull knife of jealousy jabbed inside my stomach.

"At any rate, I like your topic," William said. "And Endicott does as well. There's nothing wrong with working on something someone else has covered. You just need to make it your own, spend time with the sources. Get to know them. Intimately." I thought he was about to smile. "Listen," he said. "I know we just got here, but I'd better get on. Should we discuss further in a couple days, after you've had time to think it through?"

I nodded and stood up.

Outside, William went one way and I turned in the opposite direction. A couple passed me, their bare arms linked like doughy pretzels. The man looked so much like Adrian, with the same easy gait, the same receding hairline, that I turned around to get a better look. What would Adrian be doing in St Stephens? And just like that, I was transported back five months and four thousand miles.

It had been an unusually frigid evening. I had one last thing I'd convinced myself that I needed to communicate after five months and seven days of no contact. I'd gone to his new office right before six in the evening telling myself I was being romantic.

As I entered the parking lot to wait by his car; he came out of the building.

"We agreed it was best if we didn't see each other," he said, when we were within a few feet of each other.

It was all going according to plan. "I came here on the spur of the moment because I wanted to tell you one thing," I said. I had straightened my hair that day, and was wearing a skirt so short I couldn't bend over, paired with a low-cut top and Manolo Blahnik heels I had borrowed from a friend. I stood there shivering without a coat.

"You gave me your word . . ."

"Please," I'd said. "If you ever loved me, hear me out—"

"—I never said I loved you," he interrupted, but we both knew it was a lie.

"I'm leaving. I got into St Stephens. In Scotland."

"How wonderful!" he said as he stepped forward, extending his hand. He took mine and patted it. His touch had been cold and platonic, the relief on his face obvious.

"This is goodbye." I'd meant it as a threat, but my voice had wavered, and tears had started to swim up over my black eyeliner.

He shifted sideways. "I want nothing but the best for you. For you to be happy." After starting to walk away, he'd turned back to me, and I thought he must be feeling regretful. Then he said, "If you come back, don't do it for me."

"I won't be back," I said, spitting out the words. In the days and weeks to come, I wished I'd thought to offer him my own piece of advice. That he get over himself. But that night I just watched as he got in his car and drove away.

CHAPTER FIVE

Hidden down a side street near St. John's Quadrangle, the St Stephens Library is the town's only eyesore. The cement-and-glass Brutalism of the 1970s architecture contrasts sharply with the surrounding neo-Gothic structures and cobblestone paths. Inside I could see the walls had not been painted in quite some time. The bright orange wall-to-wall carpet had crumbled away in patches, and there was a noticeable lack of air circulation.

As I climbed to the top floor where the history section was located, breathing in old books, the irritation I had conjured up because the aesthetic did not match my idealized vision of a Venerable British Academic Institution faded away. I started thinking of William in his pink-checked shirt and steered my thoughts back to the sixteenth century.

According to the catalogue, St Stephens Library did not contain any recent publications on Catherine's court, which was good, if not surprising. I found the history section and was about to head down an aisle when I passed a carrel, piled high with a rainbow of books. Behind them a blonde-haired head was leaning in toward a tiny, white Apple computer. Rose.

She waved me over as she closed her laptop, then stood up and gave me a warm hug. She was wearing black jeans and a fuchsia sweater, its tiny fibers sticking up like feathers in the staticky air. I smelled the same floral perfume that had lingered on her book.

"Come with me," she said, tucking the laptop under her arm. I followed her into a small room near the carrels. She closed the door behind us as she straddled a chair. "I hate to distract you," she said, "but as Jerome K. Jerome once said, 'It's impossible to enjoy idling unless one has plenty of work to do.'"

"I like your sweater," I said.

"They're known as 'jumpers' here. You'll know the other essential words. Particular to Scotland there's *dreich*, which means, particularly miserable weather."

"*Dreich* . . . sounds vaguely Yiddish."

"Yeah. Oh, and don't tell anyone something is 'quite good' if you're intending to compliment them. It means just the opposite, a lesson I learned the hard way."

"Any other pointers? About St Stephens, or Scotland in general?"

"I'm still a stranger in a strange land, but at least we're a team of two now. I do know that the best scone to be had is at the Castle Café at five in the morning. If you're nostalgic for American shopping, there's a soulless mall thirty minutes away. The only pharmacy closes at five and isn't open on Sunday."

"Do you ever miss the States?"

"Yeah. I miss movie theaters that release recent films. I miss family and friends. I miss CVS and Whole Foods. I miss peanut butter. And pickles."

"I love pickles so much I dressed up as one for Halloween. Remember the deli across from campus?"

"Yes! I loved that lady at the counter! But after a while you adapt. And there are things here I'd miss if I left. Being a cheap two-hour flight from the archives. Speaking of which, how's your work going?" she asked, the center of her forehead creasing into a single attractive horseshoe of concern.

"There's a woman at Cambridge working on my topic."

"So what? Her book probably sucks."

"Unlikely. She already has a contract."

"There's only one question that matters, Isabel," she said. "Do *you* love what you're working on? A dissertation is a marathon, not a sprint. You have to care about whatever you're studying so much that you wake up in the middle of the night frustrated that it's too early to go to the archives."

"Is that how you feel about the Falcone?"

"Definitely," she said. "I'm never bored with them, with my Federico. And I get bored easily." She stood up. "Can I ask you a favor? Can I read you part of a paper I'm working on when I'm finished?" she asked. "I hate giving presentations."

"Absolutely," I said.

"Any other questions?"

"Well . . . do you have any advice about the PhD? I'm not overwhelmed yet, but I probably will be soon."

"That's normal! Everybody feels that way. As for advice. Start early every day. Don't cut corners. Make reasonable goals in a realistic timeframe. Wish someone had told me that when I started. Keep in mind you can always ask for help. It's a nice community here. For the most part."

Someone triple knocked on the window and Catrina walked in.

"Our lunch date!" Rose said. "I was catching up with Isabel. It's been, what," she looked at me, "couple a' years?"

"Back to work I go," I said. My head had begun thumping again. Ever since I spit the meds into the sink, I'd known that it would hit me sooner or later. I found a water fountain and drank as much as possible.

Back in the stacks I pulled out the *Dictionnaire de la Renaissance* and went through the familiar biographical entries of the women of the French court, then sketched out brief details of each one. When I read through the page on Thérèse Du Montour, I realized why the name Falcone had

31

sounded familiar. High-born Thérèse had caused a stir by marrying Federico Falcone, but as a wealthy widow she controlled her choices. Rose would enjoy this bit of overlap between our topics. My headache had become overpowering. I left and went back to Endicott's office.

His door was closed—was it always closed?

"Come in," he called when I knocked. I took a step into the room, and he placed a piece of paper inside the book he was holding. "Ah, Isabel. Have a seat."

His desk was covered with neat piles of papers and recent monographs. "As you know I've been planning to write my dissertation on Catherine de' Medici's female court."

"Go on."

"I was recently made aware of a student at Cambridge who will soon be publishing a monograph on my very same topic."

He smiled at me. "Someone's done a PhD on Shakespeare! Can't work on him, then, can you?"

"It's not my intention to abandon my topic," I said, "but I could adjust it."

"I see," he said. "It's not possible to tell whether this would be a good idea until you have a concrete plan." He switched off the lamp on his desk.

"I suggest that you don't abandon Catherine de' Medici's circle entirely. Your scholarship is the reason a few of us here feel that you have so much promise. It's why Madeleine wanted you to study under her supervision." His expression was cryptic, but it appeared to convey disappointment. "However, a new angle is never a bad idea." He stood up. "I don't mean to rush," he said. "And I want you to know that I'm available to meet whenever you like. But perhaps next time you could make an appointment? I'm meeting with the Chancellor of the University in five minutes."

"Of course," I said, standing up. I walked to the door and turned around. "Thanks again." But he was buttoning his coat and did not look up or even acknowledge that he'd heard me.

I went back to the library right before it closed to see if they had a book I'd seen mentioned earlier. Luke was outside on the steps with a woman I didn't recognize.

"I was sitting on the floor near her office," he said in a low voice. "She walked past without saying hi, as if she hadn't noticed me there. She was always so put together. Not that day. She had this look on her face, like fear. I heard her talking through the door. She said something I can't forget, 'I'm still deciding what to do but I'll be in touch.' A few hours later she was dead. Does that sound like an accident to you?"

It took me a few seconds to realize they were talking about Madeleine Grangier. Luke hadn't seen me. Only one of the outside lamps was on, and it was very dark. I turned around and went home. I'd pick up the book some other time.

CHAPTER SIX

For the next few weeks, I worked ten hours a day, searching for new material and ways to shape my topic. Rose or Sean and I often had early breakfasts at the Castle Café, across from the caramel-colored ruins of St Stephens Castle on a cliff overlooking the sea.

Since my arrival in St Stephens, I'd avoided coffee. Drinking tea wasn't an attempt to become more British, it was a tiny effort to redefine myself. Sean had shown me how they drank tea here, with milk but no sugar. After a while, it became the only caffeine I craved.

One week Rose told me she had to go somewhere distraction-free to work, but even when she wasn't here, we exchanged emails on a daily basis. She sent me intriguing think pieces, recipes, op-eds about U.S. politics, and amusing comics. I didn't know how she had the surplus time to sift through all of this non-thesis related material. I loved her sense of humor—I'd never met someone able to blend high and low culture references in the same breath. She knew so much about so many different things.

When my Visa bill arrived, it came to nearly $2,000. Even though I had tried to be frugal, the small expenses had added up. Supermarket shopping was twice as expensive as in the U.S., and the pound was stronger than ever. My throat knotted up. I didn't know how I was going to pay the bill. Sean had told me it was complicated for American students to work in Scotland. If Rose were in town, I would've asked her for advice, but I didn't want to bother her while she was writing. Endicott seemed as unapproachable as ever. I didn't want William to know I was feeling desperate about money. So, I just kept my head down and put in the hours.

I also didn't want William to know I was thinking about him. Assuming I would bump into him in the history building, I managed to find an excuse to walk by his office nearly every other day. I even went back to the cathedral a few times hoping for a chance meeting, but our paths didn't cross.

One day Catrina saw me lingering in front of William's door.

"You're going to wait a while, Pet," she said. "He's researching in Paris." She paused. "I wouldn't mind going with him one day, though. He's pretty easy on the eyes."

I tried to look nonplussed and said, "I was actually looking for you, Catrina! I was going to ask if you wanted to go out for tea?"

She paused before answering. "Let me save what I've been working on." She went into her office and came back out wrapped in a grey wool scarf and coat.

Catrina took me to a specialty tea place that was a bit of a walk, but they had a great selection, and the vibe was trendier than it was at Gianni's. I wanted to ask about William, but instead I asked her about Madeleine Grangier.

"I found her arrogant," Catrina said. "She and Endicott got on super-ficially, but it was always *her* students versus *his* students. We all thought they either hated each other or they were shagging, possibly both. Of course, I was gutted when she died. But he's the best in the department, so in a bizarre way you're lucky he's your supervisor now."

"That's a cruel thing to say, Catrina."

She shifted back in her seat. "Did I shock you, Pet? It was unintentional. I can be blunt sometimes."

I took another sip of tea and decided not to mention what I'd overheard Luke say on the library steps.

"Are you and Rose close?"

"Rose? I adore her. We've had some wild times."

"Wild, how?"

"I have relatives with money, so I understand her. She's always busy, claims she's close to a major discovery."

"Her topic does sound amazing. Does Rose have a boyfriend these days?"

"She says she's single, but I suspect she has someone." She sighed. "Probably a lovely Italian. She gets giggly and sings and buys racy ensembles when she's on her way to Italy. I thought you said you were friends."

The rest of the week was devoted to creating spreadsheets to track the material I had compiled on court women. A month had passed, but the withdrawal still made me sick on and off, with some days worse than others.

That Saturday I walked to a beach east of town and continued to the far end where I reached a hiking trail, which I followed to the summit. The view was stunning, and it felt good to have a new perspective on St Stephens. When I came back Sean was on the library steps. I told him about my hike and his eyes widened.

"It's certainly scenic. That's where . . . Madeleine Grangier fell by the way."

"Oh," I said. "Wish you hadn't told me."

"I can show you some other areas to walk if you'd like," he offered.

"Some other time, yeah."

My desire to hike now somewhat dispelled, I spent the rest of the weekend watching old movies I'd checked out of the library, eating bagged popcorn that was unpleasantly sweet, and drinking copious amounts of

Irn Bru, an orange-colored Scottish soda that tasted more like chemicals than oranges. Drinking it made me feel like a local. Almost.

The next morning Rose called to ask if I wanted to sign up for golf classes with her. "They're free for students. I've played but I'm terrrrrrible," Rose groaned. "But when you do such focused work, you need something physical to get out of your head, don't you think?"

The first few lessons were held out on the driving range. Rose was actually pretty good at golfing. I found that I enjoyed hitting the ball and watching it fly. The instructor's accent was difficult to understand, but when I focused on the ball I wasn't worrying about my topic, and I wasn't thinking about my dead advisor or my past. Each time, after an hour on the course I noticed that my stomach unknotted itself and I was breathing more easily, although it was so cold when the sun went down that I could barely feel my hands, and even with gloves I got blisters. After class Rose and I went to the Quaich for hot toddies.

The prospect of too much spare time scared me, so every day I went to the windowless Special Collections before they closed and stayed up late at night searching articles on JSTOR. I ignored the withdrawal headaches. By mid-October I had decided to stick with my original topic. There were many women in Catherine's circle, and many ways to approach a historical problem.

While I'd been in Special Collections, late summer had faded into autumn. The days had grown short, and what little daylight we had was faint and filtered through a wispy fog. The sun had become lazy, showing up around eight, and beginning its retreat by three o'clock. Night melted into night, melted into night. The fall colors—when I saw them—were pale varieties of beige, dull in comparison to the tapestry of vermilion and amber that I knew from my childhood in New England.

I missed October in the States. Here storms came and went, blown in by the sea. And every day, at one time or another, it rained. "Four seasons in one day," the woman in the tea shop said. To me, it felt as if there were only one. I called my mother once a week, but our conversations were tense, and full of things unsaid. I stuck to neutral topics like the weather. I didn't tell her that I was lonely.

"As long as you're alright," she'd say, but I knew she meant "as long as you're no longer in touch with him."

After going off my medication my brain would sometimes zap me awake at night or jolt me in the library. The only thing that helped was lying down with a cold washcloth over my forehead. In some ways being in a new place had become the balm I had hoped it would be. I knew that someday I'd have to face everything, but not now. I was too busy.

At the same time, I couldn't shake the feeling that something wasn't quite right here. I was still upset about my advisor's death, and I had never even met her, but no one else seemed perturbed. Had she been so disliked, as Charles had emphasized? What about her conversation Luke had overheard? It wasn't only Madeleine Grangier. The atmosphere in St Stephens felt different from other universities where I'd studied. Everywhere there was a charged silence, as if everyone were keeping some secret that I alone didn't know. Then again, I was different, too. And guarding my own secrets. It was more likely me who was not quite right.

My favorite part of the day was my regular scone breakfast with Sean, and spending time with Rose when I wasn't working felt natural, easy. I'd always been a loner, but whenever she was away, I missed her. Her energy was helping me forget the past and stop dwelling on Professor Grangier.

"You and Rose have become close," Sean said over breakfast one day.

"It's true," I said. "Aside from Rose and you, I haven't made a lot of friends. It seems like a lot of the grad students here are coupled up, or strange. Mairead and I see each other in the library and talk about going out for tea, but never do. And really, I have so much work. No time to be social!"

"You should have fun, too. Then again, I wouldn't let your guard down."

I did worry I was falling behind, that I had something to prove to Endicott. To Catrina. To Rose. And though I tried to pretend it wasn't so, I wanted William's attention and admiration.

In the past academic writing had come easily to me, and my professors had always given me high marks and a lot of praise. I'd been the top student in most of my classes without trying too hard, but that had seemed unimportant compared with the thrill of the work itself.

"Can I ask you something that's been on my mind?" I asked Sean. "It's kind of weird."

"I like weird."

"Not this. I went to the library one night and saw Luke on the steps with someone, talking about Madeleine Grangier. He said the last time he saw her she looked disheveled, and he'd overheard a conversation she had alluding to something she needed to discuss, right before she died. He sort of implied her death wasn't an accident."

"That's definitely not good weird. Who was he with?"

"I didn't recognize her. But what about you? Had you heard anything about Madeleine that sounded odd? Rumors, or?"

"I went to her office hours, couple weeks before she died. She wasn't my supervisor but she knew a lot about Catholic refugees. She was out of it, like. She shooed me out of the office, said she had another student meeting, even though I'd seen the schedule on her door and no one else's name was on it. Anyway, that was it. But I wouldn't worry. Unlikely we'll ever figure that one out, right? Best focus on your topic."

"I'm trying."

"I trust things are working out with Endicott?"

"For sure," I said. "Although every time I go to see him I feel like I'm interrupting something important."

"You probably are."

"Ha, I knew you'd say that. It's difficult separating the professor from the man. Is he married? Kids?"

"He's married to his work. Cautionary tale. But you're right, he's secretive about his personal life, even for an Englishman. They say he has a girlfriend at another Uni, but none of us has ever met her."

That Saturday night I went to the library to return some overdue books and saw William at the circulation desk. After smoothing my hair and pinching my cheeks, I got in line behind him and tapped him on the shoulder, wishing I wasn't wearing sweatpants.

"Hey, stranger."

He turned around. "Oh, hello."

"Whatcha got?" I asked, peering over his shoulder to see what book had been passed to him. The cover was worn and the words, *Oeuvres poétiques,* were written in bold Gothic letters across the top. "So, you read poetry? For fun?"

"You mustn't say a word," he whispered. "Wouldn't want to undermine my reputation as a stoic historian."

"Didn't you tell me that reading widely gives perspective?"

"Good memory."

"I didn't realize you were back. If you're free we could have coffee or a quick drink?"

"That sounds lovely, but it's Saturday night, and I've got a date."

"Oh." I looked down.

"With an older gentleman by the name of . . ." he rotated the book so I could see the spine, "Joachim du Bellay."

I smiled.

"I'll drop this and a few things off first. Meet you at the Quaich in half an hour?"

At home I put on three coats of mascara and lip gloss, brushed my teeth, and changed into a skirt and my best pair of shoes, black leather heels I had purchased after I got my first full-time job out of college, then hurried to the pub, passing two men arguing in the parking lot.

William was waiting for me at the entrance. For a few seconds he appeared to look down, approvingly, at my heels.

"The Quaich is at full capacity already. But I think I know somewhere that won't be too busy with drunken undergrads."

On a thin side street near the Castle Café we went inside a small house with a bar on ground level. We sat in the back, near the fireplace. "Nice," I said, settling into a suede armchair.

"Good to have in your back pocket in case of emergency," he smiled.

It wasn't busy for a weekend. A group of women, wearing matching pink T-shirts, feathered plastic crowns, and bright pink boas were curved around the corner of the "L" of the green-glowing bar, talking loudly.

"What can I get you?" William asked.

"Whiskey soda? No fancy whiskey though."

"I wouldn't dream of it. Mixing single malts with anything other than water is prohibited under Scottish law."

At the bar, after William placed our order, two of the women from the group approached him, a blonde and a pretty redhead. "It's my hen do," I heard the redhead say in a high voice. She leaned close to William and whispered something as she draped the feather boa over his neck. He shook his head, then looked back at me. He removed the boa and gently placed it back around the bachelorette and patted her shoulder. The women walked away.

When he returned with our drinks he sat down on the adjacent armchair.

"Gotta fend them off with sticks, I see," I said.

"Yeah, you know what it's like."

"Me? Not so much."

"I don't believe that for a second," he said. "I saw the way Sean was looking at you at the pub that night. You're not aware of the effect you have on people."

I lifted the whiskey glass to my lips and took a sip. "So back to poetry. Was that really just for fun?"

"That one, no, but I do read poetry from time to time."

"Favorite poets?"

"Pablo Neruda."

"Certainly more enjoyable than Pierre Ronsard, whose nickname used to be Ronflard, you know."

He smiled. "I didn't know that! But to be fair, Ronsard did write some beautiful verses. I'll have to find them and show you."

"Please. Speaking of, how was Paris?"

"Paris is Paris. Wonderful, as always. A lot of work this time, I'm putting together a conference in a couple months. No rest for the wicked, I suppose."

I laughed and stirred my drink.

"Have you spent a lot of time there yourself?" he asked.

"You could say that. In college I saved whatever I earned from part-time jobs and traveled to Europe during the summers, speaking English only when necessary. I worked for a while as an au pair for an Italian family, too. After graduation I spent time in Paris working on a cataloguing project with a professor."

"Oh right, the same professor Rose studied with. Viret?"

"Exactly. Do you know him?"

"Not personally but I know his work of course. Impressive that he took you on fresh out of undergrad. Anyway, now I know why your Italian and French is so good. On paper anyway. I'll have to hear for myself."

He reached out as if he were going to touch my arm, but he picked up his drink.

"I'll try my best not to disappoint." I leaned back in my seat. "Big drinking culture here. I should take it easy with the Scotch," I joked.

"It's funny, Madeleine Grangier once said she had more to drink in a weekend in Scotland than in a whole month at the Sorbonne."

I winced at the mention of her name, and William seemed to sense my discomfort. "How about where you're from . . . New York, right?"

"Close. Boston. And you?"

"Ah, you know, here, there, and everywhere."

I sipped some more of my drink, wondering why he'd evaded such a simple question.

The door opened and a draft flew inside. Catrina, followed by Bertie, acting like strangers, went up to the bar. Catrina hissed, "What a load of bollocks. It's always about her. I'm sick of it."

"You shouldn't have got so involved. I'm trying to help you."

"Piss off."

I lowered my head and turned around, then slumped down in my seat. "Maybe they won't see us," I said, draining the rest of my glass.

"Duck down and come with me," William said, in a half whisper. "I'll take you out the back entrance. One of my pals works in the kitchen."

Outside we stopped in front of a fence to contemplate the castle ruin. The streets were slick with rain, but the clouds had parted above the castle to reveal a crescent-shaped moon. Below the promontory, where the castle perched, was the tiny stretch of sand known as Castle Beach. We looked out at the calm sea, the faint moon, and the hot blue stars. The inside of my stomach felt warm.

It started to drizzle, and William offered to walk me home. We passed the quad, deserted at this hour, and the cathedral, and when I shivered, he took off his coat and wrapped it around my shoulders. I led the way to my building through the empty parking lot, littered with empty bottles and cigarettes. A car packed with six people was pulling out as we walked to the front door.

"Here we are," I said, gesturing with my eyes.

The partial moonlight painted flowing shadows across the facade where the trees were trembling, silvery. I pictured my back against the door, pulling William's jacket collar close to me and kissing him.

"Thanks for the drink," I said. "And for escorting me."

"Thank you. I had a great time. The best I've had in a while, actually."

"You sound surprised."

"Maybe I am a little."

Putting my key in the door I turned back to William. "You really should've gone for that redhead."

"Who, the bride-to-be? Call me narrow-minded, but the *droit du seigneur* has never held much appeal. Besides, she's not my type."

"What's your type?"

He lifted his chin, and said in a mock-serious tone, "Fiercely intelligent, brutally witty . . . historians."

I spent most of Sunday in bed, listening to the rain against the door, fantasizing about William.

The following freezing Monday I received an email informing me that my office was available. Rose had also written to say that she was back and would be clearing out, but she'd told me that so many times I almost deleted the message. I went to the history building and found the entrance on street level behind a small red door.

Inside, Mairead was sitting at one desk, arms crossed, headset on, lips pressed together. She jutted out her chin in the direction of the empty desk in the corner. Fluorescent bulbs in the ceiling bounced beige-yellow light up from the linoleum floor.

"Rose moved most of her stuff this morning," Mairead said, removing her headset. "Said she'd be back for the rest."

On the wall behind Rose's desk were timelines of the French and Spanish kings and queens and popes in the sixteenth and seventeenth centuries. On the desk were five or six legal pads and a stack of library books, crowned by the red book I had found in the lounge. I went closer to examine a folio-sized book on a stand. As I reached over to pick it up Mairead spoke.

"Don't touch it. She doesn't like when people touch her things."

"Oh-kay," I said, and stepped back.

As I did so, the door opened forcefully and thudded against the wall. A tall woman wearing a St Stephens fleece jacket strode in. She looked familiar. Where had I seen her before?

"You Mairead's new office mate? Isabella is it?" she asked me, clutching her broad waist with her large hand. She had a light Scottish accent. "I'm Danny." She held out her hand. She had a strong grip. "Do you play shinty?"

"What's that?"

"What's that?" she said, attempting to imitate an American accent and giggling at her efforts. "Shinty is the most marvelous field game in the world is wha' tha' is. Our team is alright, and we tour Scotland. Want to join?" Then I realized. Danny had been sitting on the library steps that night with Luke.

"I don't know, Danny. I'm taking a golf class at the moment. But . . . thanks."

"Shame about that." She bounded over to a bookcase and pulled out a folder, and said, "I'm off, then."

She slammed the door shut. Mairead stared into her screen.

"Umm, nice seeing you, Mairead," I said. Without waiting for a response, I knew would not be forthcoming, I left.

CHAPTER SEVEN

At the library Rose was returning a book at the circulation desk. "Rose!" I called, a bit too loudly. It took her a minute before she turned around. She held out her arms, then stepped over and hugged me close. She was wearing a black cashmere sweater and long fingerless gloves, jeans, and leather combat boots.

"Come with me, will you?" she said. She took my hand and led me up to the room where we had met before. She had put on weight, and her face looked fuller than before. She pulled up a chair and said, "How are you? Sorry I didn't write much in the last week. Tell me everything. But listen, they've scheduled my talk for next month. I'm freaking out. Do you have two minutes to listen to a quick overview? I was thinking about what you said about Thérèse Du Montour being married to Federico Falcone. So much intersection."

"I'm all ears."

"Well, here goes. I know you know a lot of this stuff already . . ."

"Rose, it's okay," I said. "Just start. No self-editing. I'm listening."

"You're the best," she said, her posture softening. "In the sixteenth century, the Falcone were weavers and textile merchants in Genoa. Did you know that blue jeans were invented in Genoa? They're called jeans for Gênes.

"Anyway . . . the Falcone weren't part of the high nobility, but they were strivers. Unfortunately, my branch of the family alienated themselves from Genovese movers and shakers because they were involved in an uprising to overthrow the doge, Andrea Doria. So, they fled to France.

"And thus, Giovanbattista, the *paterfamilias*, took his wife and their children to France in 1557. There was an oldest son, who died, and Federico was the second son. Then there were two daughters, Giulia and Elisabetta, and Piero, who became a bishop. Giovanbattista's first wife died and he remarried. Tommaso was Giovanbattista's son from his second marriage. Catherine de' Medici invited the whole family to court, and gave them titles, and positions in her household.

"It's a lot of characters. Just remember Federico and Tommaso for the moment. And Catherine, our connecting thread. Anyway, Federico and Tommaso Falcone sailed to the Americas on behalf of Catherine, who was interested in developing a trade route with Brazil. Federico served as an unofficial adviser to Catherine's three sons, who became the last Valois kings of France."

She stopped talking. "Questions so far?"

"Were they loyal to Rome or did they embrace Gallicism?"

"Good question. They were divided. Or maybe they were just playing both ends against the middle. The Falcone were patrons of the arts, and Federico had a Cabinet of Curiosities with natural wonders that he had found on his travels, and precious stones, including a prized emerald. There was an assassination plot. That's part of the needle-in-the-haystack information in the archives that I mentioned." She paused, watching my face for a reaction.

"Whom were they plotting to assassinate?"

"Intrigued yet, Isabel?"

"Definitely."

"It's funny. Sometimes I can't believe how lucky I was to have dis-covered this topic. Abundant, fascinating documentation, yet totally overlooked by historians."

"It does sound pretty great," I said.

She hit the top of her head with the heel of her hand. "Gosh, I'm sorry for going on and on. I could talk about the Falcone for hours—I get overly excited. Don't get me wrong, though, I've had my share of challenges, too."

"Have you?"

She flipped her hair back. "Yeah. But, what about you and your topic Isabel? How's that going? You must feel a bit lost at the moment. Which is probably how most grad students feel."

"I appreciate your concern. It's going okay, I guess?"

"Are you sure? You listened to me, I'll listen to you. I'm a good listener."

"Thanks, Rose. I'm working through something at the moment, but I'll definitely let you know when I'm ready to share."

She looked down at her watch and said, "Of course. I'll call you, later, okay?" She pressed her hand to her stomach, stood up, and kissed my cheek, and left without waiting for my response. As I left the room I walked through a cloud of her perfume.

On my way to my carrel, I went to the window to watch the sun set over the sea and looked down in the courtyard below. At the foot of the steps Rose was standing with William. As she was about to leave, Rose grazed his shoulder with her hand, just for a couple of seconds. Then they were standing close to each other and kissed on both cheeks, the European way. As William walked away Rose turned around once, then twice, to look at him.

A few hours later I listened to a voicemail from Rose.

"Darling, thanks for listening to the start of my Falcone story. What are your plans tomorrow? I have a surprise . . . but you'd need to clear your calendar. One night only. How 'bout if I pop by around ten? If that doesn't suit, ring me back. Otherwise, I'll see you then. Ciao bella!"

CHAPTER EIGHT

Early the next morning a series of loud honks in the parking lot woke me up. I remembered Rose's message and ran down the stairs.

Rose was leaning against a dark-blue Mini Cooper, smoking a cigarette that she squashed elegantly with one foot as if dancing when she saw me.

"Ready, slow coach?" she said.

"You said you'd come by at ten," I said.

"I know you're an early bird. I'll have you back at 'em tomorrow by noon. *Promis juré!*" She pronounced French words without an American accent. "Please, this means a lot to me."

"I need to work today. I'm okay with breakfast together, though."

"Isabel, are we besties? Are you up for an adventure? Or are you too important to take off part of a weekend?" She walked over and gave me a hug. Then she pushed back until her arms were out straight, holding me by the shoulders. "I just thought it would be fun. And I thought you could use some friend time. You seem a little worked up." She hugged me again. "And speaking for myself, I could use some BFF time. I am under so much pressure right now."

"Okay, okay," I said. "What kind of clothes do I need? Hiking gear?"

"No, city stuff. Nothing fancy. We'll mostly be driving and walking around."

I dashed back upstairs and stuffed a couple of wrinkled items into a sports bag.

"So where are we going, Rose?" I asked, the wind from the open windows blowing the words back in my mouth. We'd been talking for half an hour.

"You've asked me that twice now. Didn't I say it was a surprise?"

"I hate surprises," I said, with a pout she couldn't see because her eyes were on the road.

"You'll like this one. Believe me."

"You're good at driving on the left."

"You get used to it. Luckily the East Coast prepared me for driving on icy roads."

"Do you remember the Italian Society holiday party? You knew everybody, but you kept me company and helped me play cashier."

"That's right! You were so sweet to help out. We raised a ton of dough."

"And that guy, Mark. You introduced me to him, remember?"

"Mark, wait, Mark Wilson?"

"No, not Wilson. Thin, sad-eyed, tattoos, obsessed with Nietzsche?"

"Oh him! You guys hooked up? Good for you! I was with his roommate, Seth? I think. It's hard to keep track."

"Ah, the young and restless Rose. Everybody wanted you."

"Did they? Seduction is the easiest thing in the world. But for me it goes from obsession to boredom quickly. It's one or the other. Never anything in between."

"I miss Professor Viret."

"And the long lectures he kept going after class had ended?"

"Yeah, but they were great. He's the reason I love Claude Chabrol."

"I grew up watching French films with my mother," she said, glancing over at me. "She was half French. I don't know if you knew."

"That must be why your French is so good."

"She died when I was sixteen. Cancer."

"I don't think you ever told me, Rose," I said.

"Are you close with your parents?"

"My mom, sort of. My dad left when I was twelve. Haven't heard from him since."

"That's awful." She tapped the steering wheel and said nothing for a couple of minutes. "This is the Firth of Forth," Rose said as we drove onto a bridge spread over a broad river. "Firth means fjord, and Forth is the river. Firth of Forth. Wrap that around your tongue with Scottish r's. Back there we passed the river T-a-y, the Scots pronounce it 'Tee.' This bridge we're on right now is falling apart. Literally. The metal cables are breaking one by one. Plink, plink, plink."

"Isn't there another way?"

"'Fraid not. I thought you'd be into the sense of danger, the excitement! Isn't that why we chose to study history?"

I laughed in a facile manner but gripped the dashboard.

We got off the M-90 and onto the A-90. "Edinburgh," I said. "Is that where we're going? I've never been."

"You've never been to Edinburgh? What?"

Rose drove me through the city center, where the brown-stone buildings were tinged with black. We drove up hill after hill. Edinburgh looked like a darker, more compact London, with one foot firmly in the past. On what seemed to be the main commercial street, Rose parked in front of a row of posh-looking boutiques, and led me into the first one.

"Lovely to see you again, Miss Brewster," a saleswoman with a thick West Coast accent greeted Rose. I was learning how to distinguish East and West Coast. Rose had told me if I couldn't understand anything the person was saying they were probably from Glasgow.

"Hi, Vera," said Rose. She held out her hand toward me and said, "This is Isabel, my dearest friend. She's American too!" We were ushered to a seating area and one of the saleswomen brought us tea while Vera went off and then returned with a few outfits that she held up one by one. "I brought one size up from the last time you were here, Miss Brewster. I know you don't like to wear tight clothes."

"I'd better stop eating daily scones!" Rose chose two dresses and walked toward the dressing room, saying, "And now some things for Isabel, please."

An hour later we had a pile of things we had tried on, including hats and jewelry and shoes. I laughed at something Rose said and then kept laughing until I couldn't seem to stop, so I sat down and leaned my head back against the chair. Laughing turned into half-crying, and I put my head in my hands. Rose came over to me and put her arms around me.

"It's okay," she said. "Shh, shh. I get it." She rubbed my back lightly as I started to come out of it.

"I . . . I'm . . ." I said, drawing breaths between heaves.

"I think this trip was a good idea," Rose said. She stood up and walked over to another dress neither of us had yet tried on.

"The restaurant tonight is . . . smart," she said, pulling it off the hanger and handing it to me. "I should have mentioned that this morning when I picked you up."

The dress fit so well it could have been made for me. The cut was flattering, emphasizing my long waist, and the rust color set off my eyes. I looked at the price tag.

"It's 250 pounds!"

There was a quiet moment. Then Rose turned to Vera. "I'll take this," she said, holding up a black velvet jacket, "and this, and this . . . and these!"

I went outside to check my phone while waiting for Rose. She emerged and within a few minutes we were driving uphill toward Edinburgh Castle. As we passed the entrance I said, "Aren't we going to visit?"

Rose twisted her mouth to one side. "This weekend I want you to myself. Anyway, there's very little of interest inside. Right now, I'm starving. And parched!"

We drove up to the entrance of a hotel that looked like a Victorian manor on an American movie set and pulled into a spot on a sloping hill.

Rose checked in and made a reservation for tea. Our room, which turned out to be much bigger than my flat, was decorated with purple silk drapery and a four-poster bed. "Isn't this place a dream?" Rose said.

"How are we going to pay for it? Are we robbing a bank? Is that the surprise?"

"Silly you. It's on me!"

Someone knocked and Rose popped up from one of the velvet cushions and opened the door for the bellman, carrying my sports bag, Rose's garment bag and monogrammed suitcase, and four bags from the dress shop.

"This is for you," she said, passing one of the bags to me. I reached inside and pulled out the last dress that I had tried on. "I promise I'll return it if you hate it," she said. "Do you? And this bag has the pair of shoes you loved."

"Of course I don't hate it," I said. "The dress is gorgeous. And those shoes! It's way, way too generous of you. I can't accept it. I'll figure out how to pay you back."

"Let me be the judge of what's too generous," Rose said. "And you prep the bank heist."

She waved off my further protestations and we walked down to tea that was being served in a large atrium decorated with dark ferns. Two servers brought out a silver three-tiered platter with finger sandwiches, scones with clotted cream, and a bottle of pink champagne that Rose ordered, and I drank most of.

Back in the room I laid on the bed, and the room started spinning in a not unpleasant way. Rose laid down next to me, sighing as she scrolled through her phone, and I fell asleep. When I woke up, I found her on the couch near the fireplace, clicking on her laptop. "Hey, sleepyhead," she said. "Let me finish up while you get dressed."

I took a shower, dried my hair, and put on makeup. Then I slipped on the new dress. "I passed out from the champagne," I said with a yawn. "Aren't you tired?"

"Nah," she said. "I'll sleep when I'm dead."

Rose went into the bathroom and twenty minutes later came out transformed. Her eyes lined with kohl and lips a deep red shade, her hair twisted on top of her head, she looked more like an elegant hostess than a grubby graduate student. I slipped on my new shoes, and we linked arms and walked down the wide staircase, through the courtyard, to the restaurant with faux Victorian décor.

Rose wanted to order the tasting menu, but I said it would be too much food, so we settled on a salad and a local fish. "Red or white?" she asked. "Do you like Sancerre?"

"The only thing I know about wine is that I like to drink it," I said.

"Sancerre, from the Loire Valley, is the best white on the planet," she said.

"I remember royal forces laid siege to Sancerre because it was a Protestant stronghold."

"Wasn't there something about cannibals?" asked Rose.

"Montaigne's essay, *Of Cannibals*, compared the Brazilian Tupi tribe to the French in Sancerre, except unlike the French the Tupi maintained their dignity."

"Oh yes! My personal favorite Montaigne essay is *Of Friendship*. Montaigne believed that if you're lucky, you can have one true friendship. Do you believe in that kind of connection between two people?"

"I haven't found it."

"Yes you have. I have, too! With you." Rose clinked my glass with hers. "You know your Montaigne, lady."

"I feel an affinity with him. Not just because we both have Jewish mothers."

"I love that his essays began as imaginary letters to his dead friend. How poetic!" She took a gulp of water. "Speaking of cannibals, how about dessert?"

"Rose, we just had high tea and a two-course dinner. You're insane."

I leaned back in my chair, and she turned to me. "Now that we're drunk, I can tell you all my secrets and you'll forget them by tomorrow."

"Secrets?"

"In my search for original source material, I found some intriguing letters. And here's what the letters reveal." She paused and looked at me. "And what you need to keep close to the vest."

I put my hand over hers. "I may not be as pure a friend as Montaigne, but I'd never betray your confidence."

She leaned in close. "Catherine de' Medici sent Federico Falcone on a covert mission to Brazil, where she'd long wanted to set up a trade route. Federico supplied the indigenous peoples with weapons to defend themselves against the Spanish and the Portuguese. He ended up with the emerald I mentioned. Federico brought it back to Europe, intending to give it to Catherine de' Medici." She cleared her throat.

"That's really cool, Rose. So, you found the Holy Grail? The philosopher's stone?"

She smiled. "Societies like the ones Montaigne wrote about in Brazil went back thousands of years. What if I were to tell you that once upon a time, they were matrilineal, matriarchal? After the Europeans colonized the Americas, all vestiges of matriarchy were put to rest. The emerald represents a bygone era."

"What are you trying to tell me? Federico got these people to give up their most valuable possession and I'm supposed to sympathize with him?"

She quickly raised one finger to her lipstick-free lips. "The point about the emerald is what it symbolizes. Listen . . ." She took a sip of Sancerre and put her hand on her stomach. "I might need to ask you to . . . do something for me. I'm sort of in over my head and I don't know how to handle it."

"How to handle what?"

"It's difficult to explain, but I sort of got in with the wrong crowd."

"What do you need, Rose? How can I help?"

She looked over both shoulders around the emptied room and lowered her voice.

"It's complicated. I'm in a bit of trouble. But it's okay." Her phone lit up. "Just a sec," she said. She typed in something and then put her phone on the table, facedown. "Actually I, I'd rather not discuss it now." She took her hair out of its clip and let it fall on her shoulders.

"What's going on, Rose?"

"I really don't want to discuss it. Not right now. Let's gossip instead." She signaled for the check.

Back in our room she stripped off all her clothes and stretched out on the bed. Within a few minutes she was asleep.

The next morning, over a bottle of champagne at brunch, she told me Danny's story, referring to her as a "posh Scot," and talked about the other students, about what it was like before I arrived. She talked about her mother, and how much she loved her, and hated her. "It's so great you're here," she said. "I've missed being able to confide in a friend. A real friend."

I flicked over the idea of telling her about Adrian, but I'd made a deliberate decision to leave the past in the past, so it was as if it had never happened.

"I've told my dad about you," she said. "I talk about you all the time actually. I want to take you with us over school break after Christmas, if you'd like to come? Or maybe you're busy? Seeing your own family?"

"I told my mom I was staying here. I don't have a ticket to fly back to the U.S. Plus, if I went, it would just be the two of us staring at each other. Grim."

"Oh, so then you must come with me! On a skiing holiday in Cortina! My dad and his girlfriend and some Italian friends. Do you ski?"

"Nope."

"I'll teach you! Yes, yes, you must come! I insist. Don't worry about the ticket. I've got a bunch of frequent flyer miles."

"That's so sweet of you, Rose. But I don't know. I have so much work to do. And to go from one cold place to another . . . let me think about it." I laughed. "You haven't touched your champagne."

"More for you. I've got to drive, hun! Plus, I've got a hangover headache already." I hadn't seen her take more than a few sips of the Sancerre. On the way back Rose didn't want to stop by the castle and didn't want to talk. "Meditating," she said. She took me around the city, and we took a long-cut home.

She dropped me off with a cheery wave and a hug, telling me how grateful she was that I'd taken a break to spend some time together. I worked through the rest of the afternoon.

I had just undressed when I felt my phone buzzing.

I picked up. "It's meeee," Rose said.

"Hi!"

"Come downstairs?"

"Where?"

"Your parking lot. I'm here!"

"Are you okay?"

"Yeah. Want to go for a swim?"

"Now?"

"Wanted to show you the beach at night, it'll blow you away. It's mild tonight, we can see stars."

"Sure," I said. "Sounds like fun."

I went down in my PJs and a big coat and found her in her blue car. She passed me a beer and I sipped it as I listened to her chattering. It was difficult to keep up.

"Since you're not keen on the skiing idea, I called my dad and said I was bringing you to Miami with me over break for a couple weeks. He's got a condo in South Beach. I'll take you to all the best restaurants and clubs. You're right, skiing would be cold and it's too cold here during the winter anyway, not to mention lonely when the place empties out. What do you think? If you give me your birth date, I can book your ticket online. You're gonna love it."

"It . . . uh . . . sounds great. July 26, 1983."

"Oh, you're a Leo! I love Leos! You should let me do your chart sometime. I'm pretty good."

She drove, a little too fast, and parked across from the Castle Café, closed at this hour. We got out of the car. The clouds had parted above the castle revealing a nearly full moon. Along the horizon, a patch of sky changed from light to deep blue, and this spread to another patch. It wasn't much darker than it had been at teatime, but night had arrived.

We walked down toward the beach, arm in arm, and she stopped to show me the part of the castle where John Knox had been imprisoned. With the castle, the calm sea, the glowing moon and the dim stars, there was so much beauty here. On the beach Rose stood behind me and wrapped her arms around my waist.

"Look up! Ursa Major," whispered Rose. "The Great Bear. Or, as it is also known, the Big Dipper. And there," she extended a hand toward the sky, "is the North Star, Polaris. The whole northern sky moves around it, but it never moves." I let her continue.

"A lonely sailor can always orient himself facing Polaris." Still standing behind me she reached for my wrists then guided my right arm and then my left. "To your right, the east, to your left, the west. The students go swimming here on May first every year, it's a tradition! But I thought it would be fun just you and me." She pulled off her sweater and jeans, then her underwear, and left her big coat and top for last. She wasn't wearing a bra. Then she ran toward the sea, and I followed. She walked into the water.

"Ahhhh!" she screamed, drenching her ankles. "Fuck, it's cold. Come in," she said. "It's exhilarating." The enthusiasm in her voice reverberated into me.

I don't remember taking off my clothes, but then I was walking into the water toward her. I dunked my whole body in, and that woke me up. I jumped out and searched for my coat. My body felt hot and tingly. She ran out of the water toward our clothes.

"I'd never seen you naked before. Your body is beautiful," she whispered. "Isn't it refreshing? Isabel, don't you feel so alive? Isabel? Are you okay?"

I was crying. "Yes," I said. "So weird. I'm happy." I let out a sob, and my whole body was shaking. I stretched up, looking at the stars, the vastness around me. "I'm free," I said it loudly. It was just the two of us on the beach. And then again, softer, "I'm free."

"Shh," she said. She was hugging me. Her body felt warm. I hadn't been this close to anyone in months. "You're okay. I'm here for you. I've got towels in the car. I just wanted you to experience this. Sorry if it upset you." She picked up my shirt and helped me put it on, rubbing my back. Then we both tugged on the rest of our clothes, laughing.

As we started for the car, I looped my arm in hers and said, "I haven't told you about it, but I was kind of a mess back home. I feel like a person again. Thank you so much for everything. I'm so happy I came to St Stephens."

"I'm glad, Isabel. I love being with you, too. I haven't done much, not really. And I know you'd do the same for me."

We got back in the car, laughing some more. I didn't notice how cold it was, so it didn't bother me. I felt energetic, euphoric. I was really starting to like the new me.

CHAPTER NINE

I didn't hear from her again until Wednesday.

Her voicemail said, "How 'bout if I come over to your place later with a bottle and something to nibble? Seven P.M.? Looooved our swim. Hope you took a hot shower afterward. Ciao bella. Oh! PS, it's my birthday tomorrow."

When I finished at the library, I went grocery shopping and picked up a scarf for Rose at the flea market. Except for Charles, I hadn't had any visitors to my apartment, and there were papers and books and plastic shopping bags all over. On the floor were a few popcorn kernels that I had forgotten to clean up, balls of dust, and an errant pill I had missed during my purge. I vacuumed and lit candles. Rose knocked on the door at 6:59.

She kissed me on the lips and then gently pushed past me and gave herself a tour. She put down her enormous bag, which looked like a piece of vintage luggage, threw her navy pea coat on my one chair, and plunked down on the couch. I brought out a bowl of potato chips.

Rose was wearing a red silk kimono and black leggings. No makeup except bright red lipstick. Her tresses were pulled back into a low bun, curls messy but glossy. She made beauty look easy, which it had never been for me. I sat down next to her, and she opened her bag and pulled out a bottle of Scotch, "sixteen-year-old Lagavulin," and two crystal tumblers, which clunked against each other. She poured some in my glass, but not hers, and clinked my glass. I handed her my sloppily wrapped gift.

"Happy almost birthday," I said.

Rose's eyes went wide. "I adore presents," she said as she ripped open the crinkled wrapping paper.

"Fuschia's my favorite color, how did you know? Aww, Isabel, you shouldn't have." She stood up and tied it artfully around her neck.

"My mother loved her scarves. Miss her. She was good at handling my dad, without her he's kind of unmoored. Why do you think I'm in school in Scotland?" She laughed. She covered my hand with hers and kept it there, her eyes trained on mine. "Enough about me. How are you doing?"

"Work on my topic is going well, finally."

Rose dropped my hand. "Tell me all about it . . . tomorrow . . . when the whiskey wears off. I can't see totally straight. Has Endicott been supportive?" She leaned forward and added more to my glass even though I'd only had a sip.

"Very. He said he admires my work ethic. I think he's relieved I didn't switch."

"Told you! Keep going!" she said, pointing at my glass. "Endicott's had a rough time of it, poor guy. Madeleine was his closest friend. Well, maybe William is his closest friend. Anyway, I think he's still in recovery mode."

"Where is William, these days? I haven't seen him for a bit."

"Oh? He travels a ton."

"So I hear from Catrina."

"I'm sure," said Rose with a sigh. "She loves to gossip. Don't know if I'd trust her with a secret." She leaned into me and our shoulders touched and then she settled back into the chair and clasped her hands behind her head. "Do you have any?"

"Any what?"

"Secrets?"

"I, uhh . . ."

"Yeah. Let's overshare. I'll go first. The last time I was in Paris I went to a club and went home with a gorgeous couple. The sex was incredible. Okay, your turn. Come on, everyone has one. Doesn't have to be major."

I took two big gulps of Scotch and then launched into my story about Adrian. She watched me with sympathy and then leaned forward and put her hand on my shoulder.

"Thanks for trusting me with that."

"It's easy to talk to you, Rose. Thanks for listening."

"You are so welcome," she said, brightening. "You're officially my favorite person at St Stephens. Like I said, I'm as lucky as Montaigne, found my kindred spirit."

We clinked glasses again, hers still empty.

She asked where the bathroom was and staggered to it. I heard my medicine cabinet opening and she called, "Hey, do you have any Advil in here? Oh, never mind, got it." I heard water running, and she opened the door and stood in the doorframe. "You have two empty bottles of drugs under the sink. Serious."

"I told you. After Adrian and I broke up," I said, "I went through a bad time. But I stopped taking medication after I arrived here. Kept the bottles in case I need refills."

"Don't take that poisonous crap!" she said, slurring her words, cradling the doorframe with her arm. "What happened to you is not your fault. That guy took advantage of *you*."

"I told you. I'm off them now."

"Good," Rose said. "Phew." She looked down at her Rolex. "I should get going, but you haven't caught up with me, darling, and I wish you would." She swerved a bit, then sat down. She must have had a lot to drink earlier.

I took two more sips, and then her eyes went wide. "Aaaah, I almost forgot, I brought you a little housewarming gift." She reached into her big tote and took out a large, gold-glimmering gift box tied with a red ribbon.

"I was wondering what you were carrying around in there. That's for me?"

"Open it!" she said after a minute.

I pulled out a blue-and-white porcelain jar, with a growling Foo Dog on its lid. It looked antique, maybe Ming. "This is exquisite. Thank you."

She raised her empty glass. "This," she said with a giggle, "Isabel, is to mark our special friendship. There's something inside, but you are expressly forbidden to open it until we can do so together fifty years from now. Or you open it if I die before you do. In the meantime, it can brighten this room, which is really dreary."

"Thanks. It will certainly be the focal point of my entire flat. I don't know if I can wait fifty years though."

"You have to agree to it, or I won't give it to you. We need more tradition, and more mystery, in our lives. Plus, it's about delayed gratification, which I know you're better at than I am."

"Okay, I'll wait. I love the idea of opening it up together when we're colleagues at some liberal arts college, reminiscing over the old days."

Rose stood up and gave me a sloppy kiss and a long hug before she threw her coat over her shoulder and stumbled out the door. I put the jar on the living room table. It was almost ten and I soon fell asleep in a velvety haze.

CHAPTER TEN

The next morning I slept in and made it to my carrel two hours later than usual. Someone in my peripheral vision walked up to me and said, "Boo!" I jumped.

It was Danny. "Want to pop by mine on Saturday? I'm having some friends round for my birthday," she said. "I throw the best parties in this rotten village."

"Love to," I said. "Send me the details and I'll be there."

The next day I saw Mairead entering the library.

"Want to go together to Danny's party? I'm dressing as a fairy. I bought a pair of gauzy wings in the charity shop. You're coming, right?"

"A fairy?" I said. "Catrina told me that it was fancy dress."

Mairead laughed as she fished around in her pocket for her ID, and said, "Fancy dress means costumes.'"

From my carrel I called Rose, but she didn't pick up.

Saturday it snowed on and off all day. By the time Mairead met me in the parking lot below my flat it was windy and dark.

Danny lived on Fenshawe Road, outside the medieval gate, the swankiest street in St Stephens. The fresh snow crunched under my boots. When we arrived we found the red door ajar.

Danny, dressed as a pirate in a hat, corset, fishnet stockings, and over-the-knee leather boots, was standing inside the foyer. She threw her octopus arms around me and Mairead both. "Welcome, dearies! Remember not to behave tonight!" She stood back while we took off our coats and said, "Great costumes," with a laugh that might have been ironic. "That dress looks like it's painted on you, Iz."

Mairead was wearing a pink-satin dress, which looked like a girl's princess costume. She had attached wings with glittered glue to the back. As Danny straightened out one of Mairead's wings she said, "Head to the kitchen for a drink," and tossed her head toward the back of the house.

I didn't recognize any of the people in bright costumes in the high-ceilinged hallway. "I wonder what Rose will be wearing," Mairead said. "Is Sean coming? Luke?"

"Sean said Danny's circle was 'not his crowd.' Luke said he had other plans. There's a lot I'm just starting to figure out," I said. "I didn't realize there's tension between Catrina and Danny."

"Catrina's a jealous type," said Mairead. "And her closest mate Danny's hosting parties on the poshest street in town." She took a step back and closed her eyes. "'If you judge by appearances in this place, you will often be deceived, because what appears to be the case hardly ever is.'"

"Well said!" I said.

"It's from *La Princesse de Clèves*. What's true of the French court is true of our school."

In the kitchen, Catrina, in a milkmaid top, was serving drinks to a noisy crowd.

Standing in the doorway Jeff and Bertie, dressed convincingly as the Humpty Dumpty Twins, were drinking beer out of glass mugs. "Tweedledee and Tweedledum," I whispered to Mairead, and she chuckled.

Bertie poked Jeff. "Did you know that they killed King Edward II by shoving a red-hot poker up his arse?" I turned sideways away from them.

"Look, it's Isabel and Mairead," Bertie said, walking over to us. "Fancy a drink, girls?"

"Girls?" I said.

Mairead elbowed me. "What's in your mug?" she asked Bertie. "It looks like syrup with soap."

"Gulden Draak. Triple ale. The Belgians call it the champagne of Ghent. Not for the weak of heart. Fruity girly cocktails more to your liking?" he asked, looking at me.

"I'll try the Belgian beer," I said. "You, Mairead?" She nodded.

We followed him into the pantry, where he took a bottle out of the cupboard. "Why don't you start with one between you," he said, popping the cap and letting it fall on the floor. Jeff walked in and passed us each a cold mug. The taste was hoppy and bitter, complex and strange. The guys acted surprised when I asked Bertie if he would please open another bottle.

I followed Mairead through a snaking crowd of people into the living room.

Danny's adviser, Stu Carlsson, wearing a plastic Viking helmet with horns, was kneeling down on the antique rug by the fireplace attempting to make a fire. "I give up," he said, standing up and dusting his pants off. "I'm Stu." He had spiky hair, a goatee, and a mischievous expression that might have been attractive on another person.

"We've met," I said, as he shook my hand slowly and deliberately.

"Perhaps in my dreams?" he said.

"Isn't it a little early for that kind of line?" I asked, turning to look around the room for someone, anyone, else that I knew.

"Let me start again. Beautiful ladies," he said, staring down at Mairead's cleavage, and then at mine. "Where are my manners? Something to drink?" Without waiting for us to respond he walked away and toward the kitchen.

"He's Danny's advisor, right?" said Mairead.

"Right," I answered. "Be careful. Heard he gets inappropriate after a drink."

"I can take care of myself," Mairead said. Then he was back in front of us with an open bottle of champagne.

"I'm okay with my beer," I said, but Mairead poured hers into a large potted geranium plant and held out her mug. Stu filled it almost to the top.

"Great, if historically inaccurate, costume you've got," he said, turning to face me.

"Got it at a Ren fayre and figured I could get away with it." I pointed to his hat. "As you know, Vikings never had horns in their helmets."

"Touché!" he said and chugged what was left in his glass. After wiping his mouth with his sleeve, he went back to the kitchen and came out with a bottle of vodka.

"No thanks," I said as he moved close enough that I could smell various liquors lingering on his breath. He started pouring vodka inside my mug, saying, "We call this a . . . Stoli-Boli!" I pulled my glass away and a splash of vodka glugged onto the carpet.

"You're not sharing," Mairead said, pouting. He leaned over to whisper to her and then poured vodka into her glass.

Danny and Catrina were behind the kitchen counter, arguing. I turned around.

"Excuse me," Catrina said, brushing up against me on her way out of the room. I looked back at Danny, who was pouring drinks for a group of four. "Where's Rose?" Danny said. "Unlike her to miss a good party," someone responded. I walked back into the hall, willing myself to stay when all I wanted to do was leave.

I went into the bathroom and washed my hands, splashed some water on my face. The beer couldn't compete with the lingering withdrawal symptoms that had flared up, but I knew the solution wasn't more alcohol. I went upstairs and read a long article on Catherine de' Medici's library on my phone. An hour later I went down to the living room. Mairead was on the couch next to Carlsson, who was filling her mug with vodka. I bent down next to Mairead. "I'm tired, I might leave soon," I said to her. "What are you thinking?"

"Aww, come on," said Carlsson. "You juss got here! Have another dri-ink."

"I'd like to have a quick word with my friend. Could you give us a minute?" I said.

"What the . . ." he started to say as he tried to stand up from the couch, but then fell back into the cushions. "Where's Rose anyway? Yooou t-twoo are no, noo fun at-tall." He pushed himself up on the arm of the couch, then he stumbled away from us.

Mairead leaned her head back against the couch. "Spinning," she said. "Room is spinning."

"Come on," I said. "Let's go. You can crash on my couch."

"Home?" she said, her eyes rolling up to the ceiling. She lurched the top half of her body forward. "I'm going to be sick," she said, gripping her stomach. I guided her to the bathroom and seconds later heard her retching.

Jeff came up to the door. "Are you queuing?" he asked me. "I need to use the loo," he said.

"It's occupied," I said.

He bent over as he pounded the door.

"Are you almost done?" he called.

"Go away," I said to him. "Ignore him," I said to the door.

"This is practically my house," he said.

"Then you must know where the other bathroom is," I said, and he walked away.

I called a taxi company. The dispatcher had a thick Glaswegian accent that was difficult to understand but said a car would be there in fifteen minutes.

When Mairead came out, vomit in her hair, I found our coats and took her outside, where we waited, shivering in the cold, until the taxi arrived, and I helped her inside. Back at my flat I guided her to my couch, floated a sheet over it, wrapped a blanket around her, and put a glass of water and Alka-Seltzer tablets on the table in front of her. "I have Tums, too," I said.

"You're better than Boots," she said.

"This isn't the half of it," I smiled.

"Danny's advisor wanted me to go home with him."

"I'm glad we didn't stay. Let me know if you need anything," I said, on my way to the kitchen to boil water for tea and to clean her up.

"Isabel," she called after me. "Thanks."

CHAPTER ELEVEN

T hree days later, a police car was parked outside the history department. The door to my office was open, so I walked in. Mairead was sitting at her desk. She looked paler than usual.

"What's going on?" I asked, peeking through the blinds at the checkered car outside.

"It's Rose," she whispered, loudly. "Nobody's seen her since before the party. Danny reported it. They were supposed to meet for coffee and Rose never showed up, and Danny's been trying to reach her for days, but she wasn't picking up her phone or answering emails. Danny had an extra key to her flat, so she went. All of Rose's stuff is there, like her wallet, but she's missing. The police questioned me. They asked about you."

"Why are you whispering?" I whispered back.

She stood up. "Must run to the library."

"Mairead!" I called, but she was out the door. The book on the stand and the library books had been removed from Rose's desk. My desk. Someone knocked.

Two police officers, one an older man with fuzzy orange hair in plain clothes, and the other, a younger woman, in uniform, walked in and shook my hand as they introduced themselves: Detective Chief Inspector Mackenzie and Inspector Arnolds.

"Mind if we take a seat?" Mackenzie said. It wasn't a question.

"Please," I said. They pulled out two plastic chairs from against the wall. I remained standing, my backpack still on.

"Which one is your desk?" Mackenzie asked. I pointed to my desk and shifted from one foot to the other.

"It used to belong to Rose. Rose Brewster," I said, and both inspectors turned their heads to me.

"We understand you are busy with schoolwork, but we wanted to ask you a few questions," Mackenzie said.

"Is everything okay?" I asked.

"We think so," said Mackenzie, before continuing. "Do you know Rose Brewster?"

"Yes," I said. "We were in college together, but I saw her again for the first time in August, right after I first arrived. She left for Paris soon after."

"Was she often in Paris?"

"She was completing research for her PhD."

"Would you describe yourself as being close with Ms. Brewster?" Mackenzie was talking while Arnolds wrote notes.

"We've become closer than we were during college. Two Americans, you know," I said, cutting myself off when I heard my voice start to waver.

"I see. When was the last time you saw Rose Brewster?"

"Almost a week ago. Last Wednesday. She came over to my apartment. It was her birthday, and she brought some whiskey. To celebrate."

"Do you remember what time she came by your flat?"

"Right at seven," I said.

Mackenzie nodded to Arnolds, who was still taking notes.

"What time did she leave?"

"Around ten, I think. Maybe a little earlier. Is she okay?"

"Have you heard from her since that night?"

"I haven't, no," I said, shaking my head. "But Danny, Danielle, said she had seen her. Seen Rose. Before her party. Danny's party."

"And how did she seem the night of her birthday?" he said. "Did she act out of the ordinary? Did she mention being upset about anything?"

"She was in a good mood." Our conversation about sharing secrets drifted in front of me.

"So, she didn't seem preoccupied to you?"

I shook my head.

"Please give us your answers out loud, if you don't mind Ms . . ." Arnolds said, then looked down at her notes, ". . . Ms. Henley."

"Did she say where she was going after she left your flat?" Mackenzie asked.

"No," I said, then added, "No, she didn't say where she was going. After she left."

"And did you know of any trouble she was having, with her studies, with her family or her partner, if she had one?"

"Her family lives in the U.S. Her mother passed away when Rose was a teenager. Her father was somewhat . . . overprotective, although I never knew him. I'm not aware of any partner. She was a little stressed over a presentation, but other than that she was cheerful."

"The days after Danielle's party, did any of your colleagues mention Rose?"

"Let me think . . . no, no one mentioned Rose. But I don't talk to that many people."

Arnolds hummed twice.

"What about the night of the party? Was there anything unusual about that night?"

"No," I said. "Mairead and I left early. The next day I heard someone say Rose never made it. But I assumed she was getting ready for her trip."

"Her trip? Do you know where she was going?" Mackenzie asked. Arnolds looked me in the eye and raised her eyebrows.

"She talked about going somewhere to work outside of town, with no distractions."

"You say you haven't heard from her in a week. Is that unusual? You said you were close."

"Sometimes I hear from her three times a day," I said. "And sometimes three days go by without a word. Not unusual."

"Uh-huh," said Mackenzie, while Arnolds returned to her notes.

"Is there anything else we should know? That might help us?" Waiting for my answer, Mackenzie ran his eyes over me, quietly assessing me. I sucked in my stomach and shoved my hands in my pockets. I wasn't hiding anything. Why did I feel as if I were? Was this a tactic to get me to talk? To overshare. Or was I overthinking it?

I said the first thing that came into my mind. "There is one thing about Danny's party I thought was weird. Professor Carlsson was there, the only lecturer. He made some inappropriate comments to me and especially to Mairead. We reported him. Did the department chair, Professor Endicott mention that? Have you spoken with him? Could this be connected with Madeleine Grangier's case, the professor from the history department who . . . died?"

Mackenzie's mouth opened and closed quickly like a clamshell. "I'm afraid we can't answer any questions at the moment," Mackenzie said curtly, then nodded to Arnolds. He turned back to me. "Thank you very much for your time. If you think of anything else that may help us, could you please let us know? We'd be grateful." He wrote down his number on a scrap of paper and handed it to me. They each shook my hand and left, Arnolds closing the door softly behind them.

I texted Rose. "Where are you? Everyone thinks you're missing. Are you alright?"

Later that day I saw Sean alone in the lounge.

He looked concerned. "Carlsson was taken to the police station for questioning. They said Madeleine Grangier was having an affair with someone on campus. Possibly him. What happened at the party?"

"He got drunk and acted inappropriate with Mairead. Nothing happened, don't worry. I took her home with me."

"Thank goodness."

"But that's bizarre about Madeleine. I don't understand his appeal to women."

He cracked his knuckles hard.

"Well, I'm walking you home tonight." There was nothing to do but agree.

I thought about contacting William, but he was still in Paris, where he'd been invited to give an inaugural lecture at a university. I thought about the night we'd gone out for drinks. It had felt as if we'd had an immediate rapport, although I barely knew him. Reaching out to ask about Rose might've seemed intrusive.

Did he even know that his student had gone missing?

CHAPTER TWELVE

The following evening the department was hosting a reception for Professor Max Von Kaiserling and his latest book. Of overly sufficient private means, Von Kaiserling had managed to maintain an elevated profile in the academic world despite eschewing a traditional university career. He was a revered independent scholar. I'd read all of his books and had brought one with me from Boston.

At five o'clock I walked into the lecture hall where people were talking and drinks were being passed around. Before too long, Gregory Pratt, the postdoctoral fellow in our department who had arranged Von Kaiserling's visit, clinked his wineglass. Gregory had platinum hair that was cut flat and square. Everything about him was flat and square.

Gregory introduced Von Kaiserling in a formal yet intimate manner. The white-haired Austrian professor was tall and statuesque, wearing a bespoke three-piece tweed suit with red socks peeking out above polished Ferragamo shoes. He made only a few brief remarks before he waved off any questions and asked for a drink.

Gregory had a glass of something other than wine at the ready, and delivered it with yet another smile, talking nonstop until their bodies were nearly touching.

As I watched this odd dance someone said my name. It was Endicott, his coat draped over his arm. "Professor Von Kaiserling requested that you join us for dinner. He's heard about your work."

"I would be delighted."

The Howard Inn had a cozy pub with a fireplace. Professor Von Kaiserling, shadowed by Gregory Pratt, was standing at the bar. When the crowd around him drifted away I introduced myself. We exchanged a few words and then a lecturer came up to ask him to sign a book. I stood there, waiting while Von Kaiserling signed, and Gregory whispered loudly in my ear, "Isabel. If you don't mind, we need to circulate our distinguished guest speaker." He smiled wide, baring his teeth.

"Actually, Endicott let me know that Professor Von Kaiserling specifically requested I come tonight." Gregory ignored me and turned to Von Kaiserling. "We're going through to dinner now, Professor." Von Kaiserling placed his hand in the small of my back and guided me to the main table, pulled out a chair for me and then for himself. I felt Gregory's eyes on me.

"Catherine de' Medici's flying squadron," Von Kaiserling said, holding another glass of the clear liquid that Gregory had been pouring. "A fine topic merits a fine scholar. Nigel tells me you're the school of history's most promising new arrival."

"Well, for me it's an honor to work with the people whose books I've been reading for years, including yours."

"I was terribly sorry to hear about Madeleine Grangier. She had been giving the scholarly world a run for its money. Really shook up the old boys' club."

"Including an actual men's club, right?"

"Is that so?" He swirled the liquid in his glass and took a few sips.

"Just something I'd heard. Anyway, Professor Grangier's death was a tragedy, both for the university and for me personally." I took a sip of water before adding, "Although I'm grateful for the opportunity to work with Professor Endicott."

"He was competitive with Madeleine when she first arrived, but I would wager he feels regretful now." He considered me for a moment, then his eyes scanned the rest of the room. "And where is Rose Brewster?" he asked. He brought his wineglass to his lips but there was nothing left. "An excellent scholar. And quite the conversationalist." He put the glass down.

"We're friends," I said.

"Then you know she's writing about a highly significant but much-neglected historical figure, Federico Falcone."

"Yes, she's told me. And there's a nice overlap with my topic. It turns out he was married to Thérèse Du Montour, one of Catherine's ladies."

"He had one of the best *Wunderkammers* of his day. Once upon a time these collections of curiosities conveyed the owner's control of the world by reproducing it perfectly—if in microcosmic scale—by means of the most exquisite and mindboggling specimens. He took pride in displaying his treasures during his lavish banquets."

The first course was served, a soup with "neeps and tatties," and Von Kaiserling kept talking between spoonfuls. I listened and tried to look like I was paying attention.

"Among Federico's substantial holdings," said Von Kaiserling, "was a collection of Greek medals and Etruscan sarcophagi, as well as a room dedicated to what was then 'contemporary art,' that is, portrait miniatures, enameled quatrefoil boxes, mathematical instruments, astronomical clocks, automatons, and Chinese porcelain. Yet a third room contained natural wonders, fossilized shark teeth, coral, a star ruby from India, the obligatory stuffed crocodile, and even a jewel-studded unicorn horn, which we now know to be a narwhal tusk.

"He also had an enormous emerald, a gift from a Brazilian tribe. There were said to be secret mines in South America that were never revealed to the Europeans, far richer than the ones eventually discovered at Muzo."

I laid my fork down, feeling on edge. Had Rose told Von Kaiserling about the letters she'd found?

"Oh, look at this tenderloin. What is surprising, Isabel, about the Muisca, and indeed about so many tribes, is that everything was passed through the female line. In many societies, older women were the sooth-sayers, and the most powerful members. The Amazon River was named for the female warriors who had been their ancient Greek counterparts.

"Power was matrilineal. Male chiefs were chosen from the children of their father's eldest sister. The sixteenth-century writer Garcilaso de la Vega, son of an Incan princess and a Spanish conquistador, wrote about a society that worshipped the Divine Mother of All in the form of a giant emerald. During holidays the townspeople would bring smaller emeralds to pay homage to their common mother."

"Fascinating," I said, as someone cleared my plate. "I wasn't aware of this scholarship. Although Rose said that—"

"—Curiously," Von Kaiserling interrupted me, "there is a mistaken assumption that the Renaissance was an era of rigid class structures, that someone of humble birth could not become a landholding gentleman. That's not true. Federico came from a family of upstarts in Genoa, and he invented himself, rewrote his destiny in a foreign country. He made his own luck."

He paused but I had the last bite of sticky toffee pudding in my mouth.

Von Kaiserling pushed the pudding away from him but picked up the tiny glass of liqueur that had just been delivered. "Our Federico Falcone," he said as he sipped, "also had a collection of exotic animal skeletons, as well as claws and fins he had found in the course of his travels."

"Sounds a bit gruesome?" I managed to say.

"Of course. The larger, the more unusual, the more gruesome the better—but all in the name of science. As you know, such collections grew, stimulated by the discovery of bizarre fauna like the New World armadillo or its rainbow-colored parrots," he went on.

"The New World wasn't so new to the people who lived there, though. They had very advanced societies . . ."

"Yes, yes. Semantics, my dear! You are a funny one. Did you know that still today people reconstruct collections that once belonged to the great men of history? I know well a private collector who owned the only surviving Quetzal feather-headdress from a famous *cacique*. I say 'owned' because that headdress along with his collection of pre-Columbian *búcaros* were seized and returned to Mexico. A great shame, *n'est-ce pas?*"

"I think those sorts of things belong with their original owners."

"Yes, that's the *au courant* attitude. But I suspect you'd like to find something spectacular for your very own, using your fine skills as a researcher, don't deny it." With one of his long arms, he reached for my dessert liqueur, which I hadn't touched, and downed it in a gulp.

"Do you ever come to Vienna?" he asked.

"I'm sure I'll get there one day."

"Please consider yourself invited to my castle, in the Wachau hills, whenever your travels take you east. I have treasures I would like to show you. My own personal memory theater, if you will, more extensive than Aby Warburg's. In fact, let us decide on a date, and I'll arrange the transportation."

Gregory came around the table and bent down to whisper into Von Kaiserling's ear. He nodded his head up and down.

"I see," he said, "*Gewiss.*" Gregory walked away.

Then Von Kaiserling bowed slightly to me. "Now I must retire. Fare thee well. I wish you luck. I hope we will have the chance to meet again, before too long." He placed his card on the table, waited for me to stand up, and then he seemed to disappear.

The following day I knocked on Endicott's door.

"Come in, Isabel." I'm not sure how he knew it was me. "In the French court they used to scratch instead of knock, did you know that?"

"I did know that," I said.

"Well, think of bringing back the tradition."

"I wanted to thank you for including me last night."

"Kind to say, but it was Von Kaiserling who asked me to invite you. Something else must have brought you here. Let's hear it."

He didn't invite me to sit down so I stood there as I answered him. "Actually, I was wondering if we could speak about Rose. Do you have any news?"

"Don't think you're the first to ask. And I'll say what I've told the others who've asked. It's unwise to discuss it until we know more. Especially not when I have a group of students coming in." He turned his head to the door. "Agreed?"

"Agreed," I said. "But something strange is going on. First Madeleine Grangier, then Rose."

He nodded, simply. Taking the first several steps backward without turning my back on him, as if I were offering him the deference due to a monarch, I left. Three students were standing outside his door, staring into their phone screens, not bothering to move aside. Pushing past them I headed toward the library. My interlibrary loan from Edinburgh hadn't arrived yet, so I went home.

In my cold flat I covered myself with two wool blankets and lay down on the couch with my feet propped up on the armrest. I looked Von Kaiserling up online. Maybe I could arrange to review his newest book, if I was going to read all 800 pages of it. It would be good to add to my list of publications.

I was familiar with many, but not all, of his articles. He had written an article on the Falcone, "Der Palazzo de Falcone im Paris," for a German anthology, which appeared to focus on Federico Falcone's cabinet of curiosities. Rose must have known that Von Kaiserling had written about the Falcone. If she were here, I could ask her. The shiny newness of St Stephens had dulled in her absence, and everything seemed so quiet now. In two short months we'd grown so close, and I really missed her.

I emailed her. "Where are you?"

Was I the only one convinced that Rose's disappearance and Madeleine Grangier's death were linked?

I heard a loud knocking sound outside my window and my heart slammed into my chest. I peeled the blankets off my legs and stood up from the couch, turned off the light, tiptoed over to the window, pushed open two slats of the blinds, and forced myself to look out. The only light was coming from a streetlamp. Wind was slapping swathes of rain against the facade. The noise must have been a tree branch hitting the windowpane. As I stood there in the dark, afraid that someone was watching me, panic pinched my chest, and I thought about my meds. This time I needed them. But I didn't have them.

I stepped back to the window and parted two of the slats again. There were almost no cars left in the parking lot. Just one in the far corner. A small, dark-colored car. Was it blue? A Mini Cooper? Rose's car. But it couldn't be.

My nerves kept me awake most of the night, my heart racing each time I thought I heard footsteps. Every sound took on a roaring echo. Around four A.M., I sat up and leaned forward, stretching my neck to look out the window. The parking lot was empty.

CHAPTER THIRTEEN

A few hours later the hazy morning sun dissolved the shadows of my imagination. The shame I felt about the Adrian situation was worse with no one to divert my attention. Lately the headaches were bad at night, too. Even though it had been a while since I'd taken meds, I was still thinking about them every day.

While projecting an image of confidence and openness, I tried to guard my inner life, my sense of guilt. With Rose no longer here, everything I'd left behind was catching up to me. Every moment that I wasn't focused on my topic, scenes from my past played in a continuous loop in my head, and when I tried to sleep my mind felt carbonated, as if it might bubble up and spill over at any time. It would've been easier to be carefree. Like Rose.

I did, however, have something to look forward to, the department weekend in the Scottish Highlands. I'd overheard William tell Catrina that he was going. I hadn't yet had a chance to discuss Rose with him. Every time I'd wanted to bring it up there were always other people around.

When I received an email from William asking if I wanted to meet for coffee, I waited fifteen minutes before responding, "In an hour?" I dressed in a low-but-not-inappropriately-low-cut top and tight, black, spandexy pants that made my legs look slimmer and longer than they were. William was sitting in the back of the café, grinning.

"Welcome back," I said as I sat down.

On top of the table was a box wrapped in white paper with a red ribbon around it. "I hope you like it," he said.

I picked up the box and my fingers assessed what was underneath the wrapping. It felt like a book. I slid off the ribbon and opened the paper gently, aware of William watching me, and pulled out a quarto-sized book, the cover made of brown leather with a gold-stamped geometric design, and initials inscribed in the center. TDM. TDM? Inside the cover I found a penciled-in inscription, "Album de Poésie, Thérèse Du Montour."

"Wait, this isn't . . ."

"It's Thérèse Du Montour's poetry album. Do you like it?"

"*Like* isn't the word, William. I thought something like this would be in the Bibliothèque Nationale, or at least in private hands."

"It is in private hands. Yours. I came across it in a small French auction last week. Something to help with your brilliant study of Catherine's circle. I doubt Christina Yee has ever seen a copy."

"Wow," was all I could think to say. My hands were shaking.

"I'm glad you like it," he said with a wide grin.

"But . . . how much did this cost?"

He shook his head. "One should never ask a lady's age or the cost of a gift."

"Fair enough. I hope you didn't break the bank. Not for me."

He laughed. "Why not give something special to the person who can appreciate it the most? I couldn't think of a better owner. I'm touched by your concern for my finances. I just so happen to have a dear friend at an auction house in Nantes who alerts me to a potentially good bargain when she sees one."

My teeth grazed my cheek as I pictured William's pretty French auctioneer friend.

"No doubt you will be familiar with most of the poems in the album, but a few are unpublished, and some may have been penned by Thérèse herself. Technically she was rather skilled, an undiscovered genius."

"Do you think so?"

"Yes, but I'm curious to hear your opinion. I've been to her birthplace, and have seen her tomb in a town I know well. We could go together one day. A pilgrimage of sorts."

I tried not to smile too widely. "I'd like that."

Catrina waved and walked over. I quietly put the book back in the wrapping paper and inside my purse as William asked her to sit with us.

At home I took out the book and flipped through the pages. I'd read that Thérèse Du Montour had written poems, but I hadn't known that a copy of her poetry album existed. There were love poems dedicated to her by the leading poets, including Ronsard and Du Bellay, and other poems were unattributed, presumably her own.

I spent nearly an hour drafting a thank you note. After I finished writing out the final version on printer paper, my little cloud of happiness darkened when my thoughts drifted back to Rose.

Sean picked me up at nine on Saturday morning. Although we talked for the first half hour, I must have nodded off shortly after. When I looked out the window the green pastures of the south had given way to quaint towns, with shops that sold kilts for tourists and Walkers butter cookies. I fell asleep again but woke up to curving roads and dark, thick forests. Macbeth and his wife might have stepped out of the trees at any moment.

"How long have I been asleep?" I asked Sean.

"Three hours. Macbeth's castle is just up there," Sean said, as if he had heard my mental musing.

"Hungry?" I asked, reaching into my bag for a couple of sandwiches. We pulled over to the side of the road and ate them.

"You're a talented cook," he said as we munched.

"I stayed up all night baking the bread for these," I said.

Back on the road Sean sucked in some air and blew it out quickly.

"Let's address the elephant in the room, err, car, if you will." Sean said. Without waiting for me to respond he said, "You and Rose were, are close friends, yes?"

"We have a history together and being in the program together we bonded. We have a lot in common. Although on the surface we seem like opposites."

"Hmm," he said. "Rose is an odd one. Maybe she'll turn up this weekend. Maybe the joke's on us."

"What do you mean?"

"She kind of keeps to herself, friendly but at a distance. Everyone's in awe of her. Don't take my word for it—I mean—I'm a cynic, but, well, sorry to say, because she's your friend, but she's always struck me as kind of fake."

"What do you mean, fake?"

"I'm not sure if this facade of laid-back-California-blonde perfection is more than that, a facade."

"That's . . . umm . . . harsh."

"A while back she asked if I'd read one of her papers. It wasn't so great. It was fine. I gave her some comments. And then she must've overhauled it, presented something totally different a week later at our seminar. All the professors couldn't—can't—stop talking about how she's a genius, Grangier included. I guess phony's not the right word. She's curated. In it to win it. I met her brother once. He said Rose would either turn into an international success or have a breakdown. Nothing in between."

"Hmm," I said. "She's definitely not a phony. Everything the professors say about her, back when we were in college and now, is true. She speaks flawless French and is working on a great topic. Some people have it all. Any resentment is just envy."

"Are you saying I'm jealous?"

"It's unfair to judge someone because she's cool."

"She's a flirt, too, wields her sexuality."

"Whom does she flirt with?"

"Me, Luke, Bertie, William, Catrina, Danny. Endicott even! Not that he gives her the time of day. Apparently, she had a thing with Stu Carlsson. You knew that, right?"

"No and I don't believe it."

"They say academia makes strange bedfellows," he said. "I do think you two are opposites. You're easy to talk to, empathetic. I heard how you took care of Mairead," he said.

"I was looking out for a friend." I said. "Rose would've done the same."

"Whatever you say."

The road, now covered in a layer of ice, narrowed and became serpentine. Sean's car was the only one driving in the tapered lane, which didn't appear wide enough to accommodate cars going in opposing directions. Another hour passed and then Sean pulled a paper map down from the visor in front of him and asked me to give him directions. I told him where to turn left, and then right, at an unmarked road that was unpaved, until we reached a wrought-iron gate with a sign on top: Drummond House. We drove through and pulled up next to some parked cars and stepped out.

Sean pointed in the distance at rounded mountain peaks splotched with snow that were barely visible in the fading, fog-diffused light. "The name of that mountain range is the Cairngorms. I've gone climbing there before. It's beautiful."

I laughed because the visibility was so poor. "I'll have to take your word for it."

The exterior of Drummond House was made of taupe-colored stone, and many windows peeked out over a manicured lawn. I couldn't tell if the structure had been built in the nineteenth or fourteenth century. It seemed grand for a student getaway. There was no handle, so Sean pushed on the twelve-foot-high oak door. It whooshed open. He raised his arm and then scooped it down to his knees with a flourish, inviting me to go in first as he said, "Looks like we've come to the right place."

We stepped into a carpeted lobby, with red-and-grey tartan wool couches. Flames flashed and retreated in the stone fireplace in the corner of the room, but a whistling draft wrapped around us. As I went to close the door, I heard another car. Sean walked back out and then, after some hellos, Bertie came in and nodded to me. In his wake followed Catrina, lugging a bulky suitcase. I asked if she wanted a hand.

"Don't worry, Pet, I'm a strong girl," she said. Then Sean walked in with his backpack on and my heavy bag in tow. A man with orange hair and a matching beard appeared. As I pushed the big door closed, we introduced ourselves.

"Welcome to Drummond House, all of youse. My name is Duncan. Your room, Miss Henley, is the first one straight ahead a'you up the stairs, number eighteen. Mr. O'Malley, y'are in twenty-three." He consulted a clipboard and turned to Catrina and Bertie.

Sean refused to let me carry my hard-backed suitcase up the stairs, so we went together, kicking up flecks of old dust as we slid into each step, and when we found my room, I thanked Sean. Sitting at the vanity desk in front of a mirror was Mairead, applying beige lip gloss.

"Hello, roommate," she said, looking at me through the mirror. "The man downstairs says there's a problem with the heat. He's searching for a space heater."

I looked at the twin beds pushed together. "Soon we'll be more than just roommates," I said, and Mairead laughed. While I unpacked, she went down to join the others.

Our room was decorated various shades of pink—the carpet, bed-spread, and faded wallpaper. After arranging my things in the dresser, I stretched out on the bed and woke up when white light shined in my eyes.

"Are you coming down for dinner?" Mairead asked.

"Be right there," I said, and changed into my wool pants, put on all three sweaters in my suitcase, and walked downstairs to the dining room, where historians filled three large tables. Deer heads with antlers lined the high walls and light filtered in through bay windows, with a view over trees glowing black-blue in the moonlight. I sat between two students I had not met, and we talked over haggis and venison with blueberry sauce. Jessica was a fellow American who had just submitted her dissertation, and Mary, a third-year from York.

William was next to Jeff at the far table. As the staff was about to serve dessert, Mairead approached me.

"First-years are supposed to come up with a quiz. By the time everyone finishes their coffee. It's up to you and me."

"Piece of cake," I said. "Pun intended." Back in our room, pulling some notecards and a pen out of my backpack. Mairead put her head in her hands. I came up with all but two of the questions.

There were two teams, with Endicott heading one and Gregory Pratt the other. The questions were:

List the names of the wives of Henry VIII, in order.

What country gained independence from the Kalmar Union in 1523?

What English Monarch was known as the Nine Days Queen?

What Renaissance painter's surname was Sanzio?

Who invented the thermometer in 1593?

Barbary pirates invaded Provence in 1519; led by whom?

Who sacked Rome in 1527, and why?

Endicott's team was ahead by three points when my sack-of-Rome question came up.

Gregory sighed. "Students, while the questions so far were crafted *comme il faut*, explaining the 1527 sack of Rome is multifaceted. The army of the Holy Roman Emperor, Charles V, had perhaps been acting on his orders, since Pope Clement VII had sided with enemy France. Then again, the imperial troops were unpaid and included German Protestants. Frankly, the question is vague and the answer up for interpretation. Specific questions with one possible response are best. Let's move on."

"Is that your answer?" asked Endicott.

"I suppose it is. But I'd rather proceed to another question."

"Well, that's fair," said Endicott. "Next." Gregory turned to me and Mairead and with a flourish of his right arm made an exaggerated bow.

When the game was finished (a tie, made possible only by the disqualified question), we went to the bar. Our keys were attached to big wooden blocks, which we'd left out on the tables. "Don't look at your neighbor's key and charge drinks to their room, now," Endicott chided. He drank a beer with the rest of the group, but before I'd finished my first whiskey, I glanced over to see him climbing the stairs. Jan and Mairead were talking about Belgium, and Jan's experience in Scotland, so they didn't notice, and no one else seemed to, either. By one in the morning only eight of us remained and we had gone through five bottles of whiskey. Duncan had come by at one point to apologize that he hadn't found a space heater. I turned to Gregory Pratt. Studying his flat features, I tried to guess his age. Maybe a couple of years older than Rose.

No one was talking about her. Was it just too much? In addition to the relentless pressures of performing academically, the loss of one of our own seemed unbearable.

Encouraged by another gulp of whiskey I walked over to Gregory's chair. He was texting someone and smiling or smirking, I couldn't tell which. He didn't look up. I poured some whiskey in a glass and clunked it down on a coaster in front of him. "My treat," I said.

"Oh hello, Isabel," he said. "That's *very* kind," he said, and took a small sip, swishing it around in his mouth before setting the glass down. "I should have commended you earlier, for the quiz. Except for the sack-of-Rome question. But no matter. Bravo."

"Thanks, Gregory," I said. "I'm glad you enjoyed it. I've been meaning to ask, how well do you know Rose?"

He tilted his head and cleared his throat, then looked at me, his mouth slightly agape. He took another drink of whiskey.

"Rose Brewster," I said. "Maybe you don't remember her? She's a graduate student in this department who went missing a short while back. Promising scholar. Hard to forget I'd say."

"Obviously I know Rose well. There's no need to be dramatic. Likely she's on the continent doing research. Or that father of hers has taken ill."

I took a swig of whiskey and held his gaze.

"What a woman, Rose," he said. "Paleography skills, research skills. She's an exceptional writer and a poised speaker. As you said, she's beautiful. Charming."

I felt a pang of something, and it wasn't a noble feeling.

"And the last time we spoke she told me she made the most remarkable find."

"Oh."

"The story involves one of the young Falcone family men who was on a secret reconnaissance mission for Catherine de' Medici in Brazil."

Not letting on that I knew the broad outlines of this story, I moved my facial muscles into a position of rapt attention.

"The struggle in the Atlantic theater included one or two secret missions to the New World led by the best admirals, many of whom were Genoese. During that mission, Rose's Falcone chap, along with his men, traded with the inhabitants—horses and firearms in exchange for precious items, gold and jewels, jade from Central America, and . . ." He took another sip of his whiskey, and then his gaze met mine. "Even exotic animals such as parrots."

He continued. "Eventually, the Spanish forces caught Falcone's men, but he was able to escape back to France with one precious jewel, an emerald extraordinarily rare for its size and color, and, unusually for emeralds, nearly flawless."

Why had Rose shared her guarded discovery with Gregory Pratt? More likely Von Kaiserling had regaled him with the same story I had heard over dinner recently. "What happened to it?" I asked, tilting my head.

"Talk of the jewel ebbed and flowed. Jacobins claimed to have found it exhuming the tombs of the nobility at the time of the French Revolution. Then the Germans were said to have discovered its location and moved it during the Occupation of France. Others are sure the Falcone still have possession of the emerald, that it's in their collection in Genoa. I can't believe you haven't heard about all this."

"Rose did mention an emerald, but only in passing." He rolled his eyes and I asked, "Does everyone in the department know about the emerald, and if not, why did she tell you?"

"We were . . ." he paused, "we are friends, as I've told you. Anyway, I already knew about the emerald. But no one knows what happened to it. Not even Rose." I picked up my glass, but it was empty. Gregory must have taken that as a signal of disinterest on my part. "Captivating, eh?"

"Yeah," I said, yawning and putting both hands on the table, as if to push myself up. Just then Sean came over to us. I said, "Gregory was telling me how much he enjoyed the quiz."

Gregory stood up. "Indeed. But I should call it a night. Enjoy the rest of the evening. And thank you for the whiskey," he said to me before he turned and walked away.

"I'm knackered," Sean said. "Would you care to be escorted home in my horse-drawn carriage?"

"I'm going to stand by the fire and warm up before I head to the cold room," I said. "But thanks." I stood there and watched him ascend the stairs.

In what I hoped was a surreptitious manner, I had been keeping track of William, but at some point he'd left the bar. Just then the clock chimed the hour and I glanced up to see him walking toward me. When he stood close to me, he leaned in to whisper in my ear.

"I hear Drummond House is haunted. You might need protection."

"You're assuming I believe in ghosts, but I don't. Not really," I whispered back.

"Don't take my word for it. Duncan can tell us all the story." He walked out of the bar and returned with Duncan, clinked a glass, and asked for everyone's attention. I sat next to Danny as he announced, "Duncan is going to tell us about the ghosts of Drummond House."

Duncan's cheeks flushed red and he tut-tutted, "Oh, ser, I dunna ken if I wannae get into that."

"We're all historians here, Duncan. We deserve the facts. Please." The Scotsman stared at him for a moment, then began his story.

"Many years ago, in the later half a' two centuries past, there was a fair maiden. She was Catholic, engaged to a brave clansman. The clans gathered here for a ceremony in the chapel. As they were saying their vows, English soldiers arrived. The English took the husband-to-be and stripped him of his kilt." He tipped his head down. "They hung him as a traitor in front a' the guests," he said in a rush. "The soldiers took the poor young lady into this building and the lot 'a 'em did unspeakable things ta her. She went to bed and a few days la'er died a' grief.

"She still roams the halls, looking for her lost love. Last week the old piano keys started playin' a tune no one had heard before. Sometimes you feel a cold current a' air inside with all the windows closed. Other times it sounds like the wind is whistlin'. But no, it's her cryin'." He stopped.

Just then a gust of air swept through the room and goose bumps popped up on my arms.

The whole group applauded him and then he shyly went back out of the bar.

"Do you think it's true? About the ghost?" I asked.

Danny shot me a look. "We're in Scotland, luv. All our castles are haunted."

William went to the other side of the bar and walked out of the room. Catrina was sitting on the big couch with her legs draped across both Bertie and Jeff's laps. She signaled me over. They were laughing.

"Pet," she called. "Let's have a wee chat." Catrina's eyes were glazed over. It was the first time I had seen her drunk. She swung her legs around and moved toward me on the tartan-covered couch and put her hand on my knee.

"You look so innocent Pet. Place hasn't corrupted you yet?" As she grinned, I could see all of her teeth and her gums, stretched and pink.

"Drummond House? We just got here."

"No, dum-dum. St Stephens." Catrina slapped her thigh. "I've got an idea! What about a game of Never Have I Ever?' It's the right time of night. What do you say, guys?" She stood up and walked over to the bar. Jan and then Luke excused themselves.

Catrina came back from the bar with a glass for me and a bottle of whiskey; she poured a couple of fingers of brown liquid into my glass, then hers. Catrina made her way around the table with the whiskey. "All charged to Danny's room," she said.

"If we play that game, you'll drink that whole bottle because there's nothing you haven't done. Anyway, no one's in the mood," said Danny, looking up as Catrina filled her glass.

"As if you're a prude! You just don't want anyone else to know the shit that you and Jeff do," she said in a shout-whisper, loud enough for everyone to hear.

"Sod off," Danny said.

"Where *is* our life of the party? Rose," Jeff said.

Bertie whined. "If Rose were here, she'd pay for all our drinks. I've got an idea. Let's all go around and posit where she might be. I'll go first. I think Rose is in her Beverly Hills mansion. That would explain why her thesis is taking twice as long as it should."

Danny said, "I think Rose is . . ." She swigged back the last few honey-like drops of whiskey in her glass. "In the UKPPS." She looked at me. "The Witness Protection Program."

Catrina emptied her glass and picked up the bottle. We were all drinking silently.

"This is boring. Let's not all talk about Rose," Catrina said. "What's the point?"

I was about to speak when Bertie raised one eyebrow and said, "You never want to talk about Rose, Cat. Why's that? Not with me, not with anybody. Did you two have a squabble?" She pushed his arm off and swung her head around, casting a side glance toward the other side of the room.

"How should I know where she is? Probably shacked up with some wanker. Mairead," Catrina said, "you could offer a unique perspective. Our resident expert in psychiatric conditions."

She tilted her head toward Mairead.

"Why are you so eager to change the subject, Catrina?" I said.

As if she hadn't heard me, Catrina kept her eyes on Mairead. "Rose might've had a breakdown. If she were institutionalized, would we find out necessarily?"

I hadn't seen William hovering in the doorway. "That's enough, Catrina," William said, and went over to Mairead. She stood up and pushed past him and ran into the lobby and up the stairs. He followed her.

Catrina leaned in toward me and edged her hand up onto the inner part of my knee. I picked up her hand and put it on her knee. She sighed and said, "Do you think Danny's pretty, Pet?"

"Do you, Catrina?"

"No no, I asked first."

"What was that all about?" I said.

"Danny?" She slumped back in the couch and kicked her shoes off.

"No, Mairead. Why were you picking on her?"

She snort-laughed. "I was just joking around."

"It wasn't particularly funny."

"You . . . Americans take everything so seriously." She clumsily tried to put one of her shoes back on, clearly too far gone to engage in a constructive conversation. I went back to the lobby, and hovered by the fireplace, trying to figure out where William and Mairead had gone. Sean rushed down the stairs in his sweatpants. "Is everything alright? I heard a door slam, and I came out of my room and Mairead passed me in tears. I heard Catrina cackling, so can't have been good."

"I have no idea what's going on," I said, "although everybody got a little weird when we started talking about Rose. Go back to bed. I'll check on Mairead."

"Goodnight, Saint Isabel. You know," he stopped, "in the world of finance, everyone has big egos because there's a lot of money at stake but no real power. In politics, everyone has big egos because there's power but not much money. In academia, everyone has big egos because there's no money and there's no power. There are *only* egos, which makes academics the worst egomaniacs around. I don't know how I managed to get that right after all I've had to drink." He grinned.

"That's a good one. I'll remember it."

After standing in front of the fireplace for half an hour, I ran up the stairs and opened the door to my room. As I searched for the light switch with my left hand, my eyes adjusted enough so that I could see that there were two bodies in the bed. There was a larger person lying on top of a smaller person. The larger person stood up. Jan swerved around me, his head lowered, clothes in hand, and out the door. I closed it behind him.

"Sorry, I didn't know," I said after my eyes had adjusted to the darkness. I could see Mairead turned over on her side, her back facing me. "I won't say anything," I said. "Nobody's business."

Despite my three sweaters and all that whiskey, it was so cold my teeth were chattering. One of the curtains was pulled back and lacy ice patterns had formed along the windowpane. Snow was hitting the window. The snow comforted me, even as I shivered. I pulled my flannel sweatpants on, got into bed, and covered myself with all the blankets and the bedspread, which smelled of mildew. Seemingly in the next instant, my eyes snapped open as I registered the sound of a loud, drawn-out scream. It was Mairead.

Her eyes were closed but her face was contorted, and her legs were twitching. She whimpered. I touched her gently on the shoulder and she jerked.

"Wha—what are you doing?" she asked.

"Were you having a nightmare?"

It took her a minute to respond, her speech thick with sleep. "I have them sometimes."

She must have flung off her blankets, and she was dressed in a sleeveless nightshirt. One of her arms was crisscrossed with thin pink lines. It took me a moment to realize they were scars—scars reaching from her wrist to her shoulder.

She saw me and pulled the blanket up. "Car accident," she said, as she rolled back over. I lay there with my eyes closed until I heard creaking and voices. I adjusted my clothes and went down to breakfast.

Sprinklings of ash were scattered over the carpet. Catrina was sitting beside Bertie in the corner. I sat next to Danny, who looked more sober than the rest of the group.

"Wake up with a start, did you?" Danny said. "How was it spending the night next to Crazy Mairead?"

"She had a nightmare," I said. "Big deal."

"Did you know she was in an asylum before she came here? She's a bit of a nutter."

"Is 'nutter' in the DSM?"

Danny shrugged. "Don't say I didn't warn you," she said.

Bertie walked over and crouched down near us. "You should let Mairead alone. You're acting so judgmental, both of you. Grow up."

"Christ, Bertie, can you not hang about listening to all my conversations? Danny was just taking the piss, weren't you, Danny? But I'm sorry. If we've offended anybody."

"Not everything has to be a competition," Bertie continued.

"Don't take everything so literally, Bertie," said Danny, and patted his cheek.

Catrina and Danny started giggling, then Danny stood up and went to fill her plate. Bertie looked back at me and I rolled my eyes.

I walked over to the buffet. Catrina followed.

"Are you coming rambling with us?" Catrina asked.

"Where's Sean?" I asked, avoiding eye contact.

"Your lapdog? He's got a headache," said Catrina.

"My lapdog?" I said.

"I was being facetious," Catrina said, with a groan. "Nobody has a sense of humor. Anyway, it's just amusing how Sean pivoted from Rose to you."

"But . . . they aren't even friends." I said, putting my plate down and hearing it clatter.

"If you don't believe me, ask him," said Catrina.

"Why bring up a sore subject with a friend?"

"Nah, don't. Poor soul, always on the pull. Bless him. Probably shouldn't say this, but he fancied your supervisor, Grangier."

"Did he tell you that, Catrina? I didn't realize you confided in each other."

"You mean about Grangier? He didn't have to, was obvious. He'd blush and get all tongue-tied around her. Kept showing up to her office hours."

"I probably would've done the same. From everything I've understood, she was an amazing person. But I'll never have the chance to know, will I?" I said, my voice deep with a sudden loathing for both her and Danny. I didn't want to spend the next twenty-four hours anywhere near them, much less the next four years in the same small department. But I would have to. I stared Catrina straight in the eye.

She lowered her head and stepped back, seemingly disarmed.

CHAPTER FOURTEEN

Danny, Catrina, Bertie, William, and I departed at 10:30, while most of the others were still lingering over their "full Scottish" breakfasts. We walked along the black loch on the northern end of the property, which lay at the base of a round-topped mountain. Stunted evergreen trees surrounded the loch, their branches gnarled, permanently bent to one side in the direction the wind had blown them for many years. We began to climb the pebble-hewn path. As we gained elevation the trees started to thin out and bow lower, and the landscape became rocky.

Within forty minutes I could barely feel my tingling cheeks and slowed my pace. My hiking boots were covered in mud as we crossed patches of heather and streams darkened with peat. In front of a large brook, I sat down on the ground, letting Danny, Bertie, Catrina, and William walk ahead and watching their shapes and their silhouettes recede. I didn't feel like talking. Poor Mairead. At least William, and Bertie, had taken a stand. Snowflakes started falling and the wind was picking up, making me wish I'd remembered to bring gloves.

"You can't have given up already." William said. He was standing beside me. He must have crossed the heather, but I hadn't heard him.

"I'm a little out of shape," I lied, trying for winsome.

"Come on, I'll help you," he said, reaching down for my hands. "There we go."

"I've been meaning to ask," I said, but my voice trailed off. I didn't want to bring Rose into this moment. I just wanted to be close to William.

"What?"

"I wanted to thank you for the poetry album. I . . ." We stood facing each other, and he seemed taller. I studied his dark grey eyes, with their curling eyelashes, his crimson cheeks. A few flyaway hairs, speckled with tiny clusters of snow, were waving about in different directions from underneath his cashmere cap. He took off his hat and stuffed it in his pocket, then pulled off his black leather gloves and put them in his other pocket. With warm fingertips William brushed the hair away from my face and rested his fingers on my chin. He reached with his other hand for mine and held it gently between his thumb and forefinger.

"So cold," he said, blowing on one hand, then the other. He turned my right hand around and studied my palm, squinting at the inside of my wrist. He let go.

"You're sad," he said. "Why?"

I turned away from him and faced the brook.

"What happened to you, Isabel?"

"I don't want to talk about it," I said.

"You misunderstand." He met my gaze.

"What do you mean?"

"Maybe because . . . I recognize the same sadness in you that I have in myself."

"You're perceptive, has anyone ever told you that before?"

"You didn't answer my question."

"Are you sad, William?"

He stepped back and sighed. "Let's just say I've been through a lot in thirty-eight years. I'll tell you someday, maybe. If you'd like to hear."

"I would. And I don't mean to be coy. You're right. I've gone through stuff, too."

His eyes mirrored mine. "No one, especially not someone like you, deserves that."

He stepped close, reached around me, and found the small of my back. He pulled me in as he bent down to kiss me, the length of his padded body pressed against me. He cupped my face in his hands, delicately, as if he didn't want to hurt me, and kissed me again. The pressure of his lips on mine became stronger. It was like a small explosion. And then it was over. He pulled back, picked up my hand, tracing circles around it, and held it for a moment before letting go. Then he stepped back, angling his body down the hill. Catrina and Danny were calling my name.

William pulled his hat and gloves out of his pockets. Catrina was squinting as they approached.

"Tired, Pet? Highland air too much for you? I'll take your hand and lead you up the wee hill if you like."

"One of us can take you back if you want, Isabel," Danny said.

"I'm fine," I said.

"Right," said Catrina. "Let's go."

We continued in silence, up the mountainside. My heart was pounding, propelling me forward, and I was oblivious to the cold as my mind kept playing over and over the feeling of William kissing me, his warm body pressed against mine, his hands holding my head. Being seen.

When we reached the top, we stared down at the hotel and loch, at the trees around them, and at the ridge of mountains, parallel to our line of vision. By then it was one o'clock, so we started walking back, still not talking. Danny had filched a bag of oatmeal cookies and we ate them and drank from water bottles. By the time we reached the big stone house, the air was dark and full of desolate sounds. Without taking my coat off I stood in front of the fireplace to warm my numb legs and cracking hands. Before too long I slipped off my coat. As I did a crisp current of air caressed my shoulders and I heard the faint echo of a woman crying.

CHAPTER FIFTEEN

On the day of our return, William left on another research trip to Paris. We had avoided each other Sunday night. Did he have a girlfriend? Were there others? I knew I wasn't the only one who noticed how attractive he was. Although I had never seen him and Rose interacting, except for the time outside the library, it was easy to imagine them as a perfect couple, brilliant and gorgeous. Maybe that was another reason why I couldn't bring myself to discuss her disappearance with him, even though she was on my mind even more than he was.

My heat was barely working in the flat, and the biting air and somber skies matched my mood as I plodded through secondary sources.

I wasn't sleeping well, still waking up early. But rather than lying in bed imagining William's candlelit dinner with a mystery woman in France, or Rose lying in a ditch somewhere, I forced myself to go outside. On those late-autumn mornings, wrapped in a thick, wool scarf, lined gloves, a hat that covered my ears, and my black, nylon puffy coat, I walked down to Dunbar Beach. There were few people there so early, sometimes a handful of energetic joggers and someone walking a dog.

With the rising sun as my main companion, the wind swirling around me, the waves rising and crashing down, I was reminded of my small place in the world. On the beach it is difficult to think of anything but sand and ocean.

———

One morning, not a week after returning from the Highlands, I walked on the beach when the tide was out. Walking so close to the water's edge, I could smell the seaweed that lay strewn over half-submerged, glittering rocks not far off the shore. I stood there, watching the movements of the translucent, billowy sheet of sea.

The cold water rushed over my rubber boots, tugging on them as it pushed back out. Sludge crumpled under my feet. This part of the beach would be submerged in a few hours, would become the seabed again. It was impressionable, literally—not quite land, but not water. I thought about grey spaces, the indefinable, shapeless; when something is not one thing but not quite another thing, either. And then I started to think about her. About him, of course, too, but mostly about her.

Lisa. That was her name. She was the wife. His wife.

My relationship with him had taken shape, if it ever had a shape, without intention. But with Lisa's visit my relationship with him had been defined, not by what it was, but by what it was not.

A few days after the scene in the parking lot, Lisa had come to my apartment. She told me that my relationship with her husband was not a fifteen-year marriage. It was not a twenty-year commitment. It hadn't gone through three miscarriages, hadn't produced two babies—now adolescent children—and it hadn't withstood the death of three of the grandparents of those children.

I hadn't thought about Lisa or their marriage when I'd started seeing him. I'd had a vague idea of his wife, but she wasn't real to me until she showed up, calm rather than livid, that rainy afternoon.

Our affair started simply enough. At the think tank I'd been assigned to work on a project with Adrian, which was how we first got to know each other. He was a minor celebrity, but it was his charm that sparked my curiosity. Online digging revealed he was a film buff. After we had finished the project, I approached him after work and asked if he wanted to see a movie together that weekend. He said no. He was reluctant in the beginning, I remember. After the office holiday party when everybody had too much to drink, I complimented him on his tie, and asked if he wanted to have a nightcap. He accepted this time. I had worn him down.

During our first electric months, I didn't think about anything except pleasure—his and mine. We talked for hours, kindred spirits, and our conversations went far beyond our mutual love of history and languages. He told me things he had never told anybody: about his father's suicide, how it had marked him for life, and how his biggest fear was that he would fail his children in a similar way.

There was great sex, lots of it, in all sorts of places, usually suddenly. The last time had been in the conference room across from the podium behind which he often lectured, surrounded by the orange pleather seats where I used to bring paper cups of water to important people. It made me feel powerful, and so did his desire.

He was so into me, and that was part of it, too; knowing I held that sway over a brilliant, well-respected man. People recognized him when we were out together. I loved the look of reverence on their faces, their admiration for his mind. I loved that I alone knew the intimate him.

Of course, I wasn't the only one who knew him in that way. I used to wonder if he talked to his wife in bed the same way or if it was something special he only did with me; if he described what he was going to do to her before he did it. I enjoyed the anticipation, feeling something before I felt it. I had seen Lisa's picture in his office every day, and sometimes I imagined them together when he was with me.

I didn't think about the security cameras, which led to our eventual, mutual dismissal, or that my confrontation in the parking lot would prompt her visit to my apartment that day.

As I continued along the beach during low tide, thinking about indefinite things, thoughts of my father surfaced. Memories of him often wove their way into my consciousness, even when I tried to will them away.

My friends had been afraid of my father in the way that children can see through the transparent film of civility, but their parents admired him.

He could be very charming, but then something would switch, his eyes would narrow, and he would cross his arms over his chest. That's when my friends and I would grow quiet and tiptoe out of the room.

Nothing I did pleased him, including my straight As in school. Instead, he fussed over trivialities such as my messy handwriting, for which he had asked my teacher to give me extra daily exercises. I remembered going bike riding with him. The bike he had bought was too tall for my short legs. I fell off again and again, but he kept saying that when you fall you have to get up, that I'd get it eventually. Back at home, my mother couldn't conceal her surprise when she saw my knees all bloody. After I went to clean up, my father started shouting, and then I heard him stomp out of the house, slamming the door behind him. He drove away, tires squealing.

He believed my childhood allergy to peanuts was something I had faked to get attention, so once when I was six, in order to test me, he'd baked cookies without telling me there were ground peanuts inside. After just one bite I had to be rushed to the emergency room. I never forgot the feeling of my throat closing in on itself.

Although my father was a distinguished professor, the inadequacies he pointed out in me might have been a reflection of what he perceived in himself.

On the day of my twelfth birthday, my father left our house and never came back. We didn't hear from him again. For years I thought that one day he would come back, that there had been a misunderstanding. I invented all sorts of scenarios that could explain his abrupt departure from our lives. In my favorite scenario he had a top-secret job, which kept him away. Maybe he was protecting us.

My mother left all his clothes suspended in his closet, piled neatly in his drawers. She hadn't sold or donated a single T-shirt. Smiling photos of the three of us remained on the coffee table, and our image as a family froze in time in a photo on the refrigerator, anchored by an Eiffel Tower magnet.

Eleven years of our lives had passed without so much as a birthday card. Sometimes I thought about his other wife, his other children. Brothers and sisters better looking than I, better at French.

My mother rarely spoke about it, or him, to me, apart from when she noticed some little tick or habit of mine that bothered her.

My father had been a language genius—the technical term was hyper-polyglot. When I turned five my father had started reading his own translations of Perrault and Basile's fairy tales to me, the original *Cinderella* and *Little Red Riding Hood*, often frightening and different from the sugar-coated Disney films my friends watched. Until seventh grade I attended a French-language school for free because I was the daughter of a professor. I was proficient in Italian by the time I went to high school.

Studying history was a way to channel my obsessive nature into something productive, and memorizing dates and names came easily. I loved reading biographies about people of the past because their families, their decisions, their triumphs and their mistakes, and their troubled lives were great distractions from my own.

I was offered entry to every university I applied to, and scholarships to most. After moving away to college, I rarely returned home during school breaks. I wondered where well-off students like Rose went on spring break.

I stayed on campus and spent time in the library, reading history books the way I'd read biographies when I was younger—one title after another, at least four at a time.

I didn't have many close friends during my college years. What I thought at the time was my first genuinely intimate relationship came in the form of Adrian, a forty-year-old married man.

I had made coffee for Lisa the day she came over and we talked. Or, rather, she spoke and I listened. Before leaving my apartment, she said, "History always wins. You think of yourself as some sort of historian, don't you? Then it should make sense to you, of all people."

What Lisa had said made perfect sense. A few hours after she left, I reread the acceptance letter I had received from St Stephens, signed by Professor Madeleine Grangier. I would leave Adrian behind. I would make my mother proud. The medications I was taking had made me numb and listless. An ocean of distance would help, I reasoned, would save me from imploding. I reread the emails Rose had sent me—she'd made St Stephens sound like paradise. There was no reason to hesitate.

Right before I left for St Stephens, Adrian called me and left a message, saying I didn't need to leave because of him. Did I want to meet for a drink? That night I not only deleted all of his contact information, but I changed my email address and phone number.

The tide was rising faster now. It was warmer, or I pretended it was. I pulled off my boots and socks, rolled my pants up above my knees, and walked through the puddles in the sand until my shin bones started hurting. I shivered twice, then couldn't stop shaking. What would happen if I walked farther into the sea, to my waist? Or even farther than that? How long before the cold would be too much?

I retreated to dry sand and rolled down my pants before pulling on my socks with trembling fingers. I had lied to William. I did believe in ghosts.

CHAPTER SIXTEEN

Monday morning I woke at six to what sounded like an explosion but was only a garbage truck in the parking lot. Although I tried to will myself back to sleep, soon I was planning out everything I needed to do that day. Plodding through the dark to my desk, I stared out the window and waited for my computer to start up. I needed a new one, a faster one. A ding indicated a new message. It was from Endicott and addressed to the whole department.

I didn't cry at first. There was no way it was true.

They had found Rose's suicide note.

I reread the email again and again, my vision blurring as tears streamed down my cheeks. I got some tissues. I drank a bottle of water, took a long, hot shower, dressed, and walked to the department. In our office Mairead was sitting at her desk, staring at her computer screen.

"Mairead," I said. "How are you holding up?"

Violet half-moons shadowed her eyes. I dragged over one of the spare chairs and placed it next to hers. "Do you want to talk?" She didn't answer for a little while, then started to speak, slowly, as if she had forgotten how words were formed.

"I . . . need a minute," she said.

"Okay," I said. "I'll check in later." I went to Endicott's office. The door was open. Catrina, Bertie, and three students I didn't know were sitting in a circle, no one speaking. Endicott walked over to me and nodded his head gently. "Nice to see you, Isabel. Can I get you something? Tea?"

"No, thank you," I said, rubbing my stomach, which was still twisting. Catrina came over and gave me a hug.

"How are you feeling?" she asked.

"Not great," I said.

"Hmm," she said, and bowed her head. "And you're so far from home. Whatever you need, call me. Or Bertie."

"I appreciate that," I said. Endicott circled back to me and Catrina put her arm around Bertie's neck and sat down on his lap.

"What happened? Where did they find the note?" I asked Endicott.

"It was posted on my office door."

"What did it say?"

He pressed his lips together. "I cannot release that information, even if I wanted to. And I don't."

"But they haven't found the body?" I continued, undeterred.

"The police said it doesn't matter. They have . . . other evidence." He took in a deep breath and let it out quickly. "None of us realized that she was suffering. She hid it very well. You were close. How did she seem to you when you were last together? Bubbly as ever?"

I stammered. "She alluded to some problems, but nothing . . . to suggest this." Endicott shook his head as I glanced around the room. "Where's William?"

"Flying in, as we speak, he should be here sometime this evening." I nodded and went to sit in one of the empty chairs. Even though we weren't talking, the presence of other people, even strangers, all sharing the shock, was soothing. Eventually Endicott received a phone call, and everyone left to give him privacy. Catrina and Bertie linked arms and went in the direction of her office. I went to check on Mairead but the lights in our office were switched off.

I picked up groceries at the supermarket and collided with Sean after checking out. He enveloped me in a long hug and kissed me on the cheek, through my hair. "I'm sorry," he said. "All those things I said in the car on the way to the Highlands. I'm a horrible person."

"No, you're not," I said.

"Do you want to go somewhere and chat?"

"Maybe tomorrow? I need to go home and decompress. I have a splitting headache."

"Get some rest," he said. "Take the time you need." On the walk home the wind hit me from multiple directions. After putting the groceries away, I thought about going to the library, but couldn't concentrate on anything other than Rose. Rose.

The next two weeks went by in a haze. The feeling of grief that permeated not just the history department, but the campus, was palpable. I started crying at every little reminder. Even seeing someone wearing a bright scarf was enough to set it off. I'd see her around the corner, but not really. When my eyes were closed, I pictured her smiling, saying, "I'm alive."

With Rose, everything had been an adventure. Now my days seemed hollow, and loneliness began to sting for the first time since she'd reentered my life. The distance, all these things I would have dwelled on didn't make a difference when, as she'd put it, we were a team of two. Without her here, I felt far from home, from comfort and familiarity. Unmoored.

My friend was gone. I couldn't shake the feeling that I could've done something to save her. We'd shared so much, at least I had. I parsed the past for clues about what might have gone so horribly wrong. In Edinburgh she'd alluded to being in trouble. It must have been serious. But why hadn't she asked for my help?

A few days later, almost a month after we all found out that Rose was dead, on yet another foggy morning I was dusting my flat pretty much for the first time, and I started dusting the vase Rose had given me. Remembering her admonition that I not open it until we were old together, something tipped over inside of me and I curled in on myself on the couch and cried for a long time.

When I could swallow normally again, I put the jar in my lap. Could I handle this? Should I call Sean and ask him over? Tentatively I lifted the top, which was heavy, and put it down beside me. Had Rose put some sort of message inside? I pulled out what appeared to be a digital device. I pressed the play button. And there she was. Rose! Her voice.

"If you are hearing this, my life is in danger. Things have gotten pretty out of control. Remember in Edinburgh when I said I might need your help? Now I really do. I know I can trust you. Trust me, too, please. That's all I can say right now."

"Before you do anything else, put this vase in the window off the parking lot. They'll see it and know you've listened to this recording. If you don't put it there within a month after my suicide note surfaces, they'll kill me, so it's possible I'm dead right now, but I don't want to think that, knowing how smart you are you'll have figured it out."

I jumped up, pulled up the blinds, put the vase in the window, and went back to listening.

"Here's the deal. You need to find the Falcone emerald. The way to do that is to follow Federico Falcone, just as you would follow him if you were pursuing your topic. So first take over my topic, if you agree, that is, to follow through with this crazy scheme. I know the information about the emerald's whereabouts is somewhere in the archives, but I'm persona non grata in Genoa, and there are other reasons I can't go to the archives in Florence and Paris. You'll find your way. There's so much overlap with your work. And I don't know anyone more capable than you.

"You have a month to do the background research before starting the archival work, although I might be able to get them to extend that deadline if they see you're really focused on finding the emerald. And yes, you're being watched. I'm so sorry.

"Then you need to go to Genoa, where I'm praying you'll find it. But if not, then Florence. No matter what, take my place at the conference. I'll clear that with the fuckheads who want the emerald. If you don't find anything in Florence, go to Paris. I don't think there's much in the archives there, but I didn't do a thorough job of looking. If you don't find it there, we are SOL. I don't have a Plan B. I have faith in you, Isabel. I'm going to believe you'll find it. Of course you will! Once you do, go back to your flat. They'll let me contact you at that point.

"Do not, do not, do NOT tell the police or anyone else or I will be killed immediately and then you will be killed. I'm not kidding. As long as you are looking for the emerald, we'll both stay alive. I'll be in touch whenever I can so you know I'm okay.

"Put this device in a bag and leave it behind the dumpster outside your apartment. Honestly, Isabel, do exactly as I say and do not play detective. These people are professionals. My life and your life are at stake. One false move and they will not hesitate to disfigure me and let you know about it.

"Stay on task, bestie. You must promise that until you see me again, you cannot mention the emerald except in the most academic way.

'I'm sorry you're now caught up in this. I am so very sorry.

"Remember: Genoa, Florence, Paris. Present at the conference in Florence. No detours. Like I said, they are watching you.

"Bye sweetie. I love you. You are my best hope. I know all of this is totally insane, but I have to believe I will get to see you again and thank you in person. Somehow I'll make it all up to you. Not sure how but I have time to think about it."

I looked around the flat and then went into the kitchen, the room farthest from the front window. I was being watched. I had to go to the police. But I couldn't. This was crazy.

I put the recording in a bag and took it to the dumpster. Were they watching me right now? No one was around. I couldn't think about that. I had to compartmentalize. Put the situation in a box and think about it later.

Back inside I caught my breath and put my hands on either side of my head, willing myself not to scream. I was shivering so badly I made tea, and I drank it as hot as I could stand. Was Rose really asking me to do all of this? For the first time I smiled. A smile of irony.

She wasn't asking. She was telling me. She was telling me what I had to do in order to save her life, and my own.

CHAPTER SEVENTEEN

I opened my computer to set up an appointment with Endicott to tell him that I wanted to take over Rose's research. This was going to be humiliating.

An email from William was waiting for me.

> Dear Isabel,
>
> Rose's suicide has been a shock to our entire community, so I wanted to reach out and check on you, and about another matter. Please know that if there's anything you need, I am here for you.
>
> Would it be possible to meet with me and Nigel in his office this afternoon at 1 P.M.? We have a sensitive matter we'd like to discuss with you.
>
> All best,
> William

After writing back to confirm the meeting, I started thinking about what I'd say to them about taking on Rose's research. Or I could wait and meet with William after we'd talked with Endicott about whatever this "sensitive" matter was. No, I'd raise the issue immediately. It didn't matter what they thought of me. Somehow, the politics and internecine goings-on in the department now seemed irrelevant and self-indulgent. My focus had to shift to life and death matters.

Maybe I would tell William about the recording. At least he'd understand why I wanted to work on someone else's topic. But, no, I couldn't tell him. Rose was specific about that. What else had she said? I wrote out everything I'd remembered, then shredded my notes. I had to concentrate. To make a plan. I hadn't done laundry in weeks, so I threw on my last clean turtleneck with wool pants and a thick sweater and walked to Endicott's office. I knocked on the door right at one and was greeted with a double chiming of, "Come in."

Endicott and William both stood up to shake my hand. William offered me a cup of tea and Endicott began to speak.

"Isabel, I appreciate this must be a particularly difficult time for you. Everyone knows that you and Rose were close friends."

"Yes," I said, looking back and forth at one, then the other. I cleared my throat. "I need to jump in here and say that I've been giving this a lot of thought, and I'd like to take on Rose's topic. I kept hitting dead ends when I was trying to find a viable approach to my original thesis. But there's so much overlap in our topics. She and I, Rose and I, talked about that numerous times."

Endicott interlaced his fingers. "Isabel," he said, "that is precisely why we asked to talk with you today. I'll let your new supervisor explain."

"It . . . is?"

"Rose was the recipient of an exclusive scholarship," said William. "The funds benefit not only the recipient but the department and the university. Given your extensive knowledge of Catherine de' Medici and her inner circle, we thought that you would be ideally situated to work on the Falcone family."

I sat down, and the two of them did as well. William continued. "I've discussed the situation with Nigel," he said, and they exchanged glances. "You should know that while I was under the impression that Rose's work was close to completion, that is not the case. The work she did was fairly, was only, basic. I admit . . ." He walked over to the fireplace, and the light painted a shadow behind his profile. "I admit I was not a responsible advisor."

"William will oversee your work," Endicott said, "although I'd be happy to offer advice on an informal basis. I would forfeit my ability to serve as one of your thesis examiners, but we need not get ahead of ourselves."

"Thank you so much for this opportunity," I said.

"Right," said Endicott. "That settles it. You can meet and start strategizing."

"Actually, I'd like to suggest that I pull some documents together and send them to you, Isabel. You can go through them and then we'll discuss. Of course, I'll be available to you anytime."

Yesterday I would have savored those words. Today I was all business. "I assure you both that I will not disappoint you."

When I came out Sean was standing in the hallway finishing a sandwich. He stuffed the remaining bite in his mouth and looked at me as if I had caught him raiding the cookie jar.

"Hello," Sean said. "Gianni's?"

"Sounds great."

We found a table toward the back, which was empty, and after we had ordered tea, Sean said he'd heard that I'd been offered Rose's funding track if I took over her research.

"Wait, did they ask you first?" I said.

"Nah, it's nowhere near my topic. Although I like the idea of all that money."

"There's a lot? They didn't explain that part. Anyway, how did you hear? They asked me like five minutes ago."

"Catrina told me."

"Ah. She knew before I did. Guess that means everyone knows."

"Pretty much. It's about the money that the school will lose if they don't fill the spot. Catrina said it's considerable. She said Rose had missed several deadlines for her latest report. Between Rose and your late supervisor . . . it's like we're cursed."

"Sean, can we please change the subject?" I put my cup down. "How's your work on English Catholic refugees going? And have you done any climbing?"

"My own funding has me chained to the desk, as it were." He poured both of us more tea and then said, "I'm still working on my French, which isn't great. Doesn't come easily to me as it does to you. But, how are you handling all of this?"

"Wait, what about the others? Mairead, Luke? Are people okay? Do we need to check on anyone? How are you doing?" I put my hand over his, squeezed it, then pulled my hand back into my lap.

"Of course you're concerned about everyone else. Danny's doing better. Luke is calm," he said. "Catrina and Bertie are Catrina and Bertie. Mairead isn't talking about it, but, well, you know what she's like. As for me, I dunno."

"How so?"

"I feel awful about what I said on the drive north. If I had known . . ." He looked at his watch and leapt up. "Christ, I'm late. I have to run. You are so distracting. *La belle dame sans merci.*" He leaned in for an awkward hug over my chair.

After we parted I took a shortcut to the library. None of the internet-access computers were available, but a search of the St Stephens' library catalogue confirmed that there were no monographs on the Falcone here.

In the Renaissance section of the stacks, I pulled out each of the most recently published books that seemed relevant and looked for Falcone in the indices. I found only a few sentences here and there. In a reference volume on sixteenth-century Europe I saw their name in the index and read several passages. My mind was buzzing, and I'd only been there for two hours. It was difficult to believe Rose had found such an untouched subject.

Late that afternoon I stopped by my office. Mairead was at her desk, typing away.

"You're here," she said, and by the way her voice cracked I could tell she was glad. "Did they talk you into working on Rose's topic?"

"I've already started."

"What about all the work you've done in the three months you've been here? You've been living in the library. Does that get tossed?"

"It gets recycled. One of the Falcone, Federico, was married to Thérèse Du Montour."

Someone knocked. It was Catrina, in a cashmere coat and cap. It looked like . . . Rose's coat? Her grimace relaxed when she saw me. "I heard the great news," she said. She came over and gave me a little hug. "Brilliant, Isabel."

After they both left, I turned on my computer. William had emailed me a PDF file. The first of the nine pages outlined, broadly, the scope of Rose's topic: "This thesis examines the role of the Falcone family, in the context of geopolitical affairs of the European states and the family's influence on French foreign policy in the late sixteenth century." The other pages contained a detailed bibliography listing secondary literature and primary sources, which was divided into printed and archival materials.

Only rarely did Rose add additional notes next to the reference numbers, such as "Falcone Correspondence," or "letter that mentions F." It would be necessary to go back and look through the sources individually.

As I was reviewing the file for a third time, William knocked and let himself in. He gestured around the room before saying, "I'm sorry it took us so long to provide you with one of these."

I had no time for niceties and pointed to the document on my screen.

"She put together an impressive list," I said. "But other than that . . ."

"She asked for extension upon extension," he said, pulling up a chair across from me. "As you can see, she did make it to the archives in Genoa, Florence, and Paris. But when I read through everything today I could see, as you now can, that she indicated the locations of the materials but only vague descriptions of the contents."

We talked a little longer and I outlined a plan. "I'll spend a month going through whatever's here. Then the archives. Presumably there are adequate funds to cover travel expenses. I'll go to Genoa first. Three weeks? Or a month? Then Florence, coinciding with the conference there. Then Paris."

"That's a pretty ambitious program, Isabel. But clearly you're off to a great start," he said. "I'm so happy we'll be working together."

I nodded. "I am, too."

Alone at my desk I felt wave after wave of dread. Earlier I'd found out that I was singularly responsible for saving the life of one of my best friends, and my own life in the bargain. Part of me was infuriated that someone who seemed to care about me could've dragged me into this tumult. Yes, we had become close, but it had all happened so quickly. Then I remembered how low I'd felt only a few weeks ago. Rose had rescued me from all that. I thought back to the night on the beach, when I'd thanked Rose for saving my life, and she'd said she hadn't done much. That she knew I'd do the same for her. After all, I had offered to help her. I couldn't let her down. Could I? Besides, if I was able to complete the task, no one would be hurt. She'd said that.

In any case, I had thrown away three months of research and taken on a new dissertation topic. William was now my advisor, and we were linked together by work, and possibly more, yet I could tell him nothing about the enormous threat and responsibility that was now directing my every move.

Fear was not my only motivation, although it felt uncomfortable to admit, even to myself. Based on everything I'd heard and read so far the Falcone story was fascinating. I couldn't help imagining how exciting it would have been to discover the family on my own. Without pressure, without Rose. These kinds of thoughts made me feel ashamed now that serious issues were at stake. To deflect such feelings, I promised myself I would find the emerald and save my friend. For the first time ever, someone really needed me, was depending on me. My only obligation was to work hard on something captivating, something I already cared about.

I decided to spend the rest of the day in the library until it closed.

I started with the obvious, an Internet search for Falcone, and pulled up pictures of falcons as well as genealogical websites. Falcone was a common name.

After switching to Italian, the first of several pages informed me that descendants of the noble Falcone family lived in Genoa.

On the third search page I clicked a link under the heading *Collezione Falcone, Genova*. The Falcone archives appeared on Rose's outline, although the Genoa section was the least detailed part of the file William had sent. What had Rose said about Genoa? That she wasn't welcome there?

Further digging led me to a page with the following passage, written in four languages: Italian, English, French, and German.

The private archive of the Falcone family, housed in their palazzo in Genoa, was robbed, and valuable letters were taken.

If you have any information about the stolen papers, please contact the Contessa Falcone (details below). She offers a reward for their recovery.

Had Rose been to the archive before or after it had been robbed? I looked at the PDF that William had sent, but it didn't mention anything about the theft. I wrote to William and asked if he had heard anything about it. He responded right away that Rose hadn't told him.

Maybe all the original documents had been stolen, and Rose hadn't been able to work much in Genoa after all. But she told me she had worked there.

I spent the next hour researching the history of precious stones. In the early modern period, they had been used as collateral in a time when liquid assets were unreliable. The Duke of Ferrara had once pawned his most prized possession, a diamond, symbol of the Este, to finance the construction of his largest palazzo. And Isabella of Spain had used the crown jewels as collateral to fund expeditions to the Americas. The conquistadors had funded entire voyages based on metals and jewels they expected to find overseas, and their enormous bounty was heavily taxed upon arrival back in Spain when it had been declared.

The library lights dimmed overhead.

Day one was over. I had accomplished a lot, and felt calm, in control. I feared that was an illusion.

CHAPTER EIGHTEEN

For the next week I worked twelve hours a day. William had sent me an email outlining the monthly payments I'd be receiving as a stipend. At least I no longer needed to worry about how I was going to pay off my credit card. By the end of the week my full funding became official, and William invited me out for a celebratory drink, which he had to cancel at the last minute.

After a while I found that short walks were insufficient to deal with my overpowering anxiety. Ten minutes outside St Stephens' medieval city gate, I discovered a nature reserve, Glenbuck Burn, which had a public footpath surrounded by dense woods, and a river running beside it, thirty feet below. It had been constructed in the twelfth century, an artificial watercourse to transport water to the mill pond and the Priory of St Stephens.

Under the cover of the trees, it was always dusk, just light enough. The brush was so thick that water could barely penetrate, and the pathway remained clear and dry most of the time. I took long jogs there, uninterrupted except for the occasional red squirrel darting in front of me.

One rainy afternoon, I pushed myself harder than usual. A breeze from the east was shaking leaves from the trees, and a few acorns landed on my shoulder. Glenbuck Burn was deserted, and although the lack of cell phone reception had been one of its charms, today my senses were on alert. Just as it occurred to me that it might be unwise to be here by myself, I heard a crash and started running, fast. The path became wooded, and I wasn't sure where I was. When at last I came to a stop all was peaceful, and there was no one in any direction.

Of course, no one was there. The crash must have been an animal or a fallen branch. I turned around and ran most of the way back.

The next day I started running on the beach instead, which was wetter, but also less isolated. Standing on the beach, I stared at the tide that had just rolled out, exposing pink shells and glass bottles on the gray sand. After a few minutes, I bent down to pick up an unusual piece of wood and noticed someone behind me. Turning around, instinctively balling my hands into fists, I saw the outline of a person in a pale-purple windbreaker. It was Mairead.

"Sorry for sneaking up on you," she said, her windbreaker flapping in the wind.

"Don't worry. Is everything okay?"

"Relatively speaking, yeah," she said. "I wasn't going to say anything, but I overheard Endicott in his office, talking to someone. Think it was Bertie."

"Yeah?"

"You have to promise you won't say anything, Isabel, but the police have reopened Madeleine Grangier's case. They found some new evidence there was foul play involved in her death."

Sean called me to suggest we go hiking that weekend, but I declined his invitation and spent Saturday and Sunday at the library until it closed. If anyone was watching me, they would know that I was focused and on task. Work required as much energy and courage as I could muster, forcing myself into uninterrupted hours of immersion. Everything I learned about the Falcone I looked at through the lens of the mystery of the emerald and what had happened to it. I didn't want to think about what Mairead had said about Madeleine. I'd long been convinced that her death hadn't been accidental, and now I was sure it was linked to Rose and her predicament. That reality scared me into playing games with myself, pretending otherwise.

Each time I left the house, the office, or the library, I took careful note of everyone in my immediate vicinity and glanced over my shoulder frequently to see if anyone might be watching or following me. Whenever I was by myself even the slightest noise made me jump. At home I played music constantly in order to avoid being alone with creaky floorboards and a chorus of what-ifs. I couldn't fall asleep without drinking a glass or two of wine.

A few days into December, William asked for a meeting.

"Tell me how everything's going," he said.

I pulled out my notes and sat on the edge of my seat. "I've now gone through all the pertinent reference books in the library searching for references to the Falcone."

"That's a lot of volumes, Isabel," he said, his eyes widening. "Of course, it does help when there's an index."

"There wasn't always an index, so sometimes I just flipped through however many thousands of pages."

"Your dedication to your new topic is admirable."

"I'm not sure how useful this is, but my eyes are now trained to find the name 'Falcone,' even if I'm reading *The Scotsman*. Anyway, the connection with Catherine de' Medici is more than viable, so I was able to assimilate the background research. I found supporting materials via interlibrary loans. Special Collections has printed correspondence from the early modern European courts, and the letters have given me a clearer sense of the relationships between the characters. When I'm able to see the relevant archival documents, I'll be well prepared."

"Excellent," said William.

"In addition to the Calendar of State Papers and the dispatches of the Venetian ambassadors, I've read the letters from Catherine to Falcone family members and vice versa in all ten volumes of Catherine de' Medici's published correspondence," I said.

"It sounds like you've covered a tremendous amount of ground already," William said. "What's been your most crucial find? Did anything surprise you?"

I folded my arms. I wanted to tell him, so far, nothing about the emerald. But instead I said, "The Falcone were a well-oiled machine. Giovanbattista Falcone was a petty merchant, but his children made their fortunes in France. Quickly. After Giovanbattista died, Federico became head of the family. And he had the ear of the Queen Mother."

"Anything else?"

"There's so much material, as Rose indicated, which will be a great roadmap for the archives," I said. "The original sources always tell the story. Reading even a printed copy of a letter penned by Federico Falcone feels like striking gold."

He shrugged. "You're asking all the right questions," he said, "and narrowing your scope. I look forward to hearing what you discover on your first research leg on the continent. I'm off to Paris tomorrow but let's get dinner when I'm back, before break." He stood up and so did I.

"Have you heard of . . . the Falcone emerald?"

"The what?"

"Just something I ran across. I'll let you know if I corroborate. Safe travels," I said. His gaze met and held mine a few seconds too long, or maybe I just wanted to think that it did.

A week after my meeting with William I ran into Endicott outside William's office. "Isabel, while I recognize you would have written an excellent dissertation on Catherine de' Medici's female court, I greatly appreciate that you decided to prioritize the needs of the school. Please know that your decision is not lost on me. I'm genuinely sorry that we won't have the chance to work together, but I'm happy to assist in any way."

Without waiting for a reply, he continued to walk.

⸙

When I met again with William, I was relieved he didn't ask me for a progress report but instead launched into what seemed like a prepared monologue. Maybe one that he always gave his students when they were getting started.

"Think of your work as a court case, or an unsolved mystery," he told me. "The historian's first task is gathering evidence from contemporary letters, memoirs, etc. Unlike in the courtroom, hearsay evidence is welcome. You read the work of other specialists. Finally, you decide on your interpretation, remembering that no verdict on history is definitive. The past always recedes."

"I'm doing my best with what I have so far," I said.

"That's good enough," he said. "It has to be."

I put my notebook in my bag. "What do you think Federico Falcone, for example, wanted, really?"

"Wanted? What does anyone want? Power, wealth, invincibility. To have it all."

He opened his desk drawer, pulled out a blank sheet of paper, and sketched a triangle.

"A PhD is like an iceberg," he said, pointing at the top eighth of the triangle intersected by a horizontal line. "See this part underneath the line?"

"Yes," I said.

"That represents your research." He looked up at me and then moved his pen to a point above the line. "See the top? The small part?" I nodded. "That's the dissertation." He laid the paper down on the desk and tapped it with his pen. "The depth of your project, all that work, that research you put into it, may be invisible on the surface to your examiners and your readers. But it's still there."

I nodded again. "Got it," I said.

"You'll see," he said. "In time you'll see what I mean. You're onto something, though, you remind me of . . ."

"Of?"

"Of myself when I was starting out, so full of idealism, enthusiasm. It's thrilling to see in someone else."

I thanked him and literally ran down to my office. I needed to get back to work. Whenever I wasn't going through sources, I was panicking about my one-month deadline. I'd already used up more than two weeks.

I reviewed the list of things I needed to prepare for my trip to Genoa. I liked writing lists on paper, so I opened the top desk drawer and pulled out my notebook. When I tried to close the drawer, I could only push it in halfway. Inside I didn't see anything that would have kept the drawer from closing, but it was deep. I flattened my hand, reached in all the way to the back, and felt around until I touched something. Paper. Using my fingers as tweezers, I pulled out a couple of sheets, folded over several times. It was a typed letter, marked up with handwritten notes in red ink, and multiple asterisks in the margins. Rose's handwriting.

A few of the words had red question marks over them, or were blank spaces, indicating she hadn't been able to read them.

Falcone Archive AF Volume 7, Fols 12r-14v.
Transcription and Translation of letter from Tommaso to Federico Falcone, 1581

My most illustrious brother,
    I arrived in Genoa last night. The journey was long, I shall not enumerate my sufferings, but please know your emerald

is here with me, secure. Its location will be revealed to you when you arrive.

Time has given way to clarity, I now understand everything you have said. The concerns of our family must needs be our most important and only concerns. I have resigned to relegate other matters to the past, to be _____, to be forgotten.

So as to demonstrate my loyalty to our family and my intention to preserve our interests, I will disclose another crucial matter, for which I must take you into my confidence due to its extremely sensitive nature.

The most Christian King arrives in Genoa in one month and will be a guest in our palazzo.

I have had word from a contact in Spain, who has informed me that the plan to proceed is fully formed, and the moment is upon us. We must rely on the assistance of the Duke of Alba. When the matter has been concluded successfully, I understand you are to have a portion of land in_____.

Matters of the heart I have put aside in favor of the affairs of honor. What happens to M._____ concerns me no longer.

The only things of significance are strength and power, that of our family, our good name, and the future of our line. It is right and just that you, our father's eldest and head of our family, should lead this effort.

If you believe that your holy duty obliges you to help to rid this kingdom of the tyrant who knows no religion, please find and take a vial that I shall leave in _____. _____. In the _____. I acknowledge this will require much risk, but it will also grant, I assure you, rich rewards.

The glass contains a _____, a _____, prized for its qualities of strength and speed. Among its chief advantages is that it is undetectable, working quickly, painlessly, and then dissipating with equal velocity. This is a draught created by the oldest women of _____ _____, an elixir so potent that its mere fumes suffice to kill a horse, which is why only these old women are entrusted with the deadly task of brewing it.

You, who are closest to the king, know his heart. You can go near to his person and do what needs to be done to deliver us. You must kill him with ____ when he takes his dinner _____.

For what better opportunity to effectuate our plan, with the approval of _____ and the most Catholic King. You must be willing to sacrifice yourself for the cause, if indeed, the day for sacrifice comes. What say you, brother?

If you agree to carry out these tragic but necessary actions, when you arrive in the palazzo please wear your dark red doublet and attach a small white cross to the breast. Then we will know you wish to help us put an end to the shameful state of the kingdom. Do you wish for a unified Catholic kingdom, not besmirched by the evils of heresy? Act with confidence.

If you do not desire to join us, please wear your dark blue doublet. I will understand whatever you choose, although there is only one path if you care for peace.

We have written to the Duke of Alba directing him to take such steps and precautions required to carry out the plan successfully, and to instruct you. They ask you not to exceed any instructions the duke might give, as in all things you should act with utter obedience, and with the diligence that the gravity of the issue demands.

And lastly. The emerald belongs to you. I was in error to think it mine to keep or bestow. No one shall move it from its location without your knowledge. Your position, once we are delivered from the usurper, will be most great. Await word from the most Catholic King, by means of his messengers.

The time is now to take a step of great benefit to Christianity and ourselves, my good brother.

Your very devoted and admiring servant,
Tommaso F

My eyes scanned the page. Emerald! There was a lot to digest, but I was holding an English version of a letter written by Tommaso to his brother about a plot involving the king of France but most importantly about an emerald, which must be the emerald.

I read it over again, carefully. I didn't remember seeing anything suggesting this letter on the list of Rose's material, so I checked again. No reference to the letter. Rose must have already searched for the emerald in the palazzo, but the words indicating its exact location had been obscured or written in cipher. The letter suggested that after Tommaso revealed the emerald's location to his brother, Federico must have taken it, and hidden it elsewhere. Or had he never retrieved the stone in the first place?

As I was reading the letter a third time, the door opened and Mairead entered.

She walked to her desk. "You alright? You look . . . I don't know. What's that? Why are those pages so wrinkled?"

"Oh, hi, Mairead. I didn't think you'd be here so early."

"Early? It's half four." The sun had set but I hadn't noticed how dark it was.

She switched on the light, then came over to my desk and plucked the pages from my hand. "What is this?"

"Something I found. In the back of the desk," I said. "A Falcone letter that Rose transcribed and translated. It's . . . kind of remarkable."

"In what way?"

"It indicates that one of the Falcone was involved in a conspiracy, with the help of Spain, to assassinate the French king, Henri III."

"A Falcone was responsible for Henri's assassination? And this letter is the smoking gun? Wow."

"I don't think so. It was written nearly a decade before Henri's death, and the events described never transpired. Read it, Mairead."

She read the letter, flipping to the front and then back again several times. When she was finished she handed it to me. "This is sensational, Isabel. Does William know?"

"I don't think so. He must not know because otherwise he would have told me. Maybe Rose didn't put it in her notes, or tell William, because she was planning to reveal it at the conference in Florence."

"Probably. She was always one for a dramatic moment."

"You'd think a letter this incendiary would have been destroyed. Maybe it was kept for evidence? I doubt Tommaso would have made a copy. If found by the wrong person it would be an immediate, and grisly, death warrant."

"Did Rose indicate where she'd found it?"

"In the Falcone Archive."

"So a document in a private archive. But really, Isabel. An unknown plot to assassinate Henri III, with the possible collusion of the king of Spain? This is as big as the Ridolfi plot. So, you haven't shown William?"

"Not yet," I said. "He's away. And I should read the original in Genoa. Not that I don't trust Rose's transcription skills but . . ."

"Good idea. Compare it with the original. I need a coffee, can I get you anything?"

"No, thanks," I said. "And Mairead? Please don't discuss this with anyone."

"I won't tell a soul." As she headed to the door she turned back around. "There's something else I remembered. To do with Rose."

"What?"

"It was a while back, when we'd just started sharing the office. One day I came in and she was on the phone. With her dad I think. She said something like, 'No money at all? So, none of those investments were . . .' Then she hung up and started crying. I'd never seen her so upset. After she collected herself, she asked me to keep it between us. I told the police about it, because I had to, but I also . . . thought you should know."

"Thanks."

When Mairead left I tucked the folded transcription into my notebook. I wasn't sure what to make of the conversation that Mairead had overheard. Rose had never alluded to money troubles when we'd spoken, but she might have been too embarrassed to tell me. Or it had been a false alarm.

I put my notebook with the transcription back in the drawer. For some reason Tommaso had had possession of the emerald before passing it along to Federico, to whom it belonged. At least now I knew the emerald had actually existed.

In the library I took out a book on the French nobility to reacquaint myself with the details of Tommaso's life. Maybe Tommaso was the Falcone I should be following rather than Federico.

Tommaso had held minor positions in the king's household, but always in the shadow of his elder brother. There were thirteen years between them. The attempted plot could have been Tommaso's chance to prove himself. As the youngest son in a large family, he would have been under pressure to create his own wealth, as he wouldn't have been eligible for inheritance.

I found more references to the 1565 trip to the Americas that Tommaso had taken with Federico. An ambassadors' dispatch from 1579 mentioned a skirmish between French and Spanish forces off the northern coast of Brazil, during which eight French ships were lost, and 800 Frenchmen were killed. Apparently, a Falcone had been on the one ship that survived and returned to France to tell the tale of the Spanish onslaught.

If I could figure out how Tommaso had become involved with the Duke of Alba in the conspiracy, it might give me an idea about where the emerald was. Had he traded secrets or goods with the Spanish and then been forced to participate in the plot? The tone of the letter suggested it had been written with genuine conviction, but that could have been posturing. Had Federico joined his brother's so-called crusade? Had the assassination even been attempted? Obviously, it had been thwarted, since there was no record of the plot, and if it had been revealed, contemporary sources would have written of little else. Maybe the letter had been intercepted? But what if that was one of the letters that had been stolen from the Falcone archive after Rose had transcribed it?

Poor Rose. Her moment of academic glory had been taken away. But maybe she hadn't mentioned the letter to William because she hadn't done any corroborative scholarship. How could she have presented this without an enormous amount of parallel research to frame it in context? She couldn't have. That must have been why she'd put it in the back of the drawer and forgotten about it.

CHAPTER NINETEEN

The days of the rest of the year were so dark that it was difficult to wake up in the morning, not knowing if it was daytime or still night. I'd stopped jogging. I felt prepared for the Genoa, Florence, and Paris archives, but there was plenty more to do before my scheduled departure since my search for information about the emerald was paralleling my thesis and I had to keep my numerous notes and charts completely organized for both purposes.

Endicott had written to ask if I would agree to present a paper on the Falcone at the Society of Early Modern Studies conference, held in Florence that year. It was the paper Rose was supposed to give.

Four weeks after Rose's suicide note had been posted to Endicott's door neither the local police nor Scotland Yard had found her body, not surprisingly. But someone, presumably Rose, had mailed me a printed-out note that read: "Deadline extended. All OK. Genoa mid-January. Stay focused. No distractions."

I didn't freak out when I read the note, but I didn't feel relieved either. I'd accepted my role in whatever was going on and would continue to do everything possible to find the Falcone emerald. In exchange, Rose was still alive. Or so I had to believe. And as long as she was okay, I would be too.

Often fear did bubble up. Everyone at St Stephens thought Rose was dead, and the second death in our department in such a short span of time had caused a stir. Her father had stormed in one day, shouting, taking Endicott by surprise. Scotland Yard had appeared, and they'd spent several days interviewing Endicott and all of us. Both about Madeleine and about Rose.

I'd started crying, genuinely, whenever they tried to question me, and after the third attempt, when they brought a young woman in just for the purpose of talking with me and I could only hiccup through my tears, they left me alone.

Each morning over coffee—I was drinking lots of coffee by then—I went over my notes. The Palazzo Falcone in Genoa was the most logical hiding spot for the emerald, as Rose indicated, and the letter in her desk supported this theory. Then again Rose had clearly looked for it in the palazzo. I supposed "they" were sending me back, because "they" believed the emerald was still there. Had she figured out the obscured words in the Tommaso letter, or would that be up to me?

I needed to get to that archive. Rose and I were safe as long as I stayed on task and made progress. Who was watching me here in St Stephens? Would they have someone follow me in Genoa? If I did find the emerald, would they kill her or both of us after I'd told them where it was?

Whenever I started asking myself these kinds of questions, I down-shifted the rising panic by first closing my eyes and controlling my breathing, and repeating, "Don't go there, don't go there," over and over. I kept questioning why Rose had put herself, and now me, into this terrible position. How had she gotten into this mess? And why had she chosen me to pick up where she'd left off? I wanted to scream at her. If I ever saw her again, I would. But first I needed to find the emerald and make sure she stayed alive.

The Falcone family administrator had written that it would be convenient for them if I arrived in mid-January. Without going into detail, he'd let me know that the theft of documents had been significant. This Mr. Michelozzo had relayed a message from the Contessa Falcone that the rare books in the collection had not been catalogued, which was perhaps something I might be interested in doing. I'd scheduled four weeks to work in Genoa, but William thought I might not need that much time, depending on how much remained after the theft.

I made an appointment to see William the day before winter break. We had already talked about my goals for the trip, and that morning I emailed him with an update. But it would have felt odd to leave without saying goodbye, and I decided to show him Tommaso's letter. And I wanted to see him. Needed to see him.

I'd been deluding myself about managing my anxiety regarding the situation with Rose and whoever was watching me. In addition to fearing what they might do to me, I was terrified of stepping off a mental ledge without warning, because I hadn't been able to share the burden of what I was going through with anyone else. It felt so isolating. I wasn't sure I could keep it together, by myself, away from the place I now considered home. William was the person closest to the center of this maelstrom, even if he didn't know it.

Already late for our appointment, I grabbed my notebook and flipped through it to pull out the letter. But the pages weren't there. I went back to the office and searched the desk, to no avail. Had I hidden it somewhere? But three days ago I had gone over the letter again, trying to make sense of the story. I looked through my bag. Nothing. I could refer to my notes for now. The letter would turn up at home. If it didn't turn up at home that would mean someone had taken it. Whoever had taken it would have needed to break into my flat.

Each time I got home, I inspected every corner to make sure nothing looked out of place, and I double locked the door whenever I left, checking several times to make sure it couldn't be opened without keys. I had even called Charles to see if anyone else had an extra set.

By then most of the students had already left and St Stephens seemed eerily quiet. I knocked on William's door half an hour after the appointed time. His "come in" was frosty. Inside his office his neck was arched over whatever he was reading. When he looked up, his scowl softened.

"Sorry I'm late," I said. "I don't need much of your time. Just wanted to check in before leaving. Guess we won't see each other until next year. Although next year is days away." I thought he would laugh but he didn't.

"Indeed. I'm glad you came by. I was worried when you missed our appointment."

"I sent you an email this morning outlining my progress and plans," I said.

"Yes, I read it. But I would like a recap from you. Tell me about this Falcone. Sounds like you've narrowed your focus down to one. The oldest brother?"

"Yes. Federico. I've been patching together his biographical details. His early life was full of mayhem because his father, Giovanbattista, was involved in a plot against the doge. After the uprising failed Giovanbattista was forced to move his immediate family to France, and they lost the family seat, the palazzo in Genoa, where I'll be working."

"So, it's still in family hands? Did they lose it to another branch of the family?"

"Exactly. Giovanbattista's brother, Pierfrancesco, took possession of the palazzo. Then Federico's mother died. There was a fair amount of tragedy in his adult life as well. His first wife, Ginevra de' Croci, died young. He remarried Thérèse, with whom he had six daughters, and one son, who died at twelve."

"You said in your email that Federico was a controversial figure. Controversial how?"

"His involvement in the St Bartholomew's Day Massacre, for example. I have to investigate more before I can confirm or revise that line of thinking."

"Tell me about the rest of the family," William said.

"Well, his father, Giovanbattista, as I mentioned, was married twice. With his first wife he had three sons, the eldest brother died young. Then Federico, and Piero, who became a bishop. There were also three daughters. One was installed in a convent. The other two were married to what you might call entry-level French nobles.

"Tommaso, Giovanbattista's youngest, accompanied his half-brother Federico to Brazil in 1565. Federico, though, is the brother with the most agency."

I flipped through my notes to find something I'd written that morning. "People sought out Federico when they wanted a loan, despite constraints on the nobility and moneylending, because they knew about his connections with Italian bankers. He had a *Wunderkammer* and an extensive library, which landed him in trouble with the Inquisition because of books he owned about alchemy." I lifted my head.

"Federico went on at least one trip to the Americas. I'm not sure how many times he crossed the ocean. I read an ambassadors' dispatch about an accident off the coast of Brazil that involved a French fleet in the 1570s. He was a major captain by then. Eight ships were lost, an enormous undertaking during their Civil Wars, and 800 men died."

William put his elbow on the desk and rested his chin in his hand. "That all sounds fascinating! You've made a lot of progress."

"The more I've learned about Federico the more questions I have. King Henri III may have used accusations against Federico as a pretext to send him back to Genoa. Federico was close to Henry's overbearing mother,

Catherine, so maybe that's why he fell out of favor. Both he and his brother Tommaso died of the plague.

"This might sound all over the place, but as I've emphasized there's a lot of material. The blurry picture is coming into focus." I leaned back again and took in a deep breath that I let out slowly.

"It's all top-notch. When you get to Italy keep in mind that the important thing is to collect and analyze a small number of critical documents. I mean to say archival research is more about quality than quantity. That's not a criticism. Quite the contrary. You've only been at this a month, and you've accomplished so much. I was thinking about my own process starting out, and I wanted to advise you to take it step by step."

"Of course," I said. "I'm good at compartmentalizing. But I trust you, and I'll keep it in mind."

He looked at his watch and stood up gathering his papers. "I wish I had more time, but I have a plane to catch. Please email me from Genoa." He was looking around the room to see if he'd forgotten anything. "I want to know how it goes." He put everything in his satchel and walked over to his coat.

Without knocking Catrina poked her head inside and said, "Your cab's here, Will," and left, the door still ajar.

"Thanks, William," I said. "I appreciate your support. I'll send you regular updates."

I held out my hand. "See you next year!" He took my hand and held it. My cold hand in his warm one. Then his forehead creased, and he leaned in toward me and we kissed, both pulling back at the same time.

"Isabel, I'm sorry. It shouldn't be this way. It can't be. If we're to work together, we can't . . . let this happen. I can't let it. It's my fault, and I take full responsibility. But, Isabel, I . . . hope you understand."

"Yes," I said. "You're right." I walked back to the chair and picked up my bag. He slung his satchel over his shoulder, and we walked out of the office together, along the hall, down the stairs. Neither of us spoke, and I went the other way to my office.

I couldn't stop the tears that spilled out as I gathered my things. After locking up, I walked home, picking up my pace when bits of hail started needling my face. I wiped my mouth with the back of my wrist and tasted him on my lips still. The icy rain was drenching my hair now. *It's okay. Better this way. It wouldn't be healthy. Put it in a box. Place it on the shelf.*

Back home I took a hot shower, brushed my teeth, all the while feeling the ghost of William's lips. What would I do with all of this desire?

A few nights later, on the Friday before Christmas, I noticed a silhouette outside my office window. My back muscles tensed up, and I heard a couple of knocks, and saw the doorknob twisting. Someone jiggled the door, and I froze, looking around the room for a place to hide, another exit, or something I could use as a weapon. My phone was out of battery.

"Isabel? Are you in there? It's me, Sean."

My posture rigid, I opened the door. "You scared me, Sean. What are you doing here? Why didn't you call first?"

"I did ring, but you don't pick up anymore. Apologies for not fixing a proper appointment," he said with a grin.

"Oh, I'm sorry. I've been incredibly busy working on my new topic."

"No, no, I see how it is. Now you're rich and famous you forgot about your old chums, the plebs. Thanks a lot."

"That's not it at all—I just have a lot on my plate."

"Isabel, Isabel. I'm just winding you up."

"Of course you were." He was still standing in the doorway. I went back inside, threw some things in my bag, and came out, locking the door behind me.

"I was on my way out anyway," I said, trying not to seem flustered.

"Want to get a drink?"

"Can't tonight." We continued to walk in the direction of my apartment.

"You seem stressed, more than usual. Can you take a few days off? I get that you're devoted to your subject, believe me, but everyone needs a break. Specially over Christmas."

"I'm seriously fine. How's your work going?"

When we reached the parking lot, he crossed his arms as I was digging around for my keys and said, "I know it's none of my business, but whoever he is, he isn't worth it. Or *she*. Wrong of me to presume. Whoever they are, they aren't . . . Anyway, you know what I mean. Oh, fuck. Now I've really put my foot in it." He was blushing.

"Thanks, Sean. I'm just always like this before I go on a trip." I forced a smile.

"Whatever you say, Isabel. As long as you're okay. And you'll tell me if you aren't. And I can kneecap the bastard who's mistreating you."

"Thanks again," I said, with a laugh that tried too hard.

"Okay, um. Early start tomorrow. Glad you're home safe. See you next week for tea."

"Wait, see you New Year's Eve."

"Yeah. See you then."

Inside my apartment, after checking thoroughly to make sure no one else was there, I sank down on the floor. Had that been Sean's way of telling me that he, and possibly others, knew about William and me? It didn't matter. There was nothing between us anyway, and whatever might have been needed to stop. Realizing I was whimpering I stood up and poured myself first one, then another, glass of wine. After the third glass I managed to get into flannel pajamas and slip into bed.

The next day the library stayed open, exceptionally, until 9 P.M. When the librarians kicked me out at 9:06, the streets were quiet. After a minute I heard the muffled clicking of footsteps behind me, and goose bumps cropped up on my arms. I put my head down and pretended to search for an umbrella in my bag, and quickly turned to see who was behind me. It was so dark. An isolated figure, wearing a black, hooded sweatshirt and baggy pants, was walking slowly about fifteen feet behind me, then crossed over to the sidewalk. My heart pumping fast and my leg muscles tightening, I walked a circuitous route home, taking care not to slip on the ice that was forming. I turned down a small street and then another, but even when I reached the parking lot, I thought I could still hear his or her shoes on the icy pavement.

On December twenty-fourth I went to my office and found Mairead, hair pulled back into a messy bun, noisily sorting papers, like a digging mole, hundreds of sheets gathered on the floor, some scrunched up like snowballs, and more scattered across her desk.

"Hey, Mairead?"

It took her more than a few seconds to respond. "Yeah? What?"

"It's Christmas Eve."

"I'm aware."

"Would you like to come over to my flat? We could make an early dinner."

She tossed one of the balled up papers at me and it hit my shoulder. She stood up and pushed her chair in and, careful not to step on the papers, slipped on her caramel-colored mohair coat and opened the door. Turning her head back she called, "You coming?"

The grocery stores were closed, so we threw dinner together out of what I had left in the fridge.

"How's the writing going, Mairead?" I asked.

"It's fine."

"I'm embarrassed I've forgotten exactly what your thesis is on."

"Margaret of France, Duchess of Savoy, daughter of Francis I, sister of Henri II, wife of the Duke of Savoy. Isn't it terrible that we characterize women by their relation to famous men?" She tucked some strands of hair behind her ears. "Margaret wrote poetry, patronized a university chair in jurisprudence, protected the Waldensians, and was Catherine de' Medici's only true friend. Another remarkable woman buried by history. Never fear, I'm digging her back up again."

"Studying the Falcone has underscored for me just how active and important women were in early modern families. They ran their husbands' estates while they were away fighting. And occasionally gave sound battle advice. I read that Giulia Falcone exhibited 'real male courage' during the French Wars of Religion."

"Whatever that is." We laughed.

Seeing her there on the couch reminded me of my evening with Rose, and I must have given her a funny look.

"Isabel? What is it? You seemed to disappear for a second."

"I've got a lot on my mind. Mairead, can I ask you something?"

"Always."

"You alluded to some troubles with mental illness, and I was just wondering, not to go Catrina on you, but do you think that . . . it's just lately I feel like . . . I'm going out of my mind. Imagining things and seeing people . . . jump out at me. I'm a ball of nerves. Is it all in my head?"

"You want to know what I think? I think you've had a shock, that's all. First you lost your advisor, then your friend. It's a lot."

"Makes me feel better to hear you say that."

She curled her hand under her chin and put her elbow on the table. "When I was in hospital, they had to convince me that any food I saw would not randomly merge with my body cells and make me obese."

"How long were you there? In the hospital?"

"Six months." She put one hand on the table. "I've had problems since I was little. Can't watch horror films. Because that's what it feels like to have hallucinations. I see tree limbs dripping blood. Doesn't sound like you, does it?"

"Not at all. I struggled with depression, but nothing like what you're describing. That must have been so difficult, Mairead. I didn't mean to pry."

"It's no bother. You know what I found out earlier today? A friend who was with me in hospital didn't make it. You're miles away from how she was when I knew her. Lucky for you. I did love her, though."

"I'm sorry. About your friend."

She picked up her small fork and stabbed a corner of scone, which crumbled, then popped it in her mouth. "Yum," she said.

Sean had invited me, Mairead, and Luke, and a couple of his other friends from the Catholic Society, over to his flat, for "tea," which I thought was high tea but turned out to be Northern English for dinner, on Hogmanay, the Scottish term for New Year's Eve. At the last minute the friends backed out so there were only the four of us.

Sean shared a flat on the outskirts of town with a philosophy student, who had gone home to Japan for the break. He helped me take off my coat. "Would you like a bevy? The options are rather limited," he said. "I'm not really a dinner-party sort of bloke."

"How about a beer?" I said.

"Stout I can do," he said. I sat near Mairead, and we started talking. Sean brought out a bottle of Guinness that he poured into a designated Guinness glass. "Hope you don't mind it's room temperature," he said. "I know you Yanks like cold beer."

"It's my first Hogmanay. I'm happy to be an authentic Scot," I said.

"Great," Sean said. He brought over a matching glass of Guinness and said, "To your becoming a proper Scot." I didn't know if British people made New Year's resolutions, but I had already made several. The first one was to stop thinking about William.

There was a knock on the door. It was Luke. The four of us settled in, and a knot inside my chest started to loosen.

An hour later, Sean, who'd been in and out of the kitchen, ushered us over to a candlelit table. With an ease that belied his assertion he wasn't a dinner-party guy, he came out of the kitchen with a steaming hot platter of food and served each of us individually, from the left.

"Did you make this from scratch?" Mairead asked.

"Nah," he said. "It's just a jar of Patak's over some chicken and rice. I added some stuff and Bob's your uncle!"

Sean brushed off our attempts to praise him, and then he came out with a platter of steamed greens, explaining that it was mostly watercress that he'd found in a local waterway and harvested himself.

"We're not downstream from any nuclear plants, are we?" asked Luke, genuine concern playing across his face.

"I've been eating this stuff ever since I found it a couple years ago," Sean said. "It's full of vitamins." He lifted his arm and flexed his muscle. We laughed.

Somehow the conversation swung to swingers' clubs, following Mairead's confession that she'd gone to such a club with one of her professors in London.

"I was so young," she said, and the mood darkened. "Have you ever been?" she asked me.

"To London or a swinger's club?"

"Either, both."

"London, yes," I said.

"You, Sean?" Mairead asked. "Swingers' clubs?"

"Nah, not my sort of thing, although I did lose my virginity on the dance floor of a disco back home. Hardly my proudest moment." We laughed.

"Help me in the kitchen, Mairead?" asked Sean, leaping up and behind her chair to pull it out for her. I heard them giggling in the kitchen before they turned off the lights everywhere. They came out with crackling tiny sparklers on top of cups of dark chocolate pudding that Mairead said Sean had made himself. It was decadent, and Luke ate a second cup.

After dinner, Sean played "Auld Lang Syne" on an old record player, explaining that it was a Scottish song, but not typically played on New Year's Eve. "In honor of Isabel," he told us. "Isn't this what Americans listen to tonight?" he asked.

"What else is typical of New Year's Eve, err, Hogmanay, celebrations?"

"Have you ever tried *celidh* dancing?" Sean asked.

"Kaylee dancing?"

"Actually, it's uh, it's celidh, an old Gaelic word—"

"—With weird spelling?"

"C-e-l-i-d-h."

"Oh," I said. "Definitely have not danced celidhs before."

"It's similar to your line dancing, which my flat can't really accommodate, but want to give it a go? We usually celidh dance at weddings and special events, so I hope you'll forgive me for not donning a kilt."

We made two lines facing each other and Sean turned on an upbeat traditional song with flutes and fiddles that reminded me of the *Riverdance* show I had seen with my mother on Broadway. As Sean spun me around, I noticed a slight tremble in his hands.

"You're a good dancer," I said.

After dinner we kept talking, and Sean told me about his childhood in Blackburn.

"I'd like to visit," I said.

"No, you wouldn't," Sean said. "The only time you want to see Blackburn is in the mirror as you're driving away."

After midnight and toasts with all the promise of the New Year, Luke drove me and Mairead home. Back in my flat I lit a candle before undressing, trying to sustain that feeling of camaraderie. But I had too much on my mind, and too much warm Guinness in my stomach, to get more than a few uninterrupted hours of sleep.

Early the next morning, too hungover to start working, I checked my mailbox for the first time in ten days. I pulled out a blank envelope with a vintage postcard of Genoa inside, "*Come vola il tempo!*" written in red across the top. On the back were three stickers, the kind I used to collect as a child. The first sticker was a shell-shaped loaf of bread, the second was a rose, and the third was a question mark. It took a couple of minutes for my alcohol-soaked brain to grasp their meaning. The shell-shaped bread was, in fact, a *madeleine*, and apparently represented Madeleine, the rose was Rose. And the question mark must have been me.

PART TWO

CHAPTER ONE

I flew out of Edinburgh on the twelfth of January. When we crossed the Alps I pictured the land route that Falcone had traveled back and forth to France, through icy valleys, over steep, snow-covered passes. From the train station in Milan, I boarded the first train to Genoa. The *Frecciabianca* lurched and swayed as we approached the coast. The early morning fog burned off, and after we emerged from a series of tunnels I stared at the sea and the mountains speckled with scrub, at cliffs that fell sharply into that expanse of blue, the Tyrrhenian Sea.

With its many hills, Genoa is known as the most vertical city in Europe. Multicolored, modern building complexes, built after massive bombing campaigns during World War II, constituted the periphery around the city center.

The name Genoa derives from the Latin *iuana*, "gates." Genoa became an independent power in the eleventh century, and for years was rife with internecine family conflicts, suppressed in 1528 by the naval hero turned doge, Andrea Doria. He'd made an alliance with the Hapsburgs, who promoted him and his family in exchange for loyalty, even though Genoa had in the past allied with France.

In 1547, with the help of Hapsburg Emperor Charles V, Doria suppressed a pro-French rebellion led by the Fieschi family, wiping out most of them. The remaining Fieschi escaped to France, and two years later Giovanbattista Falcone, a Fieschi sympathizer, started his own unsuccessful revolt against the doge.

After Giovanbattista was forced to move to France, his brother Pierfrancesco stayed behind in Genoa, maintaining the family base there. Later Giovanbattista's sons traveled often to Genoa, establishing their own networks there.

Although Federico and Tommaso's French Falcone branch died out in the seventeenth century, their first cousin Filippo and his descendants stayed in Genoa and lived to this day in the family palazzo. The private archive was inside the palazzo, where Rose had worked. The original of the transcribed letter that I'd found in Rose's desk had come from the family archive. I hoped that whoever had stolen their documents had overlooked the ones from the sixteenth century.

At the station in Genoa, I heard something about a *sciopero*, a strike. It turned out to be a public transport strike, which meant no taxis or buses. I stopped in a kiosk and asked for directions.

Dragging my suitcase behind me, I headed east along via Andrea Doria, until I reached a series of enormous buildings that stretched for entire street blocks. Graffiti was scrawled across even the most magnificent ones. It was apparent that Genoa was a working city, with a gritty rubbed-down patina. I had read that Old Genoa was also the largest medieval city center in Europe.

I stopped to ask a woman if she could direct me to the Salita di San Paolo. She pointed across the street to a yellow wall, which led to a hidden alley. I clunked my bag down the steps to the Piazza Commenda and looked out across an enormous roadway to the harbor, full of ships bobbing up and down like plastic pool toys, masts seesawing.

Huge concrete pillars held up the *Sopraelevata*, the raised highway, its tail snaking around the city. Continuing along via Antonio Gramsci for ten minutes, I kept my eye out for a bar, thinking about a big sugary cappuccino, glancing at the buildings whose ground floors contained shops and restaurants, tired grand palazzi with trompe-l'oeil frescoes on their facades. Reminders of Christmas and the New Year lingered in the window displays.

In the harbor, I stopped in front of the Palazzo San Giorgio, where Marco Polo had composed his memoirs. A sign on my right pointed to the Porto Antico—the old port. A fishmonger, wielding a blood-tinged knife, yelled that my suitcase was making so much noise I could wake the dead. I tried to carry it but couldn't take more than a few steps, so I continued to drag it behind me over cobblestones and up hills, passing remnants of old city walls, with occasional pockets of green vegetation peeping through.

When I reached the Campopisano, pink, orange, and yellow buildings faced the square, shaped like a fan. Hanging linens spilled out of windows.

I found number eight, and just as I rang the buzzer the door swung open.

"*Buongiorno*, Isabel," said a heavyset woman with a warm smile.

She reached out and took my hands in hers, warm and smooth against my cold ones. "I am Marta." I followed her inside. "Please leave your luggage here," she said, before leading me through the foyer into a kitchen with windows overlooking the piazza, and a round table with wooden chairs around it. A bald man in a grey bow tie put aside his newspaper and came over to greet me. "This is my husband, Luigi," Marta said. I smelled garlic and basil.

The table was set with yellow plates on lace placemats with an earthenware vase filled with wildflowers in the center. Marta showed me through a tiny door to a bathroom where I could wash my hands.

It was two thirty. They must have been waiting for me for lunch. Back in the kitchen a little girl wearing oven mittens and carrying a porcelain bowl stepped out from behind the counter. She placed the bowl on a straw mat on the table and turned my way, pulling off one of the mittens and extending a tentative hand. Steam rose from the bowl. "*Che buon profumo!*" I said, stepping toward her so I could reach her hand. "My name is Isabel. What is your name?"

"Alessandra," she said, without looking up. It seemed like a big name for such a small girl.

"You can sit next to Alessandra," said Marta, pulling out a chair for me. "Would you take some wine?" she asked, and, when I nodded, Luigi poured an almost colorless liquid in my bell-shaped glass. They watched me scoop a mountain of spaghetti smothered in glistening green pesto into my bowl. It was my first real home-cooked meal in a while. After long hours at the library, I had too often settled for fish and chips or pizza.

"Delicious!"

"The wine comes from Cinque Terre. A gift from a patient," Luigi explained. "I am a doctor. And Marta is an emergency nurse, but she is also an excellent cook." For dessert, Alessandra brought out a meringue cake with a creamy center.

"*Meringata,*" she said, standing close to me and smiling up at my face.

After our espresso Marta showed me my bedroom on the second floor and pointed to a desktop computer in the hallway.

Marta said Alessandra would call me to dinner at 7:45. Luigi had brought my suitcase upstairs and I unpacked. My laptop wouldn't turn on, I'd need a new one. The computer in the hallway, an IBM, took a while to start up. The Internet connection was slow but after a few minutes I was able to open my inbox. No new messages.

I emailed Count Falcone's assistant, Emiliano Michelozzo, to let him know that I had arrived in Genoa. In Scotland it had taken three weeks and five emails before he'd responded, and he let me know that I could access the Falcone Archive in January, ten days after the family had returned from their Christmas vacation, and we'd settled on tomorrow as my start date.

Back in my room, I took out my map and started to write down the names of the streets that would take me to the Falcone Palazzo, drawing my own map. A while later the aroma of fresh herbs filled the room and Alessandra knocked on my door.

For dinner, Marta had prepared another local specialty, *torta pasqualina*, a savory pie. Luigi was making a house call, so I ate with Marta and Alessandra.

"*Torta pasqualina* is my plate favorite," said Alessandra, cutting a thick slice.

"I think the words you want to use are favorite dish, *amore*," said Marta.

"Oh, yes, my favorite *dish*," Alessandra said. "This morning we picked the *aromi* fresh from *nonna*'s garden. You will like to visit my nonna in the mountain?"

"I would love to meet your nonna," I said. "My nonna lives near Boston, where I come from," I told her.

"Your mamma and papa live in Boston?" Alessandra asked.

"Yes," I said, although it was just my mother.

"Do you have brothers and sisters?"

"No, I'm an only child," I said.

"I am only child, too!" said Alessandra.

"Let Isabel eat now, *amore*. Then we can speak," said Marta softly.

"Don't worry," I said, cutting a piece of pie with my fork. In between courses I told them that I was in graduate school in Scotland. We then talked for ten minutes in English, so that Alessandra could practice. After coffee I asked Marta, "Do you know the Falcone family who live in Genoa, the ones whose ancestors I'm studying?"

"Yes, of course, yes," she said. She looked at Alessandra, started to say something, but then looked up at the clock hanging above the door. "I did not see the time. I need to bring Alessandra to bed. But please, let me know if you need something."

I spent an hour at the computer, reading articles and waiting for a reply from the Falcone administrator. I wanted to write to William, still uneasy about the way we'd left things in Scotland. I'd heard nothing from him since our kiss, which I regretted more and more each day. I realized it was up to me to reach out, to reestablish our relationship as adviser and student. I began writing a nonchalant "checking-in" message when an email came in from an unfamiliar address.

Dear Isabel,

I know you are now in Genoa. Sorry for my silence, but they haven't let me communicate with you. I'll be brief and say that you must insist on seeing EVERYTHING in the archive. You'll need to be a sleuth as well as a scholar. Be careful with the Contessa and remember that even mentioning my name would put me in more danger than I am in currently.

IMPORTANT: Report every day on everything that you find while researching the emerald's whereabouts to the following email address: FP12001@yahoo.com. They want you to know that the more information you send, the better. Delete this email.

All my love . . . PS The bar across the street from the palazzo has the strongest and best espresso I've ever had in my life, and you're going to need to caffeinate.

I wrote back quickly: "Rose! Are you okay? What do you mean . . . ask to see everything? Please explain. I found the letter you transcribed, written by Tommaso Falcone. I hope to find the original in the Archives here. Did you send me a postcard with stickers on it?" The message bounced back. I read her email twice, deleted it, discarded the message I'd drafted to William, shut down the computer, and went into my bedroom. After a while I drifted uneasily into dreamless sleep.

CHAPTER TWO

T he next morning the house was quiet. On the kitchen counter Marta had left me a set of keys and a note explaining that she and Luigi would be home late and Alessandra would be at her grandmother's. She had also left out a pot of coffee, but it was already cold. The palazzo administrator had finally responded to my email.

> "Dottoressa Henley, the Contessa has a short opening in her schedule tomorrow at noon. Please arrive to the palazzo at 11:45 and ring the buzzer for the 3rd floor. Cordialmente, G. Michelozzo."

It was 11:00 A.M. I changed quickly and ran down the stairs and out the door. The taxi strike was ongoing, so I would have to walk.

The sky was white, and the air blew cool and wet on my face. My coat and wool tights didn't protect my legs from the wind. I consulted my map and turned onto the narrow Vico Sotto Le Murette, which ran along the old city walls, and recognized a Baroque church I had passed yesterday, San Salvatore. I kept walking, asking for directions whenever uncertain. Turning down a side street on an incline I passed three women, all with bleached hair and wearing minidresses and stilettos, in front of a doorway. One of the women, who looked to be my age, held my gaze. Five minutes before the appointed hour, my cheeks numb with cold, I entered a needlepoint studio, where a woman was knitting a red wool scarf. "Palazzo Falcone, *dov'è?*" I said impolitely and loudly.

"*Ma sei molto vicina! Qui a sinistra poi di nuovo a sinistra,*" she said, staring down at her needles while pointing left. I made a left and entered a piazza, empty except for some cooing pigeons. Turning left again I reached the Palazzo Falcone.

Painted the color of saffron, the ornate facade featured marble reliefs of grotesque heads. Offset against the rich yellow, the opaque marble seemed to shimmer, even under a thin layer of grime. Giant falcons, with talons crushing delicate creatures, were carved over the central doorway. Marble caryatids in high relief supported the protruding wall and balcony of the second floor. Off to the side, a series of doorways were almost hidden behind thick, iron-barred gates. The name "Falcone" was spelled out in heavily slanted, cursive capital letters on top of the grills.

I walked through an open gate into a dark, cool vestibule. A massive double door facing me was closed tightly, the thick oak covered with round, iron studs. In medieval times such formidable doors had been designed to keep out enemies, and the studs could damage the swords of invaders. Next to two falcon head-shaped knockers a green light glowed on a modern-style intercom.

I pressed the button for Michelozzo, *terzo piano.* The back of my ankle throbbed where my shoe had rubbed against a blister, and sweat was dribbling down my chest. I wiped my forehead and waited, trying to quiet my breath when I saw the glass eye of a camera watching me. Reaching up to buzz again I heard shoes clacking on cobblestones. The door creaked open onto a man with an outstretched arm, his body silhouetted by bright light. As I shook his hand the muscles in his arms contracted underneath his tight jacket.

"Right on time, Dottoressa. Emiliano Michelozzo," he said, and the last two Os ricocheted off the courtyard walls. His dull-blue eyes bulged, reminding me of the liquidy, lifeless eyes of the piles of fish I had passed yesterday in the market.

Michelozzo's phone rang, and he pulled it out of his pocket and answered, while covering his other ear with two thick fingers. I surveyed the courtyard, a smaller space than the outer one. In the center was a bronze fountain with dolphins and mythical sea creatures drooling water onto lower tiers. The paint on the inside walls of the palazzo courtyard, also saffron yellow, had lost its sheen, and discolored patches were flaking off. The air smelled like stagnant water in a vase of dead flowers.

Michelozzo looked top heavy. He could have been forty-five or sixty-five. His thinning hair settled on his head in a tonsure-like pattern, which lent him a certain gravitas.

"You may follow me," he said, crossing the courtyard. "*Prego*."

I walked behind him through a glass door and up a flight of marble stairs, grey and concave in the center from centuries of foot traffic. In a hallway we stopped and Michelozzo opened a door onto a small, square room with a desk by the window. The bookshelves behind the desk were empty except for a couple of thin volumes on either side of falcon-shaped bookends. The room smelled of bleach. "*Prego*," he said again, as he walked around the desk and gestured toward a metal chair. I removed my damp coat and sweater before sitting down.

I cleared my throat. "Thank you for this opportunity, Signor Michelozzo. It is a pleasure to visit the palazzo after reading so much about the Falcone. It feels like my sixteenth-century studies are coming to life." As soon as I said that rather banal sentence, I wished I could retract it.

"How long will you stay in Genoa?" He leaned forward and his jacket buckled, and . . . was he wearing a gun?

"I will be . . . I am . . . I have funding to work here for four weeks."

"Four weeks," he repeated. "To be sincere with you, Miss Henley . . . ,"
he said, pronouncing my name like a hen lays its eggs: hen-lay, "the
documentation related to the family in the sixteenth century is not vast."

"But the website—"

He raised his hand, interrupting me, "—The website is . . . I mean to
say that many documents from the archive were stolen, most horribly,
from us. And so. I am not certain why you are here."

"Yes, I was sorry to read about the theft," I said, in an even toned voice.
"As I explained in my letter, I'm looking forward to making a contribution to the study of Genoese history and to bringing recognition to the
Falcone family. I'm eager to see what the archives will reveal, and to share
my discoveries with them."

"*Allora*," he said, glancing down at his crocodile-banded watch. He
picked up the receiver of the old rotary phone on the desk and spun a
number in quick strokes. "*Sì, sì, è qui. Sì. Grazie, Contessa*," he spoke into
the phone, then replaced the handset into its cradle.

"I have been in the service of the Falcone family since before you were
born, Signorina," he said. "We have worked for them for many genera-
tions. And the Contessa is the finest woman in the city of Genoa."

I heard the clicking of heels and turned to watch the door open.
A slender woman walked in, wearing a red dress cinched at the waist
by a patent-leather belt, a white fur stole draped over her shoulders. I
stood up as she approached us. She appeared to be in her early fifties.
A gold bird of prey, with a rounded beak and tiny ruby eyes, gleamed
on her shoulder. When she didn't speak, I extended my hand. "You
must be Contessa Falcone. I'm Isabel Henley." She nodded twice and
half-smiled with closed lips and then flicked her gaze at Michelozzo. I
let my hand drop.

"I'm late for an appointment and don't have much time, but I can show
you the library quickly," she said in perfect English, with no accent. We

followed her out of the room and down a flight of stairs, stopping in front of a short door. She pulled a long key out from a concealed pocket in the folds of her dress and unlocked it. Inside the room she flipped on a light switch and closed the door behind us.

The library faced the courtyard. The air smelled stale and musty, as if the windows had not been opened in a long time. Several wide, oak bookcases lined canary-yellow walls. Enclosed behind frosted glass panels I could see the outlines of hundreds of books. Two wide desks and three brown leather chairs, the seats wrinkled and faded, were positioned in front of the bookcases. The Contessa removed her stole and draped it across one of the chairs.

"Would you like to see some of the collection?" she asked. I nodded eagerly. She walked over to the bookcase closest to me and slid the glass to one side, pulling out a thick, folio-sized book lying flat on the bottom shelf. She placed the volume, bound in ivory-colored parchment, gently down on one of the desks.

"Do you know the *Histoire de la Maison Du Fauchon*?"

"Yes. In November, when I started working on the Falcone, I ordered a copy from the British Library."

"So, you are familiar with the contents?"

"In addition to short biographies of the family members, it contains copies of printed legal documents from the sixteenth and seventeenth centuries. It was published by Antoine du Fauchon in 1702."

"You impress me with your knowledge of our family history," she said, "although you are not the only scholar who has worked on the subject. Over the years." She lifted the book and placed it back inside the cabinet, which she locked with a couple of clicks.

"Contessa Falcone," I said, "I understand you're on your way to an appointment. Perhaps we could discuss the practicalities of getting in and out of the archive, and the location of the documents?"

"Documents?" she said, walking to the chair to pick up her stole.

"Yes, I requested and received permission to work on historical documents in the Falcone archive."

"I think there may have been a misunderstanding, something lost in translation?" she said, wrapping the stole around her shoulders. "I thought you were coming to catalog the rare books in our library. You understand, we have very few documents in the archive. We once had many, but we were the victims of a tragic theft."

"I know, and I'm sorry. All I need would be to consult whatever remaining documents you have. I can then assess what would be useful for my dissertation."

"Looking at documents isn't going to be possible."

"But my PhD focuses on the Falcone and the sources are here."

"Were here," she said, glancing at her watch.

"I've unearthed some new information that I think your family will be interested in. If I could have a quick look, I'd be able to assess—"

"—The du Fauchon volume is a perfect historical record of our family in France. You say you have seen it. I do not understand why you would need to consult any documents other than those."

"Actually, du Fauchon inflated family accomplishments in order to provide proof of his noble heritage, which had been called into doubt at a time when many families were newly ennobled. The Falcone were textile merchants, they didn't have the blood of kings in their veins, as claimed. The book should be taken with a grain of salt. I need to look at the original sources directly."

"I'm afraid that won't be possible," she said, her frown flattening into a straight line. "I apologize for the misunderstanding. If you would like to look at the rare books, you are welcome to do so. But if not, Emiliano will refund you for your time. I really have to be going, but we wish you the best with your studies."

"I believe I have a right to access this archive." She reached over and gave me a curt handshake, then walked out of the room, waiting for us to come out before locking the door. She clicked down the hallway and Michelozzo led me back to his office. He sat down at the desk, opened a drawer, and pulled out a checkbook.

"Please tell me how much we owe you, Miss Hen-LAY."

"It isn't a question of owing me, Mr. Michelozzo. I have work to do here and was given permission to do it. Written permission."

"Circumstances change, as you must know. The amount please."

"There is no amount." He scratched down something on the check, tore it off, and pushed it across the table.

"Here is 3,000 euros. I'm sure you can find another topic for your studies. Genoa is a big city, with much history that can . . . come to life, as you say?"

When I didn't pick up the check, he took it himself and escorted me downstairs. Outside he extended his hand and I automatically reached up to shake it. He pressed the check into my hand and closed my fingers around it. "Arrivederci, signorina," he said, stepping back inside. The thick door in front of me groaned closed. It was starting to rain.

CHAPTER THREE

I waited in front of the door for a moment, not sure where to go. Above me opaque clouds floated in the slim gulf of sky between palazzo roofs, releasing heavy drops onto my blouse. I stepped onto the stoop, hoping the lintel would shield me from the rain, but falcon beaks and claws dripped dollops of water on me, and the metal studs pronged my back. A portal that had thwarted enemies for hundreds of years was now repelling me too. Flicking water off my shoulders, I shrugged my coat on, tied my sweater over my head, and ran. Directly across the street I saw a bar and ducked inside.

The server behind the high counter squinted at me and I squinted back, then asked for a cup of hot water and a packet of Earl Grey. After putting the cup on the closest table, I plunked down on a steel chair with no cushion.

Rose hadn't exaggerated the challenges of getting into the palazzo. But the proprietors of the archive had a legal obligation to allow me to see their documents, whether they wanted to or not. Didn't they?

The door to the bar opened and two men in khaki trench coats crossed the room, trailed by a brunette in a black leather jacket. When they sat down the woman behind the counter rushed out with a bottle of prosecco and three glasses. The woman was facing me, cropped ringlets of chestnut hair framing her round face. She was wearing burgundy lipstick and an amber pendant hung on a thin chain around her neck.

I pulled out my notebook and a pen and started to make some notes. I'd have to find out if I had any legal recourse. I knew that the Ministry of Arts and Culture was responsible for the administration of private archives because of their assumptive historical value as part of Italian cultural heritage. I'd reviewed the specific procedures regarding consultation before sending my initial request to Count Falcone. There were some gray areas, but access to scholars was an inalienable right, I remembered reading. I didn't know if there was an office of the State Archive in Genoa, but I would find out. This might have been a good excuse to email William, but first I wanted to figure out a potential solution. I would show him that I was resourceful, not needy.

After a few minutes one of the men put his coat on as he walked toward the door. The woman leaned over and whispered in the ear of the man still seated and kissed him twice before standing up to leave.

Rose had mentioned a bar across from the palazzo with great espresso, so I went back to the counter and ordered a macchiato. The man at the table addressed me.

"*Allora non sei italiana? Hai un leggero accento. Di dove sei?*"

"*Sono americana.*"

"I kneeeew it! I won fifty euros!" He laughed and slapped his thigh.

"Good for you," I said flatly.

"I'd happily spend twenty of those euros on a fine glass of *spumante* for you."

"Thanks, but I'm okay."

"It doesn't have to be spumante. What would you like?" When I didn't answer he said, "It's a drink, not a marriage proposal."

"Spumante is fine," I said, in a clipped voice meant to discourage him. He went to the bar and ordered, chatting with the server, who kept leaning forward. He carried two glasses of spumante to my table and placed one of them down next to my notes.

"*Grazie*," I grunted.

"*Ascolta*, I am sorry for disturbing you. It's only that—"

"—That it's fun to profit from my mediocre Italian accent?"

"Hah!" he said. "You've got spirit!" Then he lowered his voice. "I meant no disrespect. And it seems to me your Italian is very good. It's only that you looked like you needed cheering up." When I didn't respond he returned to his table, lifted his glass, and drained the *spumante* all at once. The server delivered a tumbler filled to the top with orange liquid and ice, which he acknowledged with a nod, barely glancing up from his phone.

The man's thick, wavy hair was many shades of blond, including platinum highlights that looked dyed. He had deep blue eyes, and some of the brunette woman's red lipstick remained on the edge of his lips. "Thank you," I said, lifting the glass. "How is it that you speak English so well? Did you study in the U.S.?"

He put down his phone and smiled. "Boarding school in Switzerland. And my mom's American. How about you? I'd like to know how you speak Italian." He leaned over and patted the chair next to him.

"I'd be happy to tell you," I said, patting the chair next to me. I then busied myself with my pages, stacking them theatrically before putting them in a folder.

"I'm Niccolò," he said, sticking out his hand and sitting down.

"Isabel," I said, shaking it.

"What brings you to Genoa, Isabel?"

"Research. For my PhD."

"Splendid! What do you study? Wait, let me guess. Italian literature?"

"No," I said, shaking my head.

"Architecture?"

"Guess again."

"Art history? That's it, yes?"

"Close."

"What then?"

"History. Just history."

"You've come to the right place. You've been to Genoa before?"

"This is my first visit." I said. "Do you live here?"

"Yes. I'm in law school." He ran his hand through his hair, his fingers snagging on one of the thick waves. "And what is your specialization?"

"I'm studying a branch of a Genovese family that moved to France in the 1500s but maintained a seat here."

"Maybe I know them, if they're still around. What is the name of the family?"

"Falcone."

He barked out a laugh and slapped his thigh again.

"So, you know them?"

"Yes, I do."

"Friends of yours?"

"The Falcone?? If I were you, I would NOT trust those people."

"Really? What . . . well, wait. First, let me apologize for being brusque. I was in the Falcone Palazzo and had a . . . let's just say an unpleasant experience."

"What happened?"

I told Niccolò about my meeting with Emiliano and the Contessa, finishing with, "Are they obligated to show me the documents? Maybe this isn't your area of the law?"

He smiled again, his blue eyes twinkling. His teeth were a little crooked and a yellowy, bright white, like the moon. "I could definitely find out for you."

"I'd be so grateful. This is very important to me."

"Are you free for a few minutes?" he asked. "Could I show you something, something related to your research?"

"Actually, I'm not free right now. I need to find a lawyer who can give me an opinion on this. In the U.S. they have dispute resolution lawyers that deal with archive issues. Do you know anyone who might advise me?"

"I have an impeccable source who can help you figure out your next steps."

He lifted his head and feigned signing a check at the woman behind the bar, who was watching his every move. *"Aggiungi cinque euro,"* he called. She batted her eyelashes.

Outside, the rain had stopped but the streets were slick and smelled like sewage. It was very cold. "Follow me," he said. "This won't take long."

In less than a minute we were standing in front of the Palazzo Falcone.

"Wait!" I said, as his finger jabbed the buzzer. "What exactly is your idea? I thought you said you wanted to show me something. I can't go back in there."

"Just . . . trust me. Okay?"

I turned around so the camera wouldn't capture my image.

As the door opened Niccolò took my hand and we squeezed into the courtyard. Emiliano gave Niccolò a firm hug and patted him twice on the back. His fish eyes widened when he saw me.

"Ci fai entrare e poi ti spiego tutto," said Niccolò.

"Niente da spiegare. Con te è sempre la stessa cosa! Ma sempre sempre!" Emiliano said, slapping Niccolò's chest.

Emiliano was Niccolò's friend?

I followed Niccolò up the stairs and past Emiliano's office. He stopped in front of a closed door and opened it just enough to stick his head in.

"Nico!" said a woman's voice. The Contessa.

He turned back to me and held up one finger, entered the room, and closed the door behind him. I heard laughter, and then he opened the door and pulled me inside.

The Contessa was seated at an inlaid-wood desk. Several geodes were perched on top of the desk like broken dragons' eggs, coarse and grey on the outside with craggy sparkling innards. On the wall behind her was an enormous genealogical tree, the family crest of falcons on either side of it. Underneath, the Falcone's motto was written in big, blaring letters: *Familia Supra Omnia.*

"See, Mamma, as I was telling you, Isabel comes from Boston. She's a good friend of Harpo's. You remember Harpo, right?" He put his arm around me.

"Harpo, yes, of course," said the Contessa. "Why didn't she say something?"

"I bet you didn't give her a chance. Plus, I don't think she likes to talk about herself—you *know* how these old Bostonians are."

"Yes, treasure, but—" Her polite smile was at odds with the tight fist around her pen.

"—So, Mamma, Isabel is visiting as my . . . guest." He hugged me closer.

"But, sweetheart, I—" she said.

"—No, there's no 'but, sweetheart.' You don't have to worry."

I was aware of the Contessa's glare and, at the same time, of Niccolò's warm body next to mine. He smelled freshly laundered and appley. "Besides," he said to his mother, "her father's a diplomat, he knows all the right people." The Contessa flicked her eyes back and forth between Niccolò and me as she traced the inner crystals of a globe-sized amethyst with manicured fingernails.

"Good," said Niccolò, "it's settled. Isabel will dine with us tonight." He blew the Contessa a kiss and ushered me out of the room.

"Wait—" I said.

"—Shh . . ." said Niccolò. He put his finger first on my lips, gently, and then on his. I followed him up the stairs. At the top he held out a long key like the one the Contessa had used earlier and unlocked the door.

"After you," he said, following me inside.

"I don't understand," I said. "You're a Falcone?"

"Yes. I'm a Falcone. And you are the daughter of a diplomat and good friend of my good friend, Harpo. And you are my special guest. My very special guest."

"This is ridiculously kind of you, Niccolò. You don't even know me. How can I thank you?"

"I'm sure we'll find a way," he winked. "Should we get started?" He helped me take off my coat.

"So, you're the Contessa's son?"

"Correct. Niccolò Falcone at your service."

"And the Contessa is American?"

"The Contessa is Elizabeth Jansen, of Columbus, Ohio."

"Seriously?"

"She was studying abroad in Italy when she met my father. They fell in love instantly, she with his title, he with her beauty, her Midwestern innocence, and her father's tidy fortune."

"So, you live here? In the palazzo?"

"This is my home, yes."

"And those people you were with at the bar. Was that your girlfriend? The beautiful woman with the red lipstick?"

"My girlfriend?! Ha! That was my sister, Severina. She doesn't have a boyfriend!" He chuckled. "Severina is *lesbica* . . . lesbian. Enough about us. Don't you have work to do? Something about a thesis on a despicable Genovese family?"

There was a knock on the door and Emiliano skulked in, noiseless as a spider, and stood in the corner.

"Nico, I wanted to see if I could do something for you. Or the signorina," he said, looking at Niccolò and opening his hands as if about to present something.

"The *dottoressa*," said Niccolò. "Yes, Emiliano. Could you please let Ottavia know Isabel will be joining us for dinner?"

"Immediately," the factotum said, and he scuffled out, shutting us inside.

Niccolò knelt down and reached under the desk. "Pretend you don't see what I'm doing," he said. He stood up holding another key and opened the bottom section of one of the cabinets. He ran his hands inside, and said, "*Eccolo!*" pulling out a white box, which he placed on the table in front of me. The box was tied tightly with a cotton string that looked new.

"*E vai*," he said. "Open it."

I untied the string and pulled the cover off the box, which exhaled dust into the air. Gently I lifted out a loosely bound stack of papers dated 1500, which turned out to be a marriage contract between Girolamo Falcone and Leonarda Fieschi. On the seventh page I found the signatures of five witnesses. Underneath the contract was a copy of Girolamo Falcone's 1506 will. The top edges were curled over, and the paper had small holes running along the center, but it was otherwise in excellent condition.

"Niccolò," I looked up. "I thought . . . Your mother said you had very few documents from the sixteenth century. That they'd been stolen."

"Before the theft she did not know how valuable the papers were. When she found out, she didn't want anyone to see them, what's left of them, even though she has no idea what they are about. She speaks Italian but cannot read these documents."

"Are there more boxes like this?" I asked.

"Yes, seven more. This is the smallest."

"There are seven whole boxes? I can probably go through two or three per week. That's perfect!"

"Is that how long you are here, three weeks?"

"I had planned to stay for four. I travel to Florence early next month. But I'd go sooner if I didn't find . . . anything of interest here."

"*Allora.* We had best make the most of your time in Genoa, yes?" He didn't wait for me to reply but stood up and took his phone out of his pocket. "Six o'clock. We should go down for drinks."

Niccolò put the contract and the will back inside the box, which he returned to the cabinet. He had just secured the key in its hiding spot when Emiliano slipped in the room. Niccolò leaned over, put his hand on my lower back, and whispered something nonsensical into my hair.

Emiliano cleared his throat. "*Chiedo scusa.* The Count and Countess are awaiting you for the *aperitivo.*"

"Tell them we'll be right there," Niccolò said, not looking up. Emiliano tottered out, leaving the door open.

Niccolò led me down another flight of stairs and through two white-tiled corridors. He twisted the brass handle of an oak-paneled door and led us into an enormous red room.

Although the dark-red velvet curtains in the room were drawn, I felt a draft. Lamps emanated a spectral light that seemed to pulsate. The walls were upholstered in red satin. Oversized divans and high-backed chairs faced a stone fireplace large enough to accommodate a pony. The last rudiments of firewood glowed orange on a grate, and Emiliano was tossing on extra logs. The fire responded immediately, popping and grabbing at the large chunks, consuming them in a frenzy.

High on the walls life-sized portraits of the Falcone forbears observed the room below. A history painting of Piero Falcone, the thirteenth-century progenitor of the family, hung over the fireplace in a gilded frame. The outfits of the men in the portraits alongside Piero's indicated that the paintings were arranged chronologically.

I counted fourteen men. On the wall opposite from Piero, next to a bishop, was Federico Falcone, dressed in a full suit of armor, its eternally shiny metal weighing down his imposing physique. He had high cheek-bones and his dark hair, moustache, and reddish beard were trimmed in the style of the day. His metal-encased fingers rested casually on his hip, from which a sword, attached to a belt, dangled. Over his stiff, white collar hung a gold chain with the insignia of the Order of the Holy Spirit. The French king Henri III had made Federico a Knight of the Order to reward him for faithful service, which seemed ironic now, knowing that his brother, Tommaso, and perhaps Federico himself, had plotted to assassinate the king. It was also ironic that the ownership of this very palazzo had been disputed by family members whose portraits were now side by side.

Federico had presided over this room for centuries. My eyes met his sharp gaze, his expression hard, proud. I imagined what it must feel like to be a Falcone in the twenty-first century, to live each day beside one's ancestors, among family ghosts.

A hand grazed my shoulder. "Isabel," said Niccolò, "I asked if you would like to meet my father."

"Yes, of course," I said. Niccolò led me over to a high-backed chair and the Conte Falcone glided forward to stand and shake my hand. He was hunched over and rotund, with a dark, reddish beard the same hue as Federico's. I recognized no further physical similarities between him and either his ancestors or his son. "As I told you, Papa, Isabel is writing a thesis about our family."

"It's a pleasure to meet you, Conte," I said. "If I had realized you were here, I wouldn't have allowed myself to become distracted by the paintings."

"Welcome to our home," he said in English, giving me the once-over, twice, and then sitting back down and crossing his ankle over his knee.

Niccolò gestured that I should sit on the silk couch. The Contessa came in holding a drink and sat next to the Count. On the Turkish carpet an Italian mastiff was lying on the floor near the Count's feet.

He sat forward and addressed Niccolò. "Has your friend seen the du Fauchon book in our library? You could show her—" he began.

"—She's familiar with it," snapped the Contessa.

"A well-educated young lady," he said with a brief nod to me and then back to Niccolò. "And *carina. Suo nome—com'è*—what was her name?"

"Papà," Niccolò said, as he felt around for his phone. He stood up. "I'll be right back," he told me. The mastiff raised his anvil-shaped head and watched Niccolò leave the room. I knelt down, and reached out to stroke the dog, who growled.

"Sorry," I whispered to the Count. "Hope I didn't upset him."

"Her. La Sweetie. She won't bite. But don't pet her," the Count warned.

The Contessa clapped her hands together. "Ah! Here's Emiliano with the champagne! Who would like a glass? We don't have guests every day, certainly not in gloomy January! A glass for each of us!" She downed the liquid in her other glass as Emiliano passed around crystal goblets and poured champagne in my glass first. The door flew open, and the pretty brunette from the bar walked in. "Sorry I'm late," she said. She stopped near my chair and bent down to take my hands. "You must be Isabel? You don't need to get up. I'm sorry my hands are so cold!" She had changed into an indigo silk blouse and black leather pants, the same amber pendant around her neck. "I'm Severina Falcone," she said.

The Contessa turned to her. "I'm glad you could join us. I hope it hasn't taken any time away from your important job and busy schedule," she said.

Severina picked up the glass of champagne intended for Niccolò and took a long drink, then tossed her head, bouncing the curls away from her face.

The Contessa looked at me. "Severina has a fancy position in the City of London. It's not often she graces us with her distinguished presence." The fire crackled, ulcerated.

"London!" I said. "What do you do Severina?"

"I manage a little fund. But it doesn't sound nearly as interesting as your work. You'll have to tell me more when we aren't in the company of these philistines." We shared a smile, and I took another sip of champagne.

Niccolò reentered the room. "Ottavia's ready for us. Shall we go in? I'm starving!" Emiliano pushed La Sweetie toward the stairs as the five of us walked through the room under the permanent stares of Niccolò's ancestors. Niccolò took my arm in his.

"You like my grandpapas?" he whispered. "*Sei molto bella*, Isabel." Just at that moment his mother turned back to look at us, so we stepped forward in unison.

French doors opened onto a dining room with walls painted a deep cerulean. In ten-foot-high gilt-framed mirrors tinged with black dots, my reflection was distorted as we moved into the center. Enormous tapestries portraying classical scenes adorned the walls, and I identified one of the motifs as the myth of Daedalus and Icarus and another as Leda and the Swan. In front of the Daedalus tapestry stood a suit of armor, the Falcone crest embossed on its breastplate. One of its studded gauntlets gripped a halberd. Niccolò squeezed my hand and looked up. I followed his gaze. The ceiling was frescoed with another classical scene, the four seasons, represented by fleshy, naked women. In the middle of the fresco an ice-blue-and-white Murano-glass chandelier was suspended from a velvet rope. It dripped ripples of glass, although instead of candles were pointed lightbulbs, most needing to be replaced.

Niccolò pulled out a blue Louis Philippe chair and I sat down, dragging the heavy arms, frosted with chipping silver paint, in as Niccolò pushed it. He slid into the chair next to me. The Contessa placed herself across the table from him, while the Count took the seat at the head. Severina sat between her parents, across from me. Candles flickered in two silver candelabras. The silverware was tarnished, splotched with black.

Three bowls of white roses in half bloom ran along the center of the table.

Emiliano appeared, wearing white gloves a size too small, and circulated with a platter piled with piping-hot pasta.

"*Per cominciare, fettuccine al tartufo,*" he announced.

"Do you prefer white truffles or black ones, Isabella?" questioned the Contessa.

"What a snob you are," Severina interrupted. "Of course, *Isabel* prefers the white."

"You were admiring my ancestors," the Count said, turning to me. "We have other pictures in the small salon and the tower of the Falcone women."

"It's a shame the women can't coexist with those mighty gents, Papa," said Severina.

"It has always been this way, *figlia mia,*" said the Count. Severina sighed. Emiliano finished pouring wine in our glasses, and the Count made a toast, welcoming me. He asked me about my work, and I outlined my findings and described my plans for research in Florence and Paris. He continued to engage me in conversation as the others ate, and we two discussed the Falcone from centuries ago. After a while I glanced over at Severina. She was watching us and listening intently.

Emiliano started to clear and Niccolò said, "I'll finish the pasta." While he ate his second serving, Severina poured herself and her father another glass of wine.

"More wine, sweetheart?" the Contessa cooed to Niccolò.

She reached across Severina for the bottle, but it was empty.

Emiliano came out with a second platter, green ravioli in cream sauce. He bent over the Contessa, who served herself two ravioli and shooed him away. After he moved to the left of Severina, the Contessa brought over a bottle with an elaborate label from the sidebar.

Severina put one hand to her forehead and raised her glass to me. She cleared the dishes after we'd finished the second pasta.

For our main course, Emiliano brought out a veal filet, and a pile of wilted greens. The meat that he served me was bright pink, bleeding rosy droplets on my plate. I pushed it around with my fork, already full and unsettled by the undercooked flesh.

The count turned to me. "Do you not eat veal? You are a vegetarian?"

"I'm just pacing myself after the pastas," I said.

The count continued, speaking slowly, "Did I mention, signorina, that my family fought alongside Charlemagne? They were brave gentlemen." I didn't respond. "But you know this. I assume you will write of their heroic deeds in your book? Yes?" He blinked twice.

"Certainly," I said. Certainly, I would not be writing about any Falcone fighting together with Charlemagne, who predated the family's existence by over five hundred years.

Niccolò helped himself to another serving of veal, which Emiliano had left on another silver platter.

"I wonder where all that food goes. You remain so nicely slim!" exclaimed the Contessa. He hadn't touched his greens.

"Skiing?" he said.

She turned to me. "What about you, Isabel? Do you ski?"

"No," I said. "I don't." Niccolò knocked his foot against mine under the table.

"But," the Contessa said, "Harpo's parents love to ski. I assume . . ."

"I—I—have terrible vertigo, Contessa," I said.

Severina interjected, "I don't blame you, Isabel. The last time I was on holiday with friends when we got off the lift I couldn't do it. And, it's dangerous."

"Severina, don't be so negative," scolded the Contessa. "Your brother does double black diamond runs, skis at night by helicopter. He's still alive, with all his bones intact."

"It's true," Niccolò said, "what's life without risk?"

Emiliano brought out a *meringata* and we ate, the only sound our forks scraping the dishes.

"You have a hearty appetite for a young woman," remarked the Contessa.

Leaving our dessert plates on the table, Emiliano poured coffee into delicate cups. I said no thank you but he served me anyway. Niccolò reached over and moved the coffee in front of his plate.

When everyone had finished, Niccolò jumped up to pull out his mother's chair. I stayed put, leaning my head back to admire the ceiling, which was flaking and needed some restoration. Severina walked around the table, sat in Niccolò's chair, brought her hand up to my shoulder, and gently pulled my face toward hers. Her ringlets smelled like jasmine. Into my ear she said softly, "Let's speak later. When we aren't subject to the regime of the watchful empress." Niccolò stepped back toward us.

"What am I missing?" he asked.

Severina said, "Oh, nothing." Touching his arm she said, "Just a woman-to-woman chat."

"Woman-to-woman? Tell me more."

"Not for you, *fratellino*," Severina said.

The Contessa was standing between the double doors, waiting for us. "Your father has gone to bed," she told Niccolò and Severina. She turned to me. "Good night, Isabel."

"Thank you so much for dinner, Contessa," I said. "And thank you Niccolò and Severina. It was lovely to meet you."

"I've emailed Harpo to thank *him*," Niccolò said to his mother.

"Where do you stay in Genoa?" asked Severina.

"Campopisano."

"Campopisano?" Severina repeated my answer as a question. "Nico, no. She shouldn't walk back by herself. Not this late."

"Of course not," Niccolò said. "She should stay here."

"Yes," said Severina, lacing her arm through Niccolò's, "that's what I was thinking."

"Niccolò, I need to talk to you," said the Contessa. "Emiliano can escort Ms. Henley home."

He leaned in close and whispered, "Tomorrow? Elevenish? See you then. Outside." In a louder voice he said, "I'll find Emiliano and ask him to meet you at the front door."

I followed Severina down another staircase. She walked quickly.

"I'm sorry I can't go with you and Emiliano. I have other plans. But I would like to speak with you. In private, if possible."

Emiliano was hobbling down the stairs with my coat. "*Pronta?*" he asked.

Severina kiss-pecked me on both cheeks and then opened the door, letting in a gust of air so cold she squealed as Emiliano and I went out into the night. I heard her double bolt the door behind us.

Even with Emiliano's slight limp, he kept a fast pace. Nothing looked as I remembered it now that it was dark. The facades of palazzi, and the tall towers casting long shadows seemed sinister at this late hour. Groups of mendicants and prostitutes lined the curving, sloping streets.

I coughed on cottony mist, spreading quickly. Without a word, Emiliano stopped. We had reached Campopisano. When I turned to thank him, he had already left.

CHAPTER FOUR

The next morning on my way out I sent a short email to William, just to check in and say all was now well in Genoa after some initial challenges that I'd dealt with. Niccolò was waiting for me on the palazzo steps outside when I arrived. He was wearing a tweed jacket, a scarf tied in a knot around his neck, tight jeans, and polished black leather shoes that looked brand new.

"Very punctual," he grinned, drumming two fingers on the back of his wrist.

"Looking forward to getting started!" I grinned back. We kissed on both cheeks as if we were old friends.

"But you have only just arrived! Before you begin work in my archive, I would like to show you my beautiful city. You can consider it . . . background research. I'm a Falcone. That counts as both background research and foreground research, wouldn't you say? All I ask is for two hours. You won't regret it. Okay?" As I started to object, he bounded down the steps, so I followed.

Walking behind Niccolò through the twisting streets of old Genoa challenged my hold on reality. It seemed surreal to be following a descendant of the Falcone through his city, much of which had existed already in the sixteenth century or earlier.

"The medieval quarter was constructed to prevent invasions," he was saying. "Between the sea, the mountains, and these narrow streets, the city center was impervious. You can understand how we preserved our Republic."

We continued through intestinal alleys until we reached a piazza and Niccolò stopped in front of a palazzo so huge I thought it was a civic building. Its *trompe-l'oeil* splendor clashed with the grime and squalor surrounding it.

"Palazzo Giustiniani," Niccolò said. "The Giustiniani were one of the most important families. Before they invented their name, they were a consortium of families with allied interests. Look at their crest, a tower from Chios, above the door. And up there," he said, pointing at a marble sculpture of a lion carved into the facade. "That lion was stolen from Croatia after a Genovese war with Venice. Imagine the intrigue of those days! The romance."

"Also, no antibiotics or anesthesia, rampant misogyny and racism," I said.

"Hmm, yes. You know very much of the history. Well, I am secure that soon I will, how do you say, stump you!"

We wandered into the courtyard.

"Pay attention to the entrances of palazzi. Note the carved sculptures over *portoni*, for instance, as they impart information about the original inhabitants." I pulled a notebook and pen out of my bag. Niccolò didn't stop talking as I took notes. "Did you learn about the *rolli* system of palazzi?"

"The what system?"

"Aha! See, already I have stumped you. When an important dignitary, or king, or cardinal, visited Genoa, the powerful families would use a lottery system to determine whose palazzo the visitor would stay in."

"So, if you 'won' the lottery, at the same time you 'lost,' right? Because wasn't it expensive, and a lot of work, for one family to host a king?" I asked.

"Ah, clever girl. However, you are off the mark. It was considered a great honor, which conferred benefits on the family, and the expenses were shared. Once the palazzo was determined, another family would loan the host the silverware, someone else would provide the plates, et cetera."

"The Falcone were supposed to host the French king in the early 1580s—have you ever read about that?"

"No."

Stopping in front of another palazzo with an imposing tower Niccolò said, "I forgot to mention, beginning in the twelfth century, having a tower attached to your house, the *casa torre*, became a status symbol. It was no longer defensive architecture."

On another street we passed a cluster of prostitutes. "So many prostitutes here," I said.

He shrugged. "We are in the *Quartiere della Maddalena*. Prostitution has been legal and protected here since medieval times."

I looked at a clock on one of the towers. "It's already twelve thirty. Shouldn't we—"

"—Ten minutes more! See this broad street," he said. "This is where families constructed flashy residences to show off their new wealth in the 1500s. The Spanish poet Quevedo said, 'Silver is born in America, dies in Spain, and is buried in Genoa.' The bankers that funded those expeditions were drowning in it. Can't you tell?" We walked by two more blocks of buildings, rivals in sumptuousness.

As we strolled down the Strada Nuova, Niccolò pointed out a wedding cake and a red velvet cake close to one another: the Palazzo Bianco and Palazzo Rosso, that I had read about. "Someday I'd love to see their Rubens and Van Dyck portraits," I said.

We kept walking and Niccolò pointed to Palazzo Grimaldi, the house of Philip II's first banker. "Nicolò Grimaldi was known to the Genovese as '*il monarca*.'"

"Thank you for showing me around, Niccolò. Knowing this background information is important. But I need to get to work. The clock is ticking."

"But I have a great hunger! I'm sure you must as well. We stop for a quick bite." He smiled and began walking. We looped around and down to the port. "This is where Genoa begins and ends," he said. "The love of the sea is in my blood."

Niccolò chose a restaurant with white-tiled walls and floors and no name. The pretty waitress frowned at me. He ordered a Genovese specialty called *farinata*, a heavy pie with a chickpea crust, and a bottle of the house wine.

"Where did you go to school in Switzerland?" I asked.

"Oh," he said with a wave of his hand, "one of those boarding schools. I learned to ski there. Among other things. With your friend Harpo. But I prefer my city, and the law faculty at the *università* is excellent. When I'm not studying, I travel with friends to the mountains, and along the coast." He refilled our wineglasses. "I should take you to one of our neighboring fishing villages—frozen in time." He clasped his fingers together, pointed them outward, and stretched.

"Your English is impeccable," I said. "I know your mom's American, but did you spend any time in the States?"

He bit his lower lip. "A little, yes." He tilted his head up to the ceiling and swigged the rest of his wine. He looked toward the door and poured himself the last of our second bottle of wine.

"To your thesis, and to your first visit to Genoa," he said, lifting his glass to toast me. He stood up. "Shall we go?"

"Don't we have to pay? May I contribute?"

"Please, Isabel. This meal will go on my account."

"Alright. *Andiamo.* Do you know if your mother is home? I'd rather hoped I wouldn't run into her today."

"We can easily avoid my mom."

I followed Niccolò down a side street that led to the harbor where his car, a Fiat with sportscar ambitions, was parked.

"Do you think you've had too much wine to drive?" I asked.

"We'll make one stop," he said, ignoring my question. "Follow me to yon churchyard, where corruption preys on the moldering remnants of mortality, and death holds his fearful banquet . . ."

"What?"

"Friedrich Schiller," he said. "I stumped you again. Hop in."

We crossed the city, driving up the hills, coiling around along the *sopraelevata*, viewing the palazzi from on high. Niccolò drove too fast on curvy stretches, and the wine lurched in my stomach.

"Where are we going?" I asked, after twenty minutes, over the roar of the engine and the ratcheting noises and thrusts of downshifted and upshifted gears.

"Soon," was all he said. After another few minutes he slowed down and we parked next to a sign that read: *Cimitero Monumentale di Staglieno.*

Niccolò nodded to the guard, and we walked under a large stone arch, entering a grassy area surrounded on four sides by long, open-air corridors. The afternoon light was waning. We walked down one of the corridors, passing ornate sculpture after ornate sculpture, funerary monuments set in salmon-pink walls.

"Designed by Carlo Barabino in 1851, the Cemetery of Staglieno is one of the largest in Europe," Niccolò said, halting in front of a group of sculpted figures in turn of the century garments. A woman with white dots on her face, tears that looked like tiny pearls, stood in the foreground holding a little boy. Niccolò spoke. "The golden age of this cemetery was the late nineteenth century, when Genoa experienced a resurgence in the shipping industry. Artists were given unlimited commissions."

"Such realistic portraits of the contemporary people," I said.

"The monuments aren't all like that," Niccolò said. He directed me to a sculpture of a winged figure pulling a disintegrating skeleton out from a tomb, its mouth twisted in a macabre grin. The portrait bust of a middle-aged man stood to the side. The donor.

"It appears to be dark but no," Niccolò said. "A symbol of the resurrection."

We continued walking, passing mourning families carved in stone. The statues were caked in a thick layer of the blackest dust, residue from car emissions mixed together with the grime of time.

I stopped in front of a monument with two women, one leading the other by the hand to a door inside a pyramid. On the right side sat a young angel holding an hourglass.

"What's behind the door?" I asked, scribbling notes.

"Nothing," Niccolò sighed. "Oblivion."

We continued strolling and I stopped again, in front of a sculpture of a winged man with a long beard, and arms crossed tightly over his naked torso. He was sitting on top of a marble sarcophagus with clawed feet, the man's own legs draped by a loose toga.

"Ah," Niccolò said. "Father Time. Telling us to remember that our time is running out, Isabel." Niccolò walked behind me. When I didn't move, he gently slid his hand along my coat at the sides of my waist. I leaned into him. "Andiamo," he whispered.

The sculptures higher up the path were dirtier, more neglected. I felt a shadow of his hands touch me as we walked in the direction of the car. I approached a statue of a young woman, eyes closed, naked to her waist, her breasts taut, one arm draped around a cloaked figure with the hollowed-out face of a skull, sheathed by bronze gauze. The woman's other wrist was gripped by a skeletal hand. I couldn't tell whether she was drawn to him or attempting to escape, but the contrast between her rounded body and the fleshless bones made me want to turn away.

"Death and the maiden," I said.

"The name is *Eternal Drama*," he said. "The tomb of Valente Celle. This is a danse macabre, the attempt to escape the final embrace of death. The woman struggles at first, but eventually she surrenders." I turned around to look at Niccolò but his eyes were closed. Then he opened them. "Beautiful, isn't it?" he asked.

"Is there a Falcone tomb here?" I asked in return.

"I'll take you to the Falcone chapel another day. Also, to our private chapel outside the city. Yes, this would interest you."

On our way out we stopped in front of one last monument. A sculpture of another young woman, seated and leaning back. She wore a billowing dress that was falling off her left shoulder. That naked shoulder made her seem vulnerable, the rest of her trapped under dense fabric. She held a bunch of flowers.

"A young widow, depicted by Saccomanno. Those poppies in her hand," Niccolò said, observing me observing her. "Emblems of eternal sleep. *Pronta?*" he asked. We crossed under the arch, away from the threshold of death, and I walked toward the car as Niccolò handed the guard some cash.

When we were fastened in, he said, "Oh no! It is four thirty. The archive will be closed by the time we return!"

"Closed? It's *your* archive! Niccolò, you promised."

"I'm sorry, Isabel. Can you forgive me? I wanted very much to bring you to Staglieno. The reward for your patience is in the glove compartment. Please open it now." He put his foot on the gas, and I found a copy of Mark Twain's *The Innocents Abroad*.

"That's so nice of you, Niccolò, thank you. I've always wanted to read this."

"That you have not read it surprises me, but I am pleased. It is an early edition."

"I can't accept it," I said, "but I would love to borrow it."

"I insist." He downshifted and passed the car in front of us around a curve. "I'm thirsty," he said. "How about an aperitivo?"

I felt like shouting NO, but said nothing, and instead opened the book to read a note written on Falcone stationery. "To Isabel, in honor of the first of her many trips to Genoa, where she will always be welcome as our guest, and friend." It was impossible to be angry with anyone who wrote such things.

Back in Genoa it was completely dark. Niccolò pulled in front of the harbor, turned off the engine, and switched on the dome light on my side. He took the book from my lap and opened it to a page with a leather bookmark inside. "Please read this section," he said, "aloud. That is, if you do not mind indulging me." He reached over and unbuckled my seatbelt, and then his own.

I started reading. "Our last sight was the cemetery (a burial place intended to accommodate 60,000 bodies), and we shall continue to remember it after we shall have forgotten the palaces. It is a vast marble colonnaded corridor extended around a great unoccupied square of ground; its broad floor is marble, and on every slab is an inscription—for every slab covers a corpse . . ."

"The language is so perfect," he said. "If only your Twain could see Genoa today."

He reached out and touched the tip of my nose before pulling his hand back and smiling again.

"Keep reading," he said. "*Per favore.*"

I continued, but from earlier pages, which had been dog-eared. I looked up at Niccolò. "It's timeless," I said.

"Now how about that aperitivo?" Niccolò asked, shifting back into drive. Buckling my seatbelt, I cracked the window open, leaned back, and closed my eyes. When I opened them, we were speeding down the highway, my ears popping. We entered a tunnel lit by blinking fluorescent lights.

Thirty minutes and twenty-one tunnels later, we turned left toward the sea. I saw a sign for Rapallo, and we drove under an old stone bridge, green weeds spiking out from irregular crevices. "Annibale," Niccolò said. "Hannibal's Bridge," he added.

"Built by *the* Hannibal?"

"No, by Hannibal Lecter." He pounded the steering wheel. "Ha! No, obviously *the* Hannibal. Hannibal was here in Liguria."

"Apparently I have a lot to learn."

"But the question is, *how* will you learn," he said as he maneuvered the small car through several short switchbacks. "I suspect that you have favored book-learning over experiences."

"Perhaps," I acknowledged.

We were driving along a narrow and curved road very close to the sea. After passing an orange church slotted between two hills, we came to a square where Niccolò parked in front of a No Parking sign.

He led me down a brick path to a village. Boutiques and restaurants occupied the ground floors of pink buildings twinkling with glowing bulbs, reflected in the now-black water, where fishing boats swayed gently. The only sound was creaking wood and the clinking of boat hardware. Hills rose in the distance, and a medieval castle, soaked in the white light of a gibbous moon, crested the ridgeline.

"This is a beautiful place," I said. "Thank you for bringing us here." I thought of William, wishing I were looking at the view with him instead.

"*Niente*," he said, smiling his big, toothy grin as he took one of my freezing hands in his. "I would like to take you for dinner in my favorite restaurant."

"That's very generous of you, Niccolò," I said. "But I'd rather return to Genoa, if that's alright. I wouldn't want my host family to worry."

We stood there for a full thirty seconds. "I will honor your wishes," he said, a little wounded. "Only one last thing. Then I will drive you home." I followed him up a steep hill of uneven cobblestones with a flat, slate path down the center. "I hope your boyfriend will not mind."

"If you're asking if I have a boyfriend, the answer is no. But you, Niccolò, you're a handsome guy, from a prominent family, with a promising career ahead of you. Certainly, you must have a girlfriend?" I paused. "Will she mind us being together in this romantic place?"

He stopped in the middle of the path. "I have many friends who are girls," he said. "But at the moment, no, I don't have a girlfriend. I'm not gay, like Sevi. I just haven't met the right person." He ran his palm over his beard stubble. "It is . . . difficult . . . to find someone who pleases my family."

"I imagine your mother would be impossible to please."

"It is not only a question of my parents. I'm the last male to bear the Falcone name."

"So you must produce heirs, the next generation of Falcone. Sounds like the sixteenth century," I said. He nodded once. "Why waste your precious time with me?"

"I enjoy your company."

"You met me yesterday."

He half-smiled, looking both older and younger than his twenty-seven years. "I'm not, I'm not *playing* with you, if that's what you think. I like you," he said, reaching over and grabbing my hand. "You are smart, and fun. Not like the normal girls I meet. The girls who are my friends."

It occurred to me that Niccolò was only *sei vecchi fa*, six old men removed, from Federico Falcone. Six centenarians didn't seem so far away. And maybe Niccolò knew where the emerald was. Maybe he would tell me.

We reached a piazza with a baroque church, the wind whipping us from every side. Niccolò took my hand as we climbed steps to a square terrace, enclosed by a thin, metal railing looking out over the sea, several hundred feet below. The water was not lit by the moon, so I could only glimpse the foamy white surf below, but I heard and felt it pounding the rock all the way down.

Niccolò steered me over to the edge of the terrace and whispered in my ear. "As a boy I used to walk down to the sea along a narrow path. Would you like to investigate?"

"It's late," I said, peering over the ledge. Stepping back, into his arms, I watched the clouds of our breath.

"Don't be afraid," Niccolò said, and wrapped one arm around my coat and over the top of my chest, just below my neck. With his other hand, he pointed in different directions. "Genoa is over there, and Rapallo there, and over there the Cinque Terre."

A rush of blood sloshed around my skull, and in a dizzied panic I disentangled myself from Niccolò's embrace and sat down. Something seemed off. I thought of Rose, how she had warned me about the Falcone, and not to say her name. She hadn't mentioned Niccolò. During cocktails the Count had referred to a pretty girl whose name he couldn't recall, probably Niccolò's intended. Someone appropriate had likely been chosen for him already. Niccolò sat next to me and put his arm around my shoulder. He waited for a few seconds, and then leaned in slowly to kiss me. I turned my head.

"Come on," he said, trying to kiss me again. I edged farther away from him. He stood up. "You are tired," he said. "I will take you home." He began walking quickly down the hill. I followed him, stumbling a few times, and losing sight of him. When I reached the car, he had Italian pop music playing at full blast. We drove back to Genoa, swerving in and out of tunnels, well above the speed limit, without speaking.

Near Campopisano he stopped the car and, idling the motor, said, "This is as far as I can go with the car."

"Oh!" I said, "Thank you for the city tour, and Staglieno, and lunch, and for showing me the exquisite coastal village. I'm so looking forward to starting work tomorrow. And Niccolò, I'm grateful to you for giving me the opportunity."

"Tomorrow on the front steps at ten," he said. "Please arrive on time. Give me your phone," he said, and I passed it to him, not thinking. He punched in his number and handed it back. I got out and climbed the hill toward Campopisano as he roared off. Inside the house was quiet but there was a note from Marta saying they had left food for me in the refrigerator. I stopped at the computer in the hallway, hoping not to wake anyone.

William had sent me an email.

> Dear Isabel,
>
> It's so nice to hear from you. I'd love to hear about your discoveries in the archives. Have you found much of use for your conference paper? I'm looking forward to seeing you in Florence!
>
> Best,
> William

The message was friendly but not flirty. I took a couple of deep breaths. At least we were interacting again. There was nothing further from Rose. I sent a note to the email address she'd given me explaining that I'd obtained access to the Falcone Archive and would start my research the next morning. The email bounced back with an automatic response instructing me to resend my message to a different address, which I did, not knowing whether that was the right thing to do, but too tired to care.

I tried to sleep but kept thinking about how I had spent an entire day acting like a tourist when I should have been in the archive searching for information about the emerald. Were the people threatening Rose watching me here in Genoa? I'd have to make progress tomorrow. My only consolation was that it seemed important to keep Niccolò on my side.

CHAPTER FIVE

The next morning, I stopped for a double espresso across the street from the Palazzo so I could arrive right at ten. Niccolò didn't appear, so at 10:06 I rang the bell, imagining the electric eye observing me. Emiliano let me in and without speaking led me to the second floor. We waited outside the study, and five minutes later, Niccolò bounded down the hall and Emiliano tottered away. Niccolò unlocked the door, then kissed me abruptly on both cheeks.

"I wanted to thank you, so much, for arranging this, Niccolò."

It was as if he hadn't heard me. "My class commences in a few minutes, but if you need something, text me." He fetched the secret key from under the desk and unlocked the cabinet with the boxes, which were numbered. He placed the first three on the end of the table closest to him.

"No one will disturb you," he said. "Emiliano will be running errands, and my parents are in Switzerland on business. I'll be back at six and can show you out." He pointed to a door in the corner. "There is a water closet, if you need."

"Thanks," I said.

He patted me once on the shoulder. "Now you can go to work."

As he pulled the door closed, I heard the lock click. I waited a few seconds then went to check the door. It was locked from the outside. I searched around the room for a key, running my hands over doorframes and cabinets, but was unable to locate a spare. I didn't want to shout into the hall. I texted Niccolò and waited a few minutes for him to respond. He didn't.

The room was quiet, with no noise from the street. A cold draft ran along my arms, as if there were an open window, but they were all tightly closed. I tried to switch on one of the old radiators but couldn't find a thermostat. I pulled my sleeves over my fingers.

I untied the string around the box, labeled "Volume I," removed the top, and gingerly opened the first folder, unsure if the tremor in my hands was due to the temperature of the room or my excitement to touch Falcone documents. Searching for the emerald in the Florentine archives might not be necessary. I might find it in these pages.

I held the first document up to the light to locate the watermark—if there was one. I had in my hand a contract, drawn up in 1497, and yes, there was the watermark. The documents underneath the contract were piled neatly and smelled a little damp, with bluish mold dotting the edges. Several pages were so thin I wondered how they had survived for hundreds of years. Most were paper, although I came across vellum documents as well. Some were bound together, and of the ones that were signed and dated, the dates were as usual the easiest to read. Engaging with the sources again felt direct, intimate.

I went through thirteenth-, fourteenth-, and fifteenth-century documents, written mostly in Latin, until I came to the sixteenth century.

I jotted down the names of the Falcone signatories. Sometimes these names were difficult to decipher, or even worse, they were abbreviated. After reading through and transcribing whatever was easy, I would go back to the unclear words. With particularly tricky hands, I wrote out entire alphabets, copying the way the writer rendered each letter, then used the alphabets as reference tools.

Back in St Stephens I had purchased a quill pen in a souvenir store and practiced writing with it to comprehend the strokes of pre-modern pens, a trick William had suggested to me. Some writers pressed down harder than others, resulting in heavy, blotchy ink in some places, and faint ink in others. Others had been dictated to, and at times scribbled everything down as quickly as possible. These pages were the most difficult to read.

Holding the papers up to the light lines became visible, created when wet wood pulp had been laid out on a mesh screen to dry. Out of all the documents created in the early modern world, how many millions had been lost, or accidentally or intentionally destroyed? The gaps in the historical record would always be vast.

Carefully making my way through the volume, I familiarized myself with the discrepancies of the various hands. Words were sometimes difficult to read because the text was written in ornate secretary hand. Although secretary hand was a standard hand, the writing was full of loops, and many letters looked similar, so it was vital to understand the context in order to determine which letters composed a certain word.

I often found remnants of a red, plastic-like substance, or just crimson traces, where wax seals had been.

Most of the documents I went through were business agreements between the Falcone and other nobles. Many pages had holes in them, and still others had ink that had bled from one side to the other, obscuring chunks of text.

In the middle of the volume, I ran my finger down one of the yellowed-white pages of a fiscal document signed by the cousins of my French branch of Falcone, who still lived in Genoa.

The next document concerned Giovanbattista. After Andrea Doria's death, the Falcone who remained in Genoa regained some of their power. Giovanbattista stayed in regular contact with his brother, Pierfrancesco, in

Genoa, throughout their lifetimes, even if Pierfrancesco had to nominally cut ties with Giovanbattista after his involvement in the uprising.

At 5:45, I put everything back in the order in which I'd found it, and exactly at six I heard the lock clicking and Niccolò appeared in the doorway.

"Ciao bella. How's the research going?"

"I appreciate everything you've done for me, Niccolò, but I do not like the idea of being locked inside a room. It doesn't seem safe."

"Cara, I did it *for* your safety. I apologize for not informing you, but I thought you would understand." He put the first of three boxes back in the cabinet.

"What do you mean, for my safety?"

"As you know, not long ago we had a theft. The perpetrator was never caught. We always keep this door locked, and Emiliano checks it from time to time." He turned to face the door, then back to me. Lowering his voice, he continued, "Additionally, I have not . . . discussed your work with my parents. I am not sure they would be pleased if they knew you were here alone with our materials."

"I understand. But couldn't you leave me with a key?"

"We don't have an extra. Only mine, Emiliano's, Severina's, and my mother's. I can't make a copy without drawing attention to the fact. You worry too much. I have to run to a dinner for my class. May I walk you downstairs?" He had placed the key back in its hiding spot and was looking around to see if anything was out of place.

I nodded hesitantly.

As Niccolò locked the front door he touched my elbow and said, "You can make it home on your own? See you tomorrow? Same time same place?" He pinched my cheek then dashed down the steps and disappeared into one of the streets.

Over the next two weeks I went to the Palazzo every day and followed the same procedure, in at ten, out at six, which agreed with me, although the room was cold, and I had to go without lunch. I moved through the documents as quickly as possible looking for anything related to the emerald. When Niccolò and I exchanged pleasantries and kissed hello and goodbye I treated him with courteous professionalism, which seemed to suit him. Entering the palazzo each day, I kept in mind Rose's words, determined to keep my promise to work diligently and find the emerald.

I began each day looking over the last page I'd finished the previous day before moving on. Running my eyes over every sheet, I stopped only if something seemed important or if it established a previously unknown connection.

In a separate notebook I was keeping notes related to my thesis, a roadmap that would help me move through the material whenever I returned to it. That was another reason I wanted to stay on Niccolò's good side.

I wished I didn't have to spend all this time searching for the emerald because some of the documents were fascinating. There was wonder in the realization, which occurred to me every so often when hunched over a manuscript, that over four hundred years ago, real people had written down with their own hands the words I was reading. There was poignancy and a small measure of terror in the recognition that, through my scholarly contribution, these souls would "speak" for the first time in centuries. I would need to reproduce faithfully what they had said all those years ago. But for now, I had to focus on the emerald.

Every fifth or sixth day I emailed William summarizing my "findings," everything relevant to my thesis, and he wrote back immediately, sounding impressed. I was starting to understand how Rose could have fooled him for almost three years about her progress. It seemed that he wanted to be impressed by what I was accomplishing.

Each night I wrote to Rose, or whoever was reading the emails I sent her, trying to make things sound promising, as if I truly thought the material I was going through would reveal the emerald's location.

I worked on both Saturdays, but it was Emiliano who unlocked and locked me into the library because Niccolò spent those two weekends skiing. On Sundays, when Emiliano had the day off, I slept in. I wasn't sleeping well, dreaming of the Contessa standing in front of the door to the library each time I arrived. Halfway through my stay in Genoa, I started to believe myself that everything I was doing would lead to a discovery, despite evidence to the contrary.

I spent most of the second Sunday working on my conference paper. Rose's name was still listed on the conference website, and the title of her paper was "Federico Falcone and the Concept of the Renaissance Man" which I hoped she'd intended to be ironic. The first draft of the paper I had written was far less deferential to him. I had uncovered more information in the archive to support my arguments. At least the documents that might reveal something about the emerald were the same ones that informed my paper.

That same Sunday in the late afternoon I took a walk in the neighborhood and visited the medieval church of San Agostino. After leaving I felt my phone buzzing in my pocket. A number I didn't recognize, the second time that day, flashed on the screen. On the second ring I answered, "Hello?" and then, because the number had an Italian area code "(39)" I said, "Pronto?"

"Isabel," said a woman's voice.

"Speaking," I said. "Who is this?"

There was static on the line, and her words morphed into something robotic, inhuman. "Udo no how much danger your rin."

"Rose!" I said. "The connection is terrible. What did you say?"

"You're seriously in danger, Isabel."

"Rose, are you okay? Where are you?

She said something inaudible. There was a beeping that sounded like a low-toned alarm, and then she said, "I don't know how much longer I can protect you. Find the emerald. Now they're threatening to kill my father. Don't mention the emerald. Don't mention my name."

"Wait. I don't understand. Who? Who will kill you?"

"They might be listening in right now, so I can't say more. Concentrate on the letters. *Please* hurry." The line cut.

That night I wrote to Rose and updated her on my progress. I didn't mention the phone call.

CHAPTER SIX

The following Wednesday I wrote down a tentative dissertation title: "The Falcone: Constructing Dynastic Identity Between Italy and France 1550–1600."

When Niccolò opened the door at the end of the day I waved him over.

"You look happy," he said.

"I've been reading about one of your ancestors, Federico Falcone." I paused, studying him for a reaction. "Do you know anything about him?"

He shook his head. "Nope."

"Federico's father, Giovanbattista, moved his family from Genoa to France. Federico, who had lived in Genoa until he was a teenager, finagled his way into high circles in Paris, and became a close adviser to the French monarchy. Federico's rise to power and wealth made him the target of envy."

"Mmm-hmm," said Niccolò, his hand reaching up to block a yawn.

"Today I was reading about Federico's trips between France and Genoa. Federico was often charged with garnering financial support from Genoese bankers. I also found a document outlining a series of debts Federico owed to the Croci, a Florentine banking family. Federico's first wife was Ginevra de' Croci, so it's not surprising, but I'd like to know what the money was used for. The Croci also lent money to the Spanish king. The French Falcone may have turned to Florentine bankers after making enemies with the doge. Federico may even have been an intermediary between the Croci and the Spanish king.

"On one trip to Genoa, Federico filed a lawsuit against his cousin, Filippo, after Filippo's father Pierfrancesco died, over the ownership of your palazzo. The new doge ruled in Federico's favor, and Federico was able to keep the property, as the eldest son of an eldest son, even though his father had been disgraced. Federico didn't live here permanently, but he stayed in the palazzo when he was in town. After Federico's death, ownership reverted once again to Filippo's family."

"*Porca puttana!*" Niccolò said, rubbing his hands together. I smiled. "It's fucking cold in here!" he said. "I'll ask Emiliano to boost the heat."

Before bed, in my daily email, I didn't mention these latest findings. Rose had told me to focus on the letters, but the letter I had found in Rose's desk outlining Tommaso's assassination plot—the original of which I hadn't yet seen—had given me an idea. Maybe the fate of the emerald was related to Federico's debts?

On Friday, the sky was full of foreboding clouds. At noon I stood up and stretched. Three weeks had passed since the day I'd spent with Niccolò.

As I was going through the final box of letters, I heard a clicking in the door and held my breath. Niccolò was still in class. Emiliano. Or the Contessa? I started gathering the papers when the door swung open, and Severina walked in. Her hair was pinned back in a bun, and she was wearing glasses and jeans. I let out my breath.

"Isabel? What are you doing here?"

"Severina, I'm *so* glad it's you."

"Why are you in this room and why is the cabinet open?" she asked. Her arms were crossed over her chest and her lips were pressed together tightly. "What's in that box?" The tone of her voice was guarded. Cold.

"Archival materials. Your family archive. I've been working on them."

"Why are you here?"

"Niccolò arranged it. He's been helping me. And also locking me in every day."

"You might have fooled my brother, but you haven't fooled me. Tell me what you want. Did somebody send you? I'll give you one more opportunity to tell me, or I call the police."

"I'm an academic. Working on my PhD thesis. On the Falcone. You seemed intrigued by my work at dinner a few weeks ago. I'd be happy to show you my notes."

I handed her my notebook, the one that focused on the Falcone as a dissertation topic, filled with detailed but sloppily organized notes and random observations about things I would return to when I was able to focus on my thesis again. Whenever I did refer to the emerald, I'd just written the letter E, which I could tell her stood for something else. She sat down and began to go through my notebook, page by page, pressing down so hard that her nails made crescent impressions on the paper. She didn't look up at me as she read, as if she were searching for something.

When she finished, she passed the notebook back to me and I said, "I'm grateful to Niccolò because, as you can see, I've made some important discoveries. Relevant to my thesis. If you look about twenty pages in, you can see an overview. I've got some other notebooks here," I gestured toward them. "One has an outline of the paper that I'll be presenting at a history conference next month. In Florence."

"So, you are here simply to write a . . . thesis?" she asked; with that word her posture relaxed, and she laced her fingers together over one knee.

"What other reason would there be?" I said, my heart furiously pumping.

"Do you truly not know?"

"Know what?"

"Why thieves robbed us."

"No, I don't. What did they steal? There are plenty of sixteenth-century documents here. What's going on, Severina? All I want to do is work."

"I believe you." Her features softened. "Intelligence and virtue are a rare combination, but that's what Nico told me you have. So, you want to write our history?"

I nodded.

"To tell our story?"

I nodded again.

"But what about the other one working on the Falcone? Rose. You must know her."

"Yes, I do. Well, I did. Rose disappeared."

"Disappeared? What does that mean?"

"One day she was at school, St Stephens. The next day she was gone. Then they found her suicide note."

"No! Does Nico know?"

"I haven't told him," I said. "We've never discussed her. I just assumed she worked here and that none of you knew her. Usually, the arrangements to work in an archive don't include, well, getting to know the family."

"You took over her PhD after she died?"

"Yes. My lead professor asked me to continue work on her topic because otherwise the school would lose funding. But that's not the only reason. The history of the Falcone overlapped with my earlier work, so it was an extension of what I'd been pursuing already. More than an extension, an expansion. Rose . . . well, not to speak ill of her, but she hadn't made much headway on actually gathering material."

"That doesn't surprise me," Severina said. "To me she did not seem to be a serious researcher."

"So, you knew her? And Niccolò did, too?"

"Yes. He knew her better than I did. Was she your friend? Well, *non importa*. I met her only after she had nearly finished her work. I returned from London unexpectedly late one night and saw her kissing Niccolò in the *salotto*. I asked Nico about it. I've seen him with a lot of women but not like that. He said he was in love with her. I believed him. She was beautiful, and attentive."

I shouldn't have been surprised, but I unconsciously squeezed my hands together.

"I stayed out of their personal affairs. But Rose and I had coffee several times across the street, and one day she said she was in trouble and asked if I could do her a favor. I didn't know her well, and said I would need to think about it. I remember she was so happy she kissed me on the lips. A long kiss. It was . . . pleasureful, I must admit.

"The next time I went to Genoa she had left, Beth kicked her out. Probably she was jealous. Not long after, someone broke into the house, and the archive. Nico said Rose was in New York at the time, so she was not the thief, something I never considered a possibility. She was flaky, but sweet. I don't think she was capable to orchestrate a theft from our well-guarded archive. For what purpose? She's a student, yes?"

"What kind of trouble could Rose have been in? Why would anyone want to steal from your archive?"

"You don't know this either, do you?" Her eyes ran over my face.

"No."

"Which is why I want to help you. Maybe you can also help me. Wait here, please, I will be back in ten minutes."

CHAPTER SEVEN

S everina came back into the room carrying a bronze box, the size of a shoebox, and gently placed it on the table. Then she locked us in the room.

"Two weeks before my dear nonna died," she said, in a low voice, "five years ago next month, may she rest in peace, she gave to me this box, and the key that opens it." Severina held up a tiny key. "She said it was important, and that I had to keep it secret. She showed me what was inside—papers, old papers, that I could not read.

"Anyway, I hid the box, and in my grief—I loved my *nonnissima* so very much, Isabel—I forgot about it. Then Rose appeared. When Nico told me she was studying documents in the archive, I thought about Nonna's box. But couldn't remember where I'd hidden it!" She reached up to push some hair away from her face.

"When I found the box, I tried to read the documents," she said, "but they are written in French, and my French is not very good. Also, the handwriting is . . . strange." She tilted her head and lay both of her hands over my hand resting on the table. "Could you try to read the papers for me, and tell me why my nonna wanted me to have them?"

I nodded. "Yes, Severina. Of course I will."

She opened the box, which squeaked in protest, and took out a document, which she passed to me. Running my eyes over it I felt a little flutter. "Well, it's a letter, but you're right. Not easy to read. You can see, here, that it was written in 1569."

"Are you kidding?" asked Severina.

"And," I said, "it was written to . . . 'Madame.' Hmm. A title, a greeting, but no name. Anyway, it was written by, you can see this loopy letter, I think it's a T, yes, a T . . . and it clearly says Falcone here. Well, not so clearly, but that's what's written."

"This is wonderful! Can you read me the letter?" asked Severina.

I glanced up at the clock. "Severina, Niccolò will be here in less than an hour. He's always on time. If you want to keep this a secret, I think you should leave now and bring the box back tomorrow after he goes to class. I don't know what else is in there, but it could take days, or even weeks, to get through. Or you could leave the box here, although I'm leaving in a few days and won't be back for a while. Probably not a good idea. Niccolò pretends he isn't interested, but he pays attention to my progress. He notices when I move a chair a few inches on the other side of the room."

"*Hai ragione!*" she said, standing up. "I should go now. But I would prefer you to take the papers with you. I'm off to London tomorrow and won't return until next weekend. Will you still be here?"

"Probably not. There's not much left. Maybe two or three days worth of work."

"Will you write out what you find? Is that asking too much? There aren't so many." She lifted the other documents out of the box and counted them. "Some of these are only short notes. There's that long letter you have and then, a shorter one, and then . . . four very short pages. So, six altogether. My nonna told me there were once other letters, too, but unfortunately they did not survive."

"I'll do my absolute best, Severina. Starting tonight." I handed her the long letter, and she closed the box.

"Whenever you have time. You do not need to start to this evening. I mean, I have had them for five years, *giusto*? Even if you need to bring them back to Scotland with you, it will not be a problem. I could take the train to see you!"

"Okay," I said.

"When you finish," she said, "we'll get together and I'll read your translation, or even just a description, that would be wonderful. Then we can tell my father, but not sooner. I don't want Beth to know, or even Nico. *Non ancora*."

"Who is Beth?" I asked.

"Beth, you know, *la Contessa*," she said, with sarcastic formality.

"Oh, right. Nico told me your mother's name is Elizabeth Jansen."

"My mother? Beth's not my mother," she said with a sour face. "My mother died in a car accident when I was ten. Beth met my papa when he was still grieving. She got pregnant with Nico to . . . how do you say, seal the deal. My nonna never trusted Beth. I am sure that is why she said this box had to be our secret."

"Did you show these documents to Rose?" I asked.

"I considered showing her, but then she left, with no warning. And also, remember that I told you she asked me for help—something to do with the archive—because she said she was in trouble? Well, there is another part of the story I have not told you. I don't know if it's connected to Rose, but I'm glad I did not show her these papers. And I am happy because now you are here, and I am not sure why, but I trust you." We both looked at the clock.

"Two years ago," she said, "a professor came to the palazzo and told my father about a jewel known as the Falcone emerald. The professor insisted that the emerald was here in our palazzo. That our ancestors had hidden it somewhere inside these walls. This was some-long ago century, I can't remember specifically. Whenever Caterina de' Medici was Queen of France. Hundreds of years ago."

My heart thump-thumped in my chest. Severina knew about the Falcone emerald! Her grandmother must have known, too. Maybe there was something in the letters about the emerald, which is why her grandmother kept it secret from Beth.

"Apparently the emerald was very valuable—because it was large and without flaws—and our Falcone ancestor wished to give it to the French queen. Or maybe to repay a debt? I cannot remember. But before he could give it to her, he died suddenly and *'mysteriously.'*" Severina crooked her forefingers. "And the professor told my father this emerald had an enormous curse on it, which led to our ancestor's death." She rolled her eyes.

"How odd," I said.

"Anyway, my father searched everywhere for the emerald. He never found it, obviously, but ever since that moment he has worried about the curse. Once he told me that the emerald caused the car accident that killed Mamma."

"Oh, Sev," I said.

She looked up at the clock again and started talking faster. "My father also thinks the theft happened because of the curse. I think it was Beth who sold them to the professor, not some stupid curse. I'll tell you the rest later. I don't want Nico to find us."

"I won't let anything happen to your documents."

"You don't need to tell me that. I already know." She hugged me, put her finger to her lips, and left, locking me in as I placed the bronze box inside my knapsack, as gently as I would have handled a living creature. I organized the documents I'd been working on and put them into their box, tying it up with the string. Then I waited for Niccolò.

The walk back to Campopisano that evening was colder and windier than it had been earlier in the week. When a few icy raindrops began to plunk down on my shoulder, I shivered and walked faster. Conscious of my precious cargo, I yanked on the straps of my backpack, holding it as close as possible. Someone I'd seen before in the neighborhood on a *motorino* roared by and I jumped back just in time to avoid being hit.

When I reached Campopisano, I surveyed the entire space around me. The dark piazza was empty except for a few cats scurrying for shelter. At home all I wanted to do was look at the letters, but I joined the family for dinner and spent an hour speaking English with Alessandra. I taught her the song about head, shoulders, knees, and toes. She thought it was very funny.

While Alessandra was brushing her teeth, Marta gave me a bottle of pepper spray, explaining in a whisper that two women had been threatened in the neighborhood in the past week. I thanked her and went upstairs.

In my room I pulled out the box. It had an abstract floral design on it, and a relief of a flame in the center, falcons on either side of the flame. The hinges squeaked as I coaxed the lid open.

I took out the letter that we'd looked at earlier, and the next sheet. Another letter, not too long. Then a third letter, very short. Severina had been right, it was a series of six personal letters, some of them unsigned and undated.

I went to the computer and dashed off an email outlining what I'd found in the archive that day but didn't mention Severina's grandmother's letters.

At six the next morning I emailed Niccolò that I wasn't feeling well and wouldn't be coming to the archive that day. He answered right away and mentioned his mother was hosting a luncheon that day, so it would be better if I wasn't there.

Feeling a shove of energy that I struggled to channel, I opened my laptop, which was acting wonky, and began to type out the letter in modern-day French, which took almost two hours. Then I translated it into English.

> *Madame,*
>
> *I hope this letter reaches you. Somehow I know it will. It is in the hands of a friend whom I trust will find you. I must beg your forgiveness for what I shall now reveal, words which cannot remain unwritten. Indeed, I could no more prevent the seas from rushing up on the shore than I can prevent myself from writing to you this day. Although I cannot blame you for it, you have set something inside me aflame, and I know that the person I was yesterday is not the same as he who writes to you now.*
>
> *You will not remember me, but I met you briefly at a large banquet hosted by the Duc de [...] . You were standing with a friend. We were introduced, but already after that moment I knew I wanted to converse more with you. You fascinated me. A friend then told me of your many accomplishments, your extraordinary wit that accompanies your uncommon beauty. This morning, as I was walking on the Rue-Monsieur-le Prince, the skies all of a sudden darkened and without warning let loose a torrent of wind and rain. I ducked under the awning of an adjacent house, expecting the storm to pass quickly. After some time the rain slowed, and I waited a while longer—how I thank the heavens that I waited a while longer—until the clouds parted to let the sun shine through. I am speaking of what happened with the elements, but also of what happened when you walked by—the sun came out and the*

world was in a moment transformed into a place of beauty beyond compare. Do I flatter myself to think that you noticed me there? I followed you with my eyes until all I could see was your shadow, and then I followed that, too. It was only after you were out of sight completely that my limbs were once again under my own command, and I ran after you but could not find you.

I know little of you, but somehow I feel that my life thus far has been leading me to you. Dear Madame, my soul is yours to do with as you please. You may perhaps laugh at such a folly, but my heart dictates while my pen writes.

How will you receive this declaration, this confession, this outburst? You know nothing of me except for the few words we exchanged and this perhaps ill-considered letter.

I know I can expect nothing in return except for your contempt. I am just another man, among many no doubt, begging for your attention. Perchance, I hope, with no reason to hope, the Fates will smile upon me and you will read this letter, one of hundreds you have no doubt received. And perhaps tomorrow you will again walk by the same building that you walked by this morning just as the rain ceased, where I will be waiting for a glimpse of your noble and most beautiful visage. I will wait in that place like a sentinel from the moment the sun crosses the horizon until it drops again in the night sky. I would do anything to see your face or even just your shadow once again.

I kiss your hands and your feet, Madame,

T. de' Falcone
Paris
The 6 day of April, 1569

About halfway through translating the letter into English, I breakfasted with the family and told them I would be working from home that day. I couldn't really concentrate again until after they had left, as Alessandra burst into my room three times to say goodbye. After finishing the first letter, I immediately started the second one.

Dear Monsieur Falcone,

Acknowledging your flattering words to me, I am afraid I cannot deign to meet you tomorrow, or ever. You must not yet know that I am a married woman, and although that should be enough of a deterrent I have yet another, which may further discourage you.

I have accepted the new learning in my heart, and made a confession of faith. I am but the humble servant of Jesus Christ and have pledged devotion to his scriptures wholeheartedly. I now reject those papal idolatries and false devotions to saints that were an important part of my previous life. This new spirituality builds in me day by day, a deep commitment to His words and His grace. But you my good sir have not so learned the holy word of Christ. It is written this is the will of the Lord that ye should be holy and abstain from indecency and every one should know how to keep his own vessel in holiness and honor.

So please, I ask you to refrain from requesting further correspondence.

May the Lord protect you, Monsieur. I wish upon you many blessings and that you should find a happiness, as I have,

M de la F.
Paris
April 19, 1569

This seemed to be a classic rejection letter. And a declaration of her devotion to Protestantism. Nothing about the emerald. Disappointment resounded through me. My laptop kept freezing, and I had to restart it several times. I saved everything every two minutes.

I went downstairs and made myself a stovetop espresso. Back at my desk, I downed it like a shot. I pulled out the next letter, and saw the word "debt" in the first line. Severina had mentioned something about a debt in connection to the emerald. I hoped something in this letter related to the emerald.

Monsieur Falcone,

I write to thank you and assure you I am in your debt. You were so kind to offer me the shelter I desperately needed, without asking any questions of me. I would not have troubled you except I believed my life and the lives of my children to be in danger. Were it not for my children, I would readily die a martyr's death, but they should not suffer simply because I have raised them in my own faith. The horrific recent events have made me understand that since my husband's death we are alone in the world, which triples my gratitude to you.

In a not too distant future I imagine I may need to rely on your kindness once again. May I call upon you?

Fortune is a fickle mistress; she readily betrays those who cling to what they believe are her promises.

I thank you again, one thousand times, my friend, if I may permit myself,

Madeleine, ??? September 1572

1572. The year of the St Bartholomew's Day Massacre. August twenty-fourth. The letter was written in September. Madeleine! Seeing the name of the elusive "Madame" sent a jolt up my spine. So, Tommaso had saved this Protestant woman Madeleine's life, and her children's lives. Why had Severina's grandmother insisted that her granddaughter keep the letters secret? They were interesting, particularly the last one, which referenced dramatic events. But there was nothing that seemed indiscreet, and no mention of the emerald.

A handful of letters remained, but I thought about calling Niccolò and asking if he could arrange for Emiliano to let me into the library for the rest of the afternoon. Then again, I didn't want to run into the Contessa and her luncheon guests, who might even be Americans.

I set my alarm for sixty minutes and took a nap. Then I started again.

At some point I heard people coming into the house, and noticed it was dark outside, but the letters had my undivided attention.

> *My dear Friend, I must thank you for the last. I assure you that I spent the night parted from you thinking of you alone. Sleep was a stranger to my eyes til morning. When absent from my sight, you remain present in my thoughts. Certainly, good Madame, I understand your meaning and wish to assure you that I do not lack courage, may you have no doubts of my devotion to you. I shall not prepare a thousand ships with curving sails, nor a mass of Danaean soldiers. I shall come myself. I kiss your feet, Madame.*
> *T. de Falcone.*

> *To my dearest friend, by my troubling you with this you may suppose the uneasiness I have felt since parting from you. But depend upon this; my future conduct shall always be to please you, for by pleasing you I please myself. The height of all my*

happiness in this life depends on your love. I could say ten thousand things more, but will conclude in the most devoted manner. Yours, Madeleine

On the very bottom of the page was one more line.

I implore you let this be burnt so it shall tell no tales.

My dearest,

I have thought of you every day and every night, treasuring your acquaintance as I have for some time. I wish to respond, yes, I will marry you. I, too, believe we could find profound happiness together for the rest of our lives. Will you meet me in _____ that we may ask the Lord to bear witness to our love? A small ceremony. Might we ask your brother for his blessing?

Until then I shall count every second not with you, until my life can once again begin, perhaps for the first time, when I will be fully yours, in body and in soul.

Who were these two correspondents?

T. de Falcone. Of course, Tommaso. Federico's brother. He had written to Federico about the assassination plot in the letter I'd found in Rose's desk. It shouldn't have taken me so long to make that connection.

Tommaso had been twenty-two in April of 1569, when he'd written the first of these letters. Madeleine was married then, and unreceptive to his love declaration. Three years later her husband was dead, and she wrote Tommaso a thank you note, referring to him as her friend.

None of the other three letters, the love letters—one from him and two from her—were dated.

The assassination plot letter I'd found in Rose's desk had been written in 1581, twelve years *after* the thank you letter. How could I guess when three undated letters had been written? At most I could surmise they'd been penned between Madeleine's thank you letter and 1581, the same year Tommaso died.

The last note indicated that Tommaso had married Madeleine. At least, she had accepted his proposal. They'd met at a banquet. He came from a prominent family and would have been a desirable husband. Then again, as the youngest son in his family, his prospects would have been meager. And although Madeleine was highly educated, as a widow with two children, she would not have been the ideal sixteenth-century wife. They had obviously fallen in love.

I hadn't found anything indicating Tommaso's marital status, but I still had a few remaining documents in the Falcone archive, as well as the archive in Florence, and the two repositories in Paris, where he had lived most of his life.

Who was the object of his affections, this eloquent and prudent correspondent? In my mind I sifted through all the Madeleines I was aware of at the French court in the relevant years. One had only been at court for a few years before she died, very young, and had never married. Another was married, but she would have been around sixty in the 1570s. Another Madeleine at the French court was Madeleine de la Fère. She'd been a peripheral part of Catherine de' Medici's circle, although she had belonged to a younger generation. A definite possibility.

I pulled up a file on my computer with all the women in the Queen's immediate and not so immediate circle and found a brief description of Madeleine de la Fère's life, taken from a 1960s reference book.

Madeleine de la Fère, Countess of Lendrienne (1551-1580).
Born in Poitou, the only child of Baron Antoine and Baroness

Catherine de la Fère. Tutored at home in cosmographic knowledge, geography, and philosophy, she grew up to be a great intellectual and married the distinguished Nicolas, Count of Lendrienne, twenty years her senior. A patron of artists and writers, she was said to have written lyric poems, none of which are extant. De la Fère knew Latin and Greek. Ten erudite noblewomen whom poets compared with muses took part in her salon, during which discussion was infused with neo-Platonic philosophy. Ronsard and Du Bellay dedicated poems to her. De la Fère died in 1580.

She was twenty-nine when she died in 1580. The year before Tommaso died at thirty-one.

She was a twenty-one-year-old widow at the time of the St Bartholomew's Day Massacre, when she first referred to Tommaso as her friend.

I read her elegant letters over again, correcting inconsistencies in my translation. She'd refused Tommaso, at least while her husband was still alive, in 1569. I didn't know when her husband had died but could find that information.

The obvious connection between these two people was affecting. A secret, cross-confessional relationship. They'd both died at what would have been considered a relatively young age.

But there was no tie-in with the emerald, and I had now lost an entire day of work. I turned on the computer in the hallway and sent an email off to the latest email address, explaining that I had not gone to the archive as the Palazzo had been inaccessible for the day due to a family occasion. I wasn't expecting to receive a response, but one came through: "No worries. R." I had stopped writing back whenever I heard from Rose, which was every five or six days, as I knew that whatever I sent would bounce back, with no forwarding address.

But after I shut down the computer, I powered it back up. It was past midnight and everyone in the house was asleep. "Love to you, R," I wrote to the email address I'd been instructed to use for my next email.

Like all the other emails it bounced back. But I knew someone would see it. I hoped that someone would be Rose.

Marta had left me dinner on a covered plate, but I put the plate in the refrigerator, and poured myself a glass of wine instead. I drank it slowly. It took me a while to calm down.

CHAPTER EIGHT

As I approached the Palazzo Falcone at ten on Monday morning, Niccolò was on the front steps holding a bouquet of white flowers. It had been drizzling but he looked perfectly dry, in a blue velvet blazer, the waves of his hair as ever fixed in place.

"I hope you like lilies," he said, handing me the heavy bouquet as I walked up the steps.

"Thanks," I said. "They're gorgeous. What's the occasion?" They smelled sweet, with a tinge of decay.

"Beautiful flowers for a beautiful woman," he said, then he took the flowers back and opened one flap of my coat, scrutinizing my clothes. I had dressed for warmth that morning as I did every day, today in a fraying sweater and wool pants. I held my bag close to me under my arm, hoping he wouldn't feel the outlines of the box. He narrowed one eye and I sucked in my breath.

"I was thinking. We should change your wardrobe." When I did not respond, he gave the flowers back to me. "Severina . . . is excited to see you. She asked me to bring you to her room."

"I'd love to see Severina, but I have a lot of work today. Perhaps, tomorrow?"

"She canceled her trip to London, I believe. She'll be insulted if we don't go see her. It won't take long. I have left you alone to work undisturbed since Staglieno, haven't I?"

"Yes," I said. "But I'm leaving soon for Florence."

"It would be impolite to remind you, *cara*, that I am the one who arranged for you to work in our library, so I won't. But you know that Severina's room is in the oldest part of our palazzo, the tower," he said. "No one from outside our family has ever seen this section. Consider it research." He turned and started walking. We climbed one flight of stairs and then another and even if I had been in that part of the palazzo before I would have been lost.

The next staircase was narrower than the others, with steep steps that spiraled up as we ascended. I had to stop and catch my breath. Niccolò stepped down, lifting the bouquet from my arms. "I apologize," he said, "I should have carried this for you. We are close, *bella* Isabella."

After a few more times around the spiral, we arrived at a partially opened door so tall and thick it looked like it would require three strong men to open it. The door behind the brand-new handle looked carved out and painted over. Niccolò called softly, "*Ci siamo, cara.*" He placed the bouquet in my arms.

As we entered Severina walked out from an anteroom crowded with piles of fabric and folded up bundles stacked on top of each other. A tawny fur shawl, curled up like a small animal, lay on the four-poster bed draped in a canopy of heavy, pink silk. Severina was dressed in a navy-velvet robe and matching slippers embellished with ostrich feathers. Her ringlets bobbed around her face, and her lips were covered in a fresh coat of burgundy.

"Oh, those flowers! Thank you, Isabel! How did you, oh! They're not for me, are they? Oh! Nico gave them to *you*. How nice!"

The grey stone walls of Severina's room had only narrow slits for windows, which allowed only a small amount of natural light in, although the drapery—swathes of cream-colored silk—was pushed back. A white wool carpet edged up to the fireplace, where only ashes remained. Several bright pashminas were thrown over the back of a silk couch. With all those fabrics, a door I couldn't open myself, and no window to escape through, I would be too frightened to sleep here, even without a fire burning in the fireplace.

Above the mantelpiece was a painting of a woman in a pink silk dress worn off the shoulder with gloves and a matching bonnet. The stern expression conveyed by her amber eyes and thin, beige mouth was at odds with her frilly attire. In one hand she gripped a cluster of pink carnations, which blended into the folds of her dress. In the other hand she held a cane. Around her neck were long gold chains connected to a red-stoned brooch. I walked over and laid my bouquet of flowers on the mantelpiece. As I began reading the inscription underneath, Severina said, "Severina Falcone, my great-grandmother, in 1883. I was named for her." She walked over and kissed me on both cheeks. "How nice to see you, Isabel. Nico said you'd agreed to play our silly game."

"What game?" I asked, but she had turned away.

"You wait outside," she told her brother, and pushed him out. "Or better yet, come back in a couple hours. Aren't you going to a meeting? I need some girl time with Isabel."

"Whatever you wish, *sorellina*. I'll be back in two hours. *A dopo*," he said, kissing her and bowing as he left the room.

After we could no longer hear him clomping down the stairs Severina locked the door and put on jazz music, turning up the volume.

"Thank you for your email. And for writing it in a sort of code that I could understand but anyone else could not. As I said, I would prefer no one else know about the letters for now. How far did you read? *Dimmi tutto*," she said.

"I transcribed all of them, and translated them into English, for you."

"All six?" she asked. "I am appreciative. And I hope it will be useful for you," she said.

"I'm not sure," I said. "They're love letters."

"*Davvero?*"

"They appear to detail a love affair between Tommaso Falcone and Madeleine de la Fère, a French Protestant noblewoman. We'd have to look at a family tree to see how you are related to Tommaso."

"*Wow,*" she said, burgundy lips closing in an "O" shape. "Tommaso is my father's name. It's an old family name."

"Until now I've been focusing on Tommaso's older brother, Federico, who was close to Queen Catherine de' Medici, the Italian widow of French King Henri II. She was de facto ruler of France for thirty years."

"Caterina, *sì,*" she nodded. "She was the one who the professor told about."

"Caterina sent Federico and Tommaso to the Americas. But Tommaso's relationship with Madeleine was news to me, and I think unknown to history. Why don't you read through my translations, and if you have questions I'll try to answer them."

"*Grazie mille,*" she said.

I opened my bag and pulled out the box with the original letters and my transcriptions on top, which I had printed out at Marta's house.

I watched Severina's face change as she read through the pages. By the time she had finished a teary veil covered her eyes.

"*Mi mancano le parole.* I have no words. Thank you—thank you!" She hugged me. "My nonna would be so happy to know that I have read these letters. I will tell my father," she sighed as I passed the box to her and watched her put it in a cupboard behind a curtain. "But will this help your research? Any time you need to look at them again, it is not a problem."

"I wanted to ask your permission to keep the electronic files, the copies of the letters that I typed out, not images of the actual letters, although if they end up pertaining to my research, I'd ask for those, too. But if you'd prefer me not to have them, I'll delete them from my computer."

She took a breath in and out. *"Certo, cara!* That is fine. I hope they make it into your book. And listen. There is something else. I did not have time to tell you the full story the other day. The box of letters was found during a restoration of our family chapel outside the city. They restored the chapel during my nonna's lifetime, but it was her father, the husband of the woman over the fireplace, who gave the box to her. My nonna was a double Falcone. She was born a Falcone, and she married her cousin, who shared the name."

"I'll have to look at a more recent family tree," I said. "Where is the chapel? Do you know whose tombs are there? And which tomb the letters were found in?"

"The chapel is located in a village on the coast, an hour north of Genoa. The reason I tell you is that with the letters my nonna gave me was a small portrait, which I believe also came from the chapel."

She handed me a plastic folder. Between two sheets of what I hoped was acid-free paper was a round portrait miniature painted on vellum, the size of a large orange, of a woman in sixteenth-century dress. The vellum was in good condition, and the woman was intricately depicted, with tiny brushstrokes. The portrait ended just below the woman's waist. She had honey-colored hair, worn in a bun, crinkled curls billowing over her forehead. She had deep hazel eyes and thin lips. Her cream-colored dress had a pattern on the bodice, which appeared to be embroidered with pearls. A high collar concealed her long neck. Gauzy sleeves, typical of the period, puffed out over her shoulders. Around her neck she wore a gold chain on which hung a large, faceted green stone set into gold: an emerald.

"What do you think?" Severina asked.

Rose had said not to mention the emerald, so I didn't, although the green stone was beaming at me like a high-wattage headlight. "Miniature portraits were often exchanged in advance of prospective marriages at the time. The artist may be François Clouet, who painted the royals and nobles at the French court. Or, more likely, one of his pupils. She is an important woman."

"Who is she? A Falcone?" she asked.

"She could be. Or maybe the woman described in the letters, Madeleine, who had a love affair with Tommaso Falcone and eventually married him, from what I've gleaned so far."

"Oh! In this moment, I remembered one more thing. Found together with these items in the family tomb was a small chest containing a dress, a woman's dress. The dress was among the things my grandma gave to me. Isn't that peculiar? I have it somewhere."

"What does the dress look like?"

"I'll have to find it. It was very dusty, and crinkled and grey, but well conserved. I did not want to allow it to get more dusty, so I put it in another container somewhere. She gave it to me in a box that was falling apart. I don't know how old it is."

Someone knocked. *"Pronte?"* It was Niccolò. Severina put the portrait in the folder and into her cupboard before opening the door a few inches.

"Nico!" Severina said. He pushed past her, carrying a tray with a teapot and cups, and set the tray down on the dresser.

"I didn't want to miss anything. Did I?" He looked around the room.

"Eh! Go back in the hall and I'll let you know when we're ready. *Dai.* Go!"

Severina turned to me and tilted her head to one side. "It's cold in here, isn't it? Oh! The fire is out! Let's warm ourselves with this tea Nico made for us." She went over to the dresser and poured the contents of the pot into a mug and said, "Oh! It's hot chocolate! My favorite!" She handed the mug to me, handle first. "Try it. It has peppermint in it," she said. I had a sip, then another. The peppermint taste was strong and astringent.

She took the mug.

"Isabel, how do you feel about wearing a corset?" she asked, and winked at me as if to say, please play along. "I think a corset would suit your curves."

"I feel fine about corsets, but I've got to get back to work—"

"—Here, try this one. I'll lace up the back for you." Severina went into her closet and came out with a bundle of ivory and pink lace and ribbons and passed it to me. I turned my back to her as I undressed, folding my clothes on the golden coverlet, aware that Niccolò was just outside. I arranged the corset around the front of my body and held it tight against my waist. It smelled faintly of smoke and lilies. "Take everything off," she said, when she saw I was still wearing my bra. After I did, she tied the strings tightly. In the mirror I could see my now hourglass shape, one that Rose had naturally.

"It's perfect for you!" She passed me a full petticoat, which I stepped into, and a velvet skirt. "Take off those pants!" she said.

"Now, some makeup!" She directed me over to a bench in front of a circular mirror. "Close your eyes." She brushed shadow on my eyelids, drew dramatic lines around my eyes, and applied a thick layer of lipstick on my lips, the same burgundy she was wearing. Finally, she tickled blush across my cheeks. "You have handsome bones," she said, and leaned over and kissed me quickly and softly on the lips.

I went over to the bed where I had piled my clothes and threw my wool scarf over my shoulders.

"You look amazing!" she said.

I drank some more hot chocolate.

Severina took off her slippers and put them on my feet. Then she walked to the door and signaled for Niccolò to come in. I shrugged my scarf back, letting it settle in the crooks of my arms. He leaned against the door as he looked at me. Then he nodded at the painting of Severina the Elder on the wall. "Dressed as you are now, you could be sisters," he said.

"We still have her cane downstairs," Severina said. "The one she is holding in the portrait. And the pink dress is in my closet. We Falcone were in the textile business and silk trade, as you know. I have several historical dresses that you have to see!"

Niccolò took one step so he was between me and Severina. He placed two warm fingertips on a patch of skin near my shoulder and moved them along my collarbone until he reached my throat. As he let his middle finger rest in the hollow where my collarbones met, he dropped his voice, "Would you like to see our cane collection?" The base of my neck was pulsating.

Severina moved around him and stood close to me. She was now wearing a corset, too. Niccolò murmured something, and I looked up into the mirror at the three of us. We could have been the subjects of a portrait from another time. It was so warm. I felt relaxed and woozy, off kilter. I reached over to Niccolò to balance myself. He leaned in. "*Dio mio . . .*"

A loud alarm started clanging. Severina pushed away and ran around the bed and switched it off.

"Shit," said Niccolò, pulling out his phone.

"I have to leave," said Severina, putting on a shirt.

"I, I really need to get to work," I said. My mouth felt funny. I pulled the scarf up around me. "Was there something in the hot chocolate?" I asked.

"Nico, did you put grappa in our hot chocolate? *Che stronzo!*"

He shrugged. "Only a little. A *caffè corretto.*"

"More like *caffè corotto.* Sorry, Isabel. It will wear off." She was fully dressed now. "Where is my phone?" she said, going back into the closet where all the fabrics were. "*Andiamo*, let's go," said Niccolò, tapping his foot. I scooped up my clothes and shoes, wrapped the scarf around my chest, and followed him downstairs, my petticoat swishing. As I moved past him through the door to the library, he touched my shoulder. His voice was soft again. "You look sexy in those clothes."

He followed me into the library, knelt down, and reached for the secret key under the desk. He unlocked the cabinet, and handed me the box I'd been working on, the last one.

Then he stepped over to an array of canes in a brass stand that I hadn't noticed. "Are those the canes you were talking about?" I asked.

He brought a wooden stick with an ivory handle over to the table and handed it to me. "The collection has been in my family for one hundred and fifty years. In the nineteenth century canes were ornaments that signified status and wealth. Power," he said, as I ran my fingers over the veiny ivory and the dark, polished wood. He went back and pulled out another cane, which he placed on the table. "This one is my favorite," he said.

I studied the detailed engraving on the handle, in the shape of a skull. "Twist the handle," he said; so I did, and it opened. "There's a knife hidden inside, isn't that marvelous?" He flipped the cane upside down and a dagger slid out onto the desk.

"Ingenious," I said, picking up the small knife.

He perched on the edge of the table and said, "Canes were used to conceal many things, including poison." He took his phone out of his pocket and scrolled through it briefly. "You can work here for a while—no one will disturb us, disturb you. My parents aren't due back until next week."

"Thanks so much, Niccolò," I said. "If I can work two long days, I know I'll finish." I untied the box. He stood up and bent over, lowering his head down to mine. I thought he was going to kiss me but instead he lifted my hair and took one of my earlobes in his teeth, gradually increasing the pressure on it until I cried out. He turned and left in one fluid motion, without saying goodbye, and locked me in.

I couldn't sort out my feelings. I was a little afraid of him, but at the same time I wished he hadn't left. I reached up and touched my ear, and then I hit the table. I pulled the scarf around me, too cold to change my clothes.

I was feeling very dizzy. In the bathroom I filled a water bottle in the sink and drank the whole thing. Back at the table I pushed the cane and the knife aside and opened the box. I sifted through the first twenty or so pages, through several long-winded marriage contracts and information about dowries. I skimmed three more wills, but there was nothing about the emerald. I had to get through the rest.

I drank some more water, and then picked up a fourth will dated 1581. Studying the first few lines of the top page I tried to figure out whose will it was. The notary had terrible handwriting. It was Tommaso's will, drawn up "on the fifth day of April 1581." Months before his death. I read through it quickly. Tommaso had left all of his possessions to his cousin, Filippo, in Genoa, the eldest son of Pierfrancesco, except for an annual stipend to a convent in Lisbon. Why had he not left anything to Federico or his immediate family? April 5. Federico would have just died.

In the will there was no mention of a wife, nor children. What of his brothers, sisters, nieces, nephews? Tommaso's will did not contain any mentions of the saints, an omission usually associated with Protestant wills. So, he had never married Madeleine. Then I remembered. She had died in 1580. The will was relatively short. The emerald was not listed among his possessions.

Underneath the will was a piece of paper that was not old. I turned it over. A note written in black, neat letters. In English.

> *N,*
>> *Last night was fun.*
>> *Yours,*
>> *R.*

R?

I leafed through the rest of the documents. Anything dated after 1581 I wasn't interested in. Toward the bottom of the box, I found one more note folded inside a seventeenth-century contract.

"My darling Nicky,

I want you to know I meant every word of what I said. Doesn't it mean anything that I broke off my engagement because I fell for you? When you act cold and dismissive it hurts my feelings.

When can we talk? Not over the phone, in person. We can figure out when to meet again . . . you know where . . . same time, same place! I'm almost finished (I can hear you laughing, but I'm serious this time!) and then . . . you'll see. After I publish my book, everything will be different. In the meantime, just know that I love you. Only you.

Ever your Rosa."

Two notes from Rose to Niccolò.

As I read the note for the third time, I heard the key click in the door. I shifted sideways in my chair, folded the note, tucked it into my cleavage, and pulled the scarf around me. As Niccolò walked in I dropped the other note inside the box, blank side up.

He plunked down next to me. "Ciao, *bellissima*. How about dinner tonight at a new place I'd like to take you? You can wear this outfit and heads will turn."

"Sure, Niccolò. That would be great."

"So agreeable! What's up? You look like a cat that swallowed a mouse. Find anything good?"

I leaned back and shook my head. "Not much. Was just reading through a will."

"Hmmm. Really? You have that slightly panicked look on your face that Severina gets when she lies. What did you find?"

"Seriously, nothing."

"At first you seemed innocent," he said, moving his face close to mine. I felt his breath on my neck. "But now I understand. You don't reveal your true self to the world. I suspect that you have things to hide. Things you've done? Things you like to do? You can tell me. Anything."

My heart was thumping. I said nothing.

"Okay," he said. "Let's start with me. I'm completely open. Would you like to know something? What would you like to know? Ask me."

"What about Rose, who worked here in the archives?"

Niccolò pulled his arm away, squeezed his hands together and stood up.

"What business is that of yours?" he said, raising his voice.

"Nothing, it's just . . . she was here. It's weird you never, we never discussed her."

"What do you know about her?" he said with a little sneer.

"She was my friend. She disappeared. I'd like to find out what happened to her. Severina said—"

"—You've talked with Severina about her? What did she say?"

"Severina said that you went out with Rose. And that Rose told her she was in some sort of trouble."

"Rosa did tell me this, yes. But as usual, she did not tell me the entire story. This was last year, I assumed she went back to the university. You said she disappeared. When?"

"A couple months ago. Was she in love with you? Were you in love with her? Are you still in love with her?"

"In love with her? What are you talking about?"

"You said I could ask you anything!"

He scowled, then his face relaxed, and he crossed his arms and lowered his voice. "She was here in the archive. Yes, I was with her for a time. But I never loved her. She had . . . problems." He tapped his temple twice with his index finger.

"What do you mean?"

"She was a manipulative person. Everyone loved her because she was beautiful, intelligent. Charismatic. She knew so much about history and about my family. It was a pleasure to speak to her about any topic. She bewitched Severina and our whole family, even my mother, into . . . into . . ."

"Into?"

He walked to the window and looked out. "I fell under her spell. Soon after she arrived . . . we became involved. After she'd been here more than a month, six weeks maybe, a rare book dealer came to the palazzo. A few years older than I am. James was his name. James something. Harris? Yes, that was it. James Harris was interested in our documents. He met with my mother to talk about our archive. I could see that he was . . . appealing to women.

"A week or so after I met him, I saw him on the street, far from here. With Rose. They were holding hands. I surprised them, said I would tell my mother. My mother was furious. I don't know what she said to him, but she told Rose she could no longer work here. And then . . . some weeks later . . . the theft.

"After we advertised the reward, a French woman wrote that she had Falcone papers, very old ones. My mother had me call her and demand the return of the stolen documents, but this woman said they were not our documents. I thought it might be Rose, you see, but it was not."

"Do you know who the woman was?" He turned back to me and sat down on the table.

"I called her, but she never answered her phone."

"I'd like to contact her, if possible."

"I have no idea how to reach her, Isabel. I'm only telling you, so you know I'm telling you everything I know about Rose." He reached out and took my hand.

"When you said Rose was manipulative, what did you mean?"

"It's more that she was strange. And she had a dark side."

"Dark side?"

"A cruel sense of humor. She made fun of people behind their backs, she asked me to do things for her. And things to her."

"What things?"

"I did whatever she wanted. I was infatuated with her." He let go of my hand and tipped back in his chair. "She was into rough sex. She used to beg me to tie her up, to hit her with the cane. But more than that, after all that . . . well." He let the chair down with a thud. "You say she is your friend. You should know that the documents were not the only things stolen. I'm not saying she stole them, but the timing is suspect, isn't it?"

"What do you mean? And what else got stolen?"

"The palazzo was . . . not exactly ransacked, but things were damaged. Our suit of armor, the one you saw in the dining room, was broken apart. We had to hire a restorer to piece it together. The door to Sevi's room was damaged, but the intruder was unable to get in. And not only here in the palazzo. That same week two of our family chapels were broken into, and several family monuments were . . . desecrated. The whole situation was a disgrace for my family."

He moved to the chair next to mine, so close our legs were touching. "What about you, mystery lady? What do you like?" He took hold of my left shoulder and kissed my neck, scraping it with his teeth. The scarf fell down, off my shoulders.

"What's this?" he asked, looking at the piece of paper sticking out of the corset. He tossed it onto the desk as he stood up and put his hands on either side of my head. In a quiet voice he said, "Naughty girl! Were you trying to steal from our archive?" He raised his voice. "That is a crime!"

At first I thought he was kidding, but then he grabbed my arms and pulled me up from the chair and forced me facedown on the table, ramming his elbow into my back. I tried to stand but he pulled my hands behind my back and held my wrists in one hand, pushing me back down with the other. I cried out and he released the hand on my back, but only to reach for something, the string next to the document, which he used to tie my hands together.

"Get off me!" I yelled. The room was spinning, but not so much that I couldn't see him grab the knife, which was lying in front of me. I struggled and kicked my legs out against him, but he was very strong. He hiked the skirt and petticoat up, still pressing down on my back with his elbow, and yanked my underwear down.

"No!" I said, trying to scream. "NO!"

"Go ahead and scream," he said. "Severina's gone and Emiliano doesn't care." I whimpered and held my breath.

"Don't fucking move." He put down the knife and slid his hand roughly from my neck to the middle of my back as he positioned himself behind me. I heard him unbuckle his belt, felt the cold metal brush my skin. "You want this, don't you?"

There was a knock on the door.

"Nico? Isabel? Are you in there?" It was Severina. Niccolò relaxed his grip. "Yes, Sevi, we're here." He picked up the knife again and cut the string around my hands, then reached over to the cane and slipped the blade inside the handle.

CHAPTER NINE

Severina banged on the door and wiggled the doorknob. "What are you guys doing in there?" she yelled, even though we could barely hear her. "Why is the door locked?"

Niccolò buckled his belt as he walked to the door. He opened it just a crack, through which I could see half of Severina, in a grey suit.

I opened my mouth, "Sev . . ." was all I could manage before Niccolò spoke.

"Ciao, *cara*. I was just showing Izzie some private documents."

"Private documents, eh? I haven't heard *that* one before." Severina laughed.

"Yes, truly! Isabel's finishing up with the old papers, and I wanted to show her this other stuff while my mom is away. We didn't want Emiliano to discover us."

My arms and my legs were shaking, and I felt very cold. I stretched the scarf out and wrapped it around me. I had bitten my tongue, and could taste blood in my mouth.

"Okay, Nico," Severina said, but then leaned to the side, looking into the room. We made eye contact. "Well, you guys enjoy, and be careful." She winked. "See you when I get back? Are you going to the osteria tonight?"

I stood up and walked to the door, smoothing the velvet skirt. "Actually Severina, I'll leave with you. My host family is making me a farewell dinner."

"So early?"

"They're preparing some traditional dishes. I need to. Help them. I'll walk out with you."

"That's fine," Severina said.

"I'll join you," said Niccolò, lacing his arm through mine, squeezing it. I wriggled away from him.

"Let me get my notebooks," I said.

"We'll wait for you in the hall," said Severina.

"I can help you," Niccolò offered.

"I'm fine," I said. They both stayed in the room, watching me. I quickly put the letters back in their original folders, and when Severina whispered something to Niccolò I slipped Rose's two notes back inside one of the contracts. I put the top on the box but couldn't tie it, since the string had been cut. Niccolò grunted as he picked up the box.

"Severina, do you mind if I run upstairs to your room and change back into my clothes quickly?"

"You can borrow those things for now, Isabel. Just bring them with you when you come tomorrow. Or next week is fine."

Over his shoulder Niccolò said, "I think she should leave the corset here."

"I'll be back tomorrow," I said.

"Wouldn't want it to get misplaced," he continued. "Then again, Florence is very close. Only an hour or two by train?"

"I can change now, in here," I said. "Will you wait for me, Severina?"

Severina affectionately stroked Niccolò's cheek. Then she turned to me. "Yes, whatever you like. But be quick, please, because I'm late already." They left the room, but I couldn't get out of the corset by myself. I opened the door a couple inches and said, "I need you to untie me, Severina."

"I can do it," Niccolò said, but Severina was ahead of him, and she pushed into the room. I tried, but I couldn't get the door to click shut.

As she loosened the tight strings, she must have felt me shaking.

"Are you okay?" she asked, putting her hand on my shoulder.

At her touch I flinched and brushed away a tear with the back of my hand.

"Yeah. Totally fine," I said, my voice cracking.

"You sure?"

"He . . . I . . ." I said, swallowing hard, trying to keep it together.

She bent over me and whispered in my ear. "He seems like he's this big *donnaiuolo*, a ladies' man," she said. "But he's not," she said. "He has a good heart. Women have broken it over the years. Go easy on him."

"No," I said, "it's not that. It's—"

"—What's taking so long?" Niccolò shouted from the hallway.

I lifted my head and looked at the ceiling so the tears would stay in my eyes. "Isabel," she said. "Ignore Beth. Nico's a *mammone*, a mamma's boy. But more importantly, I am so excited about the love letters, I can't stop thinking about them. Let's meet outside the palazzo for a coffee tomorrow, okay? And maybe I come visit you in Scotland so we have time away from my crazy family, mmh?" She put her arm around me and then let go.

I finished putting on my clothes and we left the room holding hands.

We passed Niccolò and I moved ahead of Severina and started down the first of the staircases, clutching the bannister and watching my feet so as not to lose my balance. Severina followed behind me, and I was hyperaware of the sound of her high heels. When we finally exited the palazzo, I willed myself to stand up straight.

"I'll walk with you, Severina," I said.

"But we're going in opposite directions! Campopisano is that way!" She stretched out her arm and pointed. "You'd be late for the cooking lesson."

"No, I just . . ."

"I'm so late I should run there. I shouldn't have worn heels." She laughed. "*A domani!*" She started clattering down the steps and I took off without looking back, gripping my bag against my body and beginning to run.

After a couple of streets, I stopped running. Soon Niccolò caught up to me. He put his hand on my shoulder, but I knocked it off. "Get away from me," I yelled in a low voice.

He maneuvered in front of me, blocking my path. He made a puppy-dog frown as he walked backward. I pushed him out of the way and kept going.

"Oh come *on*," Niccolò said. "It was a joke. I wasn't actually going to do anything. I was only teasing you. Teaching you a little lesson. Didn't you think it was fun?"

I wrapped my coat tightly around my body and walked faster.

"I *said* I wasn't going to do anything," he repeated, keeping my pace.

I stopped, turned, and broke into a run, down the street in the opposite direction. As I followed a curving part of the street, I remembered the pepper spray Marta had given me. I found it in my pocket, stopped, and turned around. No Niccolò.

I followed a different route to Campopisano, half-running, but it was drizzling, and I skidded on some wet pavement. The streets glowed shiny black, slick, glimmering and grotesque at the same time. I just stood there. After a minute my whole body was shaking again, and I began sobbing. My face and clothes were soaked. I wrapped my arms around myself and started walking. Soon the tears subsided, replaced by fury.

When I arrived, no one was home. I dropped my coat on the floor upstairs and went to take a shower. Waves of nausea and vertigo ran through me. I sat down on the white-and-black tile bathroom floor. The spinning got worse, so I crawled to the toilet and vomited. When I felt strong enough to stand, I turned the dial in the shower to the hottest setting and waited until steam filled the room. I stripped off my clothes, stepped in, and let the scalding water wash over my body for several minutes, until my skin was purple and raw. I toweled off, and in the bedroom pulled on a pair of leggings, a turtleneck, and the warmest sweater I had. I wrapped my wet hair in a towel, then climbed into bed under the covers, where I started to shiver again.

I woke to the sound of the front door closing. I crept out of bed, picked up my coat and searched the pockets until I found the pepper spray. I pointed it at the door, my finger on the spray button. Then I heard Marta's voice.

"Isabel? Are you here?"

After a few seconds I called back down. "Yes. I'm upstairs!" I pulled the towel off my head, brushed my damp hair back, and tied it into a ponytail. Then I went downstairs. Marta and Alessandra were in the kitchen standing at the counter. I went over and took Marta's hand and held it, smiling. "I'm so glad to see you," I said.

Marta studied my face. She bent down and whispered to Alessandra, who turned to me and said, "I have to start my homework now, Isabel. We will see you later."

"*Che c'è*, Isabel?" Marta asked when Alessandra was upstairs. She put her arm around me and guided me to the table.

"I'm okay, I'm okay," I said, biting down on my lip. Tears began streaming down my face. I brushed them away with my fingers, then my wrists.

"What happened?" she asked.

"I . . . went to the palazzo to work. I . . . he. He used to lock me in the room and today he . . ."

"Who? Who locked you in what room?"

"Niccolò. The library. To protect me. Because of the theft. And because the Contessa didn't want me there. But he let me in and showed me documents. I needed to read them and was grateful. I found a note from my friend, but he thought I was trying to steal, and got very angry. He pushed me on the desk, and tied my hands, and he . . . he . . ."

Marta grimaced and leaned in toward me. "What did he do to you?" she asked in a quiet voice with staccato syllables.

"I felt so helpless. There was nothing I could do! I fought him . . ."

"What did he do to you, Isabel?" she asked again.

"Nothing, but only because Severina knocked on the door."

"It doesn't sound like nothing. He violated you!" She gently stroked my back.

"It would have been worse if Severina hadn't come in."

"It was wrong what he did! It was criminal." She hugged me and I sobbed into her shoulder. "You must not go back there."

"I have to. I still need to go over a few last things."

Alessandra stomped down the stairs and stood in the doorway. "Mamma, can you help me?" she asked.

"*Arrivo, amore*," said Marta. "Isabel is leaving us soon." She put her arm around me and pulled me close.

"Oh no! You will miss us," chimed in Alessandra.

"She means she will miss you," Marta said, correcting her daughter's error.

"Alessandra, you weren't wrong. I will miss you, all of you," I said, looking at Marta, "very much." Alessandra hugged me, then ran upstairs. Luigi, dressed in his lab coat, entered the kitchen.

"Isabel, how nice to see you here," he said.

Marta turned to her husband, "Can you go help Alessandra with her homework?"

"*Certo*," he said. As he walked toward the stairs I turned to Marta.

"You're right," I said. "I can't go back to the palazzo. I'll go to Florence a few days early." I looked at her. "I don't know how to thank you for everything you've done for me. I want to return your kindness. All of you are welcome to visit me in Scotland."

We hugged again. Her hair smelled like the citrus-scented shampoo that I used in the shower, and it soothed me. Marta gave me a bottle of homemade limoncello just before I left the next day.

CHAPTER TEN

As we approached Florence, I glanced out the train window at the rolling hills of Tuscany. The ride was quick, but my neck hurt, and I had a bruise on the underside of one of my ribs, and the pain reminded me of getting slammed down on the table every time I inhaled even a small breath.

I had rented an apartment in town, courtesy of my stipend, and I'd written to the owner, who didn't mind me arriving early. Number twenty-three *nero*, on the via Guicciardini, was a modern low-rise like its neighbors, which had risen up where older buildings had been bombed away during World War II. I punched in the code for the main door and found the keys in the mailbox. The apartment was on the second floor. After putting my things away, I went to a pizzeria and ate a slice as I wrote out everything I needed to see and do. Back at the apartment I worked on my conference paper until I fell asleep, but was woken up every hour by the ringing of bells from nearby Santa Felicità.

At 8:30 A.M. I walked to the Archivio di Stato, stopping often to study my map, placed inside yesterday's *La Repubblica*. I walked along the river until I reached an intersection and crossed onto the sidewalk along the broad Viale della Giovine Italia.

With its blackened cinder block facade and pigeon's-blood-colored staircases visible from the outside, the Archivio di Stato looked like an enormous digestive system, the ugliest building I'd ever seen in Italy. Inside two archivists behind a window instructed me to take the elevator upstairs. I pressed the button.

"*Deve insistere!*" called out one of the women. Okay, I insist, I said, pressing the button again and again until the door shook open.

In the high-ceilinged reading room, archivists wearing white lab coats and serious expressions walked back and forth between the rows of scholars. I entered an annex where, I was informed, the *funzionario* would issue my ID. I approached a man with a fluffy moustache, seated in front of a circa 1984 computer.

I greeted him in Italian and produced Endicott's letter of recommendation. He gestured for me to sit across from him. Leaning in he spoke slowly. "What are you researching?"

I told him that my dissertation focused on the Falcone family. His hands arched up into a prayer gesture.

"*Dottoressa! L'Americana! Lo sapevo.* I knew you would come back . . ."

I decided to play along. "*Certo,*" I said, "*Dottore.*"

He looked at my letter and slowly typed, poking at the keyboard. "Henley? *Ti sei sposata?*" He peeked away, and after he'd printed out the card, he gave it to me and said, "*Ben tornata!*"

"*Grazie, Dottore,*" I said.

I sneezed twice, which I sometimes did when anxious. I realized what he had said. "*Rohza,*" he'd said. Rosa, Italian for Rose. Apparently, he had mistaken me for Rose.

I sat down at a computer terminal, but before it could boot up, I felt someone tap me on the shoulder, a young woman who politely reminded me that purses were not allowed in the reading room. She directed me to an ill-lit locker room. Back at the computer, I created a username and password: Falcone.

The first items on my list were the five Croci account books.

Only three items could be requested per day, so I placed a request for volumes one, two, and three. They wouldn't arrive for another two hours, so I went out to an electronics store, bought their cheapest laptop, and took it to an internet café to configure it before returning.

At the circulation desk the archivist, Dottoressa Bruni, reviewed my request. On the carrels behind her were at least thirty manuscripts, each a different size, shape, and age, most of them in paper boxes and tied up with orange string, like unusual gifts.

She passed me a folio-sized account book, nearly three feet tall and two feet wide. I carried the heavy book to the closest desk and dropped it as I was setting it down. It landed with a boom. I looked around and mouthed, "Sorry!" to everyone who had looked up. Thick clumps of caked-on dirt had fallen onto the desk and dust poofed up, coating my face and arms and chest. No scholar had consulted these books in quite some time. I coughed and brushed myself off.

The book was too large to fit on a stand, so I opened it on the table and flipped through the first ten of the hundreds-of-pages-long book. Every page contained neatly written entries in black ink. The writing was Italian, but at first glance it looked like an unrecognizable alphabet. I had to ease myself into reading the entries.

I went to the end. The last page dealt with the year 1520, which was too early for my purposes. The front cover flopped shut, and I brought it back to the circulation desk.

"*Già finita?*" asked Dottoressa Bruni.

The second book ended with entries in 1530, and the third book covered 1530 through 1550. I needed the last two volumes. My manuscript quota was up for the day, but I convinced Dottoressa Bruni to let me order them when I told her I was only in Florence for a short time.

While waiting in the locker room, I installed more programs on my computer. I wasn't able to access the archive's catalogues, so I went back upstairs and signed in on a computer. I started cross-checking the Archivio di Stato references with Rose's bibliography.

There were at least fifteen items that mentioned the Falcone but weren't on Rose's list. Had she seen them but not listed them because she believed they wouldn't be relevant to the emerald search? I would have to look at all the volumes in the collection that had to do with the Falcone, but I would start with the ones on Rose's list.

When I saw the fourth book being wheeled to the circulation desk, I went up to retrieve it. I started going through the volume, which covered the early 1560s, searching for Federico's name. I would not find Catherine de' Medici here, since the Croci were allied with Catherine's cousin, Cosimo de' Medici, Duke of Tuscany, whom Catherine was fighting with. The Duchy of Tuscany was a vassal state of Spain in those years, further complicating Catherine's interactions with her cousin.

About halfway in, I found my first mention of Federico.

On my new laptop I began to type out the relevant entry as written:

Dare

Federico Falcone, of Genoa, on 28 June, is debited 300 scudi d'oro, paid in cash to _____ towards the 800 scudi d'oro our Iacopo Filli ordered us to pay him [Falcone] so that he could go and find _____ in the new land. Debited to Expenditures, f. 82 credited to the Cash account herein, f. 210

And on 2 July, 250 scudi, paid in cash to _____ _____

for the balance of the above mentioned 300 scudi. Debited to expenditures, f. 82.

Avere

This side was blank. Federico had not repaid his debt.

I began typing a summary, which I planned to email to William.

"Since Federico's voyages to the Americas were not fully funded by the French monarchy, he needed to seek support elsewhere. This entry identifies the Croci as Federico's main financial backers. Via his first marriage to Ginevra de' Croci, Federico was able to secure key support. The account book indicates Federico didn't repay his debts to the Croci."

I withdrew my hands from the keyboard. Perhaps he had given the emerald to the Croci to pay off his debt, and it was recorded elsewhere? Or not recorded at all? 1000 scudi was a significant sum in the 1560s, enough to fund a voyage.

> Dear William, I hope this message finds you well! My research trip in Italy has been productive. In Genoa I found intriguing documents providing evidence of a love affair between Tommaso Falcone and a French noblewoman, and more pertinent to my dissertation, Tommaso Falcone's will.
>
> It's my first day here in Florence. So far, I've found records of the Florentine bankers who financed Federico's first and possibly second voyage to the Americas, the Croci family. Federico's first wife was Ginevra de' Croci. Can't wait to discuss. See you at the conference!

I attached the file with my summary and sent it to the email address as well, explaining that I had gone to Florence early, having finished in Genoa.

Overhead lights clicked off in quick succession and a loud bell startled me. It was five P.M. The archive was closing. I shut my laptop, handed in the account book, and headed back to the apartment, stopping for gelato on the way. As I walked out of the *gelateria* I noticed three missed calls from an Italian number I didn't recognize.

I dialed the number. Rose answered on the first ring.

CHAPTER ELEVEN

She was crying. "I told you they threatened my dad . . . Why are you wasting time on the account books of a different family?"

"Rose! Are you okay? The account books? Wait, you know what I'm looking at? Are you here in Florence? At the Archive?"

I could hear her take a deep breath. "It's not me who's watching you! Listen, the things you need to focus on are on my list, the one I sent William. No tangents. The list, the conference, then Paris."

"Everything Federico related should be on your list. Federico's voyage was funded by his first wife's family. I'm following the money."

"Forget that stuff. Focus on the emerald. My life depends on it."

"Rose, I'm doing the best I can. I'm filing a report every night. I'm making progress. But you're stressing me out right now. Why aren't you doing some of this work? Why can't you help me?"

"They want everyone to think I'm dead. I burned a lot of bridges trying to find the emerald and I can't go back to any of the archives. I told them you would find it and they believed me. But they're watching. Both of our lives are on the line. Isabel, thank you so much. How am I ever going to repay you?" She hung up.

I called back three times, but the signal dropped each time the call went through.

I looked around me. The wind had picked up, but the streets were quiet. A man in a black overcoat beside a bicycle was looking toward me, about twenty feet away. I put my head down and started walking in the direction of the apartment, holding my phone up to my ear, pretending I was talking to someone as I passed him.

"*Si*," I said to the imaginary person. "*Arrivo adesso. Non ti preoccupare.*"

I was relieved that Rose was still alive, but at the same time a slow-building anger gnawed at me. Rose didn't, and couldn't, appreciate how hard I'd been working to help her. She had put the entire task of keeping us both alive on me, and she wasn't doing anything to help in return. She claimed she couldn't go back to the archives, but to burden me with all this responsibility wasn't fair. There was no way to reach her even, nowhere to put my frustration. As I walked, I realized that my body was hunched over. I was like a tightly coiled spring. Even my fingers were curled, ready to punch through a glass window. I stopped, stood up straight, and unclenched my fists. I had to continue along the path. Rose's path.

The next morning, I was waiting at the entrance to the Archives when they opened. The desks in the reading room were nearly all occupied.

Before bed I'd ordered three volumes that contained "*Lettere Varie*" of the Falcone, the first items on Rose's list, using the archive's online system. The first I brought to my desk was not a bound volume, but a grey box. I unraveled the small knot in the string and opened the box to pull out the loose pages. There were hundreds. I worked without breaking for lunch or coffee. Looking for Falcone references took all morning and most of the afternoon.

I raised my head now and then to check if anyone was watching me. The researchers came and went. No one I recognized. The archive staff looked bored. No one appeared to be paying attention to me. When I was in the documents, I was in the sixteenth century, and I wasn't thinking about how to keep Rose alive, or whether my own life was in danger. I couldn't allow myself to think about her father, that he might have been threatened because of me.

By 4:30, I had only found three letters that Giovanbattista had exchanged with the Medici in Florence, trying to garner support in the aftermath of the failed plot against the doge, and one referencing a falling out with his brother, Pierfrancesco. I didn't understand why this volume was even on Rose's list, or why she had considered it more important than the Croci account books. Back in Scotland I had worried that I'd find out while working in the archives that Rose actually *had* made progress on her topic, and that I wouldn't genuinely be able to claim it as my own, although for now it didn't matter because I was focusing on the emerald. But after going through the two account books and this first volume, I could see that it was entirely possible she hadn't consulted any of the volumes in depth and had only conducted a survey of the materials housed in the archive. No wonder she thought that information about the emerald could be anywhere.

I turned in the volume and collected my belongings from my locker.

Walking along the Arno, I made my way home wondering who was watching me. I did not want to think about Rose and her beautiful, smiling eyes. I did not want to think about her father. Thoughts of Niccolò, Adrian, and finally William—all equally unwelcome—fought with each other to position themselves in the forefront of my mind. My phone vibrated in my pocket, an unlisted number, but when I answered, there was only silence.

Before unlocking the door to my building, I looked around. No guy wearing an overcoat on a bike. No one who wasn't walking quickly, going somewhere. I opened the door to the apartment and walked inside.

The contents of my suitcase were strewn around the room. I stepped back and out into the hallway and looked in each direction. I reached into my jacket and clutched the canister of pepper spray in my hand, then I went inside again, walked around one step at a time, tiptoed to the bathroom, and stood still for a moment, listening. The only thing I could hear was my breathing, shallow and erratic, and my heart beating fast and hard. With my extended arm, I pushed the door open slowly. No one in the shower or behind the door. I leaned over and checked inside the closet, and underneath the bed, my heart still pumping frantically. No one was here.

What could they have been looking for? Did they think I had information on the emerald that I wasn't telling them about? I opened the front door. The area around the doorknob was obviously scratched. Someone had picked the lock. I quietly walked down the hallway. No other doors were open or appeared to have been broken into.

Back in my apartment I double locked the door. Whoever had gone through my things didn't care if I knew they'd been here. Or they'd been in a hurry. I wanted to call the police, but whoever was watching me would see the police come, and then Rose would die. And I would be killed, too? I thought of going to a hotel, but I didn't want to leave.

I called William.

"Isabel! So nice to hear from you! I just went through the document you sent me," he said, before I had a chance to speak. "You're making real progress—"

"—William, something terrible happened. Someone broke into my apartment in Florence."

"What? Are you okay? Did anything get stolen?"

"No, but my clothes were all over the floor, as if whoever it was was looking for something." With no preamble, I launched into a breathless, slightly incoherent summary of the past couple of months, Rose's disappearance, her messages, the emerald, the threat against her father, and ended with the break-in.

"Slow down," he said. "Are you saying Rose is alive?"

"Well, she was alive as of last night when she called."

"Jesus, Isabel, why didn't you tell me sooner? What did the St Stephens police say? Is Scotland Yard involved? Does Endicott know?"

"Nobody knows. She told me they would kill her if I told anyone."

"Who is 'they'? Why would anyone want to kill Rose? Why are they threatening you? Do you know where she is now? Why isn't she looking for that emerald? Why you?"

"I'm not sure why I'm involved now. Everyone's supposed to think she's dead, so she can't be seen in the archives. Not in Florence, or Genoa, or Paris. Or they'll kill her."

"Really? It's unbelievable. I mean, difficult to believe." Neither of us spoke. I felt relieved. I didn't need him to solve anything, but just telling him removed some of the terrible burden of keeping the knowledge to myself.

"Isabel," he said, "I don't want to downplay any of your concerns, but are you sure Rose didn't . . . I mean are you sure Rose isn't creating some high-level drama here? I hate to say it, but at your expense? You know Rose."

"I do know Rose, and no, I can't imagine that she would make me think that her life, and my life, and her dad's life, were in danger, if that weren't the case."

"Maybe she just needed to get away from it all?"

"William, I can't believe you're not taking this seriously. You're not taking me seriously. You don't need to fix this for me. I just wanted to confide in someone about this situation. I'm scared."

"I'm sorry, it's just . . . who are these people watching you? Breaking into your flat? Are you sure it's related to the situation with Rose? Did you check to see if there had been other break-ins recently in your area?"

"No other apartments on my floor were broken into. Just mine. But I thought of something. When I was in Genoa, the daughter of the count said a professor had come looking for the emerald at the Palazzo Falcone. At that dinner at school, Von Kaiserling told me about the Falcone emerald. And later Gregory. Maybe it was Von Kaiserling! Could he be threatening Rose?"

"I doubt it's Von Kaiserling—he's eccentric, sure, but he'd never threaten anybody. Also, he adores Rose. The last time I saw him he was genuinely distraught that she'd gone missing."

"I don't need to know who broke into my apartment. I need to find the emerald. I now know that someone really is watching me, whether or not you believe me."

"Look, I do believe you. I'm sorry! It's just, well, maybe I don't believe Rose. But, Isabel, please be careful. Do whatever you need to do to make these people happy. Presumably if you find evidence that there is no emerald, everything will go back to normal, right?"

"I have no idea. But I'm exhausted. I need sleep more than anything. Thanks for listening. I feel better. I'm just going to focus on work. As you can tell, looking into Federico Falcone has really been about looking for the emerald, so I'll just keep doing that. I'll put it all in my paper, assuming I get through this."

"You'll get through it, Isabel. If anyone could handle this crazy situation, it's you. And I want to help! What can I do?"

"For starters, don't tell anyone I called you, please."

"Of course not," he said. "You have my word."

We hung up, and I pulled out my new laptop and sent my nightly missive, describing the three things I'd found that day at the archive. After I pushed "send," and sent it to two more computer-generated addresses, I realized I'd have to lug both my old laptop and my new one with me wherever I went, as I couldn't risk leaving either of them in the apartment.

Feeling even more overwhelmed, I went to bed too tired to eat. My last thoughts were of Rose's father. I wished I had met him back when we were at school, Rose always told great stories about him.

CHAPTER TWELVE

I spent Friday and Saturday systematically ordering volumes from Rose's list and going through them one by one. I found nothing related to the emerald in the manuscripts.

For every letter I read that was addressed to or sent by a Falcone, I noted the reference number, the addressee, and the recipient, and, if interesting, briefly summarized the contents. I didn't bother transcribing them. I could go back to them if I decided later that they were relevant to my thesis.

On her list, Rose had placed an asterisk next to number 3789 of the Medici Archive. I cross-checked the reference in the catalogue, which noted that 3789 contained "diverse letters of Federico Falcone." I ordered 3789 and the two that followed, 3790 and 3791, because the catalogue described them as a three-volume set. The next day, Sunday, I worked on my conference paper at home, getting up every ten minutes to make sure the door was locked.

On Monday, an archivist handed me 3789, which was tied up with twine and had a thick vellum cover. Over certain patches were black dots where animal hair had been removed. The spine was soft and flexible, and some of the leaves were loose. It seemed alive, or as if it had been alive once. I placed the volume on the stand; it didn't give off an odor, but it looked like it should smell musty.

Since there was no index or table of contents, I would need to leaf through the signatures on every letter in order to find anything written by Federico, just as I'd done the previous week. Inside the front cover the dates "1565–1592" were penciled in. Though bound as a book, the volume was a random assortment of letters.

One page had a strange sequence of letters and numbers. It began *f i m 3 7 9 b n q 1 3 8*. I was about halfway through the volume. I paused. When I next looked up at the clock it was 4:35. I hadn't taken a break and had almost finished the volume. I hadn't found any correspondence written by, about, or to Federico. There were twenty or so pages left. How could I possibly save Rose going so slowly?

I collected my things, including my old and new computer, and walked out of the archive. A tall man standing alone about fifteen feet from the main entrance moved toward me. I froze, then squinted. "William!" I called, walking out to meet him.

He seemed hesitant to embrace me.

"Ciao, Isabel," he said, as we air kissed on both sides of our faces. "Would you like to join me for an aperitivo?"

"I'll join you," I said. "But I'm not drinking."

"You're looking skinny," he said.

"I suppose you mean that in a nice way?"

"Isabel, have you been eating? Sleeping?"

"Yes," I lied.

"What have you been eating?"

"Panini. And other stuff." My stomach grumbled.

"Haven't you been taking breaks?"

"Of course."

"I'm talking about a proper lunch break, with real food, not just coffee. The sixteenth century isn't going anywhere. Slow and steady wins the race."

"Alright then," I said. "Let's go." I took him to Bar Antonio, on the Oltrarno, a place I'd only ever walked by. After so much time in the stagnant ether of the archive I enjoyed the fresh breeze, noticing the bite of cold air on my face. I wasn't sure if I'd brushed my hair.

The bar was small and lit by candles, unusual for Italy. A woman with freckles like flecks of dust on the bridge of her nose found us a window seat, squeezed next to another table of Americans.

"It's busy," I said.

"Many Italians consider the aperitivo the best part of the day," said William.

The pretty server asked for our order.

"*Formaggi misti* for me," he said. I thought he might flirt, or glance at her tiny waist, but he didn't.

"*Lo stesso per me, per favore,*" I said.

"*Niente da bere?*" she asked.

"*No, grazie,*" we both said in unison.

I arranged the three types of pecorino cheese onto saltless, Tuscan bread and ate them, followed by the pickled vegetables that came as a side dish, in under three minutes. When I had finished, William offered me the rest of his, which I accepted without hesitation. He ordered a third serving, which we split.

"So, bringing you here wasn't such a terrible idea. You know, you'll be more efficient if you take breaks to eat," he said, wiping his chin with his napkin.

"Most of the people here can go for three-hour-long lunches if they want to."

"As you well know I'm all for hard work. But you need to take care of yourself. I'm not saying this as your advisor, or colleague, I'm saying it as your friend," he said.

"I'm a first-year PhD student. Am I really your colleague?" I asked. "Or your friend?"

"Yes," he said. "You're both."

"You know what? I don't need your pity," I said.

He grimaced a little. "I'm sorry if you heard it that way. I just want you to keep going, and to . . . succeed. PhDs are stressful, to put it mildly. Nutrition, sleep, these things are invaluable. And—"

"—And?"

"I have enormous respect for you, Isabel. Your language skills, your talent for research, your dedication. I'd never speak condescendingly to you. Never."

"I didn't mean to sound uncharitable."

He continued, "It's my fault if I seemed heavy-handed. But I've been in your position. You should have seen the beard I grew when I was finishing my thesis. I looked like Rip Van Winkle. My diet consisted of cereal straight from the box, poured directly in my mouth. I had no time for anything but work. I know what it's like to spend endless hours in an archive, communing with the voices of the past. As if you know them. These historical companions become more alive than your real ones."

"That's how it feels to me."

"And there's that sense of . . . invincibility, am I correct?"

"Yes. Completely."

He chuckled.

"What's funny?" I asked.

"When the letters start dancing on the page," he said, "the loops in an 'S' for instance, that means you've had enough for the day."

"So that's what that means," I said, managing to smile.

The server came back, and I ordered a tiramisu.

"Make it two," said William.

My blood sugar surging, I told him about Genoa, and the search for the emerald, and what had happened with Niccolò.

He rolled up one of his sleeves. "He did *what?*"

"I was terrified. And I felt completely helpless. Powerless. It was so violent. I think—I know—it would have been worse if his sister hadn't interrupted him. His parents were away. He thought we were alone. That he could get away with it."

"Shit. I'm glad you told me. I'm so relieved you . . . escaped. I'm furious that anyone would do that to you, would frighten you, threaten you, worse. If he were here, I don't know what I'd do to him. Oh, Isabel. I'm so, so sorry." He reached out and put his hand over mine.

"It's okay," I said. "I must admit, though, I'm feeling overwhelmed. I can't get Rose's father out of my head. I just want to be a normal PhD student, and instead I have to focus on the emerald. The emerald and my thesis are linked, but there is so much I'll have to come back and work on."

"I wish I could help. But it seems like you're doing all the right things. Have you seen anything suspicious? Or anyone? Do you still think you're being watched?"

"Not sure. I'm putting all those thoughts in a box and putting the box on a shelf. It's a technique that's worked in the past."

"What happens if you find the emerald? How will you tell Rose, or whoever is watching you? Or if you can't find it? When will this be over?"

"I email them every night, tell them my progress. Sometimes I hear from Rose . . ." My voice trailed off.

"The thing is," I continued, "I know I called you in a panic the other day, but I'd rather not talk about it right now, okay? I'm feeling more . . . normal . . . than I've felt in a long time. I'd like to hold onto that feeling. What about you? Why are you in Florence, and why didn't you tell me you were coming?"

"I had to look at a few sources at the Biblioteca Nazionale to prepare for the Machiavelli conference in Paris in a few weeks. The bad news is that they need me to arrive a little sooner to prepare, which means missing the conference here, and your paper. And well, really, I came because I wanted you to know that I took you seriously when you called me about Rose and the emerald and . . . your lives are in danger. Especially your life. Isabel, I believe you. And I want to help. If I can. I'd offer to come to the archives, but maybe we shouldn't draw attention to the fact that we're working together just in case you are being followed. I know you're perfectly capable of handling archival challenges on your own, but I'll be here as moral support. We can have coffee together. Every morning. If you want."

"That sounds really great, but I wouldn't want to burden you. I'm making good progress, although I'll let you know if I get stuck."

"It's not a burden," he said, eyes on me.

The tiramisus arrived and we dug into them. Then we had two espressos, each. An hour later, William paid above my protestations, and he accompanied me back to my apartment, each of us under the cover of our own umbrellas. Near the Ponte Vecchio, a gust of wind snapped my umbrella inside out. I held onto it, and then looked at it in my hands, crumpled, a limp bird with broken wings.

"Oh!" I said, and everything that had been held at bay by William and his sparkling eyes rushed back at me.

"Come here," he said, holding his large umbrella over both of us. It was the closest we'd been since our kiss before break, close enough that I could smell his cologne. When we reached my building, he handed me the umbrella. "Please take it," he said. "I insist."

"Thanks," I said. "What about you, though?"

"I won't melt."

"I can pay you for it."

"Not a chance," William said. "But in exchange, do me a favor. Stay focused, but don't forget about your health. I'm staying with a friend in Settignano, so I'm right around the corner if you need anything."

"Well, thanks so much," I said, "for the umbrella, for the aperitivo, for your company. All of it."

"It was my pleasure," he said. "Really. Now, go get some sleep."

"Sounds good," I said, starting up the steps. Then I half turned. "Do you want to come up?"

"Would you like me to? Are you still worried about the break-in?"

"No, it's not that," I said, sounding braver than I felt. "Thanks for the lovely evening."

I went to bed thinking of William, but I was too worked up to fall into a deep sleep.

CHAPTER THIRTEEN

The next morning my wrists and temples pulsed energetically. The aperitivo with William had buoyed my spirits. I was plowing my way through the last twenty pages of the volume when a signature caught my eye.

F. Falc---.

A stream of blood throbbed into my skull, and I sat up straight.

I skimmed through the eight-page letter, written on April 7, 1573. Federico himself had penned the text himself rather than dictating it, since the handwriting in the letter was the same as in the signature. The letters sloped to the right and the words ran together, indicating that Federico had barely lifted his pen between words. There were areas where the ink was heavy and blotchy, and others where it was faded, barely visible. I imagined Federico pressing down on his pen, ink flowing onto the page in spurts.

I went back to the beginning and started copying it out into readable Italian. I would translate it into English back in Scotland.

The letter concerned a delivery made to the Grand Duke Cosimo de' Medici. He had purchased a black stallion from Spain, and arrangements for getting it from Spain to Florence involved an intermediary at the court of the Spanish king, Philip II. Federico was traveling to Spain himself to supervise the transaction. It didn't make sense to me that he would go to Spain to supervise the transportation of a horse. It seemed beneath his rank. And why was he involved in a transaction with Catherine de' Medici's two sworn enemies, her cousin the Grand Duke and the Spanish king?

I thought back to Tommaso's letter that I'd found in Rose's desk. Contemporary pamphlets contained rumors that Federico had been secretly loyal to Spain, although such conjectures had been dismissed as attempts by his rivals to discredit him. But maybe there was something to it? Then again, perhaps the stallion in question had been a Trojan horse of some sort? Could he have used the excuse of the delivery to spy on Florence and Spain for Catherine? Or—another or—maybe the stallion was a code word for the emerald. *Semental* in Spanish . . . *Smeraldo* in Italian.

I continued plodding through the pages. Halfway through, a large section of text was comprised of numbers. Written in code. I turned the pages to see if the rest of the letter was enciphered. After three pages of numbers, the information about the stallion delivery started up again. The middle pages were written in the same hand, with the same flourishes to the individual letters on the rest of Federico's letter. The same ink was used from start to finish. There was a final half page that appeared to have been cut away.

I leafed through the remaining pages, finding nothing Falcone related, but several other coded documents. I handed in the volume and brought the next one in the set, 3790, to my desk. There were a handful of letters written in code here, too. Three quarters of the way through I came to an undated document that was not a letter. The top of the page began, "To facilitate intelligence of the present cipher." The next two pages were instructions, referring to an alphabet, at least in the beginning:

"It is composed of three types of alphabet characters, or one of three types of numerals, simples, doubles, or triples.

"The simple characters each have a small mark above them, and each signifies a simple letter of the normal alphabet, under which is noted in this table, for example, S signifies ____.

"The doubles of the ten first numbers up to 10 or up to 19 each signify a simple letter of the said alphabet which is figured in the said table, for example 10 signifies 'i,' 12 signifies 'b' . . ."

The document used the following an example, "If I would like to write, 'I have heard that the emperor is managing his affairs terribly in Hungary,' I would encipher it, '2619. 1477. 108231064786601539 148 116 149."

The following pages consisted of tables with translations of various coded letter and number combinations. For example, in the simple category, the letter "a" was expressed as 5, "b" was 12, "c" was 7. In the double category the letters "ba" signified 20, "be" was 28, "ca" was 21, etc. Same for a third category.

Then there was a category of words that had their own numbers, unrelated to the simples, doubles, and triples.

Voyage was 183

Negotiation was 169

Siege was 177

116 was the Queen of England

118 was the King or Queen of France

155, danger

149, money

Huguenots were 163

170 was help

Countries were identified by numbers. Italy was 140. I wasn't surprised that family names were expressed in code. I skimmed down until I found "Falcone," which was 22. Then there were more complicated symbols. A large "O" with a cross though it and two dots on either side signified betrayal. A large capital "L" with two dots on either side was the pope. To convey a real number, the number was written with a bar over the top.

I looked back at the alphabet singles, doubles, and triples at the top. The word emerald would be expressed in Italian as "es" + "me" + "r" + "aldo." I filled half a page of writing variations, so I could easily recognize it if I came across it.

I wanted to tell someone, anyone, perhaps the researcher at the table next to mine, that I had discovered a guide to deciphering coded letters from the sixteenth century. But mostly I wanted to tell Rose. The lights were going off around me, but I kept on writing. One more line! I looked up to see one of the archivists standing next to me. I closed the book and turned my notes over so she couldn't see them, and then clicked them into a neat stack. "It is time to leave," she said. "Now."

I went to a deserted café near the Piazza Beccaria, and started to research ciphers.

I read about the Caesar monoalphabetic cipher and the later polyalphabetic "shift" ciphers such as the one invented by the fifteenth-century humanist Leon Battista Alberti that used a cipher wheel consisting of two disks, the inner one rotating and containing twenty-four possible characters. The plaintext characters on the outer disk were twenty of the twenty-six capital letters in our alphabet, which were followed by the digits one through four in order. Francis Bacon's 1605 cipher was the most well-known, but the one I'd found pre-dated it. The simple decoders seemed to be a passe-partout, used among aristocrats and between courts in the sixteenth through eighteenth centuries.

Such codes were not impregnable, and a weak cipher was dangerous since it gave the sender a false sense of security. Apparently, the French were better encoders than the Spanish, and the French had master cryptographers, able to break even complex codes.

In my daily summary I mentioned the enciphered letters and the decoder, and said that I hadn't decoded anything yet, but hoped a coded letter would lead me to the emerald.

I had decided to try out the key on one of the number-filled letters that I'd come across in the first volume, 3789. If this led to the emerald, it would all be worth it. I couldn't wait to tell William. But first I wanted to work it out. I spent the night falling in and out of vivid dreams.

The next day I practically yanked the Medici volume from the archivist. I found the coded letter near the middle of the volume, which had the date 1574 scribbled diagonally in one of the margins. After looking it over and not identifying what I thought was the combination of numbers for the word emerald, I began to transcribe it, first writing the numbers out in my notebook, leaving them clumped in what I presumed were words. After half an hour, only partway through the first page, I attempted to decode it. But the words I came up with were nonsensical, with nothing to do with French, Italian, or Latin words. I selected another coded letter and tried again. The decoder wasn't working. Or I was doing something incorrectly.

I sifted through the pages looking for more coded documents. When the archive closed, I went home. Every night I performed the same ritual. With my phone in one hand and the pepper spray in the other, I walked slowly into the building and inside my apartment. I was ready to convince myself that there was no reason to suspect the break-in had anything to do with me. It could have been a random crime that could have happened in any city. The thieves had probably been disappointed to find a suitcase full of cheap clothes and notes on obscure historical subjects. I decided to wait to tell the building management about the scratched-up door, just in case.

I sent an email summarizing the few things I'd found in the volume related to the Falcone and explaining that I hadn't yet figured out the decoder but knew I would have a breakthrough. Tomorrow.

I was making progress. I was sure they could see that. I hadn't heard from Rose since my first full day in Florence, over a week ago.

The next day I decided to try to decipher two more letters I hadn't yet worked on. If I could decode the first few words, then I'd keep going. If not, I'd move on.

I found two coded letters and checked to see if they contained anything that might represent the word emerald. They didn't, and after writing out and decoding the first ten "words" of each one, neither produced anything intelligible, only gibberish. I handed in the volume, and left, stopping at a bar for a panino. If William asked me, I'd be able to say I was eating well.

Back inside the archive I rolled my shoulders and settled into the chair, foam oozing from its back. Feeling discouraged, I picked up the third volume, 3791, from the circulation desk. I flicked through the first few pages, scanning the names in the greetings and the signatures. Nothing about an emerald. Nothing related to the Falcone.

About three quarters of the way through 3791, I found a simple decoding key, tucked inside a piece of paper folded over itself. I had read about these kinds of simple keys, this one with number-per-letter substitution. I wanted to feel some measure of excitement, but after the dead end with the other decoder I only felt frustration. If I wasn't under so much pressure to find the emerald, I would have been thrilled to follow this wherever it might lead, but whatever decision I made could be life-altering.

Since it was impossible to take photos in the archive without advance permission, and photocopying wasn't allowed, I spent the remainder of the day copying out the new, simple key. When I finished, I went through a few more pages, found a coded letter, and attempted to decode it. But I couldn't produce any words that made sense.

I'd been seesawing between gloom and elation and was heading back toward gloom when I had an idea. Unfortunately, the lights flickered before I could act on it.

Outside I saw a text from William saying he was still in town because his *alluvionato*, or flood-damaged, Biblioteca Nazionale reference had been held up by the conservators. It was Friday night, so I invited him to meet me for an aperitivo at Bar Antonio.

"I could get used to this," I said, when we greeted each other.

"It doesn't take much to fall into Italian routines," he said. We ordered a carafe of the house wine and, after agreeing to avoid discussing Rose or the emerald, we talked about Italian musical artists we'd seen perform. I told him about the decoders I'd found.

"Is that unusual, William?"

"I'd say. You'll have to show me."

"Certainly, I will. But should I keep going?"

"Most scholars wouldn't bother. I admire your perseverance," he said with a slight nod. "Next time we'll go to the Biblioteca Nazionale together."

"I'll look forward to that," I said, half-batting my eyelashes, but he didn't seem to notice.

It was late when we left, and the street outside the bar was empty.

"Let me walk you back," William said, and I didn't say no.

I could feel the pull of him in the center of my stomach as we walked together. "Do you want to come up?" I asked when we reached my building.

"Sure, I'd be happy to take a look around," he said.

"No, I mean. Would you like to have a drink? A little homemade limoncello?"

His eyes widened. "I'd love to."

I took his hand and we walked into the building and up the stairs. In front of my door, he put his hands on either side of my face and began kissing me. I could taste the red wine on his tongue.

I unlocked the door and pulled him inside the apartment and we stayed there, in the vestibule, kissing, deeper and deeper. After a while I stood back, my chin scratched by the shadow of his beard.

I took two shot glasses out of the kitchen cupboard and slipped a Jobim CD that I found into an old stereo, which surprisingly still worked. We sipped the sweet limoncello, listening to low, languorous cadences, our pinkies only grazing.

"Isabel," he said, after he had swallowed the last pulpy yellow drops in his glass.

"Yes?"

"Would you like to dance?" I nodded. Taking my hands, he pulled me up and we began to move together to the music. When the song ended, we stopped dancing and just swayed. I thought he was going to kiss me, but he stepped back and dragged his hand through his hair.

"I've been trying, all this time, I mean, for a while, to contain my feelings for you. I was concerned it was inappropriate, since you're my student now, but I . . . I can't stand it," he said. "I like you, Isabel. Actually, I don't like you, like is not sufficient to describe my feelings." His expression was wild, insistent. He looked away.

I took his hand, and he tickled my palm with his thumb. I stood on my tiptoes and craned my head up to kiss him. He leaned forward, knocking his lips into mine, then lifted me up and carried me, my arms around his neck.

"Where's the bedroom?" he said with a coy smile, walking toward it. He lay me down on the bed and shook off his shoes, began to undress me slowly, and then unbuttoned his shirt. Starting with my ankles, he kissed me everywhere, finally nestling his head between my knees. My legs fell open and I took in a deep breath. "I want you so badly," he said. "Is that okay?"

"Very okay."

He pushed himself up and over me, running his hands through my hair, kissing my neck. When I looked up his eyes were closed. "I'm worried if I look at you it'll be over too quickly," he whispered. "And I want this to last."

That night I didn't think at all about Adrian or Niccolò or Rose or the emerald. The world was only as large as our two bodies, a tumble of limbs and hands. I loved feeling close to William. I could tell he was making an effort to restrain himself, to be gentle. My body kept trembling the whole time.

I couldn't sleep afterward, distracted by his warmth and the scent of his cologne on the sheets. I watched him sleep, and several times heard him talking, and twitching dramatically. I wanted to comfort him but wasn't sure how.

I fell asleep for a couple of hours and when I woke up smelled something cooking. I felt around in bed. William wasn't there. I wrapped a sheet around me just as he appeared with a tray and two plates of eggs and toast, and a mug of tea for me.

"I couldn't find any food in the apartment, so I went out for a coffee and tea and the bar sold me the eggs and bread. I thought maybe you'd be hungry."

"Famished," I said as he set the tray down beside me. "I do drink coffee now," I said. "You were right, it's impossible to do without."

"Take mine," he said, passing me his mug. He sat next to me, and we ate—plates in hand, silverware clinking—without talking but looking at each other. He reached over and traced a line down the side of my face. When I finished, he stacked our plates on the tray and took it to the kitchen. I heard the water running and snuggled under the covers.

Soon he came back and sat on the edge of the bed and took my hands in his.

"Thank you. For everything. I'm enjoying getting to know you."

"Yes," I said. "Me, too."

"Isabel, you're just . . ." he took my hand in his ". . . you're perfect."

We kissed goodbye, not lingering this time, and he slipped out.

I knew concentrating on work would prove challenging, with my head humming, suffused with secret pleasure. Even though I hadn't slept much, I was full of energy and electricity. My body felt warm and fulfilled. I couldn't stop smiling, practically dancing to the archive.

At the circulation desk, I picked up the first volume of the three-volume Medici set, and back at my table I selected one of the coded letters I'd found. I copied out four lines into my notebook, then tried the simple device. Number by number corresponding to letter by letter, I began to build words on top of the groupings of numbers. Spacing helped, or else the words would have been difficult to distinguish. A flush fell over me as I transcribed the first three words.

I went back and copied out more of the coded letter into my notebook. Then I decoded a few lines. I kept shifting farther out toward the edge of my seat as the letter unfolded in front of me. Although the words were appearing, the letter itself lacked context, referred to another letter, and seemed irrelevant to my work. I couldn't figure out the signature, but it wasn't Falcone. I didn't bother translating it. I just moved on.

At six William sent me a text.

"Hey, just wanted to say hi and see how you're doing."

"Great day! You?"

That night I didn't send a summary email because the Internet at my apartment wasn't working, and I had sent one the night before, when William had stayed with me. I'd try again in the morning. They'd be happy to know about my decoding, even if I hadn't yet found the emerald. The panic that I lived with on a daily basis began to subside. William texted back. "Glad to hear. I had a wonderful time last night."

I had planned to visit the Bargello on Sunday, when the archives were closed, but instead I slept in, and spent a few hours researching codes on my laptop. I had turned my phone on silent. Looking over I saw a missed call from William. I called back but he didn't pick up. I took a nap, then went for a walk. I wandered for a while, thinking of William's hands on me as I walked beside the Arno in a dreamlike state.

The streets were dark and quiet. I made several turns and tried to get my bearings. Everything looked so different at night. A hooded figure drove up the street on a motorino, stopped, and waited—the engine rumbling quietly—watching me. I turned and walked down a side street at a regular pace, went around the next corner, and stopped. I stepped into the middle of the street and put my hands on my hips, facing the direction I'd come from. I felt invincible, with thoughts of William and the decoding of the letters twin currents running through my body. I was ready to confront anyone who might be following me.

But no one came, and I was deep in a labyrinth of narrow streets, so I continued in what I thought was the direction of the river. My phone thrummed in my pocket.

The number that flashed on the screen started with the British country code (44).

"Pronto?" I answered, "Hello?"

"Isabel," whispered a woman's voice with an English accent.

There was static on the line.

"Who is this?" I said.

"Catrina."

"Catrina! Everything okay?"

"They have Rose. You've got to finish your work, Isabel. Rose tried, but she can't protect us any longer."

"Us? What do you mean? Who has Rose?"

"They're tracking you. You haven't sent an email in two days, and they're concerned you're not taking the assignment seriously. If you don't find something soon, they'll kill Rose. If you contact the police, they'll kill Rose. If they haven't already. They said I should tell you that I'm next, then you. Are you listening? The only reason you're still alive is they want you to find it. Your only allowance is the conference. They know you're giving a paper, which is why they've been lenient. Please, Iz . . ."

Then nothing except static. The call had dropped. I looked at my phone and called her back every ten minutes for an hour, but she didn't pick up.

CHAPTER FOURTEEN

B ack at the apartment I sent off an email explaining what I'd found on Friday and Saturday, about the decoders, and the research I'd done on ciphers. I went to bed late and couldn't fall asleep, wanting to tell William about Catrina's call.

In the middle of the night, I texted Sean, "Can you check on Catrina? I got a weird call from her. Let's connect soon."

Nervous sweat ran down my face. I considered my options. Right now, I wanted nothing more than to drop out of the program, and run away somewhere far from all of this, but I was too far in.

I needed to keep working, to decode more letters, solve the puzzle, find the emerald, and save Rose's life, my life, and now, it seemed, Catrina's life.

The next morning at the archive I looked for more letters, planning to copy out the ciphered letter in the afternoon, when I could concentrate better. Two hours into my day, I found another encoded letter. I tried the simple decoder. It worked. I skipped down to the bottom to decode the signature. Federico Falcone.

In the first sentence of the letter, I decoded the word *smeraldo*. A surge of electricity ran through me, even more electric than what I felt with William. I spent the rest of the day and the following day unraveling Federico's letter. I had to switch around a few sentences, but I finished decoding it, then transcribed it from sixteenth-century Italian to modern, and the next day I translated it into English.

Magnifico Signor Duca,

I should wish to tell your excellency that on the occasion of my last voyage to the new world, so-called because it was not yet known to our ancestors, I traded handsomely with the people, exchanging a finely crafted Milanese harquebus and an astrolabe for a precious emerald, most rare in size and perfect in color and clarity, wholly without flaws or obscurities, unique. The stone had been mined from a hidden site in the New Kingdom of Granada and composed the center of the crown of one of the kings. It is said the stone had lain in the sepulcher of this king, until his tomb was opened by Spaniards. American peoples consider the soul immortal and believe in the resurrection of the body. Thus, the locals, upon seeing the Spaniards opening the tomb and scattering the bones of the dead king to access his gold and riches, warned them not to disperse the bones in such a way, lest the bodies inside the tombs would not be resurrected. Such peoples have no fear of death, confident they will come back to life, so long as their bones remained untouched. Horrible fates met the Spaniards as a result of their disrupting the tombs, and the great emerald stone ended in the hands of the Brazilian Americans, who see no use for such precious objects. Such men would rather possess weapons to vanquish their enemies and thus exchanged the very precious jewel for the harquebus offered by us.

Your excellency must know there is no better stone than the emerald, and none more pleasing to the eyes. Of the special properties of the emerald, I refer you to the Natural History of our Pliny, in which the great Pliny writes that emeralds are the most valuable stones, second only to diamonds, and that the Emperor Nero, who had failing eyesight, used the emerald to watch gladiatorial fights. Nero princeps gladiatorum pugnas spectabat in smargardo. The healing and mystical properties of these stones were well known to the ancients in Greece and Rome as indeed they are today. Given only very slight assistance from your excellency, I would be proud to sail once again to the Americas in order to bring as back as much gold and as many precious jewels and spices as you should desire.

    Federico de' Falcone

I sat back and read the letter over a few times. I had found my first archival reference to the emerald. Federico had traded weapons with local inhabitants in exchange for the precious stone, believing it might entice the Duke of Tuscany to fund future expeditions. I typed up the letter and my conclusions and sent it to the email address. I hadn't found out where the emerald was, but I had found a description of it.

I emailed William, limiting myself to academic matters and added a PS.

> Can't wait to present at the conference. Say hello to Sean and Mairead, and also CATRINA.

I hoped he'd find it peculiar I put her name in capital letters. At around one A.M., I was hovering on the edge of sleep when the phone rang. It was Catrina.

"We need to meet in Florence before the conference. In person."

"Of course."

"Somewhere quiet. Private. Text me back when and where." She hung up.

I texted her back. "Day after tomorrow? Bar Antonio? 9 P.M.?"

The next morning, I woke up to my phone ringing. It was Sean.

"Isabel," he said, after a perfunctory hello. "It's about Catrina. No one's seen her in a couple of days. Bertie has no idea where she is. But even worse . . . her wallet and her phone and everything is still at her house."

"Oh no, oh no."

"I didn't tell the police that you'd texted me about her. I thought we should . . ."

Just then my battery clipped out.

CHAPTER FIFTEEN

A n hour later I checked my phone, which was now charged. There
was no text from Catrina, but three from Sean asking if I was okay.
I wrote back, explaining that my phone battery had run out, and suggested
we talk later. He responded that he was flying to Florence the next day,
very late. He'd see me at the conference, but I could call him any time.

I opened my laptop and typed out another email to the latest email
address.

"I've finished going through all of the items on Rose's list. A
cache of Federico's letters are in the Département des Manu-
scrits at the Bibliothèque Nationale in Paris. In addition, the
French Archives Nationales has the only existing inventory of
Federico's household. As soon as the conference ends, I will
leave for Paris, although I'm still waiting for my travel grant
request to be processed. As you can see, I'm making steady
progress."

I wanted to finalize my talk, but I had scheduled a coffee with Endicott,
who was already in Florence for pre-conference events, and we'd agreed
to meet at a bar in Piazza Santo Spirito.

I ordered a milky cappuccino and found him waiting at a table in the back, flipping through a stack of papers. When I sat down, he put the papers on the chair next to him and said, "Good morning, Isabel. I trust you are well."

"Thank you, Professor Endicott. I hope your flight was uneventful."

"I should let you know something serious has happened in St Stephens," he said in reply.

"Catrina?"

He pushed his glasses up his nose. "Do you mean to tell me you already knew?"

"Sean phoned me this morning. Let me guess, you don't think it's a good idea to discuss it."

He leaned forward in his chair and squinted at me over his empty cup. "No. We don't know anything yet."

I wondered if the police would be able to find out from her phone that she had called me. "She called me recently," I said. "We made tentative plans to meet here in Florence."

"Well, that doesn't seem out of the ordinary. You are colleagues," he said, "although I suppose we should let the police know, on the off chance she doesn't turn up." A look of concern played across his face. "How is everything going? Are you looking forward to the conference?"

"I am. And research is going well. I discovered a series of coded letters and a deciphering key here in Florence."

"William mentioned yesterday," Endicott said, smoothing one of the pages with his hand. So, William had received my message. "Well done, Isabel. Although I caution you to stay focused on your topic. Did you turn up useful material in Genoa?"

"The account books are no longer there," I said. "But lots of useful documents. Marriage contracts, land purchases, baptismal registers, et cetera. I found two letters from two different popes and other notables.

Correspondence with other families the Falcone tried to make alliances with in Genoa after their rift with the Doria."

"All this material in the family archive? I wonder what was stolen."

"Something doesn't add up about that story. It may have been . . . an inside job."

"Have I ever told you Nigel Endicott's first rule? It's always an inside job."

I smiled. "I've pieced together the information I compiled previously with what I found in Genoa and Florence. Although Genoa became a Spanish vassal state, half of the Falcone family remained loyal to France, starting with Giovanbattista. The money Catherine de' Medici sent to finance Federico's voyages to the Americas was in the form of loans. Federico did not reimburse the crown."

"That's not unusual. Did the monarchy receive anything in return for their assistance? Have you seen enough material to make conclusions? I saw from your travel request that you have plans to go to Paris. Perhaps you'll find documents to complete the picture. What will you talk about at the conference?"

"My paper is focused on Federico. His relationship with Catherine de' Medici was close, but also transactional. Federico was using Catherine, and she was certainly also using him. To answer your question, I'm not entirely sure what Catherine received in return. Reading Federico's letters to her, his endless affirmations of fidelity, it's all piled on so thick. At the same time, he was trying to raise money from her cousin, Duke Cosimo, to fund voyages to the Americas, according to a letter I deciphered here in the archive."

"I see you're developing your decoding skills already. Well, exactly what Federico and Catherine had in mind will become clear as you continue to sift through more material. All we can do as historians is make assumptions based on the sources," he said. "And add a pinch of skepticism."

"How do we begin to assess a historical figure's character, if we have no choice but to base our assumptions on the way they present themselves in letters they wrote? Or the way biased others wrote about them did? How can we ever know the truth about someone who lived so long ago? Or hope to figure out a disputed event?"

"You are familiar with the Biblical quote: 'we all see through a glass darkly.' Writing 'what happened' is problematic. Scholars have debated and will continue to debate the events of the St Bartholomew's Day Massacre ad infinitum."

"We don't see things as they are, but as we are."

"Precisely." He pushed back in his chair. "It's a mistake to assume a great familiarity with the past. It is ever a foreign country."

"The past that we deal with is more like an alien planet, of which only a few traces remain. I'm trying to maintain a requisite sense of detachment."

"Good, I look forward to hearing your paper. William is very impressed with what you've done thus far. And I trust his judgment."

I wanted to tell him I could have made more progress by now, but I'd been focusing on the emerald. "Well, I've certainly collected a lot of information, although I don't have a solid idea of where it's taking me. There's more to do in Paris. I've taken tons of notes, but I'm sure I'll have to come back to Florence at some point."

"You've warmed to the topic, haven't you? I know you had your misgivings when we first offered it to you."

"I so appreciate the opportunity you gave me to work on the Falcone. You and William. He's been a supportive advisor, and I . . . know how much he respects you," I said, slightly flustered at the thought of just how supportive William had been.

"We're a good team."

"How long have you two been working together?"

"He was my hire, so it's been four years. I'm proud of what he's done. Not only is he a terrific researcher, but he's great with students. He's come so far."

"What do you mean?"

"Has he ever spoken to you about himself?"

"He hasn't."

"Everyone else in the department knows. It's a sad story, but ultimately one of redemption. When I first met William, he had nothing. He was living out of his car."

"Really? He's always so well-groomed and seems so . . . perfect," I said.

"He was born in your country, although he's of Scottish descent."

"William's American?"

"He's been living in the UK for such a long time he must have lost the American accent. He comes from a comfortable background, but his father died when William was eight or nine. His mother remarried an abusive brute. William suffered mostly from benign neglect, or so he says. He went to good schools but was bullied throughout secondary school."

"High school?" I said.

"High school. Mocked for hand-me-down clothes and for being a 'nerd.' Then he discovered history, literature. These alternative universes, they . . . saved him."

"Sounds familiar."

"William had a talent for maths. He was offered scholarships to attend the college of his choice. He settled on a uni in Canada and made the dean's list every term. He continued on to graduate school in the States, and soon developed a brilliant understanding of the early modern period. They practically threw money at him. A true *wunderkind*. And then . . ."

"And then?"

"William was passed up for tenure in the United States. Despite publications, teaching accolades, et cetera. It was . . . inexplicable. But I saw in him great promise and told him he could count on a steady position. I've not regretted that decision. His enthusiasm for history is, well, infectious. He's been a real boon to the department."

"Your heir, perhaps."

"Ah, perceptive Isabel. Yes, that's correct." He stood up. "It's time for me to leave for my next committee meeting," he said, tucking his hat under his elbow. "If not before, I'll see you at the conference, certainly at your panel." And then he was off.

Ten minutes later, when I went to pay my bill, they told me it had been taken care of.

Although I had attended conferences while working on my masters, this would be my first time presenting my own research. I was a little wary about sharing my latest insights about the Falcone, but I was looking forward to seeing people and meeting legendary scholars. I felt relieved that "they" had allowed me this reprieve. The annual Society of Early Modern Studies conference was the largest academic conference in the field. The rest of my colleagues would arrive over the next days. Back at the apartment, I worked on my paper without a break, confident I could finish it in one day and then practice reading it. At six P.M. I sent another email to the address: "Met with Professor Endicott this morning. Worked on my conference paper the rest of the day."

On Wednesday morning I received an email informing me that my travel grant request had been accepted. It included a generous per diem allotment, which would allow me to rent an apartment in Paris.

There was another email from Niccolò. The first one I'd received from him, right after I'd arrived in Florence, I had deleted without reading. But I opened up this second one.

Subject: Your sudden departure

Dear Isabel, it has been two weeks since you left, and I have been trying to reach you. You must excuse me if things took an unfortunate turn for us.

I think it is a great shame, your anger towards me, over a small misunderstanding. I would like to see you and talk in person. It would be easy for me to arrive to Florence. Also, next month I will visit Sevi in London, and I could travel through to St Stephens.

As a token of my regard for your work, here is the address of the French woman I told you about, the one who may have Falcone related materials. Marie-Christine—she can be reached at MCC1965@yahoo.fr. There is more I should explain to you.

Regards,

Niccolò

I was glad I had the pepper spray, in case Niccolò decided to surprise me. Or had he been here already? I shivered.

I emailed Marie-Christine immediately, introducing myself and my research. I asked whether we could arrange to meet in Paris the following week.

———

The conference was being held just outside Florence in a villa in Fiesole that once belonged to a famous art historian, now home to an American university. I took the bus there and walked up through a path lined by majestic cypress trees. Inside the villa, I found the registration area.

I checked in and flipped through the thick conference booklet.

My panel, "Transnational Contexts II, International Relations in Renaissance Italy and France," was scheduled for eight thirty the first morning. Rose's name was still listed along with two American PhD candidates from universities in Florida. Rose should be giving this talk. But she wouldn't have been able to present something comprehensive.

I wandered around the booths of publishers, their tables covered with colorful hardbacks that ranged from under $100 to almost $500. Beautiful books unaffordable for graduate students.

I glanced up and saw Gregory Pratt on the opposite side of the room, talking to one of the publishers. On the back wall there was a table with thermoses and a half-empty platter of finger sandwiches. I helped myself to two cups of herbal tea, hoping that would settle my stomach and my nerves. It didn't.

I took a bus back to the city center. As I approached my building, I recognized the same man I'd seen with the motorino lingering near the entrance. I spun around and began to walk briskly in the opposite direction. I reached inside my purse but couldn't find the pepper spray. My two laptops were in here, and they were heavy. I kept my quick pace until I found a broad artery, with several groups of people. It felt safer here. I looked behind me and spun around in a circle. I couldn't see the man; he hadn't followed me. I took in a few deep breaths, struggling to get enough air.

I wasn't imagining anything. Someone was following me. How long had they been observing me, and how much did they know? Catrina had sounded really upset on the phone.

Why hadn't they attacked me in some overt way rather than shadowing me and breaking into my apartment? Apparently, they wanted me to know that they could strike at any time. I reasoned that I must be safe so long as I continued to send those emails and made progress in my search for the emerald.

But if I stopped making progress, or told anyone else, like I'd told William, I couldn't count on staying safe. They obviously wanted me to know that they were watching. A power play. I spun around, my palms felt clammy, although the air was freezing. I needed to write another email to the address.

I could no longer allow myself spare time that wasn't accounted for, and I'd have to check in more often. But they knew I was going to the conference. Rose had told me that, and Catrina had confirmed. I wasn't sure what I was doing wrong. I walked home slowly, checking behind me and to the side every few feet. At the opposite end of the street, I looked all around me, gripping my keys in my hand. A few students were near my building, laughing. The man was nowhere in sight.

CHAPTER SIXTEEN

F inally, I sat down with my paper.

"Federico Falcone: Brother, Advisor, Explorer. Spy?"

Rose would not appreciate my lack of reverence for her academic heart-throb. Her fascination with Federico seemed in direct opposition to her feminist sensibility. My paper stressed that his letters had revealed him to be a bigot and an extreme racist, notably in his opinions about the indigenous peoples of the Americas. He expressed contempt for anyone who was not Catholic. In a time not recognized for its openness to other religions or cultures, Federico stood out as being particularly vehement in his intolerance.

I didn't have a full picture after only six weeks, but Federico's worldview seemed clear. He always put his own interests, and those of his family, first. I gave examples and emphasized the importance of reading what others had written about him. Maybe the stolen documents contained crucial information, but I would probably never find out.

As I'd emphasized to Endicott, it was becoming clear that Federico had been at once trying to influence Catherine's rule and at the same time soliciting support for his overseas ventures from other European leaders—Catherine's enemies.

I didn't include any of the material about Tommaso and Madeleine, or what I'd found out about the emerald, but I did add a line about the Croci family investing in his trips to the Americas and noted that he had also solicited the Medici in Florence.

I had finished the paper but read through it again and made minor adjustments. Then I stood up and practiced reading it aloud in front of the mirror. It took just over thirty minutes, five minutes longer than my allotted time. I read it over for the rest of the afternoon. After a quick dinner and three more read-throughs, my phone rang.

"They found Catrina's body."

"No!"

"A farmer walking his dog found her at the foot of one of the cliffs on a small, rocky beach. About five miles away. She left a note. They haven't . . . released it yet."

"Listen, Sean, let's not discuss this now."

"I don't understand."

"I'll . . . see you at the conference. Thanks for calling." I hung up, then started pacing back and forth. Was I somehow responsible for what had happened? The thought was devastating. My mind ran over the conversations I'd had with Catrina. She'd said I needed to finish my work. Were Rose's captors threatening me?

I kept pacing, unable to stop, unable to go back to my paper. Eventually I collapsed on the couch and fell into a half-sleep. The buzzer woke me up. I looked at the clock. 10:30.

"Sì," I said tentatively into the intercom.

"It's William."

I buzzed him in and turned off all the lights, removed the chair from behind the door, and walked to the tall window that looked out over the street.

When he knocked, I peered out the window, hiding half of my face. The street was empty. I closed the curtains, turned on a table lamp, and opened the door. William wheeled a suitcase and backpack inside that he left behind the door. He hugged me close for a long time, and even when I tried to pull back, he wouldn't let go.

"Sorry for showing up like this," he said.

"Sean called a few hours ago and told me about Catrina. I'm speechless."

"I came as quickly as I could because I wanted to tell you myself. Isabel, I'm so sorry about what I said on the phone that day. I owe you more than an apology."

"Catrina called a few days back and told me that 'they' have Rose. They think I haven't been working hard enough on finding the emerald. Now, Catrina's dead because of me."

He took my hand. "None of this is your fault."

"Catrina said they were going to kill Rose, too, if I didn't find the emerald. I cannot believe this is happening. Nothing seems real."

He put his hand up to my shoulder and I jerked away. "We have to get back to St Stephens," he said, "and talk to the police. That's why I brought my bags with me. Can you pack quickly? We need to go. Tonight."

"I can't leave, William. Don't you get it? Catrina's death was a warning. If I give up the search for the emerald, they'll kill Rose, too. Anyway, I'm presenting tomorrow."

"Isabel, it's not safe for you to be here anymore. Someone's following you, breaking into your apartment. And now Catrina."

"And it's safe to be in Scotland with a murderer on the loose? We don't know that whoever it is who killed Catrina hadn't also targeted Madeleine Grangier. Her so-called accident seems more and more suspicious. They said they'd kill Rose if I went to the police. If there's any chance Rose is still alive, I can't risk telling anyone. I shouldn't have even told you."

He put his head in his hands. When he looked up, he said, "Isabel, I want to help you, in whatever way I can. If you don't want to go to the police, that's your decision. I meant everything I said the other night. I . . . I love you, we're in this together now."

I took his hand. "I'm grateful for your help, but also really worked up right now."

"Do you want me to go?"

"No."

We talked until two, and for a while he held me on the couch. We didn't take off our clothes. I wanted him, but my unease overpowered my desire for sex. When the clouds dissipated, I thought it might calm me down, and started to take my shirt off, but he stopped me. "I want you, of course, but I don't want you to feel like I'm taking advantage. There'll be plenty of time," he said, embracing me.

Around five I said he should probably leave before sunrise.

"I'll go," he whispered. "But only if you promise you'll be okay. I feel terrible leaving you."

I hugged him again. "It's for the best. I wouldn't want whoever is following me to think we're working together. I'll be okay. They know I'm giving the conference paper. I'll see you in Paris soon."

"You're going to stay with me, right? I think that's the safest option."

"Yes," I said, "I will." I hadn't planned on staying with him but was thrilled. I felt a pain deep in my chest as he hugged me once more, tightly, and turned to go.

At six thirty I showered, dressed, and took the bus to Fiesole. In a bar in the main square, I drank a cappuccino and a double espresso. I wasn't ready to interact with anyone, but wanted to go in with the right attitude. By seven thirty the conference attendees, identifiable by badges with the

SEMS logo, were starting to gather at the villa. I saw Sean pick up his badge. His face softened when he saw me.

"Nice place, Florence," he said, after we'd hugged. "This is my first time in Italy. Maybe I should change topics, too."

"Aww Sean how did you know I could use a laugh?" I said. "Catrina's death has totally thrown me. I can barely put one foot in front of the other, and I've got to present this morning, at the same time you're giving your talk."

"I know," he said. "I almost decided to skip the conference, what with everything that's happened, and now I'm going to miss your paper, pretty much the only reason I decided to come down. Well, and to see you."

"You have to give your talk! Anyway, I'm glad you're here. Where's Mairead?"

"Missed her flight."

"That's a shame."

"She hopped on the next one, hope she's here in time for her panel. Bertie and Danny were looking for an excuse to skip the conference, so they stayed behind, supposedly to help with the investigation." We hugged again, wished each other good luck, and headed off in opposite directions.

I walked through a glass gallery with terracotta floors and entered the room where my panel was to take place. It looked like a classroom but with Renaissance frescoes on the ceiling. Only in Florence.

By 8:20 a few people had trickled into the room. I flipped through my pages, making sure everything was in order. When I looked up Endicott was there, in the front row. The other presenters and I took our seats behind a table facing the audience. I was the last speaker, which would give me time to slow my fluttering heartbeat. I thought about Sean, and wished he were here.

The two others presented their papers, but I didn't hear more than the odd word or two as I quickly scanned down the first page of my talk, sweating underneath my scarf.

"Good morning. My name is Isabel Henley, and I will be speaking today in place of Rose Brewster, with a slight modification of the title printed in your booklets." At the mention of Rose's name, I heard whispering and shuffling in the audience and looked up to see Endicott shushing someone behind him. I drank some water, and began, reminding myself to speak slowly.

My paper received generous applause, and it looked like no one in the audience had fallen asleep.

When it was time for the Q and A, a hand went up in the back row. Gregory Pratt. Next to him was a man with white hair and an impeccable, tailored grey-wool suit: Von Kaiserling.

Gregory stood up and cleared his throat. "Thank you for your paper, Isabel. You've done a remarkable amount of work in a short time. Do you believe in what you have presented today?"

I took a sip of water. "Believe in it?" I said. "I'm not sure I understand your question. But yes, to the best of my abilities, I try to present history accurately."

"Consider your notion that Federico Falcone acted unethically on numerous occasions. Surely, by the standards of the time, his political acumen was admirably astute, and he led the French crown through many turbulent times, wouldn't you say?"

"I would say that Catherine de' Medici, the de facto ruler of France for thirty years, was adept at statecraft. Her inclusion of Federico in her circle was incidental in the context of her navigation of a system where the odds were stacked against her. Because she was a widow. And an Italian. And a woman."

I continued, "Federico did not always guide her wisely. She strove time and again for conciliation, even assembling Protestant and Catholic leaders to dialogue at the Colloquy of Poissy. Federico advised against appeasement, against peace treaties, and encouraged Catherine to take a hard-line position at every turn."

Gregory nodded. "Your research is sound, although at times your paper took on a rather . . . judgmental tone. Might your bias against Federico be a product of your own views, perhaps?"

"Bias? It's my intention to remain objective. But who among us is not aware that history has long prioritized hungry colonialists willing to exploit others, whether indigenous peoples or even those closest to them, in order to achieve their goals of wealth or power, or both? The literal blood of the indigenous populations of the Americas financed the rise of capitalism in Europe."

He paused and said, "Aha! So perhaps you have chosen the wrong century?"

"The phenomenon is hardly unique to the sixteenth century," I answered, swallowing hard. "It's possible, I'm sure you would agree, to study the horrors of despotism, slavery, the Holocaust, and the like without being sympathetic to the perpetrators. History should be studied, even when it's painful. Especially when it's painful."

"You're courageous to stand up for your convictions," he said, sitting down as other arms shot up. I glanced at Endicott, who raised one of his eyebrows.

After some questions about our methodology, none directed at me, thank goodness, and another round of applause, we stood up and began to file out of the room. Endicott approached me. "You handled yourself admirably, Isabel. It's a shame William wasn't here to hear you. He was detained in Paris, I'm afraid."

"Oh, really?" I said, adjusting my scarf.

Another group was congregating outside an adjacent room. Gregory Pratt was standing with the leading expert on technology in sixteenth-century Spain. He threw his head back, laughing heartily at something she had said. His eyes floated past me as if I were a wall fixture, and he re-focused his attention on the professor.

It was 11:03. The second morning session had just started, and I had decided to attend a panel on diplomatic history. But when I pushed the door open there were so many people crammed inside that I couldn't see or even hear the speakers. I tiptoed out and into another panel, "Perceptions of Foreign Women in Early Modern Courts." I learned about other immigrant families that had struggled with the same prejudices that the Falcone had encountered. After the panel I traded cards with one of the speakers.

During the lunch break I was perusing new titles at a booth in the book sales room when a man with a badge identifying him as a vendor asked me to describe what I was working on. I explained briefly, adding that I was only in the first year of a PhD program. "That would make an excellent book," he said. "I'm the acquisitions editor. Here's my card. Please contact me when you have a manuscript."

"Thank you," I said, putting his card in my jacket pocket and feeling it glow there.

I met Sean for coffee in the piazza. After twenty minutes, Mairead joined us. She was wearing an inch of makeup, and her hands were jittering. Sean and I did our best to keep her distracted and walked her to the room where she was presenting. We sat in the front row so she could see some friendly faces.

She did more than a decent job—better than anyone else on her panel—and most of the audience questions were aimed at her. She fumbled the first one but then redeemed herself.

After congratulating Mairead I went back to the book exhibit and took a moment to absent myself mentally from the conference, watching the attendees as an outsider would have.

I recognized myself in the awkward graduate student who bumped into me accidentally as she, practicing what she was going to say, made her way to the distinguished professor she had only ever seen on the flap of a dust jacket. I recognized the flushed excitement on scholars' faces as they discussed their research with other like-minded people.

After a while I stepped out into the garden. Staring across at the rows of cypress trees as the sun melted into the horizon of Florence calmed my thumping temples. I turned around to go back inside and noticed Von Kaiserling standing a few feet away by himself. We made eye contact and he walked over to me.

"I enjoyed your talk earlier," he said. "I hope you didn't feel that Pratt's question was polemical. I'm interested in your topic and wish to understand further the depth of your commitment, which is clearly extensive."

"I did not find his question provocative, Professor. To the contrary. I think working out ideas in a venue such as this is extremely helpful, invigorating even."

A gold ring with a blue stone, incised with his coat of arms, glittered on his pinky.

"Once again, my compliments on a job well done." He took a breath before continuing. "I myself am working on a new study of Mary, Queen of Scots. It will bring me to your campus much more often, as I told Nigel earlier. Have you heard of the Babington plot, my dear?"

"Yes. It paved the way for Mary's execution."

"You know what they say in France, if you want to kill your dog you accuse it of having rabies."

"Is that what they say?" I asked but he had already started his next question.

"And did you know that Sir Francis Walsingham entrapped the good queen through a method he developed from his best cryptanalysts to break her personal code, and that he had her letters copied and sent back to her with their original seals?"

"I did not know that," I said. "Fascinating. I found some enciphered documents here at the archives."

His eyes fell down to my hands. "Did you now?"

"Yes," I said. "I've begun to read through Federico Falcone's letters in cipher."

"Tell me, you were able to decode them yourself?"

"With a simple decoder, yes. It was fairly straightforward."

"That's marvelous, my dear. Few scholars have the requisite skills or patience. That is most impressive."

"Professor Von Kaiserling—"

"—Max, please. We are colleagues."

"I was thinking about the first time we met in St Stephens, at your book launch."

"Yes, my dear."

"We talked about Rose Brewster. Do you remember?"

He raised an eyebrow.

"A brilliant student," he said. "Her dissertation was perhaps the best MA thesis I've ever read. Endicott's second-in-command, is it Thorson? Thorson advised me she'd gone missing, presumed suicide, is that right?"

"Anderson? Dr. William Anderson?"

"Yes. Anderson. She did not strike me as a depressed person, so I found it most peculiar."

"We were all shocked," I said. "It was tragic. It is tragic. And now a second student has died. Another presumed suicide. They found her body two days ago."

"Indeed. And Nigel tells me you are going to finish Ms. Brewster's thesis on the Falcone. Run the last kilometer, as it were. Will you be finishing this other student's thesis, as well?"

"Yes and no. I have taken on the Falcone topic," I said. "Which is plenty of work. Although it turns out that while Rose had done a fine job indicating the locations of an array of archival sources, there is little evidence she was able to analyze many of them.

"At dinner following the launch," I continued, "you told me about Federico Falcone's *Wunderkammer*. And then I read your article."

"How good of you to read it, although I'm surprised the St Stephens library has a copy. Very few were printed."

"I found it online."

"Commendable. Do go on." I looked around before continuing. We were alone except for a caterer setting up for the evening cocktail.

"You told me that one of the items in the *Wunderkammer* was a rare emerald."

"Yes."

"Gregory Pratt also told me about the Falcone emerald, making it sound as if it were common knowledge, at least among historians, that this emerald existed, and no one knew where it was."

"Ah, dear Pratt. He is attracted by things that shine and sparkle. Rarely does he reach beyond the superficial. And you, young scholar, are you, too, now dreaming of mythical jewels? Is that why you were so eager to take on Ms. Brewster's research?"

"I'm more interested in the Falcone, Federico, as you know from my talk earlier. But I was curious about the emerald. No one seems to know where it is, what happened to it. Maybe it wasn't that valuable. You described it as large. Maybe it was a fake? Otherwise, wouldn't we know where it is? You'd think it would have been donated to a museum."

He twisted the ring on his finger. "To call it a fake is to call into question my scholarship, but fear not, you haven't offended me. What happened to it remains a mystery, one I hope is solved in my lifetime.

But the emerald's real value is not monetary, although certainly there are those who would be willing to pay tens of millions for it.

"There are even some who believe it may provide clues about . . . occult things. Alchemical secrets. It is a very storied, old stone with a staggering provenance. Valuable beyond measure, in many diverse ways. And yes, Isabel, it is real. Of this I'm certain. No one has seen it for centuries, but it will be found. Perhaps you will find it."

"First, I'd have to start looking. Maybe I'll have time after I finish my thesis."

"Something I'm curious about. Do you know where . . . where they found Rose's body? Thorson did not mention."

"Anderson. Dr. Anderson. They didn't," I said. "Find her body."

"Oh, my. Might it be possible she's still alive?" He shook his head.

"Perhaps I could help with the investigation," he went on. "I have connections and resources."

"They did find the body of the second suicide in our department. Maybe she was actually the third. After Madeleine Grangier, the professor who fell to her death right before I arrived. She was supposed to be my thesis advisor."

"Oh yes, of course. I will reach out to Nigel," he said. A man in an oversized suit had entered the garden and was hovering near us. Von Kaiserling looked over at him and nodded.

He turned back to me. "Do you have plans this evening? Would you like to join me and a few friends for dinner at my favorite trattoria?"

"Thank you for the invitation," I said, wondering who else would be there. "I would love to come, but I'm leaving very early for Paris tomorrow morning and have to pack."

Von Kaiserling blinked. "Off so soon?"

"Unfortunately, yes. I'm sorry to miss the dinner."

"As you wish," he said. He pulled out a silver case and handed me his business card, heavy, cream-colored stock edged with gold, which included his coat of arms: a crown flanked by two birds of prey. Eagles. Or falcons. "May I have yours?"

I had mine at the ready and handed it to him. It had been laser-printed on the department's machine and one of the corners had already folded in on itself. "Thanks again for the invitation to dinner," I said. He turned and held up my card as he waved, and then handed it to the man still standing near us. Von Kaiserling and the man walked in the direction of a cluster of five eager-looking students who had just appeared.

Gregory came up just then and we exchanged pleasantries. He then excused himself, no doubt to trail after Von Kaiserling.

I went back to the book exhibit, planning how I'd get back to the flat without anyone following me. My flight was at seven thirty the next morning so I'd arranged for a taxi to pick me up at four. In one of the stands Sean was opening book covers and putting them back gently. I waved him over.

"Anything interesting?" I said.

"Just ogling books I can't possibly afford."

"You know Maximilian Von Kaiserling? He came to my paper earlier and just invited me to a dinner, so I must've done something right. We had a strange talk out in the garden. I'm not sure what to make of it to be honest."

"Ha, only you, Isabel. I'd be wary of him though. Did you know he purchased an aristocratic title? He's Baron Von Kaiserling, although he has no noble lineage. He's obsessed with heraldry."

"Sounds very sixteenth century."

"He underwrote a lot of this conference, but I don't trust him. His motivations are unclear."

"You don't trust anybody."

He shrugged.

"Anyway, I'm not going to the dinner."

"Good." He put the book down he'd been holding. "Have you been enjoying the conference?" he asked.

"Very much," I said. "Sad to leave early."

"Do you have to?"

"Yeah. You'll have to let me know how the rest goes. How about you, Sean? Enjoying the conference?"

"I met some solid people for sure. Just think, for a few hours in Florence, or somewhere equally brilliant, specialists can connect with other specialists trying to commune with the several-hundred-year-old dead. Before returning to teaching jobs in isolated places. This kind of thing will keep us going when we're professors, Isabel. Right?"

"Yes, but talking with Von Kaiserling clarified more cynical aspects about academia. Scholars, too, go to great lengths to obtain what they desire: career advancement, money, fame."

He shot me a cryptic glance. "And not nearly enough to go around."

CHAPTER EIGHTEEN

On the plane ride, to slow my fast-churning thoughts, I called back memories of my first trip to Paris with my father when I was eight. I remembered waking up before landing and seeing historic mansions, tree-lined avenues, and the Eiffel Tower sticking up like an upside down "Y."

"You're going to love it," he said, and I did. I loved the curvy buildings draped in sleek grey. I loved the Jardin de Luxembourg, its magical statues and the fountain, my first introduction to the Medici. While my father did research, I stayed with his colleague, Madame Géraud. On the plane it occurred to me that he and Madame Géraud had been more than colleagues—of course they were.

But not even Paris with William would be enjoyable. I needed to spend all my hours focused on finding the emerald.

The questions repeated themselves in a loop. Had I seen everything in Florence? Or could I have been more thorough? I had gone through all the items on Rose's list and additional manuscripts, but in the end had only found Federico's deciphering key and one letter related to the emerald. I kept worrying that I'd overlooked something crucial.

I had outlined a battle plan for Paris, with multiple lists of cascading priorities of must-see items, and knew the location and details of every source I needed to see. Marie-Christine Clément, whose email address Niccolò had sent me, had finally responded to my query, and we scheduled a meeting at her house to see her "Falcone" documents. It seemed as promising an avenue as anything else.

My detailed schedule allowed for only six hours of sleep, and no downtime. If I worked hard enough, I could find the emerald, and save Rose. I cursed her silently for putting me in this predicament, but I would deal with that later. When we were both safe.

After landing I checked my phone. There was a missed call from an American number. It turned out to be my mom. We hadn't spoken for over a month, and I hadn't told her about the Italy trip, or anything about Rose, or about my advisor, or the fact that I had embarked on a wild-goose chase to save my own and my friend's life. I hadn't wanted her to worry. But I nearly broke down when she asked where I was, and I said in Paris for research, and then went on to describe my new, fascinating, and fully funded PhD topic. On the surface, it all sounded idyllic, an opportunity that would've been any scholar's lifelong dream. Only I knew the truth.

William's friends' beautiful apartment was in a Belle Epoque building in the fifth arrondissement. Everything was painted white, including the wooden beams in the ceiling. There were floor-to-ceiling bookcases stuffed with new books, and a smaller glass-paneled cabinet filled with antique books.

"Who lives here?" I asked William after he gave me the tour.

"German classicists. They teach at the Sorbonne, but they're currently on sabbatical in Athens."

"So that's why there are no clothes in the closets."

"Did you think they were spies?" he asked, whispering the word "spies." "I'll introduce you next time. They're great and let me come and go as I please."

"Now I see why you're in Paris so often. How can professors afford this place?"

"Family apartment. Pretty sweet deal, right?"

"To say the least."

"I think you need to follow me back into the bedroom for a moment, *chère mademoiselle*. There is something I neglected to show you," he said, walking backward with an impish grin, loosening his tie.

William's conference started that week.

My own ambitious program would begin in the Bibliothèque Nationale, Site Richelieu, housed in a former private mansion, or *hôtel particulier*. Although I'd written to request permission to consult their collections months ago, in order to obtain a reader's card I needed to be interviewed, which ended up costing me a day of work because the interviews were held in the other location of the Bibliothèque Nationale on the opposite side of Paris. The following day I was standing in the entrance holding up my card when they opened.

The reading room was the most elegant I'd ever seen—long, stained-glass windows flanked by dark-wood panels, wide desks with individual green glass lamps. I was given a number and a spot near the window. Readers were allowed to consult five manuscripts per day, and requests were made by hand, in pencil. Because the catalogues for the collection I was focusing on weren't online, I was consulting them here for the first time, and discovered numerous letters written by Federico that I had been unaware of.

I was deeply frustrated by the item quota here, just as I'd been in Florence, since often only one of Federico's letters was buried inside any given manuscript, leaving me with only four more possibilities that day. During the first week I ordered five items every day, sweet-talking my way into a sixth manuscript on Thursday, Friday, and Saturday. I tore through Federico's correspondence, filled with his habitual obsequious affirmations of loyalty to prominent figures, his eagerly dispensed battle advice, and even a treatise penned by him, which he dedicated to King Henry III, Federico's own Mirror of Princes. I had known there was an abundance of material in the French archives, but I had overestimated my ability to move through it quickly. I worked every day continuously until they closed. The archivists squinted at me, curious about this eager young *Américaine* who didn't leave for the customary two-hour lunch. By the end of the week, I'd gone through twenty-seven manuscripts but had found no mention of the emerald. The odds of me discovering anything were dwindling, but I didn't lose heart. Still, I wondered why Rose had insisted I look here.

Each night after the Bibliothèque closed, I took the metro back to the apartment where William greeted me with a three-course dinner. After six evenings of feasts worthy of Vatel, we stood in the kitchen as he prepared *risotto allo zafferano*. He had a large pot of water on to boil, and a small cup of broth to the side into which he dropped saffron threads. I watched him slice an onion with great precision.

"How do you have the surplus energy for all this cooking?" I asked.

"Relaxes me after a long day of intellectual work."

"You're good at it." I patted my stomach. "And I love seeing a man in an apron."

"Copying recipes from cookbooks at the library was my first foray into research," he said. "I had to learn to cook from an early age, because I didn't like peanut butter."

"Same," I said. "My mother asked a neighbor to give me lessons. And then I was anointed the chef. That said, we ate a lot of frozen food. I was never an inspired cook. I don't have the patience."

"Patience is important, but so is passion." He put his knife down and rinsed his hands, wiped them on a dishtowel, and stroked my cheek.

"How's the conference?" I asked.

He spooned butter into a pan and when the foaming subsided, he pushed the onions inside. "All goes smoothly, thanks. We've organized a follow-up in Lyon in November."

"Let's wake up early and take a walk before breakfast. We'll have to say goodbye before you leave."

"Turns out there's only one paper tomorrow since the other speaker canceled. I'm going to skip it as I've heard her talk already. One of the other organizers is going to take care of the last day wrap-up since I did so much on the front end. So, if you have the morning free, I'm yours. My flight is at two so I'll have to leave at noon."

"That's wonderful news!"

"And maybe we could rethink that early walk," he said.

He poured in the plump risotto. "Arborio," he said. "I couldn't find carnaroli."

"I've never asked what *you* think of Machiavelli," I said, pouring more wine into my glass. "Was he as cunning and evil as his reputation would imply?"

"No." He reached toward me and put his hands on my waist, then positioned me so our hips were aligned. He kissed me on the forehead and went back to the stove. "He was a man of his time, a product of his circumstances. A brilliant one."

"Machiavelli wasn't a philosopher, but a historian, analyzing the past, using hindsight to apply lessons in his own time." While I knew the history, I was mesmerized by the way he spoke about Machiavelli, his eyes flashing between me and the risotto.

He poured one ladle of broth into the pot and stirred. "Will you take over?" he asked, offering me the spoon. "Need a little fresh air." We kissed and traded places.

William opened a window. "Consider the following," he said, sounding more professorial than I'd ever heard him sound, watching me as if I were his eager pupil. And then with a bit of drama he continued, "'At night-fall I enter the courts of bygone men. I inquire into the reasons for their actions; and they answer me. And so, for four hours I feel no annoyance, I forget all troubles, poverty holds no fears, and death loses its terrors. I become entirely one of them.'" He paused, and although he was looking at me, he was seeing something else.

Then he came back. "Communing with the past enabled Machiavelli to forget his troubles. The life of the *mind* offered a way forward."

"That appeals to all academics. But what about the idea that his writings motivated the St Bartholomew's Day massacre?" I asked, walking around the counter, handing him the spoon. "Your turn."

Stirring the risotto he said, "It's a matter of interpretation, and fashion. In the early sixteenth century, nobles bragged about owning copies of *The Prince*, dedicated, as you know, to Catherine de' Medici's father Lorenzo, Duke of Urbino. Later, French jurists accused Italian immigrants, including the Falcone, of using *The Prince* as a handbook for plotting the massacre. But Machiavelli is not the monster he's made out to be."

"People rarely are," I said.

He tilted his head. "I wish we'd met years ago," he said, and picked up the bottle of Iranian saffron from the counter before resuming cooking. "Do you know how much a few strands of this would have been worth in the sixteenth century? We take it for granted today, like everything."

We talked for another few minutes.

He turned off the stove, stirred a cup of parmesan into the risotto, then pulled two bowls out of the oven. "Light the candles, please," he said, and he filled each bowl and sprinkled cheese over the pale-gold rice. We ate in silence, slowly.

I offered to do the dishes while he took a shower, and then I showered, letting the hot water melt the tension in my shoulders, my scalp, and my hands. I went into the bedroom to find it lit by dozens of tea candles.

William stood up and found the corner of my towel tucked under my arm and tugged at it until it slid off onto the floor. "Will you lie with me?" he asked, pulling me into bed. And with the flickering light of the tiny flames illuminating our skin, I watched his beautiful hands move with great precision up and down my body.

William woke me up in the middle of the night, rubbing my back because he said I'd been having a nightmare. I vaguely remembered dreaming about Rose.

"The archives are closed tomorrow, what are your afternoon plans? I have an open ticket; I could stay past lunch. I could stay past dinner," he said.

"Actually, I made plans to meet with this woman, Marie-Christine Clément."

"Who?"

"Someone who claims to have found letters with the name Falcone in her attic. Niccolò sent me her contact info."

"Niccolò? I didn't realize you were still in touch with him."

"I'm not. He emailed me when I was in Florence. Obviously, I never answered."

"I see. Does Endicott know about this woman and her letters?"

"Nobody does."

"I'll come with you, if you'd like me to," he said.

"That would be great."

"As I said, I have an open ticket. And I can't imagine anything I'd rather do than spend the afternoon with you." He hugged me close. I felt moored. It was all going to be okay.

CHAPTER NINETEEN

After an early lunch we took the metro to Saint-Cloud. Following the directions I'd been given, we crossed a stone bridge and continued along an almost-rural road until we reached a standalone house. William rang the bell, and I smoothed my sweaty hair while we waited in the hot breeze.

The petite woman who greeted us had silky grey hair that gleamed iridescent in the afternoon sun, like a spider's web. After we introduced ourselves, she whispered her greeting as if someone were asleep nearby and led us down a thin corridor into her kitchen. She motioned toward some wicker chairs at the counter and served us darjeeling tea that had steeped for too long and was bitter and hot.

"Speak to me of your work," Marie-Christine said, addressing me.

I put my teacup down. "My dissertation focuses on a branch of the Falcone family, who emigrated from Genoa to France in the sixteenth century and rose to fame and fortune. I'm hoping to shed light on how the broader patronage system functioned." Marie-Christine nodded, with a look of slight interest but noncomprehension, reminding me that I was dealing with a nonspecialist.

William added, "At the same time the Falcone were denounced by French families who considered these successful immigrants to be usurpers."

"Is this your work as well, *monsieur*?" Marie-Christine asked William.

"He's in a related field," I said.

She took one last puff from a shortened cigarette before squashing it in an overflowing ashtray. "My mother died some years ago," Marie-Christine said. "In her attic I found an old trunk that had ancient things inside, including many letters. I saw the word 'Falcone' written on an envelope containing some letters, but I was unable to read any of them, they could have been written in hieroglyphics. Only this word, Falcone, seemed legible. I must admit I only spent an hour or two on a few occasions. When I searched the word online, I discovered it was the name of a family. I contacted the only Falcone I could find, in Genoa, but never received a reply. I suppose they were not interested."

She lit another cigarette, inhaled in and out, and sent more smoke spiraling around the room. "You were very kind to send me an email, Isabel." She folded her hands in her lap. "Excuse me just one second," she said.

We listened to her walk up the creaking stairs. I hoped I was about to view original documents that no other scholar knew about. Then again, the letters could have been written by a Falcone that had nothing to do with my research. And Marie-Christine might not let me read them, might want to sell them to me first. I had to act nonchalant. Why hadn't I discussed this with William beforehand? I leaned over and whispered, "Let's not seem too interested, okay?" Marie-Christine returned to the kitchen cradling a large, grimy box, the cigarette dangling from her lips. She set the box down on the counter and opened the lid, then pulled out a series of documents in various shapes and sizes—their top edges curled over like dying petals—and laid them on the table.

The papers were covered with mold spores and black splotches where the ink had bled through to the other side. The handwriting on the pages on the top of the pile was more modern, probably eighteenth century.

As she went through the pages, they dipped into the seventeenth and sixteenth centuries, then back to the eighteenth and nineteenth.

"*Et voilà*. Here they are! They start here. There are several," she said, humming contentedly. "Can you, please, tell me what is written in these pages?" she asked. She handed me one small sheet, the size of a three-by-five-inch index card, and leaned in to watch as I flipped it over to the other side and then back again.

"I need more light. Would it be possible to open the blinds, or switch on a lamp?"

She opened one of the blinds and my eyes scanned down the page.

"This is . . . a receipt for . . . three chickens and one cow," I said.

"Ha!" she said. "You are good at reading difficult writing. How can you do that?"

"She's an expert," said William.

"There are more pages," she said. "I hope they are not all about chickens and cows." We shared a laugh and she pulled up another chair and sat next to me. She took more papers out of the box, handing them to me one by one, not waiting for me to finish one before giving me the next. Further down in the pile, the documents were in even worse condition: mold spots consuming whole pages, larger ink stains obscuring paragraphs, the paper itself often torn or breaking or thin, seemingly about to disintegrate. I held each document up to the light. William picked up every page that I put down and glanced over it before replacing it.

"I'm still having trouble seeing," I said. Marie-Christine stood up and switched on a lamp with a dark blue lampshade that rendered it ineffective.

Worse than the mold or ink stains that obscured words, the pages felt cold and damp. I coughed. "Moisture," I murmured.

Marie-Christine gazed up at the ceiling. "The attic," she said. "The roof is in need of repair. It should have been fixed ten years ago. But I have not the money."

"They need to be dried out. And then handled and stored carefully. Somewhere they won't be exposed to humidity."

"There are many of these in the box. Why don't you continue to read," Marie-Christine said. "*S'il vous plaît.*"

Trying my best to handle the documents in a way that would not damage them, I skimmed the first few lines of each page. There were records of financial transactions including real estate purchases, loan notices, and more receipts for livestock and produce. Only a handful of them were from the sixteenth century, and none were coded. After about thirty pages I picked up a thick cluster loosely gathered in silk cloth and unwrapped it. Moisture had stained the edges of a paper envelope on top. The name Falcone was written in pencil on the envelope.

"*Et voilà,*" said Marie-Christine. "Falcone."

Under the envelope was a stack of pages. I teased the first one away from the others and looked at it. It was written in code. I scanned the rest of them quickly but gently, looking at the last page before going back to the first. They were all enciphered. I counted twelve of them. There was no date that I could discern, but they appeared to be from the late sixteenth century. They weren't as damp as the other pages, fortunately.

"These are written in code," I said to Marie-Christine. "I have a few decoding keys on my computer, and I can try them on these letters the next time I'm here."

She looked up at the clock ticking on the wall like a metronome. The air in the kitchen was stale and hazy with smoke.

The doorbell rang and Marie-Christine left the kitchen.

"Enciphered letters," said William. Marie-Christine was speaking with a male visitor. When she came back in, she said, "It's getting late. Could you come back another day? Another day soon. If that is convenient."

Then Marie-Christine's phone rang, and she went into the other room to answer it.

312

William squeezed my hand tenderly. I squeezed it back and walked over to open the kitchen window to let the cigarette smell escape. A cat was slinking through the back garden, pouncing on a tiny bird. Inside there was dust everywhere, more apparent in the dim sunlight, darting through the edges around the blinds. The papers in Marie-Christine's trunk were being stored in the worst possible conditions. Perhaps I could convince her to donate the documents to the Bibliothèque Nationale, with their expert conservators.

As soon as William left, I'd be able to focus on nothing but the letters. I'd bring the decoders and go through each one systematically. Maybe I could find a room to let for a few days out here, close by. If the letters contained anything related to the emerald, I would be the first to find out, as clearly no one else had seen them except those who'd written and received them, and maybe Marie-Christine's family members, who wouldn't have been able to read them. I heard the front door close and closed the window right before Marie-Christine came back in. "When can you return?" she asked.

"Tuesday?" I wanted to spend the next day with William. "Tuesday at ten in the morning? Or nine, if that works. The earlier the better, for me."

"Let us agree on ten on Tuesday," she said, nodding her head. "You'll come with your computer." She lowered her voice. "But I must insist that you do not photograph the documents when you are here, Isabel. *Compris?*"

"*Bien sûr*," I said. "I promise."

CHAPTER TWENTY

As William and I walked to the station we didn't speak to or even look at each other. The streets emptied as it started to drizzle. In the metro I was pushed up against William as more people entered, feeling the pull of him, but it was quieter now.

Upstairs I sat on the couch and stared at the void in the center of the room, trying not to cry.

William put his hand on my shoulder, but I turned away. "Don't look so excited. This could be a big deal, but it could also be a waste of time. It's just as possible I'm not going to find the emerald, and I'm not going to save Rose." By now tears were coming out in streams.

"Wai—wait. Today was a great day! I think there's real potential. Twelve coded letters!"

I sat up. "Yeah, but no key. I'll try mine when I go back to Saint-Cloud and see if either of them works, but that's a *pretty big* if."

William moved closer and pulled me into his embrace. He lowered his voice. "I think you need a night off. You've been under so much stress for—how long—since October? Feeling that you are alone responsible for Rose's life. . . . That's too much for any single person."

I crossed my arms over my chest. "It's not just Rose. There's also Catrina, whose death I'm probably responsible for."

"Shh, shh," he said, rubbing my head. "Isabel, you don't know that. If you do want to save Rose, you simply can't think that about Catrina right now. It's toxic. Let's instead think about dinner. I know this great place, a five-minute walk. *Très intime.* Put it all out of your mind for three hours. I have an idea. We could pretend . . . that we are lovers in Paris!"

"Okay, but just this once."

I took a shower and tried on a skirt and white shirt before deciding to wear the only dress I'd brought, black, the lower part embroidered with tiny red flowers.

"Zip me up?" I asked William after I had adjusted the lining.

He walked behind me and said, "With pleasure." He ran the fingers of one hand up my spine, preceding the zipper, which he tugged up with his other hand, giving me a small chill.

"Mmm," I said, not moving. "You do that so . . . expertly."

He softly kissed the back of my neck, then stepped back.

I twirled around and put my hands on my hips.

"You look gorgeous," he said. "You are gorgeous."

Outside, arm in arm, we walked along narrow streets, William's wool jacket sometimes snagging on the delicate embroidery of my dress. We reached a row of three cafés that all looked similar. A man standing in the doorway of the first café waved and called out, "Hello, Monsieur Anderson!" William returned his greeting with a "*bonsoir!*" We kept walking and I glanced up at him, raising one eyebrow.

"I often eat there when I'm in town," said William. He leaned down and whispered, "But where we're going is much more romantic," and squeezed my arm.

We approached the only restaurant on the block with no outdoor seating and stepped into a cozy room with white tablecloths and red-leather booths. There was one French family with two children, but the other customers were all couples. We were seated next to each other at a banquette table tucked into a corner near a small, empty fireplace with dried flowers inside it.

"*Très romantique!*" I said. "Did you request these seats?"

"*Ah mais oui!*" he said.

I couldn't eat more than one course, so we ordered the special, provençal stew. William put his arm around me and drew me close. "That's better," he said. "You're smiling again."

In front of William on the table was a thick, red, leather-bound wine list. Its cover brought to mind Rose's book where I had first read the name "Falcone." Without opening it, William signaled to the closest server.

"We'll have a bottle of the Château Talbot. The 1998."

The server wiggled his glasses down the bridge of his nose. "Monsieur et madame are celebrating something, an anniversary perhaps?"

William took my hand in his. "Not an anniversary, but we are celebrating." He squeezed my hand.

"Well," I said, after the server left. "We're celebrating our last night together, at least for a while."

"I've decided to stay on a few extra days actually. Didn't feel right, leaving you. Not again. And I want to be around when you make the discovery that sends your career into the stratosphere!"

My heart fluttered and I took a sip of water.

Another server, the sommelier, walked up with the bottle of wine, and she uncorked it in front of us. William swirled the red-black liquid around in his glass and stuck his nose inside and inhaled.

"*Très bon*," he said. The sommelier poured wine into my glass, filling it just slightly less than halfway, and then poured some into William's glass.

The bordeaux tasted smooth and sultry. We talked and held hands until our stew arrived steaming and aromatic. After he had taken a few bites William said, "Tell me something about you that no one else knows." He poured more wine into my glass. Again, I thought of Rose, of that night in her apartment, "Tell me a secret," she had said.

"I'm not sure I can think of anything that fits that description," I said, and gulped down some wine. "I don't have any real secrets."

"Alright," he said. "What makes you happiest, and conversely, what troubles you in the middle of the night?"

I eased back into the banquette. "My father left us when I was twelve. That doesn't make me happy, nor does it trouble me anymore, but it's something important I haven't told you."

"That's terrible. I'm so sorry. That must have been very difficult as a young person." He ran his fingers over mine. "And your mother?"

"She's fine, she lives in Boston. I'm an only child."

"What else has . . . shaped you?"

"School mostly . . . . I've been focused for as long as I can remember."

"I mean relationships. What other relationships have shaped you?"

"After college I had an affair with a married man. It went on for a while, then one day his wife came to visit me, and I realized how crazy the whole thing had been. So, I ended it. It was difficult, but I think the scars have healed."

He patted my hand. "I'm honored by your candor. Thank you." We were quiet for a moment and then he asked, "Is that why you chose St Stephens? To escape? Don't worry, I don't judge other people's choices. Machiavelli wouldn't approve."

"That was part of it. And the opportunity to work with Madeleine Grangier. And to study alongside Rose. I wanted to be like her. Be careful what you wish for." As I leaned back the leather squeaked. "How about you, William? What was it like for you growing up?"

He raked some hair back from his forehead and took a swig of wine. "My mom was a professor. It was another time. Universities didn't want to hire her because they assumed she'd get pregnant, but she found a position anyway; she was that smart. If any of her competitive colleagues asked, she'd tell them, 'Fuck you, I don't want kids.' Then I came along. And my dad died. My mother remarried. My stepfather was . . . mean. In both the Scottish and the American sense." He swirled the wine in his glass, looked down at his plate, then at the glass. His face was pale, and his eyebrows scrunched together. "And my . . . I've never told anybody this before but . . . my mother . . . she . . . abused me."

"Oh no, I'm so, so sorry," I said, taking his hand.

He sipped more wine and looked toward the other tables. "She has severe bipolar depression with bouts of psychosis. Lives in an institution. The only treatment that's ever worked is electric shock therapy. I've never told anyone that either."

"I'm so sorry," I said again. "That's really heavy. But I'm glad you know you can trust me. I want to support you as much as you support me. I'm a good listener."

He looked at me. "I know you are. You're a good person. I could tell when we first met, and like I told you then, I could see your sadness. It drew me to you. Anyway, it's all in the past. I left home at seventeen. Although I do still pay her bills."

"Seventeen is so young," I said, squeezing his hand again.

"I've always supported myself. Odd jobs, factory work, even gambling. Recently online poker."

"You can make money that way?"

His voice took a lighter tone. "If you're talented, yes. Enough about me, though. How do you feel? Hopefully this break has been good for you. I can't believe we've been in Paris for an entire week, and this is our first dinner out! As though I've been hiding you away."

"It's nice to relax for a few hours," I said. "How long will you stay in Paris? Will you be working on your paper for Glasgow?"

"I've written most of it," he said. "To answer your first question, I'm not sure when I'll leave. How long would you like me to stay?"

"Forever?" I said, "But you might distract me."

"I promise I won't. Unless you want me to." Our hands met under the tablecloth, and we twined and untwined our fingers as our eyes locked.

He tapped on the table and when he caught someone's attention he signaled for the check.

We walked back home along the *quais* that ran beside the Seine, letting the breeze escort us back to the apartment. It was hot inside, so I opened all the windows and asked William to unzip my dress. I then slid it off along with my underwear and tossed them on the bed. I helped William out of his clothes and pulled him into a cold shower, thinking it would cool us down, but it didn't. A couple of minutes later we toppled into bed, woozy from the wine and the cold water. I straddled him, crushing my hips into his. He held my face in his hands the whole time.

"Do you want to take a break?" I asked, after a while.

"We can go on all night if you want," William said, brushing my hair out of my eyes. We fell asleep in each other's arms, but soon separated. At around three A.M., when I was still wide awake, he brushed my shoulder.

"You're going to find the emerald," he said. "I have a good feeling."

The next morning in the kitchen he passed me a cup of freshly brewed coffee. "You didn't sleep at all, did you?"

"Not much. I shouldn't have had all that wine."

"How long do you think it will take at Marie-Christine's?"

"All day, for several days in a row. As long as she'll have me."

"I can help you, even if it's just bouncing ideas back and forth. We could work ten or twelve hours. Or I could be quiet. I'll bring a book."

My phone rang.

"Hallo, Isabel? It's Marie-Christine. I'm in Lille. A friend of mine has taken ill and is in hospital," she said. "I don't know when I will return. Tuesday will not work."

"Oh, I'm so sorry! I hope your friend is okay."

"I am not sure," she said.

"Excuse me for bringing this up right now, Marie-Christine, but I'm still trying to figure out why Falcone letters might be in your attic. Your last name is Clément, right?"

"Yes, but the house belongs—belonged—to my mother."

"And her name was? Her maiden name."

"De la Fère."

We spoke for a few minutes and said goodbye after she assured me she would be in touch when she returned home.

I turned to William after I hung up. "Her mother's last name was de la Fère, like Madeleine! I'm definitely on the right track. But what am I going to do now? She's in Lille with a friend who needs her. Who knows when she'll be back."

"We'll find a solution. I promise," William said. "Actually, I may already have one."

I spent the rest of the afternoon writing up all my notes and going over the list of all the remaining documents I still needed to see. William went out for a few hours, to "stay out of my hair," and I was grateful to be alone and organize my thoughts. I wanted to follow up with Marie-Christine for more details about her mother's family and ask if she had any idea when she'd be back, so I dialed her number. But the call didn't go through because my phone had run out of battery. I looked around for a charger. Nothing in any of the cabinets or drawers. Maybe William had one? I opened his briefcase, which thankfully, but oddly, he'd left behind. No charger in the big pocket. I searched a smaller pocket. My fingers felt a stack of damp papers. I pulled out Marie-Christine's coded letters, all twelve of them.

I found the charger and plugged in my phone, then sat on the couch and tossed explanations around in my head until William arrived half an hour later. He was carrying a bouquet of what looked like three dozen long stemmed red roses, which he put in the kitchen sink. Then he plunked down next to me. "You're very quiet. What's wrong?"

"William, I found the packet of Marie-Christine's letters in your briefcase."

He turned away and then back. A flash of anger pulsed through his eyes. "What? Did you—did you look through my things while I was out?"

"I was trying to find a phone charger."

"You shouldn't go through someone else's belongings without asking. I shared some personal things with you last night, and it's upsetting to think you don't trust me."

"I do trust you—it sounds like you don't trust me."

"Yeah, okay. I can't believe you'd snoop through my things. What next, did you hack into my computer?"

"How many times do I have to tell you, I was looking for a charger? You're welcome to look through my things anytime. I have nothing to hide. Why are you blaming me for something trivial and avoiding my question? I'm sure you have a good reason for taking Marie-Christine's letters, but I'd like to know what it is. And why didn't you tell me after I hung up with her?"

"Trivial? I'm a very private person, Isabel. That's something you should know. Why didn't I tell you right away? I was planning on surprising you. When I said I might have a solution, this was it." He threw his hands up in the air and slapped them down, then pointed toward the kitchen. "That's why I brought roses. I'd planned an entire evening. I thought you'd be thrilled. You needed those documents, Isabel, and now we have them . . . . Who knows when Marie-Claire will be back." He cracked his knuckles. "This entire time I've been killing myself to help you, Isabel. A little gratitude might be nice."

"I know you have, William," I said. "And I am grateful." Then I added, "Her name is Marie-Christine."

"Not to mention it was our responsibility as historians to intervene," he said. "The documents were in danger. All the knowledge in those letters could go up in flames. Can you believe how much she smoked?"

321

"It wasn't our call to make," I said. "I'm going to return her letters as soon as she's back!"

"The irony is you care about her family legacy more than she does," William said. "Well, when you're there you need to battle for them to make sure they're preserved. For posterity. You're close to a real breakthrough. And to finding the emerald. And saving Rose. Let's focus on those things, especially the last point. Someone's life."

"Yes," I said. "But not by stealing."

He took a deep breath. "I would rather borrow—*borrow*—a handful of papers from someone to whom they mean *nothing* than risk your life and Rose's life. Do you want to end up like Catrina? Do you want Rose to? Is that what you want? Time is running out, and you're attacking me. Do you think I wanted to take those letters? I honestly don't give a shit about whatever the hell her name is, or her letters. I did it to help you. I don't know what else to say."

I sucked in my breath. "I understand you were doing it to help. But you should've just told me!"

"Not just to help. To save your fucking life, Isabel. What is this really about? Yes, it's a stressful time, but it seems like your blaming me has more to do with your own trust issues. Because your father abandoned your family? I can't think of another reason you'd react so irrationally. Carrying the past with you is destructive. Take it from someone who knows." He stood up and walked to the front door. "Maybe you should do a little soul searching and tell me that's not what this is. I'll be back in an hour with dinner."

That night we had sex with special urgency, as if we were both aware of how easy it would be to lose each other.

CHAPTER TWENTY-ONE

T he following day I went to the Archives Nationales in a state-of-
the-art building in the Marais. I ran a search on their computerized
but offline catalogue and found the call number for Federico's inventory.
It was located in the Minutier Central, which housed notarial records.
Underneath the entry in the catalogue there was a note specifying that
the inventory was in poor condition and required special permission to
consult. I applied by contacting the email address listed at the bottom of
the screen. I spent the rest of the day copying out six of Marie-Christine's
letters and writing a long email to my mother. By the end of the workday,
no one had responded to my query. The following morning, I tried
again—in person this time.

"The official who can help you is not available," said the receptionist.
"Would you care to wait?"

"I'll be back in a minute," I said. I stepped outside and called Marie-
Christine. She didn't answer, but her voicemail said she was out of
town. So, she was broadcasting the fact that her home was empty and
unguarded. I worried about all the other documents in her house. Rose's
captors might steal them anytime. I needed to get back to work so my
mind could stop swerving in a thousand different directions.

I returned to the office and was told that the person I needed to speak with had been in briefly but had now gone to lunch. I cracked my knuckles. While waiting, I looked again through the catalogue. Later, William took me to his favorite English bookstore, and we read passages to each other from a few favorite novels. I could tell he was trying to distract me.

Back at the apartment William said he had a headache and went to bed. I took out the letters and laid them on the kitchen counter, then copied out the remaining six. I'd try to decipher them using copies of the decoders I'd found in Florence. I tried transcribing the first few lines of the first letter. Neither decoder worked. Same for the second. After two hours, I had reached a dead end. I couldn't read any of the letters without a functioning key.

The third day William called somebody on the inside at the Archives Nationales who got us the special permission. He came with me just in case, and I squeezed his hand and mouthed "thank you" as we went into the building together. We sat at a carrel away from the other desks and waited for a few minutes until two archivists brought out a white box. As they walked away, he stood up, kissed me on the forehead, and said, "I'll be back in half an hour."

I lifted the inventory out and placed it gently on the stand. The cover was made of parchment. The spine was damaged and loose leaves of paper jutted out from its gaps like misaligned vertebrae. The title inside read "Inventory of Federico Falcone, Baron of Neilly and Counselor of the King in his State and Private Council." The pages were dusty and thin, flakes threatened to disintegrate between my fingertips.

The inventory listed all of the items in Federico's palatial villa near the Louvre, which had been destroyed during the French Revolution. Although most inventories were created after someone died, this one had been compiled during Federico's lifetime. Inventories were composed room by room, describing each space and its contents with their approximate value, thus enabling detailed reconstructions of sixteenth-century households. Working through such material provided a privileged glimpse into the inner workings of any given individual or family.

The inventory was over sixty pages long. I skimmed through many pages listing Federico's furniture, including hundreds of oak tables and chairs, and only wrote down elaborate and unusual items.

The section on the *salle des tableaux*, Federico's painting gallery, itemized his paintings. He owned perhaps seventy canvases, which he would have shown off during the lavish banquets he was famous for hosting, according to contemporary sources. My eyes moved over the individual entries, which included religious as well as mythological works, and portraits of French kings and queens. Perhaps some had been painted by famous artists. I came to a series of family portraits, starting with a six-and-a-half-foot portrait of the *paterfamilias*, Giovanbattista.

Some of the paintings had been returned to the family in Genoa and were hanging on the walls of the palazzo. Sure enough, the next entry described the portrait of Federico, which I had seen there, unless the one in Genoa was a copy. Six feet tall in a gilded frame.

On the next page, in "a room with a garden view," I read about chairs covered with morocco leather embossed with gold, and a stone intarsia table with marble, agate, and other semiprecious stones in the center.

By then, forty minutes had passed, and William circled back to me and slid into the chair next to mine while I read through six pages describing bed linens, including linen sheets and silk blankets, green velvet pillows, feather mattresses, and damask covers with "golden embroidery of birds and flowers."

"Talk about a laundry list," I whispered to William.

I skimmed through the contents of several rooms before coming to Federico's wardrobe, which listed his clothing and armor.

"In Federico's bedroom there were two Milanese swords and a dagger," I said. "The Milanese were master sword smiths. And an *écritoire*, that's a . . ."

"Writing desk," William and I said at the same time.

"With an inkwell and two drawers," I said. "Which locked."

"Ooh," William said. "For secret correspondence."

"Two mirrors, which were very rare. I'm sure Federico was vain. Then an *horloge*, a clock, I suppose. 'In the German style,' with a figure of Saint George. But with two dragons in gold-coated silver. I wonder why two?"

William said, "In the Northern European tradition, a small dragon is often depicted next to the large dragon that St George slays. The small one signifies that, despite our best efforts, evil persists."

"The Northern Europeans were wisely cynical."

Next to Federico's bedroom was a small room where he kept special items, including his collection of objects from the Americas: shells, an entire shelf of coral objects, one hundred vessels of agate and crystal, twenty-five "*chinoiseries*," twelve astronomical instruments, seven geometrical instruments; a gilded metal and steel mechanical armillary sphere, showing the movements of the sun, moon, and planets; and reliquaries of Brazilwood, amber, and silver; and skeletons of a bird of paradise, a crocodile, and a chameleon. On folio 46v a section on "precious stones" listed a glass cabinet made for a "precious emerald, very large."

I edged as close as possible to William and pointed at what I was reading and gave him a thumbs up. After copying down the rest of the contents of the room, I released the inventory.

Outside William lifted me up and spun me around.

"Darling," he said. "I'm so proud of you."

"I'm glad to have found this," I said. "But it's nothing to get excited about. Even if the inventory is now out of circulation, scholars before me, including Von Kaiserling, must have seen it, or a copy of it, because he published an article in German about Federico's *Wunderkammer*. And it doesn't give any indication as to where the emerald is, just that Federico had one. This particular one." I sighed.

I went back to the Bibliothèque Nationale the next day. I worked there on Friday and Saturday, and again on Monday and Tuesday. On Wednesday I'd gone through three of my five daily manuscripts and found a handful of letters penned by Federico, but they contained nothing of value.

I called up the fourth volume. About a third of the way in was a coded letter. I pulled up the decoders on my screen, including Federico's simple decoder. Then I slowly began to build words.

The next day I decoded the entire letter, which turned out to be a letter Federico had addressed to Catherine de' Medici.

CHAPTER TWENTY-TWO

Madame Catherine de Médicis, Most Illustrious Queen
Mother of the King of France etc.]

*Excuse the late arrival of this letter. Serving you and your son,
the Most Christian King, you must know, has forever been and
continues to be my principal concern. Not for one moment of my
time aboard your grand ship, notwithstanding thirst, hunger and
pungent rain, has my mind veered away from the service of your
most exalted majesties and the completion of the mission with
which you so munificently entrusted me.*

*It is with great sadness and regret that I am forced, out of
duty toward you and the unwavering respect I bear your majesties, to report to you the loss of eight of our own ships off the coast
of Brazil. 70 pieces of artillery were seized, and it is believed
that over eight hundred souls have perished. Evil Spaniards are
to blame for our misfortune. How grateful am I that I escaped
with my own life in order to deliver this letter to a faithful
friend traveling to my most beloved France. I have assurances
that he will deliver this letter to the hands of your majesties
with whatsoever possible speed as can be afforded to us in these
days of inconstancy.*

I should wish to inform you, as well, of the loss of my dearest friend Jacques [. . .]. Carried on his person I know to have been a map detailing a most secret passage deep into one of those great forests far inland from the coast. He had good reason to believe that the map would have led him to a hidden wonder, the greatest potential discovery in that land of a thousand new discoveries.

I believe the map to be burned or sunk to the bottom of the sea because my cherished friend promised that he would destroy it, and himself, willingly, rather than hand it over to the hands of our enemies. But, most fortunately, my now-defunct friend confided in me the details of the said map, which I shall convey to your majesties when I return, when the winds of this treacherous sea blow benevolently in your direction, and above all when the good Lord wills it.

Upon my return know that I will urgently invoke the never-ending charity of your most generous majesties to request a further allotment of men and artillery for our next voyage, that it may be victorious and that I may load your triumphant ships with abundant bounty. In further pursuit of this end, I will most humbly beseech your majesties to grant me a small sum, with the reassurance that such a sum will re-pay itself ten thousand fold.

A small consolation I may offer to your most honored majesties is that among the dead were many souls infected with the heresy. The next voyage, I can assure you, if my wishes are granted, will be superior to the first. Upon my return, I shall handpick a pure contingent of sailors, inspired by the one true Catholic faith, to claim this verdant land in the blessed name of your majesties. Once the ample monies reaped from these prizes begin to flow into the coffers of your kingdom, the perfect health of the state shall finally be restored as the heresy will be cut out completely.

May the good Lord protect and preserve you always in good health. I humbly kiss your hands.

Your most obedient and affectionate servant,
Federico de' Falcone

While the letter didn't mention the emerald directly, it did refer to the trip Federico had taken to Brazil in late 1579. How had the Spanish discovered the secret voyage? Had someone alerted them? It had been a spectacular naval disaster. And yet Federico had remained intent on fundraising. The letter provided an accurate depiction of his character. I texted William, "Intriguing stuff," and typed out the letter in full on my laptop. My sixth-and-final manuscript of the day yielded nothing. I decided to leave early.

On my way home I stopped at a local market and bought a baguette, cheese, and ingredients to make homemade mayonnaise, pleased with the idea of surprising William when he arrived home after his meeting with a professor at the Sorbonne.

Back in the apartment I arranged the baguette and cheeses on a platter, then set out to make mayonnaise, using the recipe in the only cookbook in the apartment. I broke an egg over a bowl and poured the contents back and forth between each half of the shell until only the yolk remained, then repeated the process. I whisked the yolks with lemon and olive oil. The mixture turned out curdled, lumpy. I tasted it, laughed at myself, then washed my failed attempt down the drain and went out to buy a jar at the Monoprix across the street. They were having a rosé special, so I stuck a bottle in my cart along with *mâche* and herbs that looked very fresh.

Crossing the street, I felt giddy, lost in my thoughts. Outside the building I stopped. Niccolò was standing on the front steps. I didn't retreat, but slowly put the bags down on the pavement and pulled out my phone.

"I'm calling the police," I said in a flat tone.

"Go ahead," he said. "It's not 9-1-1 over here. It's 1-7."

"What?"

"To dial the police. Dial 1-7. *Diciasette.*"

"What do you want, Niccolò? Why are you here?"

"I think you know something about missing papers and property. Belonging to my family," he said, taking a few steps toward me.

I dialed the police, explaining in French that my life was in danger, and gave them the address.

I stood still as he came closer. "William will be here any minute."

"William?"

"Professor William Anderson. My advisor. The apartment where we're staying belongs to his friends."

"Oh, him? William? This is his name? His real name? Ask Rosa about him." He said and barked out a short laugh. "Ask my mother!"

"The Contessa? Why would I ask her about William?"

"Let's start with why you should ask Rosa. First of all, this is her apartment. Aren't you curious how I found you? I called your school and told them I was your brother looking for you and they told me you were in Paris. Where else would you be in Paris but here?"

"Next Willem, the handsome professor. This is also his apartment. Rosa and I met here when he was in Scotland. The two are lovers. Or they were until Rosa came to Genoa. Or maybe they were until you came along. Or maybe you're doing a threesome thing? Now it's all making sense.

"As for my mother . . ." We both looked up as two cars with flashing lights, but no sirens, stopped dramatically at each end of the street, and then four police were charging toward us from different directions, guns drawn.

CHAPTER TWENTY-THREE

Three hours later I was back at the apartment, trying to gather my thoughts and assess how much of Niccolò's story seemed believable, and what I would ask William. My forehead was throbbing. After taking a shower I drank a glass of rosé and was starting to pull some semblance of a meal together when William let himself in.

"Oh, darling," he said. He poured himself a glass of wine.

I put my glass down and stared toward the window.

"Darling," he said. "Everything okay? You seem agitated."

"Do I?" I turned to face the wall, took a deep breath, and then turned back to him.

"We had a visitor. Niccolò."

"Niccolò?"

"Yes. He told me this is Rose's apartment. Is that true?"

He answered without hesitating. "No—yes."

"No, or yes, which one is it?"

"It is the apartment where Rose stayed when she came to Paris. It does belong to friends, though."

I folded my arms. "He said it was also your apartment, yours together. You and Rose. That you stayed here. Together. That you were . . . that you were lovers."

He slowly shook his head. "Remember," he said, "everything Niccolò says is motivated by his own agenda."

"You bastard," I said in a low growl as I edged past him.

"No!" he said, and dropped to his knees on the floor. "Isabel, no!" he screamed. "Isabel! I—I love you."

I turned at the front door. He shot me a look deep with anguish. Why was I worried about hurting him?

"Please," he said. "Please listen to my side of it."

I'd forgotten my purse. I crossed the room, and yanked it from the chair, slinging the long strap over my shoulder.

"I'm leaving," I said, nodding, convincing myself.

"Isabel," he said. "Darling." That word was like a secret password that changed the direction of my blood flow. "Please," he said quietly, and I could see his arms start to shake.

I let my shoulders sag and walked over to the couch. "Tell me," I said as I sat down. "Only, don't draw it out. And do not try to stop me if I decide to leave."

He lowered himself down to the floor, his eyes on mine. "I wanted to tell you. I actually have told you, all of it, but only in my mind. I didn't think you would believe me. I thought you would believe her. I thought you would believe Rose.

"She was my student in a summer study abroad program in Florence. Seven years ago. On the last night the teachers and the students went out drinking. Soon, Rose and I were the only two people left in the bar. Rose went quiet. Then she told me she couldn't stop thinking about me.

"I fell completely. Every day with her was an adventure. She was so full of energy, so smart. When I was offered the job at St Stephens, I encouraged her to apply."

A corkscrew twisted inside the soft space between my ribs. "Go on," I said.

"When she first arrived, we kept the relationship secret, and then we broke up. Her father had made it clear that he couldn't stand me. He threatened to disinherit her. Once she told him that we'd broken up the money flow was turned back on. For a while. After Christmas she told me that she couldn't live without me, but that we'd have to pretend we were colleagues and nothing more.

"Rose was fishing around for a topic when she met Von Kaiserling at a book launch. He fell for her just as I did, just like anyone who got within twenty feet of her, like you did. At dinner the next night he told her about the Falcone family. He said they would make a great topic, especially Federico. He had a lot of material from Genoa already, and she was welcome to use it. She loved the idea, and he became her unofficial advisor. He offered her a full scholarship, and a big stipend.

"Rose told him about me, and he gave us his blessing. He owns this apartment. He treated us to first-class plane tickets, expensive dinners, shopping sprees. Heady stuff. Rose and I always had 'research' to do, and practically lived here.

"About three months in, he told us about the Falcone Emerald, something he wanted to add to his old-timey cabinet of curiosities. He said if we could find it, he'd be willing to pay us a lot of money. Ten million dollars. At first, we didn't believe him, but when he wired each of us $250,000, we knew he wasn't messing around.

"He steered us to the Falcone Archive in the palazzo. Rose went to Genoa, sweet-talked her way in after meeting Niccolò 'by chance.' She ended up staying with the Falcone for a couple of weeks. Which turned into a month. She and Niccolò started sleeping together, she claimed it was to further the cause. But she wasn't conducting any research. She had no leads on the emerald, and she wasn't answering Von Kaiserling's emails.

"He turned nasty and one of his minions started threatening her. She begged me to come to Genoa. She said she would steal a few pages each day and I could work on them. I went to Genoa, and Von Kaiserling put me up at the San Rocco Palace Hotel. Rose said she couldn't drop Niccolò, and I never saw her. I came up with my own plan. I sent a note to the Palazzo Falcone on the hotel letterhead and said I was a rare book dealer and invited the Contessa for a drink. She accepted. It was only in an attempt to find out about the emerald that I flirted with Beth. Contessa Falcone.

"She agreed to sell their whole collection of sixteenth-century documents to me. Von Kaiserling was thrilled and had the courier bring down $500,000 US dollars, with another 10 for spending money. The Contessa kept re-negotiating the details of the deal, always over dinner in my hotel room. She brought a stack of pages to keep me reeled in, and two days later I found a letter written in mirror code that mentioned the Falcone Emerald. The letter said the emerald was hidden in a suit of armor at the palazzo. Rose asked to meet me, and apologized for letting me down. She and Niccolò had been fighting and he followed her, showing up just as I was accepting her apology with a friendly hug. There was quite the scene. Niccolò threatened us both and Rose took a taxi to the airport. Where she went, I have no idea. Probably back to daddy.

"The next day Niccolò's family left to go skiing but the Contessa backed out at the last minute, pretending to be sick. The factotum drove them up, so I had free reign of the palazzo and eventually looked inside the suit of armor and found the emerald."

"You found the emerald?"

"Well, there's more to the story."

"You spent the weekend there with the Contessa I guess."

"Yes, but listen. The emerald looked like a piece of cheap glass. I gave it to Von Kaiserling and he had it polished, then mounted in a cabinet he'd had custom built for it years ago. He had no interest in us after we delivered the stone, but he did deposit a million dollars into a Swiss account that Rose had opened up, promising the rest at the beginning of the following year.

"Back in St Stephens Rose was rearranging Von Kaiserling's documents and the pages from the Falcone Archive to construct her thesis. But she never did any real work. Even that list I gave you was the original list that Von Kaiserling gave her. She had told me she wanted to put the word 'doctor' in front of her name. She rented a place in New York, in the West Village, started throwing parties for a new crowd she wanted to get in with. She flew back to St Stephens every once in a while to keep up the appearance of being in the program. She began writing a novel, never told me what it was about, but said I wouldn't like it.

"Then came the call. From Von Kaiserling's lawyer. We had sold him a fake. The lawyer explained it was not a modern fake, but a fake that had been made in the sixteenth century or after, so Von Kaiserling realized we'd been duped as well. Luckily. We asked for time and fended him off by saying we had some fresh leads. He got distracted by something in Iceland for a few months. Obviously neither of us could go back to the Palazzo Falcone. Rose had daddy's checks flowing in again and wasn't willing to go to the Florence or Paris archives. Those rich girls really feel invulnerable. She just dropped out of sight and mind."

"Where do I come into all of this?"

"You had just arrived, and you had that problem with your topic. It was actually Von Kaiserling's idea. He came to St Stephens to meet you after Endicott raved about you. Von Kaiserling wanted Rose out of the picture, and we tried to dissuade him, but he insisted he wanted you to proceed where Rose had left off, for you to find the emerald. He swore to me that he wouldn't lay a hand on you, or any of us, as long as you didn't know what was going on. Even if you came up with nothing, he promised never to hurt you. He believed you were his best hope for finding the emerald, and, to be honest, I did, too. But then, he wasn't true to his word. At first, I thought Rose was making up everything she told you. But I was genuinely shocked when you called to say your apartment had been broken into. And then, of course, about Catrina."

He stood up and walked around the room twice, on his second pass glugging down the rest of the glass of wine I'd poured myself earlier. "I would have gone to those archives myself, but the Contessa had put out that reward, and I knew she was searching for me, tentacles everywhere, including in Florence and Paris. She even sent her goon Emiliano sniffing around the Archivio di Stato. And Paris was a different problem."

"What do you mean?"

"I accompanied Rose to the BN the last time we were here, because she was in panic mode, totally freaking out by that point. To such an extent that she actually tried to sneak out a letter that she thought had to do with the emerald. She slipped the letter inside my laptop, as we were on our way out, and they discovered it. I took the heat for her, explaining she was my student, that it had been an accident. All we got was a slap on the wrist, but I was expressly forbidden to return to the library until otherwise notified. I think my name is on a blacklist or something."

"Wait. Rose tried to steal a document from the Bibliothèque Nationale?"

"Yes, but only because she was desperate. And the threats from Von Kaiserling kept coming. And eventually, things got really ugly. Uglier than I could have imagined.

"Rose shared with Catrina some of what was going on, and she decided to out Von Kaiserling, who threatened her. But then to hedge his bet he recruited her, said she had to get to you, because you weren't taking your task seriously. He told her to tell you his people had kidnapped Rose, that both her life and Rose's life were in danger.

"Catrina disappeared, thinking she could elude him, I guess. And her second call to you must have been trying to warn you. But they caught her, obviously, and killed her. Her murder was no doubt meant to serve as a warning to Rose, to you, and to me. Von Kaiserling contacted me and said as much."

I spoke again, but my voice was not as hard as it had been. "This is a lot to take in."

"I know," he said. "Believe me, I know." He shook his head and tried to pretend he wasn't crying. I went over to him and took him in my arms.

We rocked each other for a while until he said, "I mean it when I say I will never stop begging your forgiveness. For this and everything else."

"There's more?" I asked, as I stepped back.

"There's more, yes," he said.

"What is it?" I asked. "What happened to Rose?"

"Months ago, I told her she could stay in my place on the Isle of Lewis, which would allow her to disappear for a while. And there was another thing. She was pregnant."

"Your child?"

"Isabel! Jesus! Don't you get it? I love you! I have loved you since I met you. I remember seeing you in the rain that very first day. I remember every detail of every encounter we've ever had. I could quote everything you've ever said to me. No. I haven't slept with Rose since you arrived in St Stephens."

"Where is Rose now?"

"Rose and I had agreed there would be no communication between us while she was in Lewis, for her safety. Then Rose started calling me, messaging me. She was bored. I told her the calls could be traced, to be careful, but she didn't care. She was running out of money—her dad was withholding her allowance. One day a Lewis neighbor called and left me a message saying it was urgent I go there. I assumed Von Kaiserling's team was watching me, or trying to, so I made sure no one could track my movements.

"When I got to the house, Rose wasn't in any danger. This is where you come in, actually. She found something I'd written to you, but never sent. She figured out I was in love with you.

"When I didn't deny it, she attacked me, and you. She said you were mentally unstable, and started yelling and throwing things at me, then took a knife from the kitchen and tried to stab me. She actually managed to knock me out with a frying pan, I think, and when I came to, she was gone. I don't know if she went to Von Kaiserling, or if he found her, but he's got her now. He left me a voicemail with her screaming on the phone."

"So Rose was in the Hebrides at your grandmother's house, and now Von Kaiserling has got her. Jesus. Anything else? Has Von Kaiserling threatened you recently? Are you in danger now?"

"Yes, I am. He's been threatening me ever since the fiasco with the fake emerald. I've almost completely reimbursed him for everything, but it hasn't been easy. And anyway, it doesn't matter if I reimburse him. He's still after me. I was angry with Rose for a long time, but when I heard her voice on the phone, it was kind of harrowing."

"And you didn't tell me any of this? I cannot believe you have been keeping all of this from me."

"Look, I couldn't tell you, not any part of it, okay?"

"Nothing? Why not?"

He made two fists, took a deep breath, and looked as though he couldn't continue. "Because he told me if I told you . . . he said he would find out, and he . . . he would kill you. He's having other people watch you, watch me, and he's watching you himself. That's why he went to Florence."

"And he wasn't worried about us staying together here, that you'd slip up?

This is his apartment. You're telling me now, does that mean we're both going to die?" I gripped his hand.

"I had to tell you, you didn't give me a choice. I can't afford to lose you, Isabel. Don't worry, though, I switched off the bugs when we arrived. I had set some up for Von Kaiserling before, so I know how it's done. He keeps asking me what's going on, but I've told him the building manager found the extra wires and hardware in the utility room on this floor, and he didn't know what they were, so he removed them."

"What about Madeleine Grangier, William? Do you know what happened to her?"

He shook his head.

"I can take it," I said, although my teeth had started to chatter. "Tell me."

"I'm sure she was another of Von Kaiserling's victims, although he refuses to discuss her with me."

"I want to know everything," I said, sensing he was holding something back. "All of it." I was clasping my hands together so tightly my fingertips had turned white.

He glanced toward the window, and angled his body away from me. "Madeleine called me. The day she died. I've been carrying that around. She said she needed to make an important decision and that she'd . . . be in touch soon." His voice was cracking.

"Why did she call you?"

"We were friends. And she knew she could trust me."

"So Von Kaiserling killed Madeleine himself?"

"No. Never himself. One of his people."

"Who?"

"No clue. Now you know everything I do. Please, I can't stand to talk about this anymore. I—I've never felt so bad in my life."

By this time, I was kneeling right next to him. He took me by the shoulders.

"You believe me, don't you?" he whispered. "I couldn't have made something like this up."

I held his face in my hands. "I believe you."

He took my hands in his and kissed the inside of my wrists. He was shaking again, and he looked at me as if to say, here it is, the truth stripped down. I searched his eyes. All of it was true.

"What do we do now?" I asked.

"There's still time to find out what happened to the emerald. We've got the coded letters, and although none of the keys you, or I, tried work on them, I can do basic decoding using frequency analysis. It's time consuming, but it's our best shot. We'd better go back to Scotland. For now, tell Von Kaiserling you found coded Falcone documents that you believe will indicate the location of the emerald, but you need a few days to decode them. You can write that tonight in your email."

Later, when we were still, William rolled on top of me and pushed the hair back from my face. "Tell me that we'll be together. Forever." His expression was tender, generous. "I want to hear you say the words."

"Forever," I said.

"All of it," he said.

"Together forever."

"Darling, please. I want to hear you say the words."

"We'll be together forever." I ran my finger over his lips. "Okay?"

He rolled back down on the bed and pulled me in to fit next to him. "Yes," he said. "Good."

PART THREE

CHAPTER ONE

William and I flew back to Scotland together but parted ways in Edinburgh. I continued east to St Stephens on the train and William drove west to Glasgow, with Marie-Christine's letters. He said he'd start decoding them, even without a key. His mathematical skills made it easier, but he said anybody could do it, given enough time.

After checking in with Endicott and agreeing to have tea with Mairead, I went home. That night I lay in bed for many hours with my eyes open, because when I closed them, I felt worse. I couldn't help replaying the events of the past few months in my mind. I knew I loved William, but his confession had shocked me and made me question everything that had happened since my arrival in Scotland.

Resentment had turned to anger, and it was directed toward Rose. It was to save her life that I'd changed my topic and was now following the emerald. My life had been endangered because of her, I'd risked everything for someone who had deceived me.

Why had she never told me that she and William had been a couple? Or any of it? The betrayal struck in a profound way because she was my friend. The thought of her with William, the thought of them loving each other, hurt the most. I wanted claim on all of him, not just his present, but his past, too. This retroactive jealousy might have been irrational, but that didn't make it feel any less real.

Von Kaiserling should have been the target of my ire, and to some extent he was. While I was furious with Rose, I was at the same time tormented by the idea that she was being held somewhere against her will.

On my second day back at the office I found a package from Marie-Christine, which had been there for a week. It contained the files from her entire archive, saying she had thought about it and wanted them to be transcribed and conserved. William's theft of the letters now seemed inconsequential. But I didn't want to get my hopes up for what might turn out to be another dead end.

At home I unfolded all the documents and laid them out individually on box trays. After letting them dry out for twenty-four hours, I began to sift through them. This was the de la Fère archive, and I found the signatures of various family members on nearly all of the pages.

Most of documents were from the eighteenth and nineteenth centuries, although there were a few older ones, from the sixteenth century, or earlier. Most were undated, but I was familiar enough with the handwriting to guess when they'd been written. If I were not so completely involved with the emerald search, I would have been captivated by the idea of exploring the untouched archive of an old French family. But I didn't have time to think about the de la Fère, and the secrets their papers might contain.

I sorted through the pages.

Among the files were a handful of letters in cipher. I decided to start with those.

I chose one at random, with only a few lines of text.

There was no decoder. I tried mine but they didn't work. I might need to ask William. Sifting through the other pages I eventually found a key. I tried it on the first coded letter I had looked at. It worked.

It was a note from Madeleine de la Fère to Catherine de' Medici. This was Madeleine's key! The note was undated. Madeleine had requested a private audience with the queen mother. I picked up a second letter, a longer one.

This was a longer letter addressed to Catherine de' Medici. What was it doing in the de la Fère archive? It was possible the original version of the letter had already been sent, since important dispatches were often sent twice. Or it was a copy. The other explanation was that it had never been sent.

In three hours, I deciphered the parts of it that could be deciphered. Several words were obscured by blotches of ink, and there were other areas where the paper had worn thin and was broken, making the numbers illegible. By the time I finished reading and transcribing it was late, the sun floating over the horizon like a closed eyelid. I had forgotten all about dinner, all about William. I couldn't lift my eyes from the pages.

To Madame the Queen Mother of the Most Christian King,

Excuse the writing of this missive from your most humble subject. A matter the highest urgency has become apparent to me, and I cannot be silent. If this is my last act in the world, I must disclose the information to you.

I have proof that Federico Falcone has entered into the pay of the Catholic King [Philip II of Spain.], your enemy. He is conducting business in the Indies to aid the king of Spain. Monsieur Falcone is a dangerous man, loyal to no one but himself. I must write to you of the danger for he [unclear] . . . and . . . supports the usurpation . . . . the Duke of Guise and . . . the assistance of the Catholic King, and he now plots to poison your son the king of France. In order to settle his debts, and to lay claim to new territory beyond the seas, Federico is trying to procure for the king of Spain a precious emerald gifted to me by his brother who brought it from the Americas.

If I am found [. . . obscured words . . .] by strange means please [. . . obscured . . .] I enclose a letter here that refers to a deadly poison from the Americas, made from the skin of poisonous toads. Such a poison is untraceable. I fear he [. . . obscured words . . .] wishes to do harm to the Christian King [Henri III.] Please take heed. His first wife, Ginevra de' Croci died from violent convulsions, which I believe may have been caused by this poison, although the cause of this poor woman's death remains unknown.

Thank you, Madame. It has been a great honor to render service to you . . . the love that I bear for . . . have served you such that I might have served a king . . . I know you have always striven to act justly . . . for your children and for our country.

Your most humble and devoted servant,

Madeleine de la F

Having transcribed it I went back over it, correcting my work, then walked to my office. Mairead wasn't there. I made a timeline of Madeleine, Tommaso, and Federico's last years, taking note of the dates of important life events. I went home and called William. During the week he was in Glasgow, we had decided not to be in contact, in case our calls were being traced, but I knew he'd be as thrilled as I was about finding the letter.

"Yes," he answered on the first ring.

"It's me," I said.

"Oh, darling," he said, and I could hear the smile.

"I know we said we wouldn't speak, but Marie-Christine sent me a box of letters. It's the rest of her archive!"

"That's fantastic! What's in there?"

"Lots of stuff, but nothing seemingly related to the Falcone. But I found coded letters as well, including one that Madeleine de la Fère sent to Catherine de' Medici."

"How were you able to transcribe it, if it was coded?"

"There was a decoder in the box. Madeleine's key! The letter was a warning about Federico. The text is obscured in places but seems to indicate Madeleine's warning that if anything happened to her, Federico might have poisoned her. He had obtained an undetectable poison from South America and was planning on using it on King Henri III!"

"King Henri III was assassinated in 1589 with a dagger, not poisoned."

"That's true, but we know that Madeleine died later that year. We also know that Federico never returned to France after Madeleine's death. He died in Genoa. From the letters I've seen in Genoa, Florence, and Paris, I believe Madeleine's claims are substantiated. Federico was working as a double-agent, spying for the Spanish king, who was paying him, all the while Catherine de' Medici considered him one of her most trusted advisors.

"Remember when I told you that Catherine's fleet was intercepted by Spanish forces? I think Federico may have leaked the information about the secret mission to the Spanish. So, he was profiting from his relationship with King Philip and at the same time trying to get funding from the French crown to finance future voyages, and maybe enticing Catherine with the emerald that he was going to give her in repayment.

"Tommaso described all of this to Madeleine, so Federico killed Madeleine, not just for the emerald Tommaso had given her, but because he knew Madeleine could expose him."

"But she did expose him. You just described the letter that she wrote to Catherine de' Medici."

"I don't think the letter to Catherine ever got sent, which is why it was preserved in the de la Fère archive. Federico killed Madeleine before she could send it. If it had been sent, Federico would have been executed. Probably drawn and quartered and disemboweled. That's how Catherine dealt with other would-be regicides.

"In her letter, Madeleine suggests that Federico may have poisoned his first wife, Ginevra de' Croci, who officially died of convulsions. This was the same Croci family who'd paid for Federico's first trip to the Americas, the same family who worked as Philip II's bankers."

"Seems at odds with that letter from Tommaso you found in Rose's desk."

"It is. That's something I don't understand."

"Wow. But right now we have to focus on searching for the emerald. Our lives, and Rose's life, depend on it. Let's go to Lewis. It would be safest for us there, together, where no one would be able to track or find us. Also, I miss you. It's only been a few days, but I can't stop thinking about you, about that little dimple on your back that drives me insane. Plus, we'd be . . . uninterrupted."

"I miss you, too," I said. "Oh, Sean's texting me. He's outside. We're going out for a drink. I tried to say no but didn't want to act suspicious."

"I'll send you a note with instructions. Use the simple decoder. In your email tonight say you're expecting me back in St Stephens, and then you're going to lay low and stay in your flat for the next week. You have one of those timer things, so your lights go off and on, right?"

"Yes, all good. I'm walking out my door now," I said.

"I love you, my Isabel," he whispered.

When I returned home from my drink with Sean there was an encrypted note from William.

"Pack tonight: warm, weatherproof clothing. Leave lights on timer. Keep flat dark. Call for taxi to meet you at bus station at 3:30 A.M. Walk there. Taxi to Glenross station. Train 5:48. Text XOX as train pulls out. In Glasgow, no talking until on road and sure no one following us."

CHAPTER TWO

The next morning, I stepped off the train and followed the platform into the station. William appeared from behind a pillar, and we walked toward the exit without acknowledging each other. "I'm so crazy about you, Isabel," he said under his breath as he backed the rental car out of the parking spot.

Waiting at the third traffic light he took my hand. "It's impossible to spend even a night apart. I want to pull over to the side of the road and have my way with you."

I crossed my arms. "I don't think anyone followed me. And they presume you'll be heading to St Stephens today, so no point in keeping track of you here, right?"

"Life is . . . brighter when you're around," he said, as we continued along the road. "I can't wait to show you my gran's place."

"How can you do this?"

"Do what?"

"Pretend like everything is normal! Do you realize how much deep shit we're in?"

"Yes, Isabel, I do realize. That is precisely why I'm taking you to a safe place."

"But I told them I would translate the letters and tell them where the emerald was after a few days."

"And you can email them tonight and give them an update. They think you're holed up in your flat."

My vision blurred for a few seconds, and I said nothing. "Sorry," I said. "I had no sleep last night. I'm so wound up. I'm going to close my eyes."

When I woke up, we were at the ferry terminal. We had to wait in line in the car for the boat, so I pulled out the letter I'd transcribed, from Madeleine to Catherine de' Medici, and read it to William, finishing just before we were allowed to board. We parked and climbed up a ladder to the top deck. The ferry was nearly empty, with only a handful of couples and families.

The trip started out like a ride at an amusement park, but soon the wind kicked up and the boat was yawing and groaning and almost everyone went inside. William tried to keep me comfortable, but I was miserable the entire time. Spring felt so far away.

CHAPTER THREE

The wind died down as we approached the coast, and the horizon grew into rocky promontories cascading down to the sea, a coastline of stubby fingers reaching out into shallow water. As we pulled into the harbor, I made my way to the main deck and disembarked like a drunk person, swerving over to a bench, where William found me after he'd driven the car off the ferry. He wrapped me in a blanket, then went away and returned with a thermos of strong tea with sugar. "Sip this," he said. "We'll wait here until you feel better." He edged in close to me. Gradually my equilibrium was restored.

Pulling me up from the bench he put his arms around me. "The house is on the other side of the island. It'll take an hour and a half to get there."

"I'd like to lie down in the back seat," I said. "I still feel woozy."

In the car I fell asleep, but the gears rumbled as we climbed and descended hills, William accelerating rather than decelerating at the summits. I sat up and looked out at the horizon, glancing at my phone now and then.

"Still no reception. Are we in the Outer Hebrides, or outer space?" I asked.

We continued along the coast on narrow roads that hugged high cliffs, rarely passing another car. I must have drifted to sleep again, because I woke up when the car was crunching over gravel. Thirty feet in front of us stood a grey, granite house, with a turret, which bestowed a medieval character on the structure. The house was situated high up on its own hill. In the distance a range of green mountains with rounded peaks rolled east. I couldn't see any neighbors. Getting out of the car the wind plucked my scarf off my shoulders, and I chased after it. The lawn under my boots was damp and sparse. Gusts hissed around me, whistling in my ear. About a hundred feet to the right of the house was a small cottage.

"What's that?" I asked William as he began unloading. "The little house."

"Smokehouse. Did I tell you we smoke salmon? I can show you tomorrow." He opened an unlocked cobalt-blue door. "After you," he said.

Inside the entry hall, the walls above us on both sides were lined with the skulls of large animals, some with antlers.

"The house was built in the 1880s as a hunting lodge," William said. "Directly ahead is the kitchen. On your left, the dining room. On your right, the living room—with a view of the beach. Upstairs, the first door on your right is the bedroom. Our bedroom."

He threw my backpack over his shoulder and lifted my duffel and tote along with his own suitcase, then followed me up the stairs. The bedroom door was wide open, revealing a coffered ceiling and a king-sized brass bed against the back wall. A dressing table in front of bay windows overlooked a sprawling beach of sunset-pinkened sand a hundred feet below.

"It's actually not freezing in here," I said. "Doesn't it cost a fortune to heat the place?"

"I had a neighbor come in and turn on the heat in advance. I've thought of everything, you see. Now, should we get you out of those wet clothes?" William asked. He walked into the adjacent room and a few moments later I heard water spilling into a basin. I followed him into a bathroom where an old-fashioned tub rested on bronze claws. William was naked already and the tub was filling up. He turned off the taps, then stepped close to me and unbuttoned my shirt one button at a time, threw it on the floor, and knelt down, kissing my waist as he pulled off my pants and underwear. He helped me step into the water, then slipped in and sat down so we were facing each other. He reached for the bar of soap and washed my feet, before leaning forward onto his knees and lathering the rest of my body.

When we were clean, he clambered out of the tub and helped me out. We toweled each other dry, although my skin still felt slimy with soap. He lifted me up and lay me on the bed and then he was over me, supporting himself on his forearms. We continued kissing, deeply. He kept looking in my eyes, his gaze becoming so intense I had to look away.

The northern sun was so bright. I climbed on top of him, kissing his neck. Then he rolled me over, so he was on top again, watching my face as before, and for a few seconds, he held down my wrists. I'd forgotten how strong he was.

Then he flipped me over onto my stomach, my face in the pillow. He kissed my neck before entering me, slowly at first, and then moving faster, harder, pinning my hips, until he finished with a loud, "Yes." He leaned over me, gathered my hair in his hands and kissed the side of my neck, and rolled off. I turned on my side.

"Sorry," he said. "I just wanted you so badly."

"It's okay but, I'm still not feeling like myself after the ferry."

"I'm sorry," he said again.

He inched off the bed and left the room, returning with a pot and two teacups on a black-lacquer tray.

"Fresh chamomile," he said. We laid there and cuddled, and I fell asleep. When I woke up the door was closed, and William was gone. I looked at the clock. I'd been sleeping for half an hour. I was hungry. That was a good sign.

Wrapping myself in a terrycloth bathrobe I found in the closet, I wandered into the hall, the sound of my footsteps muffled by the tartan carpet. I heard clicking on a keyboard coming from the other side of a door that was almost closed. I knocked softly, before pushing it open.

The room had no windows, only floor-to-ceiling bookcases covering four walls. Where there were no books there was a desk; William, dressed in khaki pants and a black cashmere turtleneck, was sitting in front of a computer. He started when he saw me and pulled some earbuds from his ears.

"She has stirred!" he said. "Just give me a second to close up." He picked up the old document he'd been working on and put it in a folder. "I made a bit of progress on building a decoder for those letters from Saint-Cloud," he said, "but I'm not there yet." He stood up and reached for my hand, then brought it up to his lips. "I also have a fourth decoder, the one Rose and I used to decode the letter about the assassination plot. So far, it's not useful. Maybe it will be for another letter, though, especially anything with the de la Fère woman. But no more talk of work, not tonight!

"Dinner was scheduled to arrive twenty minutes ago, but I just got a call saying their driver got stuck in some mud on the other side of the island. So, I need to retrieve it. Take me about an hour round trip. Will you starve before then?"

"I'll throw on clothes and come with you."

"Absolutely not. You didn't sleep last night. We have a lot of work ahead of us. Put your feet up. And let's also go to bed early so we can start early tomorrow," he said. "We should get up with the sunrise."

"Deal," I said. "I'll send my nightly missive to Von Kaiserling."

"Good idea. And I'm sorry about earlier, Isabel. I hope you'll forgive me."

"It's okay," I said. His phone alarm went off and he silenced it.

"Our dinner awaits," he said as we walked out of his office. He gently steered me to the bedroom, and we kissed goodbye.

"One hour!" he said.

I glanced out the bedroom window, down to the beach. It was still light outside. I opened my duffel and took out my makeup bag and applied a light coat of silvery eye shadow, mascara, and nude lipstick. I'd forgotten my hairbrush so I looked inside the drawers in the dressing table and closest nightstand, but only found some bookmarks and an old lipstick that must have been William's grandmother's. In the nightstand on William's side of the bed I pulled out what looked like a fuchsia-colored hair scrunchy but turned out to be a lace thong. Probably not his grandmother's.

I stuffed the thong back inside the drawer and slammed it closed. Rose must have stayed in this room when she was here.

I switched on the TV. There were three channels, all of them in Gaelic, so I turned it off.

CHAPTER FOUR

I took Marie-Christine's papers out of my bag. Before going through them, I wanted to organize everything else, starting with my notes and Madeleine's first letter that I had transcribed. I must have left the original in the car because I could only find my transcription. I couldn't focus, was still thinking about Rose. So, she had stayed in this room. Were things between her and William truly over? Where was she now? Thinking about her constantly was exhausting. I laid down on the bed again and put my hands behind my head. I must have fallen asleep again because I woke to the smell of something delicious, mixed in with the piney fragrance of burning wood.

"Isabel," William called. "Dinner is served."

"Coming!" I said.

In the dining room, two porcelain plates, monogrammed silverware, silver-rimmed goblets, and linen napkins were arranged on the oak table, which could have seated ten, and a candelabra with lit candles sat in the center, a fire roaring in the fireplace.

"This feels very grand," I said, as William pulled out a chair with velvet arms for me.

"I'm thrilled," he said, raising his glass of red wine, "to have you as my guest." He pointed down at our plates. "Smoked on property."

"Looks wonderful," I said. I took a few small bites.

The next course was fish and potatoes, resting on sauce flecked with green.

"Halibut," William said, smiling. "Caught yesterday. With beurre blanc sauce."

"Mmm," I said smacking my lips. I ate the potatoes as William described the drive to the other side of the island. "There's a storm raging outside. It's not easy to drive in gale-force winds," he said. He stared at my plate. "Don't you like it?"

"I'm still feeling queasy from the ferry. And . . . there's a bitter aftertaste."

"Bitter? Hmm . . . must've added too much parsley." He cleared our dishes and brought out small bowls with strawberries sprinkled with powdered sugar. I ate two strawberries, coughing on the sugar. After William had eaten the last strawberry, he brought out a box of chocolates and whiskey with two glasses.

"Aged Talisker. Older than you," he said, tipping the bottle to show me the label.

"Not by much," I said. The liquid was as dark as maple syrup and the alcohol smell was overpowering.

"It's cask-strength." William said, and clinked my glass, "To your discoveries." He rubbed my knee. The wind had picked up, it was rattling the windows. Outside fog was blowing over the sea. "Oh, darling," he said. "Get thee to bed. I'll do the dishes."

In the bedroom I undressed and didn't even remember falling asleep.

I woke up alone and started working at the dressing table. I took out two documents, which were not useful. Then there were three letters, and although not encoded, they were difficult to read. In order to go through them in chronological order I checked the dates before beginning to transcribe.

Dear Madame,

In truth my brother cannot marry you for another reason other than your choice to embrace the heresy that you dare call religion. My brother cannot marry you because he is, in fact, already married. During our last voyage, together in the Americas, he married a young woman, with all the gifts that youth bring and a terrible desire to tie herself to one of our men. She was not unhandsome, it bears saying, and she seduced my young brother without difficulty. And, as frivolous young people do, not caring for the reputations of their families, he acted upon a whim and married the said person on the spot. She has borne his child, and if you should wish for proof, I attach a copy the Bishop of____'s . . . approval of their union, for which he had to petition the French Crown. Thus I ask you to please return the gifts that he has bestowed upon you, which belong to me, the head of our family. Madame, I remain very humbly yours etc. etc.

Federico

Before I started the next letter William brought breakfast in on a tray. As I was about to tell him about the letter, he said he'd received a call from a neighbor and had to run out to help dry-dock a boat before the big storm. He'd be back in a few hours.

Back at my desk I continued with the next letter.

My dear friend,

I suppose by your long silence I am to understand that my brother has revealed to you that which I had kept hidden to my great regret. With this letter I shall explain the truth of the events as they were. Judge me on this telling, which I promise to be the veracity. I hope you know that I am a man of my word.

On our last voyage to the Americas, in 1565, I accompanied my brother Federico.

Our fellow men had too oft supported one side against the other of these peoples in order to rule over their conquered lands, which they did with much cruelty and violence. The French settlement was almost destroyed and fighting between Lutherans and Catholics meant that all men were in a constant state of conflict.

Deep in the forest outside the camp where we docked our ship, my brother happened one day upon a young Indian woman. Seeing her modest quarters, he assumed she was of low birth. He seduced her. After some weeks she sought him out to explain, in despair, that he had left her with child.

In order to preserve her reputation, and on the condition that she agreed to convert to Christianity and that she would be my wife in name only, I married her in a small Catholic ceremony. We lived apart, she with her family. Because I continued to spend time with her father, I began to learn some of their language. I came to understand that the young woman was not the daughter of my friend, but she was the granddaughter of a king and queen of a land far away in the mountains. She had fled her home due to civil war there. She wanted to make an alliance with us, in the hope that we could help restore her lands and kingdom, by right of inheritance. Of course, this was not possible, even if I wished we could help her, but I was moved by her plight. Although I did not see the young woman again, my friend let me know that she wished to bestow upon me a single green emerald. I protested and refused to take it, but aboard ship on our return trip home, I found it hidden inside a small chest in my trunk. This was the stone that I gave to you as a gift. Why did I not give it to you sooner? This, too, is a long story.

My brother, perhaps afraid that she might tell the world that he was the father of her daughter, had obtained a dispensation sanctifying the union between her and myself, as I had in haste married her in a Catholic Church.

In my youth and foolishness I believed that marrying her was a good and necessary service in order to protect her and my friend's family from dishonor.

Upon our return to France, and although it was my own property, my brother seized the emerald from me, and it has been in his possession since, although he has promised to gift it to Queen Catherine.

In truth I do not see him ever parting with anything precious. He thinks he has a right to all things on the good earth. Besides, he believes the emerald bestows power upon him, wisdom and strength, that it will restore his vision. Perhaps he believes he will never die.

I therefore supplicate you, please, to understand my actions and better comprehend the reasons for my conduct.

I admit that I have behaved shamefully and deceitfully. But my love for you during these years has been constant, and I have always been true to you alone. Still, I expect and accept your scorn, as the situation warrants no other action.

If you wish to hear this story from my own lips, say the word and I will meet you at the time and place you choose.

I remain yours, for life,
Your Tommaso.

William hadn't returned so I went downstairs, made lunch, and went back to work.

There was another letter addressed to Madeleine, the contents in cipher, and not with the code used in Madeleine's letter to Catherine de' Medici. William had mentioned Tommaso's deciphering key, so I went to his office to retrieve it. If he had been working with it maybe he had a hard copy on his desk. Otherwise, I'd have to wait until he got back. The door was locked. I went downstairs and looked around for a key. Nothing. I remembered a trick I'd learned in college. From Rose. I found a bobby pin, went back to the study, and coaxed the old door open.

The decoding key was sitting on his desk.

I used the key on the letter. The first word I recognized was emerald.

On heightened alert, I flew through the decoding and translated it from French to English.

> *My dear friend,*
>
> *I write in code so that my brother will not read these words. When I did not receive a response to my last letters, I visited your home in Paris attempting to explain my conduct in person.*
>
> *Thank you for sending Mme de . . . to my hotel, to deliver the silk dress that I had given to you, the one you wear, beautifully, in your portrait. Mme de . . . said you wished to tell me that you were returning all of my letters, all my gifts, and that I would understand from the dress your secret message for me. If I still possessed your portrait, I was instructed to destroy it along with your letters. Dearest, I could no sooner destroy your letters and portrait than I could destroy a holy relic. I understood you wished to erase all memory of us, but how could I erase my love, oh my*

cherished one? How could you ask me to be so cruel? I will not. I cannot. How to convince you that I will never love another so long as I breathe?

In the privacy of my bedroom, I unfolded the dress. You are so clever, my love, although your message shatters my heart. When I saw my letters, and the emerald necklace and two rings I had given to you had been sewn inside the dress, then and only then was I to understand that you never wished to see me again. I write now to tell you that I am bringing your dress with me to Genoa. Perhaps one day after my death they shall turn it into a holy cloth or other garment. Or perhaps they will permit me to be buried with it. You dress must remain intact. I never want anyone else to touch it, if not you. I hope, against hope, that you will respond to this message. I wish that I was bringing you, and not your dress, back to Genoa with me, and it breaks my heart that this will be the closest I will ever be to you, perhaps ever again, although it is not for me to make predictions. In these uncertain times everything and nothing seems possible.

Yours forever,
T.

Madeleine had sewn the emerald inside her dress when she gave it back to Tommaso after she'd broken up with him when she'd discovered he was already married. I remembered the miniature portrait of Madeleine, how Severina had told me that the box of letters had been found in a tomb along with the portrait and a woman's dress. Severina still had the dress. The emerald was probably still inside it!

I took out my phone to call William, but the battery was dead. The house line started ringing, three short trills.

"I'm an hour and a half away," I thought he said, although the line was cutting in and out and it sounded windy. "Right near . . . castle in Stornaway."

"William, I know where the emerald is!"

"What? You're breaking up."

"One of the new letters explains where the emerald was hidden."

"Where . . ." I heard him say. Then the call dropped.

I went back to the letter and started to go through it again as I'd skipped over a few words. I heard footsteps and looked at the clock. Only five minutes had passed since William's call. It must have been the house creaking in the wind. I had found the emerald! The information had been in Marie-Christine's attic this whole time.

The door swished open. A figure was standing in the doorway.

It was Rose.

CHAPTER FIVE

"**R**ose!" I said. "Rose!" She smiled and held out her arms. I went to her without hesitating and hugged her. Then I pulled back. "You're here! You're alive, and in one piece!"

"Did someone tell you I was dead?"

"William said you had a fight, and you left, and Von Kaiserling had you."

"Not surprising. William's been playing us off each other, lady. I'll explain but we need to leave before he gets back. Grab the documents, your computer, warm clothes, and a raincoat. Walking shoes. I have a plan, but we've gotta go. Like, now."

I glared at her. The scene in Paris played somewhere in my peripheral vision.

"You listened in on the phone," I said. "You want the emerald. The money."

She laughed. "It's not about the money, honey. My dad sends me checks whenever I ask. But I am afraid of Von Kaiserling, that's why I'm here. At the moment, however, I'm more afraid of William, and you should be too."

"Why would William tell me Von Kaiserling had you?"

"I don't . . . . Maybe he was afraid someone would tell you we were a couple? And you'd figure out he'd been lying to you? I don't know. We really have to go now. If we don't, we're going to get killed."

"Wait. Are you and William still together?"

"Isabel, focus. William is a psychopath. He killed your advisor, Madeleine. I had a fight with him—about her! I found a love letter she sent him and confronted him about it. I heard you tell him that you'd found the emerald. Don't you get it? As soon as you show him that letter, he'll kill you. He said he'd be back in ninety minutes, and fifteen of them have already gone by. We need to leave."

"So, the two of you are not together."

"How can I make this clear? William trapped me here! The only reason he's keeping me alive is in case he needs to extort the money from my father. William is using you to find the emerald. He has no intention of giving it to Von Kaiserling, by the way, he's got somebody on the line in Sweden who's willing to pay twenty million dollars for it. I just want to give it to Von Kaiserling and get on with my life."

"This is . . . crazy!"

"I have no idea what he's told you, but as soon as he saw your application and I told him we were friends, he hatched his plan. He didn't even tell me about it until after I found out I was pregnant and said I was going to tell you everything and ask you to help me find the emerald. He said he'd take over, and that I needed to take care of the baby, but we should pretend my life was in danger or you'd never agree to it. I'm sorry, Isabel. Being pregnant messed with my head. I cried all the time. I did whatever he told me. He convinced me it would be the best thing for you. For everyone.

"But that's over. I had a miscarriage, and . . . as horrible and tragic as that was, right now I want to save myself and you. Get your stuff. Hurry up."

"I don't know why I should believe you." I said. "William's story is completely different. And he loves me."

"He doesn't love . . . hang on. Why should you believe me? Because you're my friend. We've known each other since college. How long have you known William? Six months? Look at his track record. His fancy clothes and lifestyle. On a lecturer's salary? He's made all his money stealing rare books and manuscripts, including that poetry book by Thérèse Du Montour. He lied about who he was and stole the fake emerald from the Palazzo Falcone and took my transcriptions. He stole a shitload of documents from the Bibliothèque Nationale that they don't even know are missing. He stole the papers from the woman in France. He's been lying to you about all that, no doubt. He broke into your apartment in Florence! As I said, I want to give the emerald to Von Kaiserling. William is fine with leaving him empty-handed. If he told you Von Kaiserling had me, he's either planning to kill me or he'll make sure that Von Kaiserling will."

"Shit," I said. "Holy shit."

She looked around. "Where's your stuff? Get the documents." I started throwing things inside my duffel. Where were my sneakers?

"Rose, why did you go to all this trouble to have me study the Falcone?"

"Isabel, none of this was my idea. I was about to tell you everything and ask for your help, remember? William promised to explain everything."

"Did Von Kaiserling murder Catrina?"

"What? Catrina's dead? When?"

"I thought William decoded the pages the Contessa gave him. He's the one who discovered that the emerald was in the armor."

"Is that what he told you? That's not what happened. Nico told me about it one night when I got him drunk. That weekend I went skiing with him and his dad so William would be able to get in and take the emerald. Listen. You're my best friend. I need you to trust me."

I threw my bag over my shoulder, and we started down the stairs.

"I also wanted to say how incredibly grateful I am for what you're doing, what you've done for me, Isabel."

"I should be thanking you for introducing me to the Falcone."

"Right? We get attached to the people we study, don't we? These worlds are totally immersive. Sometimes our subjects become more real to us than everyday reality. Just think. Now you'll be able to look at the Flying Squadron with fresh eyes."

I stopped on the landing and grabbed her arm. "Wait a second, Rose. You're suggesting I give up my thesis now? That I turn over to you everything I've found?"

"*Your* thesis? I'm so sorry, Isabel! William was supposed to explain that it was temporary. And that you'd be compensated for your time. He didn't tell you?"

"I switched topics and have been looking for the emerald because I was trying to save your life!"

She said nothing.

"You did no work and I've been working furiously for five months. Admittedly, I've been focused on the emerald, but I have a roadmap. You didn't even come up with a list of sources! Even that was from Von Kaiserling."

"I've done a ton of work. What did you think I was doing during those three years at St Stephens? You can't possibly believe I would have given up the Falcone."

Somewhere a clock started clanging the hour.

"Isabel," she said. "Okay, okay, it's your thesis. I don't give a fuck about the emerald, or the thesis. Are you coming with me? Or would you prefer to wait for William to kill you?"

At the entrance I slipped into my boots and Rose pulled on a large parka with a fur-lined hood. "I don't see my coat," I said.

"Here's mine," she said, handing me a wool coat from the rack. It felt tight around the shoulders as I wriggled inside.

I took a scarf out of my duffel and some documents spilled onto the floor. "Isabel, let's go!" Rose shouted. "I can take that stuff if you want."

"I got it," I said, tucking as many pages as would fit into the mini duffel under the coat rack. She struggled to zip my duffel and I folded the original and the decoded version of the letter about the emerald over twice and tucked them inside my shirt, then zipped up the coat.

The rain was coming down in doughy lumps. As we left the house, Rose took my hand and we started to walk quickly. "Hold on, darlin'," she said, squeezing my hand. We stopped when we reached the smokehouse.

"Let's duck in here and I'll find the car keys," Rose said. "They're not in my pocket. Hopefully the rain will let up." I turned the door handle. It was unlocked.

"William said there's a storm coming. Maybe it's already started."

"Don't turn on the lights," Rose said. She had started pawing through the small pockets of her backpack.

"Dammit," she said.

"Where's the car?"

"Hundred feet up the road. It's his grandma's old wreck, and he thinks it's dead, but I had it repaired while he was away." She stood up. "I've got to run back to the house. Can you put my things back in the bags? I shouldn't have brought so much crap. Push this stuff in farther so I can close the door."

"Okay," I said. We moved everything and I started putting her clothes back in her backpack.

My eyes ran over her. She looked so small, so vulnerable.

"I understand you, Isabel. You loved it. The chance to work on my topic. To be me. Original, daring, spontaneous. So different from you."

Without giving me a chance to respond she ran out, pulling the door closed behind her. The rain was coming down even harder now. I snapped her backpack shut, and went through a vestibule, lit by a series of nightlights. In the next room white lab coats hung from metal hooks on the wall. The interior seemed ascetic, clinical. The smoker looked like a large oven. In the next room there were buckets of salt, and a refrigerator. Another room had a long steel table beside a sink. The cottage was much bigger than it appeared from the outside. Then there was yet another room, with two desks side by side, and shelves filled with books, and a table, with a puzzle half-assembled on it. This was someone's office. I opened the drawer and found a few knickknacks, including a gold ring with a red stone in it. Where had I seen it before? Then I realized. It was Catrina's ring!

I looked out a window and saw the beach and a hint of whitecaps, tiny clouds blowing through black water. The rain had slowed to a drizzle. I searched for a window with a view of the main house. The lights were on. Had we turned them off? I heard a car start up in the distance. Or maybe it was crashing waves.

CHAPTER SIX

Fifteen minutes passed. Footsteps. I walked out of the room. The rain and wind had quieted down.

A knock on the door. Why didn't Rose just walk in? Had it locked when she closed it? My eyes had adjusted but I didn't know where the front door was. I walked in and out of the few rooms until I saw the luggage down the hall.

Then I heard William's voice. "I got your message, darling." I reached for the doorknob but stopped. Where was Rose? Had William killed her? I took a step back and knocked into the luggage. I would grab my backpack with the Marie-Christine papers and the bag with the loose pages and head out the back door. I looked down. My bags weren't here. Had Rose taken them? I turned to reach for the doorknob a second time.

William spoke again, his voice raised. "Rose! Let me in! She found the emerald! And Max is dead."

I felt the room dip and spin and reached out to steady myself against the cold wall.

"Rose? Are you okay?" A pause. "You're not still upset, are you? It's all worked out. We can do whatever we want now! Rewrite our own history."

I took another step away from the door. I needed to make sure the other entrance was locked but felt frozen in place. He jiggled the doorknob, knocked four times.

"Rose? What kind of game are you playing? Are you okay?" A pause. "Did you lock yourself in?" He kicked the door.

"Fuck it," he said. "I know you're upset but I need you to help me with Isabel. We have to kill her tonight, during this storm."

Light flooded the vestibule and I let out a little scream. The door was still locked. I'd accidentally switched on the light, so I turned it off.

"Rose! Is that a signal? Are you okay, darling?"

With that word my thoughts became laser focused. I'd been feeling a swirl of confusion and terror, but now felt only rage.

"I hope you're okay. I'm going up to the house to get the key," said William.

I heard crunching on the gravel. I unzipped the coat and patted my shirt. I still had the letter about the emerald and my decoded version. I zipped the coat back up and felt around for a spare key, along the walls and doorframes, and inside the desk drawers. I couldn't find one anywhere. There was no other way out.

After ten minutes there was more crunching on the gravel. "I know you're in there," he said. "Open the door, Isabel." I held my breath. "I realized that Rose took the car, but she won't get very far, not in this weather." I heard him breathing. In and out.

So, I *had* heard the car start up. Had Rose lied to me? She had taken the documents. "There's a spare key under the doormat. Find it?" I reached under the mat and felt for the key, then stood up and slid the key into the lock and unlocked it, but the top was bolted.

Apparently he didn't have a key to the top lock.

I heard myself speak in a low voice. "Did you trap Rose here? I'm not opening the door."

"I absolutely did not trap Rose. Don't you realize? This was her plan. All of it. She's been here, hiding from the Contessa and Niccolò. Trying to conceal her pregnancy from her father. And she's been writing, waiting on you to complete her work. That's why she locked you in my smokehouse."

"I found Catrina's ring in the desk drawer. What's it doing here?"

"Rose killed her. She'd started blackmailing Rose. Rose had convinced Catrina to play along, but then she wanted in on the profit. After Rose stopped paying her off she overheard Catrina trying to call you. I was in Florence. Rose spiked her drink."

"You've lied about everything. Why would I believe you?"

"Because you still love me."

"But I don't trust you."

"I know things don't look good for me right now, but Rose was a monster, and everything you overheard was an attempt to get her to—I was doing it to protect you."

"To protect me?"

"Yes, I can explain."

"I'm sure you can. But I'd rather if you didn't."

"Aren't you curious about her dissertation? She was my best student, everything she submitted was perfect. Want to know why? Because she was a fraud. Von Kaiserling found out that she had plagiarized her MA thesis. He threatened to expose her, to ruin her career. Don't you understand? She looked the part, but that was all. The only person who was ever in any danger was you, Isabel. You can stay in the smokehouse by all means. You should know, it gets very cold in there, freezing."

"Just because I don't believe what Rose told me doesn't mean I believe you."

"Let me in so I can tell you everything. I loved you very much, you know. I believed in you. Your faith in the project. You . . . reminded me of Rose when she was just starting out. The Rose I believed existed, not the real Rose."

"You just said you were going to kill me!"

"Because that's what Rose wanted to hear."

"I know you killed Madeleine, William."

His voice went hard. "You were planning on running away with Rose. Until she locked you in there. You see, Rose told me you were unhinged and on a ton of meds. She'd been planning to poison you and tell everyone you'd OD'd, then pass your work off as her own. She could finally live the life of her dreams, courtesy of her tragic best friend. Stay, Isabel. Or go. You've ruined everything."

"I have the document about the emerald. I hid it under my sweater. Rose might have the bag with the rest, but I have the one that matters."

There was a long pause before he said, "Nice try. The bag's with me."

"You don't have this letter. I wanted it to be *my* surprise for you. I'm looking at it *now*, it's in my hand. Unless I decide to burn or shred it while you're getting the keys. Then you'll never know."

"Come out. If I was going to do something to you, don't you think I would've done it already?"

"I'm holding the pages in one hand and a lighter in the other."

He didn't answer. I heard him clumping across the ground. He was going for the extra key after all—or to get a gun? Unless he was pretending and waiting outside.

I slowly opened the door. No William. I closed it quietly and headed in the direction of the road. It had started raining again, hard. I sloshed along, barely seeing what was ahead of me, stumbling over rocks and trying to stay on level ground.

I tripped over something and flew forward onto my stomach, shouting as I hit the ground. It took me a minute to stand up and start moving again.

Behind me I began to hear thudding footfalls and grunts. "Isabel!" William yelled. "Wait!" The ground was uneven, littered with small rocks and deep, soggy patches that slowed me down. He caught up to me and knocked me over. I fell facedown on the ground again, my palms landing on soft, wet soil, the taste of mud and grass filling my mouth. Then he was on top of me. I tried to flip around and claw at his face, but he was too strong. He reached around me, trying to pin my arms as I kicked at him, then flailed on the ground, freeing one of my arms and thrusting it forward. I bent my arm toward me and threw my elbow back as hard as I could, but only hit his shoulder. I pulled my arm forward again and slammed my elbow back. Something crunched and William yelped. I wrested free from his grip and pushed myself up. William was clutching his face, blood streaming out of his nose. I ran.

"Stop running!" he shouted.

I ran away from the road and toward the sound of the ocean, but after only a minute or two my legs slowed. I could hardly breathe. Stopping, I half-turned. He was running toward me, blood covering his face, pouring out of him.

I started running again but slowed to a jog then stopped, dry heaving, hands on my knees. I still had the pages. Over the echo of the surf, William's voice was calling me, soft and consoling. The voice I remembered from Paris.

Could he see me? I couldn't see him. "Don't be frightened, darling. I'm glad Rose is gone. She wanted everything, all for herself." He was out of breath now, too. "We'll find the emerald together. It'll be romantic, like before. We'll have everything . . . just you . . . and me."

I darted ahead, away from the fog, away from the cliffs—or toward them, I wasn't sure. William was in my wake, four boots clumping in time across the soft ground. My heart felt ready to spring out of my chest. I wished for even a sliver of moon obscured by clouds. I thought I'd lost him and slowed down before stopping to catch my breath. The fog swirled thickly, and it was impossible to know where I was stepping.

"Now, now," William said, his voice even softer, soothing. He was close.

I turned toward his voice and he stepped into view. I pulled my arm in close and swept it across my body, releasing the letter into the wind, which gusted just then, snapping the page up and away.

William was reaching toward me, but he turned, seemingly in mid-air, and grasped at the air where the letter was twirling about. I crouched down and froze in a lunge position, my arms out in front of me, unable to move, gasping for air. I had to decide which way to run.

William leapt for the letter but missed it. I could hear the pounding of the surf louder than ever. I turned away from the sound of the waves and staggered for two steps, but then the toe of my shoe lodged into fleshy soil. I slammed into the ground for a third time, my hands slashing across gravel, my face pressed into the slimy mud.

Pushing myself up, William landed on me, knocking me over and onto my back, bashing my head back against sharp pebbles. His hands found my neck and began to squeeze. With all my strength I thrust my pelvis up in the air, managing to fling him off me. I turned over and crawled along on all fours, scrambling to stand. I heard a rain of rocks, followed by a high-pitched gasp.

In the darkness William's voice rang out, desperate and panicked. "Isabel!" I turned. "Help me!"

Was this a trick?

I looked around me. "Over here!" His voice cried out. "I'm going to fall!! I can't hold . . . I'm . . . HELP me! NOW! YOU BITCH!!!"

Not able to stay standing, I sank to my hands and knees and made my way toward the sound of his still shouting voice. Then it stopped. The fog had lifted. I was almost at the edge of the cliff. I inched forward and looked over. William was right there, trying to climb up. I crouched down, intending to start running again. He reached his hand up toward me.

Then he slipped, and the hand that had reached out shot up and out behind him. "Rose!" he shouted, as he floated off into the air, bellowing out her name in one long cry into the night. And then he was gone. He was gone!

I stood up and took a step back. Something was flapping around my ankle. The letter. The last page. I reached down to retrieve it, but it was mostly pulp by then. The original, the page I'd copied out, and the transcribed page with the details of the emerald were nothing more than mush.

Trudging back uphill toward the house, I followed the curve of the cliffs in the now-moonlit night. All I could hear was the thunder of waves heaving, as they always had, as they always would, against the shoreline hundreds of feet below. The steady reverberations of a conquering army.

EPILOGUE

Back in St Stephens, the news about William, Rose, and Von Kaiserling had spread quickly, infecting every department. And then it was all over the international news. Rose had driven William's grandmother's car around an icy curve and crashed into one of the lochs. In the car they found my bag with the documents, but water had gotten into it and the documents inside had all disintegrated. Rose was in the hospital, but under arrest, with twenty-four-hour police surveillance. William had died from his injuries. It took a helicopter and a team of divers to retrieve his body. His skull had cracked open and almost all of his bones had broken.

For the first few days after returning to St Stephens I saw William in every tall, dark-haired man entering the history department. I saw him walking away from me on the street, and ahead of me in line at the supermarket.

On my second day back, I reached out to Marie-Christine. "Please tell me what I can do to compensate you for your loss. Anything," I pleaded.

"No," she said, with a small hum, tears in her voice. "But no, no," she kept repeating. "It's . . . too late now. They are gone."

The next day I met with Endicott.

"I just submitted a proposal to give a paper at next year's Society of Early Modern Studies conference in Chicago," I said. "The title is 'The

Cross-Confessional Epistolary Relationship Between Tommaso Falcone and Madeleine de la Fère.' I'm putting together a panel, so please let me know if anyone might be interested in participating."

"Will do," said Endicott, watching me across his desk, as he had on my very first day at St Stephens. Then he leaned in. "I may have seemed skeptical of you when we first met. Perhaps I feared you'd turn out to be like your American compatriot, Rose, whose work ethic I found wanting. I hope you can forgive me for the jeopardy in which I placed you because of my misplaced trust in William. You should know there is evidence that he murdered Madeleine Grangier. And Catrina's autopsy report revealed that she was poisoned. At this time, they're unsure about the degree of Rose's involvement." He shook his head. "It will take some time to sort it all out."

I sat back and after a few minutes of silence he continued. "One of the detectives discovered that William was dealing in manuscripts on the black market. His trade apparently extended across Europe, so as a known entity he couldn't return to the Archivio di Stato in Florence, or the BN in Paris. He was helping Von Kaiserling to construct a *Wunderkammer*. And so was Rose."

"Do we know if one of them took the Newton book from the library?"

"Oh, you heard about that, did you? No, they caught the thief. Unrelated. William wasn't daft enough to steal something here."

"Do you wonder why none of us could see through his charming mask?"

"I suppose there was always an . . . iciness in his soul that none of us paid attention to. That obsession with Machiavelli, not just the historical figure, but Machiavelli as teacher, what William referred to as 'the practical application of Machiavelli's genius in today's world.'" He crossed his ankle over his knee and pushed his glasses up his nose.

"Maybe we, as historians, should give up," I said. "Too many lacunae. And since history is written by the winners, as it were, we might do a disservice to the people of the past by misunderstanding what really took place."

He smiled a knowing smile. "Probably, but it's all too compelling, isn't it? I must say I'm impressed with how you handled yourself, how you managed to best him. And . . . you've changed somehow. You seem more self-confident, which is good. And a bit world-weary, which is less good. Or maybe you're just weary. Which is understandable."

"I'm weary of talking about it constantly," I said. "Just now I'm trying to focus on the future for once."

"Why don't you take some time off? Head to London. Do you have friends there? Or Seville? Rome? Somewhere warm and sunny?"

"I moved to Scotland for warm and sunny," I said, and we both laughed.

"Thanks for the suggestion, but I've got to keep working. Otherwise, I might never start again," I said, and he nodded because he understood.

I left his office and went down into the broad street. I walked to the cathedral, and ambled for a while between its bare ribs. A woman with blonde hair was standing in front of one of the tombstones. From behind she could have been Rose, but as I got closer, she turned slightly, revealing a much younger woman. When she noticed me glaring, she scuttled away.

Rose would be out of the hospital soon. She had called me twice, but instead of answering I blocked her number. I knew she didn't believe she had done anything wrong, and if we spoke, she would just continue to lie to me. Her father had called several times, too, leaving long-winded voicemails about his saintly daughter, an innocent victim of William and The System. I had even received a few messages from his lawyer. I'd decided the next conversation I'd have with or about Rose would take place together with the police. In the next few months, I'd testify against her. It wasn't revenge I sought, not exactly, and I'd given up the idea of trying to make her feel guilty or even responsible for her actions. But the people whose lives had been affected or destroyed because of her deserved justice.

The worst part was realizing I'd never be free from her. Then again, was anyone ever free from anyone else?

At home, later that day, I called Severina Falcone. She picked up on the first ring. "Severina, it's Isabel."

"Oh the woman in the news. What is it you want?"

"Severina, I would've reached out sooner, but I couldn't. I'll tell you the whole story whenever you want."

"You never said goodbye. You have not been in touch. And I'm confused by your behavior with Niccolò, who has a new girlfriend, by the way. Even Beth likes her. But you, you disappointed me. You were using us. Just like Rose. The three of you together, you, Rose, and that professor."

"No, Severina. Rose used me. She was using you, me, Niccolò, your father and Beth, all of us. And the professor was, too. There is so much—too much—to tell you over the phone. Rose did ask for my help, and it's true I didn't tell you, but she'd led me to believe our lives were in danger. I'm sorry for all the hurt I caused. If you want no more to do with me, I would understand. But I'm calling about something important. Are you in London or Genoa?"

"Genoa. For Easter. My father is unwell, his heart. He needs an operation. Of course, he goes on and on about the bloody curse."

"I'm sorry to hear that. But Sevi . . . Severina. The dress in your closet, the one found during the excavation of the Falcone chapel, along with the portrait of the woman with the emerald necklace. Does the dress in your closet match the dress in the portrait?"

"Why do you ask this?"

"I found a document that says . . . the Falcone emerald is inside the dress!"

"The one in the portrait? The cursed emerald? Inside the dress? In my closet . . . hold on I will look. Okay, okay I'm bringing you inside the closet with me. I'm here now, let me look." She put the phone down, and I listened until I heard her say, "Here! Yes!" She picked up the phone. "It is the same as the portrait. I have this dress. *Ma non ci credo.* It has been here all this time. But what do you mean by this? That the emerald is *inside* the dress?"

"Start with the top part. It might be hidden along one of the whale-bones. You should be able to feel if something is sewn inside. Can you?"

"I cannot feel anything, although the whalebones are talking to me. It's crunching, or, crinkling rather. Some of them are flattened. Hold on. You know what, let me look and I will call you back."

I sat by the window. In thirty minutes, she called. "My nonna would kill me if she knew that I destroyed our family heirloom. But Isabel . . ."

"Did you find it?"

"I did not find an emerald. But there are very old papers folded up that appear to be a long letter. In Italian. Old Italian."

"Can you read the handwriting?"

"No. Just like I cannot read the other letters."

"Could you look at the signature?"

"I have done that," she said. "It is signed Tommaso Falcone."

"Incredible!" I said.

"I can scan and email the letter to you. Or will the scanner hurt the paper?"

"Thank you, Severina. The scan shouldn't damage it."

"Give me a couple of hours, okay? I'll be back in London when my father feels better. I'll come to Scotland. We could discuss everything then."

"I'd like that," I said. "Send it whenever you can."

A few hours later Severina's scan arrived. I made a cup of English breakfast and started to read.

My dear cousin Filippo,

I entrusted this mission to a close friend and trust you will read this letter.

Please allow me to apologize. You expected to find not words, but an emerald, hidden between the layers of this fine silk dress. Yet the story you are about to read will provide you with something more valuable: the truth about your family.

I start with my condolences. I am sorry for the death of your father, Pierfrancesco. It is my hope that you will learn from his noble deeds, and from my errors. You are still young, cousin, and the young have time.

Although our fathers were brothers, our families lived in different countries, and because we did not know each other until recently I share the details of my life.

After my father was exiled, I had a happy childhood alongside my brothers and sisters in France. My brother Federico and I went on a voyage to Brazil in the year 1565 on behalf of Queen Catherine. It was there that my brother's true character was revealed to me. Although I cannot recount all the sinful acts Federico committed during our stay, he did father a child with a woman whose honor I attempted to preserve through ill-considered nuptials. The woman, descended from royalty and living in exile, gifted me a single great emerald, perhaps in the hope that we would help her raise an army to reclaim her lost kingdom. We did not help her.

When Federico and I returned to France we were spoiled by royal favor. Privilege granted me the attention of women. I was vain, some weeks I cannot remember for lack of sobriety, and I courted women who did not return my affections. As for those who did love me, I soon tired of them. The youngest son in my family, I was always the last to know the plans they had for me.

One evening, attending a ball I had meant to leave early, I met for the first time the sister of my soul, Madeleine de La Fère. That very evening, I wrote to her, revealing my feelings for her, but Madeleine, a married woman, refused to meet me.

Not long after, her husband died. And yet she refused to respond to my letters. Three years passed. Still, I wrote to her. Still, I loved her.

During the disastrous night of St Bartholomew, she came late to my house, for I had supplied her with my address in every letter I sent. She required shelter for herself and her children and had no friends who would come to her aid. Without hesitation I hid them in my home until the troubles passed. She thanked me, and after a while deigned to be my friend.

There was the matter of her religion, that my brother called the heresy. But her faith never concerned me, rather I became intrigued by the new learning. She could quote the Bible, and recited long passages in Latin and Greek.

She knew Italian better than I and introduced me to Petrarch and Dante. Reading books she loaned me from her library, I culti-vated a love of poetry, painting, and philosophy. Art, beauty, and wisdom filled the letters we exchanged. She was the most learned person I had ever met, and I constantly strove for her esteem.

One afternoon she confessed that she knew of my feelings for her, and told me, at last, that she felt the same. As the natural expression of my long-standing love, I proposed marriage and bestowed upon her many gifts, among them the most valuable of my possessions, the emerald. Upon my instructions, the finest jeweler in France set the stone inside a necklace. I commissioned *a portrait of Madeleine wearing the necklace, a portrait that became dearer to me than any other object.*

But when Federico learned that I had given my beloved the emerald, which he claimed, without merit, for himself, I saw the extent of his wrath. He made haste to tell Madeleine that I was not fit to marry, expressing to her that I was already married to a woman in the country of the emerald and that she had borne my child. So convincing was his false story, that Madeleine refused to see me.

In a letter to her I explained that the union was with a woman who had never been my wife in body nor in soul, that the child was Federico's. But Madeleine sent back the dress I had given to her.

Sewn inside the dress were the letters I had sent her, and the necklace, along with instructions to destroy her portrait and all the letters we had exchanged. No trace of us was to remain.

A day later my heart rejoiced when a courier delivered a letter from Madeleine. But it contained only one final instruction: to take the emerald to my wife across the seas.

With great resolve I set out to fulfill Madeleine's wish. Fearing you or other cousins might inform my brother of my whereabouts, I could not depart from Genoa. I did not know then that Federico had stolen your palazzo from you, claiming his birthright. In haste I went to Lisbon, making my way to the docks, and became acquainted with a ship captain, an admiral still sympathetic to France. Fancying myself a knight of old on a quest, I volunteered to accompany his ship, destined for Brazil. They were to depart immediately, in search of red wood. I told the captain I came from a humble background, convincing him I knew my way around a galleon.

"I know you," he said at once, seeing through my shaved face
and heavy cloak. *"Do you not remember me?"* We were near
the same age, but he looked an old man, his eyes heavy and skin
leathery. He said I would not recognize the land I'd once visited,
what was once lush and verdant had turned to a heap of mud as
if pillaged by hordes of grasshoppers. Everything had been stricken
by rot, the beautiful country overrun by rats, pigs, and mosquitoes.

He seemed so distraught by the treatment of the inhabitants
that I felt an instant affinity for this man. And so, I explained
that all those years ago I had married a woman in Brazil and
now wished to return to her, and perhaps bring her back to
France with me.

For a moment he stopped speaking. *"Yes,"* he said. *"I remember
now."* Shaking his head, he informed me that my wife had been
taken by a fever the previous year.

"And the baby? Her child?"

He laughed. *"She is no longer a baby."*

"Do you by chance know what happened to my wife's daughter?"

"Your daughter," he said, pointing at me and slapping my
chest.

He told me the story of Federico's daughter, whom he believed
to be mine. She was here in Lisbon, for she was engaged to marry
a Portuguese man. Her name, the name my niece had been given,
was Mariana.

I had not known the name of my own niece! What a terrible
truth. But here she was, in this very city. The man told me the
name of her future husband.

I begged him not to reveal to a single soul that he had seen
me, and in exchange for his silence I gave him a copy of a prized
map by Cantino.

My search for the man Mariana was to marry was not at once fruitful. Spending days and nights in taverns, I listened to stories told by city dwellers and travelers, nobles and simple men. In one small inn, late at night, I overheard a conversation between two Frenchmen, who did not know I understood their language. They spoke of the wickedness of the Duke of Alba, who had some business with an Italian man, a certain Falcone. Falcone was described as an evil man, an accomplice of the Spanish king. There was talk of a plot, which involved the murder of the king of France, and poison to be administered by the hand of this Falcone.

When I thought they could speak no worse words against my brother they talked of how he had informed upon Queen Catherine's fleet. 8 French ships had been captured due to his treachery. I knew that I must make haste and inform my sacred lieges, but allowed myself one week to fulfill my promise, and find my niece. But first, I wrote to Madeleine asking her to warn the Queen Mother in case I should not return before he could begin to enact the evil. As fate would decide, the very next day as I searched for the man Mariana was engaged to, I discovered that the man had died, and his fiancée had been moved to a convent. I found out the name of the convent, asked for directions, and walked there. What joy I felt! I had feared finding Mariana would have proven impossible or worse, that she, too, had died.

As soon as I arrived at the convent, I arranged to speak with the abbess, introducing myself as Mariana's uncle. The abbess said she prized my niece although Mariana had only recently arrived, for she was devout, and possessed a strong will.

I requested to speak with Mariana, and the abbess bade me wait, and then I was brought to the cloister's parlatorium to wait for Mariana to finish her afternoon prayer. A girl walked toward the grated window near me, and the other girls stood at a distance.

Mariana did not smile as she approached the window but looked upon me as if I were a stranger, which in truth I was.

I introduced myself, and explained in broken Portuguese that I was her uncle. Mariana did not step closer. I began to weep then, tears of relief, but my tears did not impress her. She regarded me with pity, as though I were a strange creature, one she could not understand. Looking closely, I saw that she did not have the features of a person in good health. It pained me to think how difficult her life must have been, how many she had lost, how cruelly they had been treated.

I said our family in France had many blessings and that I could provide for her, promising that she would never want for anything. "I know your father," I said, and she stiffened. "I have something special to give you, something that belongs to you alone."

Then she spoke, her voice detached but without reproach. "Ereiout," she said. "You have come. You," she continued, "are the man who abandoned my mother. She told me that someday you might come."

I produced the emerald from my pocket and passed the stone to her. She held it up, that she might examine it in the light. As she twisted it around in her fingers, the green shone bright against the white stone, the old world and the new.

She held out her hand, and passed the stone to me again, and nodded once.

"You may go, sir. Thank you for your visit," she said.

"This is your inheritance," I said. "From the land of your birth. It belonged to your mother. Now it belongs to you. It is . . . a treasure."

"Possessing this trinket will force me to recall great unhappiness. I do not care for earthly possessions, for the life I lived then. I now live with purpose. To serve our Holy Father."

"It was my duty to deliver this to you," I said. "You may do with it as you wish." I passed the emerald to her once more and stepped back. I bade her farewell, although I could see she no longer wanted to look upon me, instead seeming to dismiss me as a queen would have dismissed an unworthy subject.

Without saying more, she lifted the emerald and threw it onto the stone floor close to my feet with so much force that it broke apart. Then she turned from me and did not look back. I picked up a few of the jagged pieces and put them inside my pocket.

After taking leave of her I was overcome with sadness and left the convent in a hurry. As I walked, beggars, young mothers and old men alike, reached out to me. I distributed all that remained of the emerald, shrugging off their attempts to thank me.

I could not bear to look at the pieces. Even the beautiful color, its brightness blinking at me like an evil spirit, held no temptation. A gem that most men would strive their entire lives to obtain to me meant only suffering. As it had reminded Mariana, so the emerald reminded me of everything I had once possessed, of everything I had lost. The emerald had proven unlucky, cursed, as we had once been warned.

And thus, the stone that had traveled across the seas had been destroyed at the hands of its true owner. I do not fault her, knowing how many sorrows were caused by its existence in a short life full of more horror than I would ever know.

I returned to the convent one last time and requested to speak with the abbess. I pledged to send money for Mariana but insisted my gifts should remain anonymous.

Now I had fulfilled my promise to Madeleine and hastened back to France. I did not know if she could love me again but prayed that time would dull her anger. Even my brother could not prevent me from marrying her if she would have me.

But it was not to be. No sooner had I arrived in Paris when I learned the disastrous news. Madeleine was dead. The pain hit me like a blow from a boulder, then cut beneath my skin with the force of a thousand daggers.

But when I spoke to Mme de . . . and she recounted how my Madeleine had come to die, my ire became such that I can scarcely describe. Mme de . . . told me Madeleine had written to the Queen Mother about my brother's designs against the king. Mme de . . . claimed the convulsions that had led to Madeleine's death had been caused by poison, disguised as a gift of sweetmeats, delivered by Federico!

I went to meet with my brother and told him of my sojourn. Leaving aside what I believed had happened to my beloved, I asked if the rumors I had heard were true.

All he said was, "You have no proof. Where is my emerald? Is that not why you are here? I demand what belongs to me."

"You shall have all what belongs to you, brother," I said.

I requested an audience with the Queen Mother and when she had dismissed her guards, I told her what I had overheard in Lisbon. With somber fortitude she said that she had once held my brother in great esteem. But she now recognized the rumors about Federico to be true and assured me that I need not worry for the safety of her son the king. She conveyed gratitude for my honesty and expressed her intention to fulfill any reasonable request that I might have. And that is how the good Queen came to countenance my desire for meting out

Federico's punishment, commensurate with the evils he had committed on the earth.

I explained my wish to preserve the reputation of the Falcone name, that we might be remembered by our children's children without the stain of treachery that one member of the family had visited upon us. I asked her, must one burn an entire orchard for but one rotten apple? I thanked her for the blessings she had bestowed upon us, assuring her that living as her loyal subject had been my greatest source of pride.

And then, though I was meant to leave, she stayed with me, and began to speak of Madeleine. The Queen told me that Madeleine's intelligence and goodness had distinguished her among her ladies. But all this I knew.

Then the Queen Mother bestowed upon me the greatest treasure I have ever possessed, worth untold numbers of emeralds. She told me that in the years since the death of her husband, Madeleine had turned away many suitors, and confessed to love only one man. "I know without doubt," said the Queen Mother, "that she must have meant you."

I saw great anguish in her face then, for I suppose she was sad to see me go, and sadder still for the terrible knowledge I had imparted. She shook her head and said, "My son, how you have grown."

Our meeting gave me further resolve to fulfill my plan. When I arrived in Genoa to Federico's palazzo, seized from your father, I wrote a letter to lure Federico, claiming that I sought his assistance in a plan to kill the king of France, asking him to wear specific clothing to signal his agreement to be involved in the dreadful deed. I told him that we were to discuss the matter in the palazzo tower, where I had placed the emerald and a vial of poison inside of our grandfather's suit of armor. Before the arrival of my brother, I carefully laid a stone of glass inside the suit, glass so carefully crafted by an expert counterfeiter, that one might mistake it for an emerald.

I told your brother were he to help me arrange to deliver Federico's justice, or at least not obstruct me from doing so, the palazzo would return to your hands. It belonged to your father, and so it should belong to you. I waited for Federico in your father's old room in the tower. When he entered, I lay upon him and strangled him, for I was younger and stronger than he, and my hatred for him was greater than his own, for his hatred was diffuse, applied to everyone and everything that he could neither own nor conquer.

The cause of death would not be discovered, for although I left marks on Federico's body, I paid to have my secrets kept, distributing sums among you, my cousins, and your allies, that you might give out that Federico had died from plague. It was a year of plague, and none would care to question what had happened to him. Besides, he would not be missed. I, like Cain, now had the stain of Abel.

I have tried to act honorably, to defend the homeland that had been kind to its adopted son. With the deed I have described I avenged those who had suffered by Federico's hand, and especially Madeleine.

And now you, my cousin, know the history of my life, the good and bad I have done. You know my heart. You may judge me. Probably you should. I hope these lines do not disappoint. And that they explain what I must now do.

I hope by the time you read these words that my Madeleine and I will be together once again. As Michel de Montaigne, whom

Madeleine hosted in her salon, wrote, "As I do not offend the law against thieves when I embezzle my own money and cut my own purse; nor that against incendiaries when I burn my own wood; so am I not under the lash of those made against murderers for having deprived myself of my own life."

Now gladly shall I consume the poison, that it may hasten my final journey to join her there where I know she lives with all the good souls who have come this way before.

Yours in humility, Tommaso.

When, at the end of the day, I finished transcribing the letter, I put the pages down and bundled up in my winter coat. Outside, fat snowflakes filled the air, dusting streets flooded with students trying to get their bearings, to find their way.

I took a long walk, past the cathedral, down to the beach, and finally up to the cliff where Madeleine Grangier had been pushed to her death. A chill passed over me as I imagined her last moments in this peaceful place. There were so many questions I had wanted to ask her. I resolved to do whatever was possible to honor the memory of someone I'd never know. I'd organize a memorial for Madeleine, and I would dedicate my future book to her. The thought that she or her scholarship would be forgotten was unbearable.

I continued to walk, beyond the old city walls, and I climbed to the top of a medieval lookout tower with a panoramic view of St Stephens and the dark sea below. For several moments I let the faded sun and briny wind wash over my face.

Then, instead of going home, I went to my office. Mairead was still there. She stood up and came over to me. Without saying anything, she wrapped her arms around me, and held me firmly against her small frame even as I tried to stand tall and collect myself. Her tenderness pierced all my determination to remain stoic, and I began to cry, to sob, for the first time since that night on the Isle of Lewis. "I feel like such a fool," was all I could manage.

"'A woman sees in the world what she carries in her heart,'" she said, and for once I didn't ask the source of the quote, and she didn't offer it.

We sat down.

"I've just discovered something extraordinary, Mairead. A previously unknown historical source."

She raised her eyebrows. "The best kind. Tell me about it."

"I'm still putting my thoughts together, but to start, remember when I found that letter in Rose's desk? The one that indicated Tommaso Falcone was involved in a plot to kill the French king?"

She blinked. "Yes."

"It turns out to have been an entrapment letter. Tommaso was never planning on killing the king. But he knew his brother, Federico, was, and Tommaso wrote that letter to get his brother to come to Genoa, where he murdered him."

"To protect the French monarchy? That's some extreme loyalty right there."

"It was really because Federico had poisoned Tommaso's fiancée. And there's more. A lot more. Did I tell you about the Falcone emerald? No? We have a lot of catching up to do. Anyway—"

Just then the door opened partway, and Sean stuck his head inside.

"Sean!" I said.

"I've been looking for ya," he smiled, walking through the door. "Give us a hug," he said as he approached us, and I started crying all over again. "Looks like someone could use a pint. On me this time." The three of us linked arms and walked to the Quaich where we stayed drinking and talking until they kicked us out.

Afterward Mairead turned down a side street to go home, and Sean and I watched her. At this hour, lit only by gas lamps and moonlight,

St Stephens looked picturesque, the way I'd imagined it before I'd arrived.

Sean took a step toward me and said, "Isabel, might I take you out for tea next week? Tea, as in dinner. If you have time, of course. There's a restaurant where I've always wanted to go, and . . . I thought maybe we could try it. Together."

"Sure," I said. "I'd love to."

"Really? I mean, great. Great."

He hugged me again, tighter than he had in my office, and as we stood there in the cold, embracing on the cobblestones, the events of the past few days and weeks and months seemed to drift away, I hoped for good.

ACKNOWLEDGMENTS

I would like to thank everyone who has helped make this book a reality. First and foremost, thank you to Joyce Carol Oates, for believing in me and my writing. Joyce is not only an extraordinary writer, but also the greatest teacher and mentor anyone could ever hope to have.

Many thanks to Deborah Landau and the entire NYU Creative Writing program, my professors Nathan Englander, Darin Strauss, Zadie Smith, Rick Moody, Anne Enright, and Chuck Wachtel, as well as the insightful writers in my workshops, who offered useful feedback on early drafts.

Heartfelt thanks to my amazing agent, Jody Kahn of Brandt and Hochman. Jody's guidance has been crucial during this entire process—she is a dream agent.

A million thank yous to my brilliant editor, Luisa Smith, who saw this novel's potential and helped me transform it into its best incarnation.

I would like to express my deepest gratitude to Otto Penzler. It is an honor to be published by a true legend. Many thanks also to Charles Perry, and the exceptional team at Mysterious Press/Scarlet.

Thank you to my family and friends across continents who have given me much encouragement and love over the past seven years. I could not have written this novel without them. In particular, my mother has supported me and this project from day one. Thank you for reading stories to me from a young age and for teaching me everything I know.

And to my wonderful husband, Bjørn, who understands more than most the lifestyle and crazy hours of working artists, thank you for being with me every step of the way.